ADVENTURE TIME

BRAIN ROBBERS

ROSS RICHIE CEO & Founder • MATT GAGNON Editor-in-Chief • FILIP SABLIK President of Publishing & Marketing • STEPHEN CHRISTY President of Development • LANCE KREITER VP of Licensing & Merchandising
PHIL BARBARO VP of Finance • BRYCE CARLSON Managing Editor • MEL CAYLO Marketing Manager • SCOTT NEWMAN Production Design Manager • SIERRA HAHN Senior Editor • DAFNA PLEBAN Editor, Talent Development
SHANNON WATTERS Editor • ERIC HARBURN Editor • WHITNEY LEOPARD Associate Editor • JASMINE AMIRI Associate Editor • CHRIS ROSA Associate Editor • ALEX GALER Associate Editor
CAMERON CHITTOCK Associate Editor • MATTHEW LEVINE Assistant Editor • KELSEY DIETERICH Production Designer • JILLIAN CRAB Production Designer • MICHELLE ANKLEY Production Designer
GRACE PARK Production Design Assistant • AARON FERRARA Operations Coordinator • ELIZABETH LOUGHRIDGE Accounting Coordinator • STEPHANIE HOCUTT Social Media Coordinator
JOSÉ MEZA Sales Assistant • JAMES ARRIOLA Mailroom Assistant • HOLLY AITCHISON Operations Assistant • SAM KUSEK Direct Market Representative • AMBER PARKER Administrative Assistant

ADVENTURE TIME: BRAIN ROBBERS, February 2017. Published by KaBOOM!, a division of Boom Entertainment, Inc.
ADVENTURE TIME, CARTOON NETWORK, the logos, and all related characters and elements are trademarks of and © Cartoon
Network. (S17) All rights reserved. KaBOOM!™ and the KaBOOM! logo are trademarks of Boom Entertainment, Inc., registered in
various countries and categories. All characters, events, and institutions depicted herein are fictional. Any similarity between any of the
names, characters, persons, events, and/or institutions in this publication to actual names, characters, and persons, whether living or
dead, events, and/or institutions is unintended and purely coincidental. KaBOOM! does not read or accept unsolicited submissions of
ideas, stories, or artwork.

A catalog record of this book is available from OCLC and from the BOOM! website, www.boom-studios.com, on the Librarians Page.

BOOM! Studios, 5670 Wilshire Boulevard, Suite 450, Los Angeles, CA 90036-5679. Printed in China. First Printing.
ISBN:978-1-60886-875-9, eISBN:978-1-61398-546-5

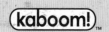

Created by Pendleton Ward

Written by **Josh Trujillo**

Pencils by **Zachary Sterling**

Inks by **Jenna Ayoub & Phil Murphy**

Colors by **Joie Foster**

with **Laura Langston**

Letters by **Warren Montgomery**

Cover by **Scott Maynard**

Designer **Grace Park**
Associate Editor **Whitney Leopard**
Editor **Shannon Watters**

With Special Thanks to Marisa Marionakis, Janet No, Curtis Lelash, Conrad Montgomery, Meghan Bradley, Kelly Crews, Scott Malchus, Adam Muto and the wonderful folks at Cartoon Network.

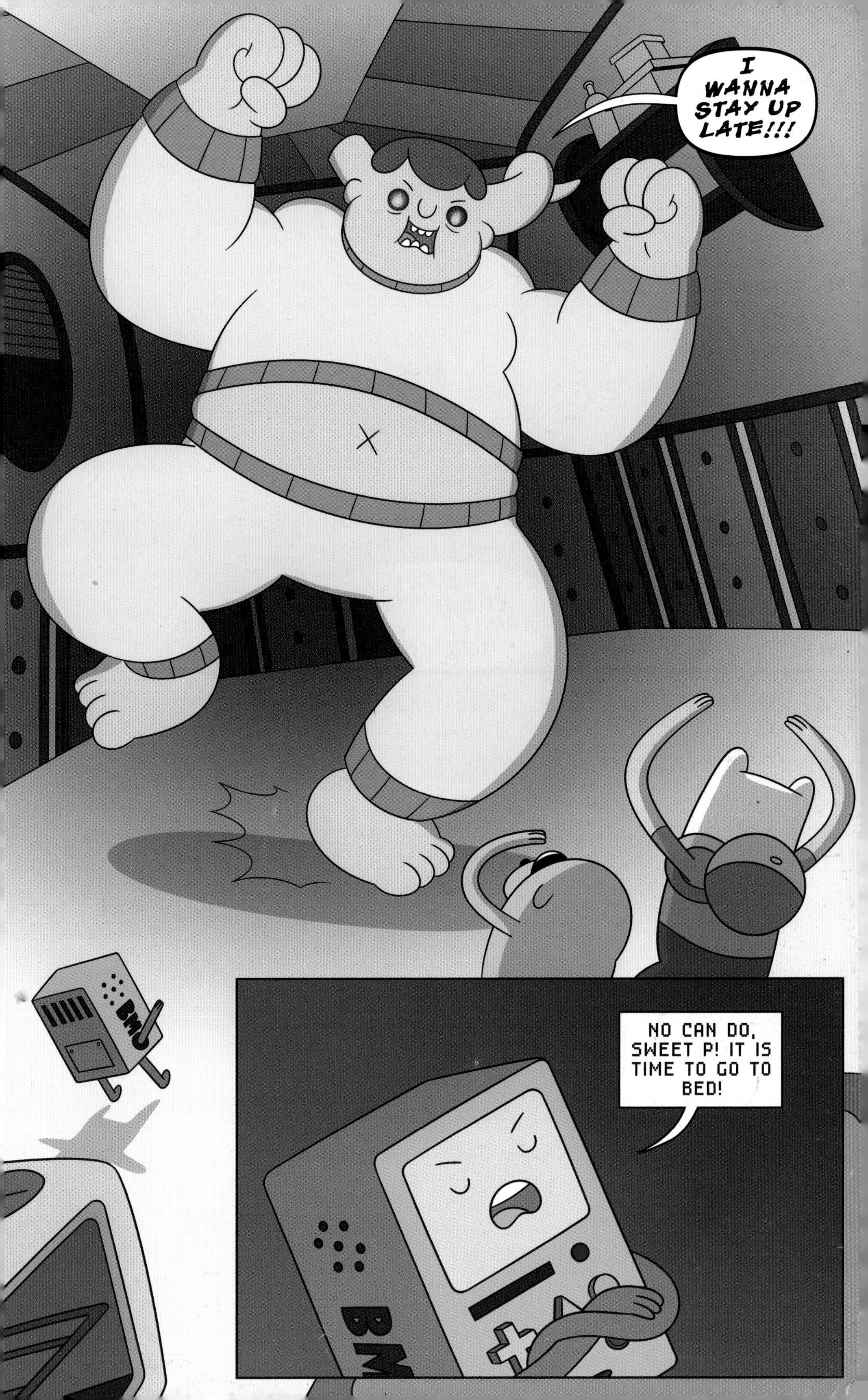
I WANNA STAY UP LATE!!!
NO CAN DO, SWEET P! IT IS TIME TO GO TO BED!
BMO

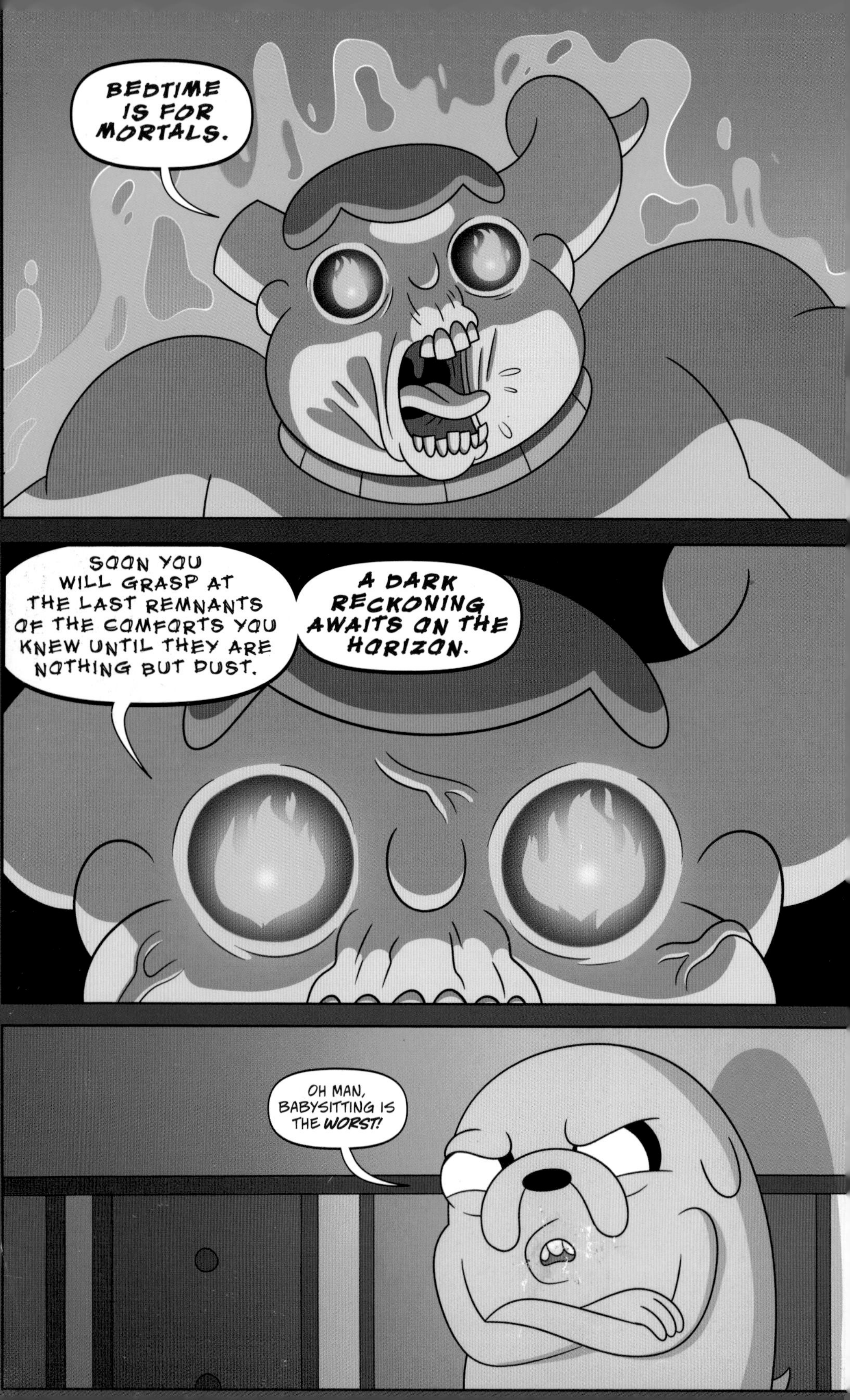
BEDTIME IS FOR MORTALS.
SOON YOU WILL GRASP AT THE LAST REMNANTS OF THE COMFORTS YOU KNEW UNTIL THEY ARE NOTHING BUT DUST.
A DARK RECKONING AWAITS ON THE HORIZON.
OH MAN, BABYSITTING IS THE WORST!

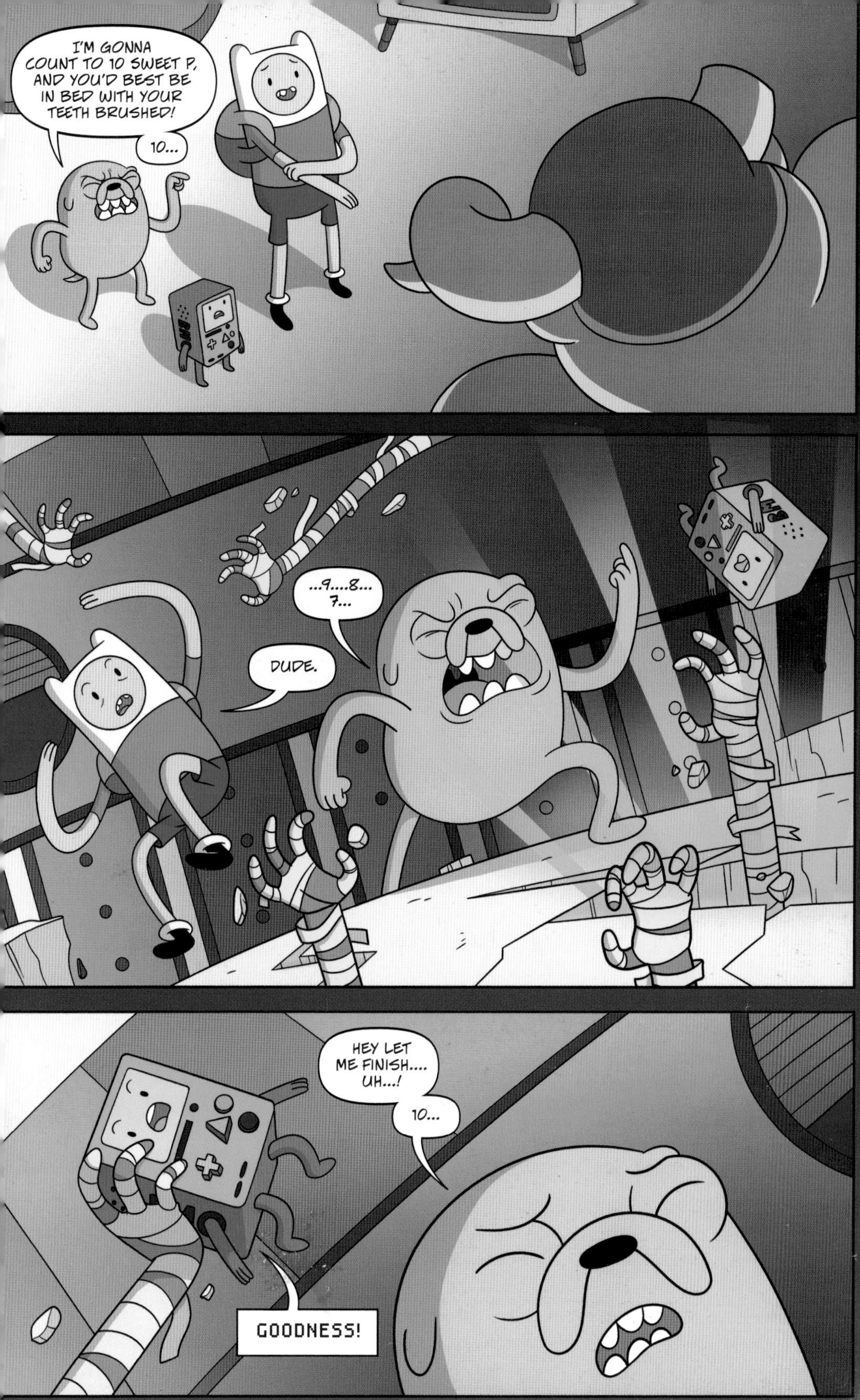
I'M GONNA COUNT TO 10 SWEET P, AND YOU'D BEST BE IN BED WITH YOUR TEETH BRUSHED!
10...
...9....8... 7...
DUDE.
HEY LET ME FINISH.... UH...!
10...
GOODNESS!

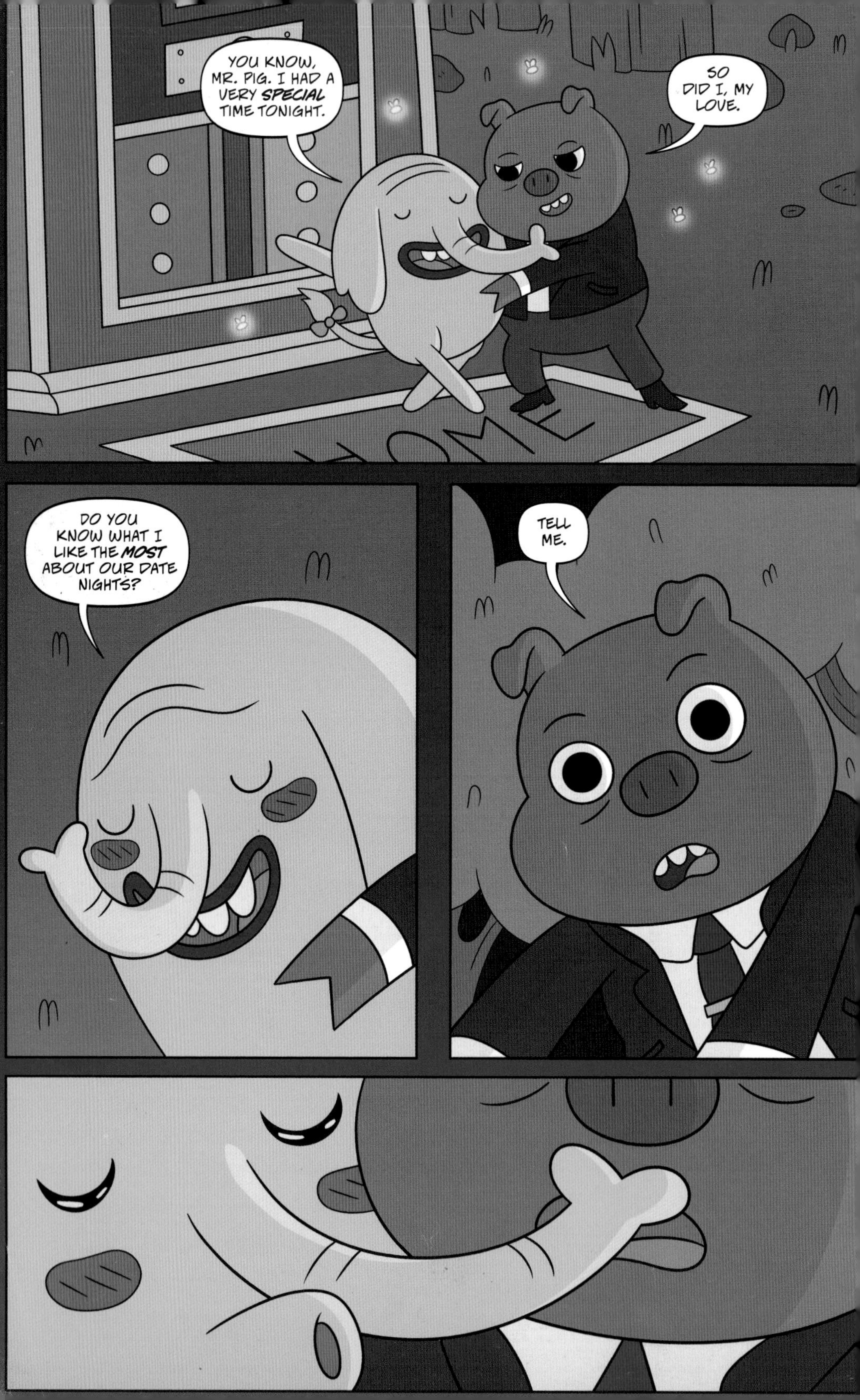
YOU KNOW, MR. PIG. I HAD A VERY **SPECIAL** TIME TONIGHT.
SO DID I, MY LOVE.
DO YOU KNOW WHAT I LIKE THE **MOST** ABOUT OUR DATE NIGHTS?
TELL ME.

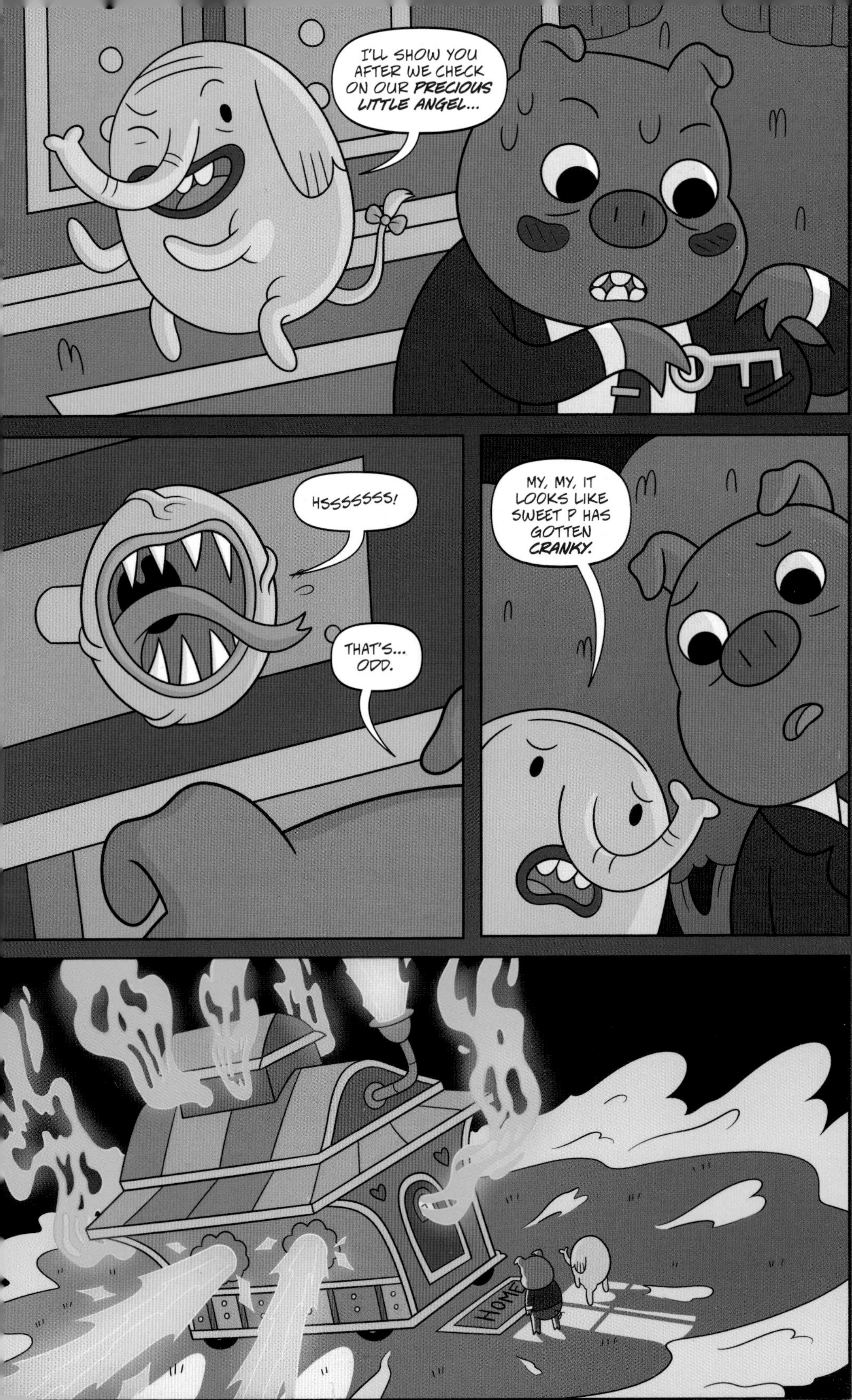
I'LL SHOW YOU AFTER WE CHECK ON OUR PRECIOUS LITTLE ANGEL...
HSSSSSSS!
THAT'S... ODD.
MY, MY, IT LOOKS LIKE SWEET P HAS GOTTEN CRANKY.
HOME

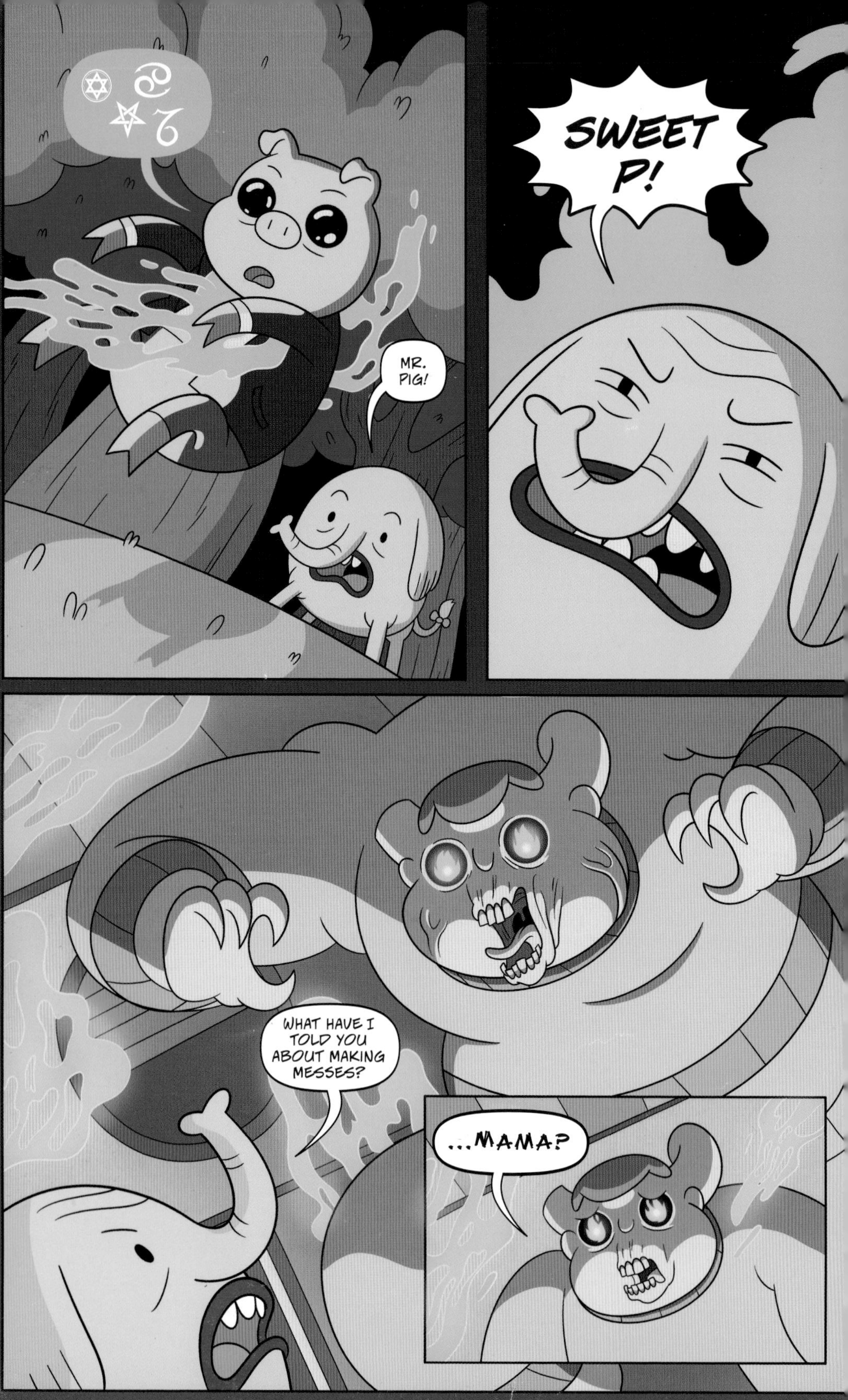
MR. PIG!
SWEET P!
WHAT HAVE I TOLD YOU ABOUT MAKING MESSES?
...MAMA?

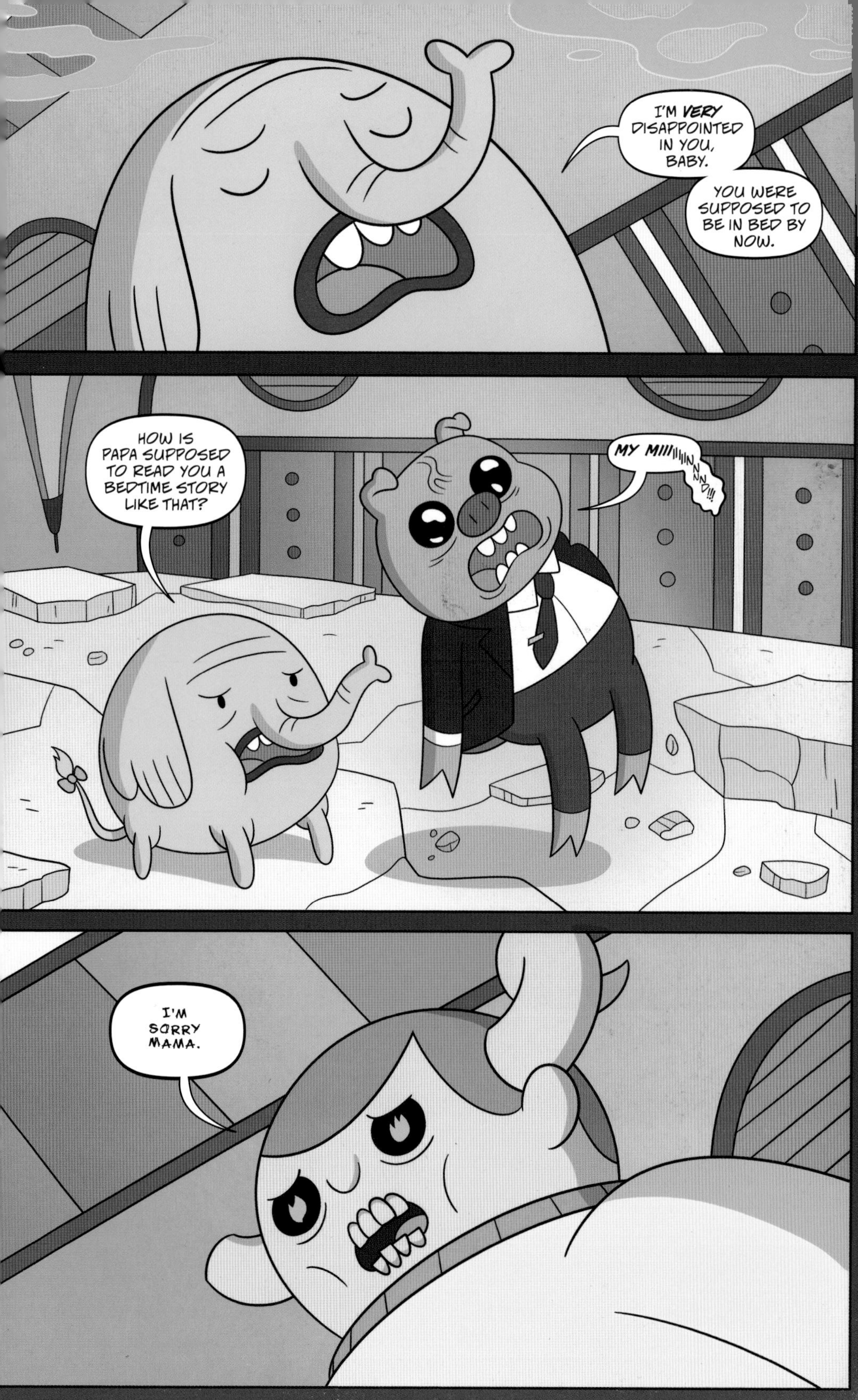
I'M VERY DISAPPOINTED IN YOU, BABY.
YOU WERE SUPPOSED TO BE IN BED BY NOW.
HOW IS PAPA SUPPOSED TO READ YOU A BEDTIME STORY LIKE THAT?
MY MIIIIIIIINNNND!!!
I'M SORRY MAMA.

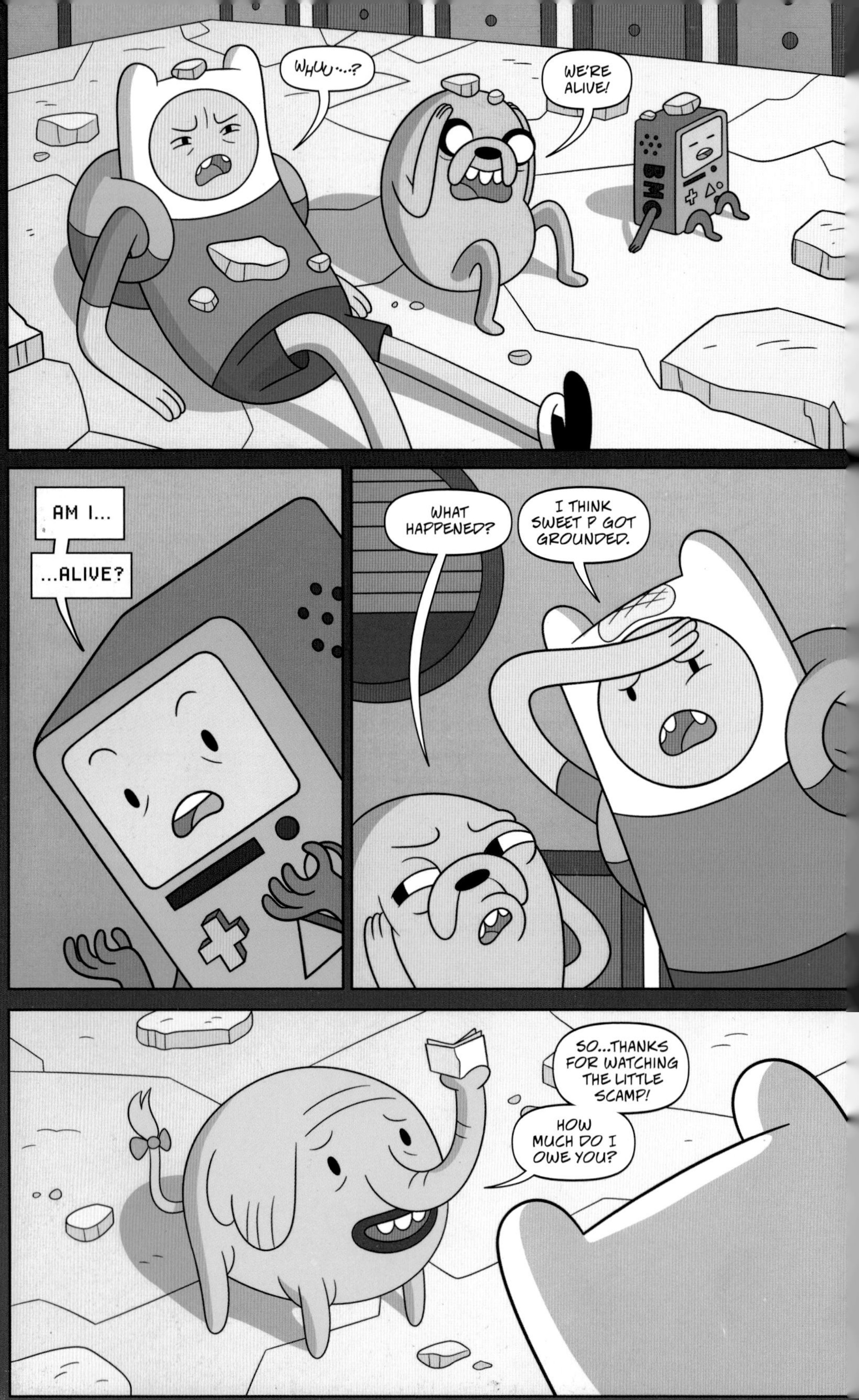
WHUU...?
WE'RE ALIVE!
AM I...
...ALIVE?
WHAT HAPPENED?
I THINK SWEET P GOT GROUNDED.
SO...THANKS FOR WATCHING THE LITTLE SCAMP!
HOW MUCH DO I OWE YOU?

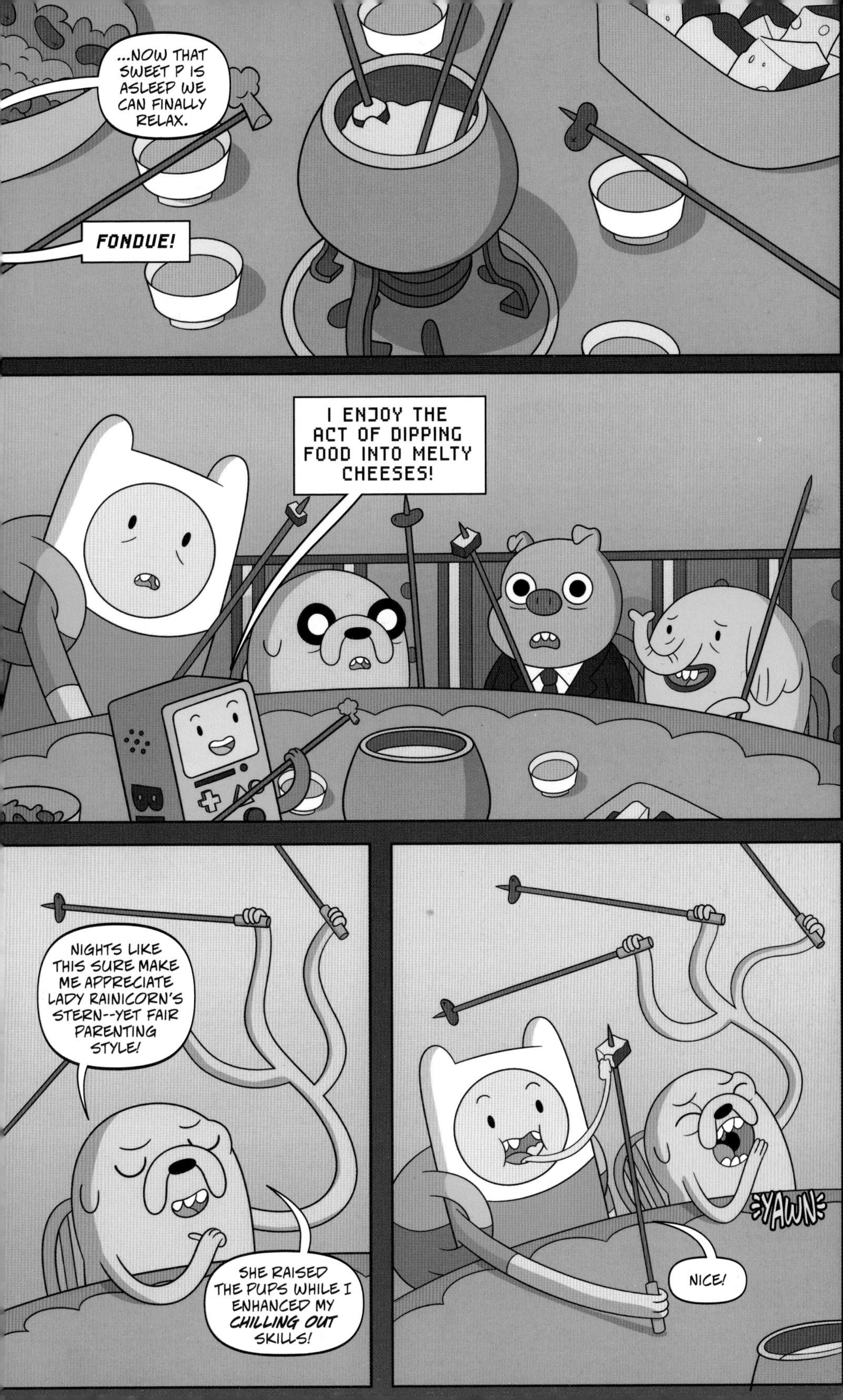
...NOW THAT SWEET P IS ASLEEP WE CAN FINALLY RELAX.
FONDUE!
I ENJOY THE ACT OF DIPPING FOOD INTO MELTY CHEESES!
NIGHTS LIKE THIS SURE MAKE ME APPRECIATE LADY RAINICORN'S STERN--YET FAIR PARENTING STYLE!
SHE RAISED THE PUPS WHILE I ENHANCED MY CHILLING OUT SKILLS!
YAWN
NICE!

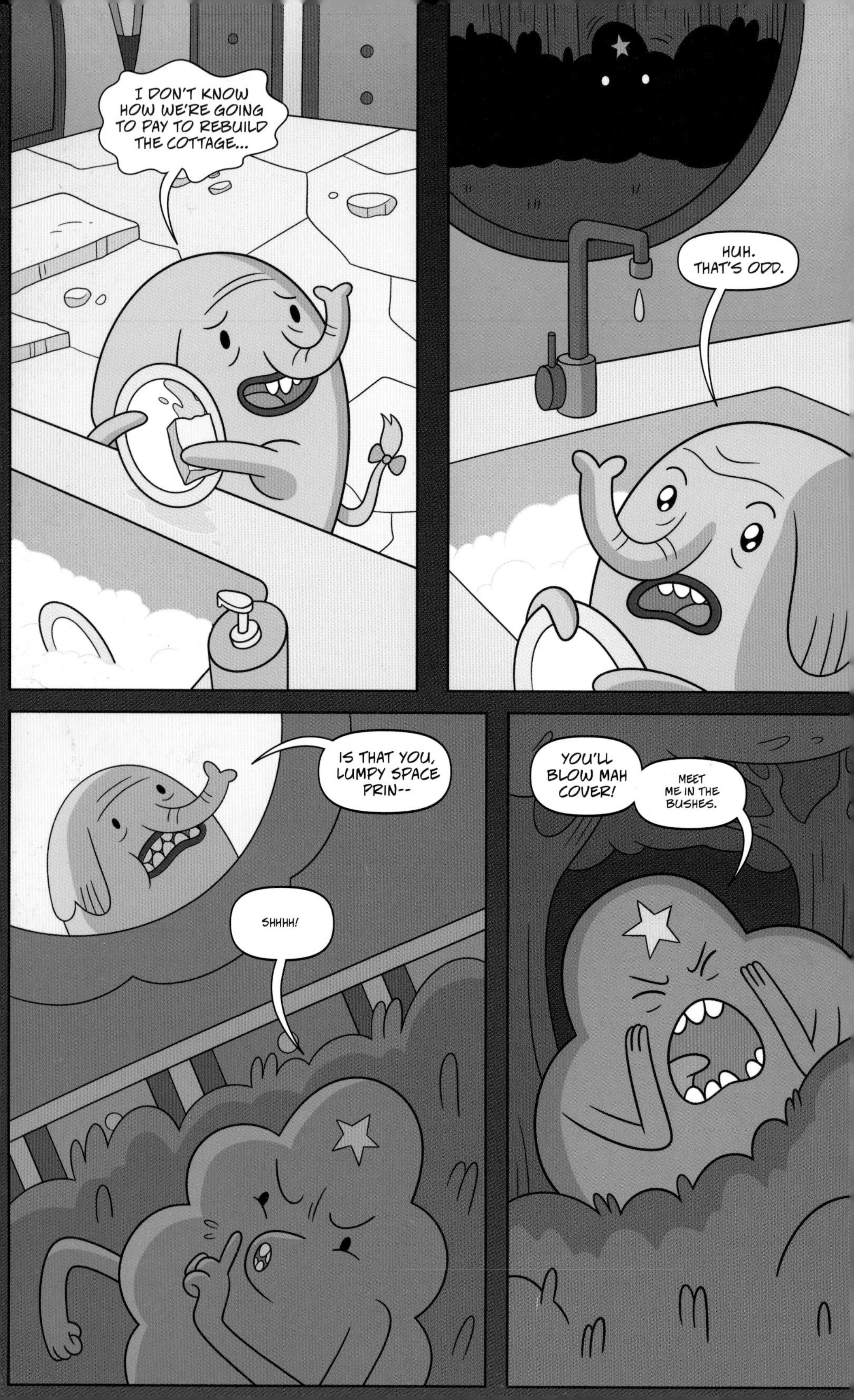
I DON'T KNOW HOW WE'RE GOING TO PAY TO REBUILD THE COTTAGE...
HUH. THAT'S ODD.
IS THAT YOU, LUMPY SPACE PRIN--
SHHHH!
YOU'LL BLOW MAH COVER!
MEET ME IN THE BUSHES.

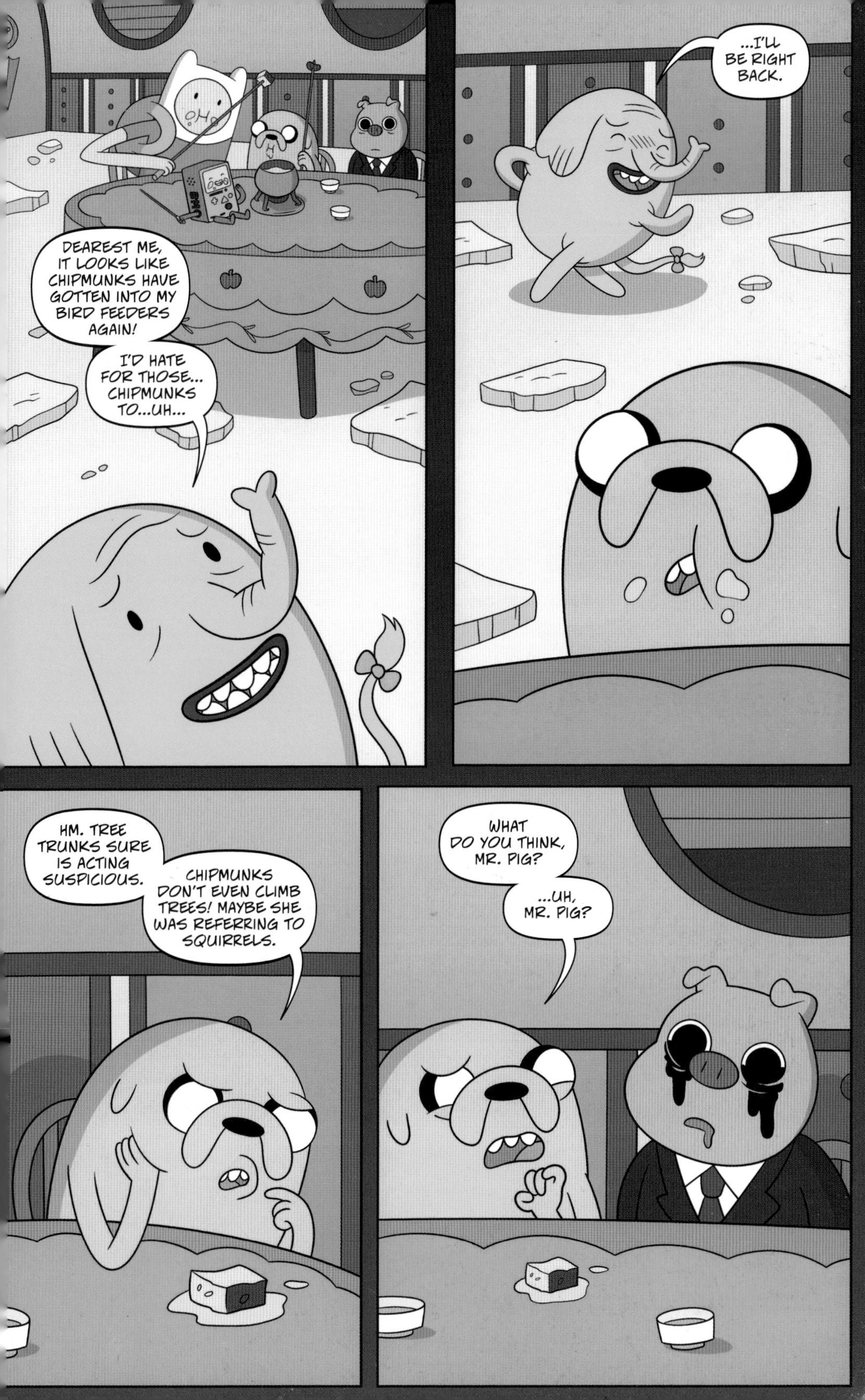
DEAREST ME, IT LOOKS LIKE CHIPMUNKS HAVE GOTTEN INTO MY BIRD FEEDERS AGAIN!
I'D HATE FOR THOSE... CHIPMUNKS TO...UH...
...I'LL BE RIGHT BACK.
HM. TREE TRUNKS SURE IS ACTING SUSPICIOUS.
CHIPMUNKS DON'T EVEN CLIMB TREES! MAYBE SHE WAS REFERRING TO SQUIRRELS.
WHAT DO YOU THINK, MR. PIG?
...UH, MR. PIG?

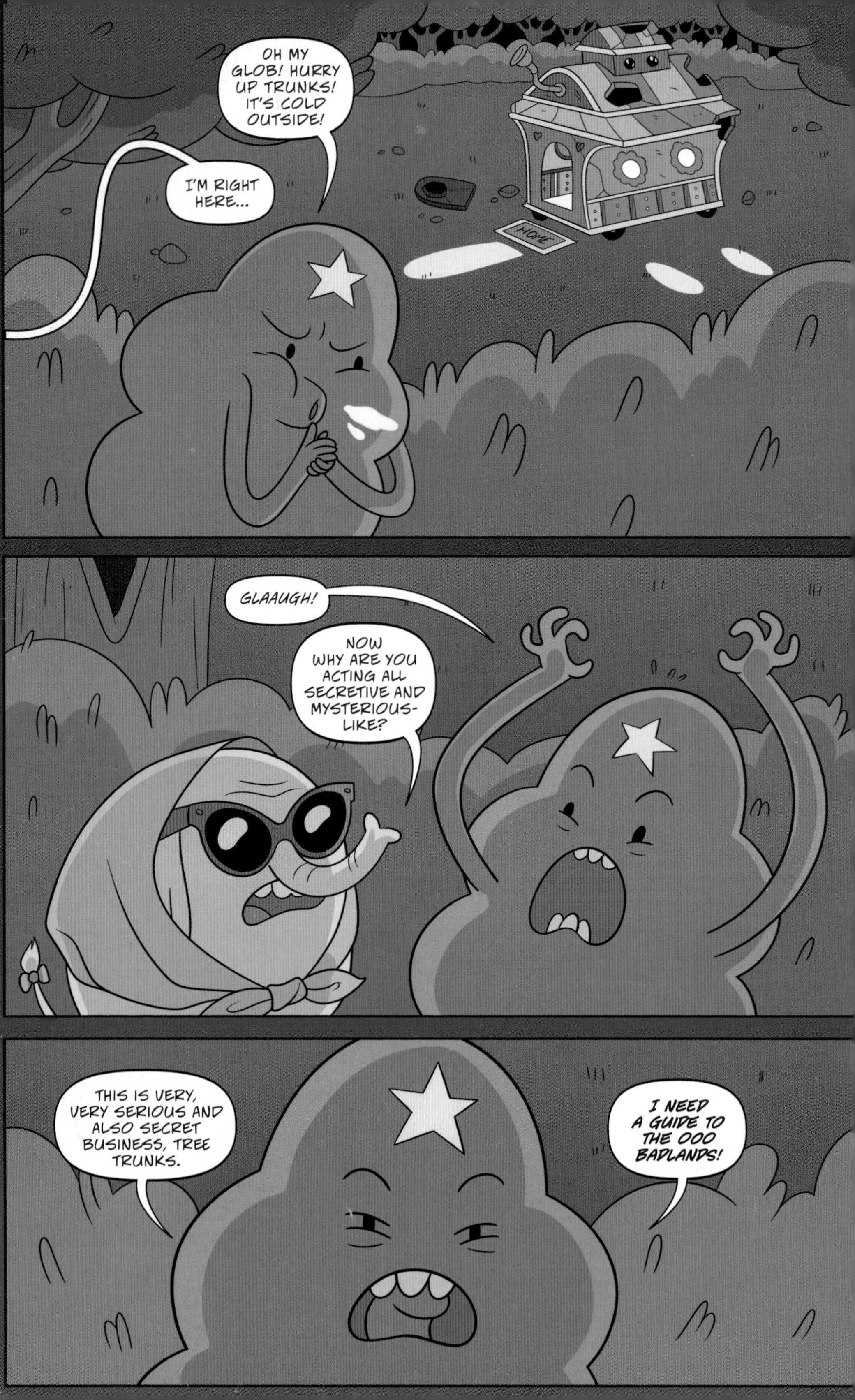
OH MY GLOB! HURRY UP TRUNKS! IT'S COLD OUTSIDE!
I'M RIGHT HERE...
HOME
GLAAUGH!
NOW WHY ARE YOU ACTING ALL SECRETIVE AND MYSTERIOUS-LIKE?
THIS IS VERY, VERY SERIOUS AND ALSO SECRET BUSINESS, TREE TRUNKS.
I NEED A GUIDE TO THE OOO BADLANDS!

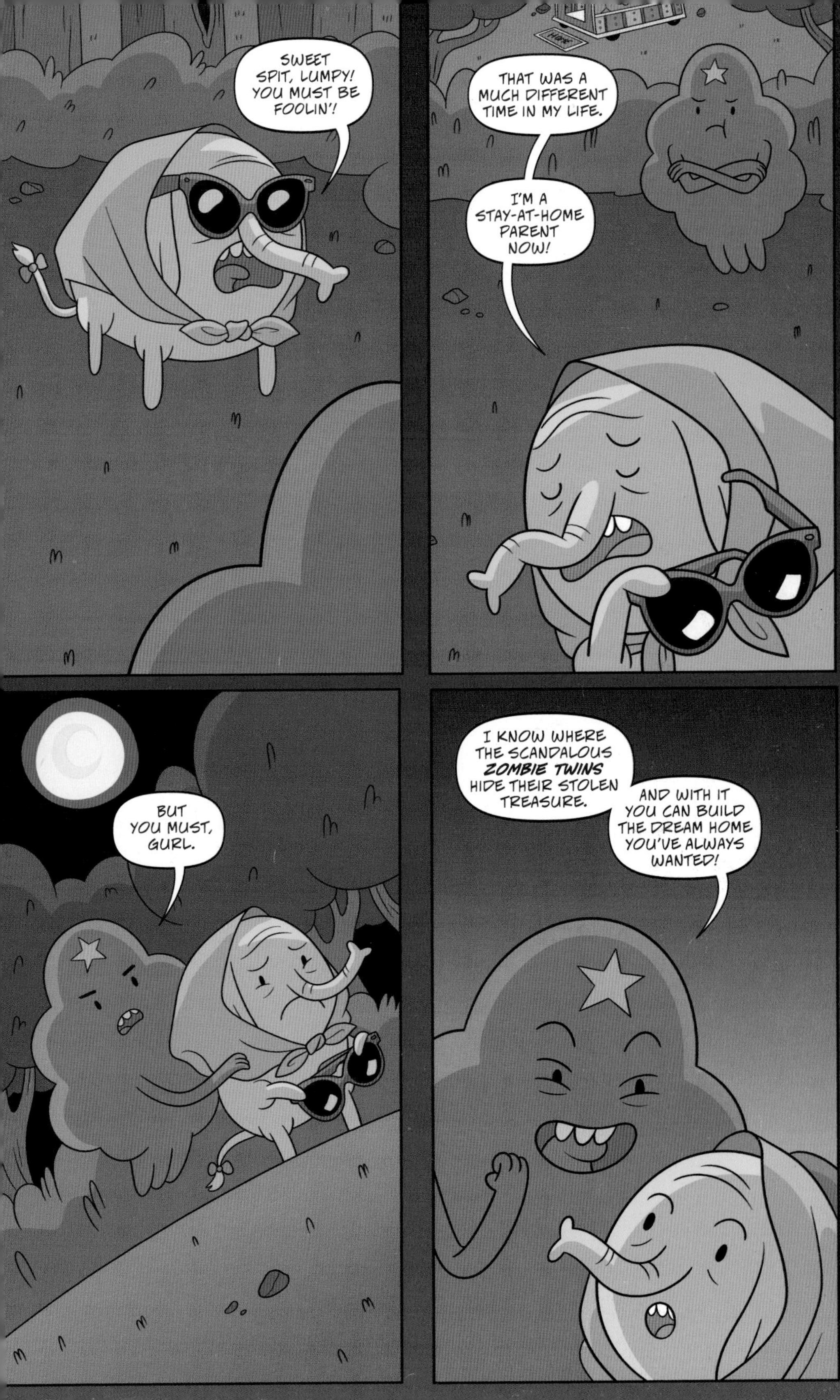
SWEET SPIT, LUMPY! YOU MUST BE FOOLIN'!
THAT WAS A MUCH DIFFERENT TIME IN MY LIFE.
I'M A STAY-AT-HOME PARENT NOW!
BUT YOU MUST, GURL.
I KNOW WHERE THE SCANDALOUS **ZOMBIE TWINS** HIDE THEIR STOLEN TREASURE.
AND WITH IT YOU CAN BUILD THE DREAM HOME YOU'VE ALWAYS WANTED!

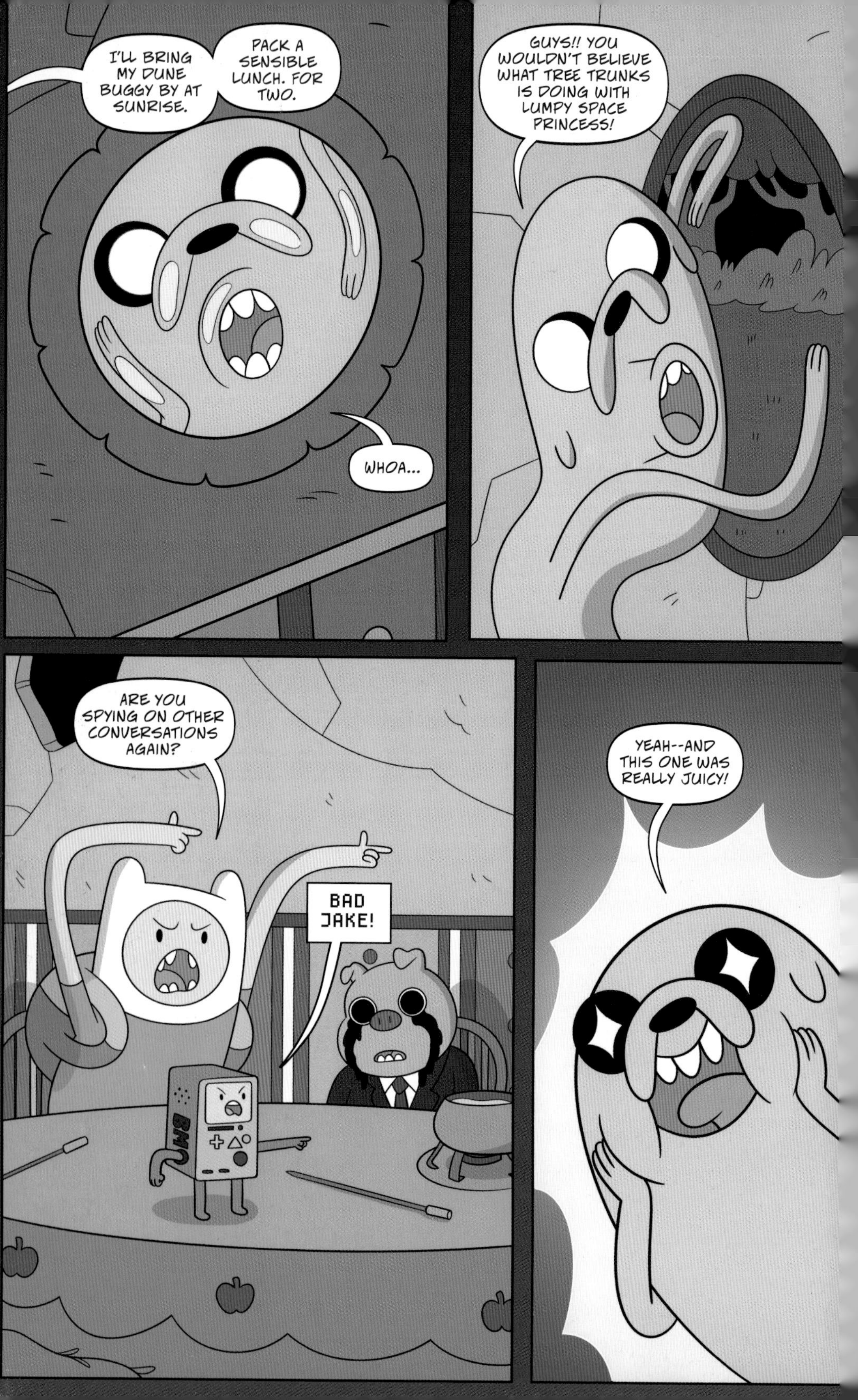

I'LL BRING MY DUNE BUGGY BY AT SUNRISE.
PACK A SENSIBLE LUNCH. FOR TWO.
WHOA...
GUYS!! YOU WOULDN'T BELIEVE WHAT TREE TRUNKS IS DOING WITH LUMPY SPACE PRINCESS!
ARE YOU SPYING ON OTHER CONVERSATIONS AGAIN?
BAD JAKE!
BMO
YEAH--AND THIS ONE WAS REALLY JUICY!

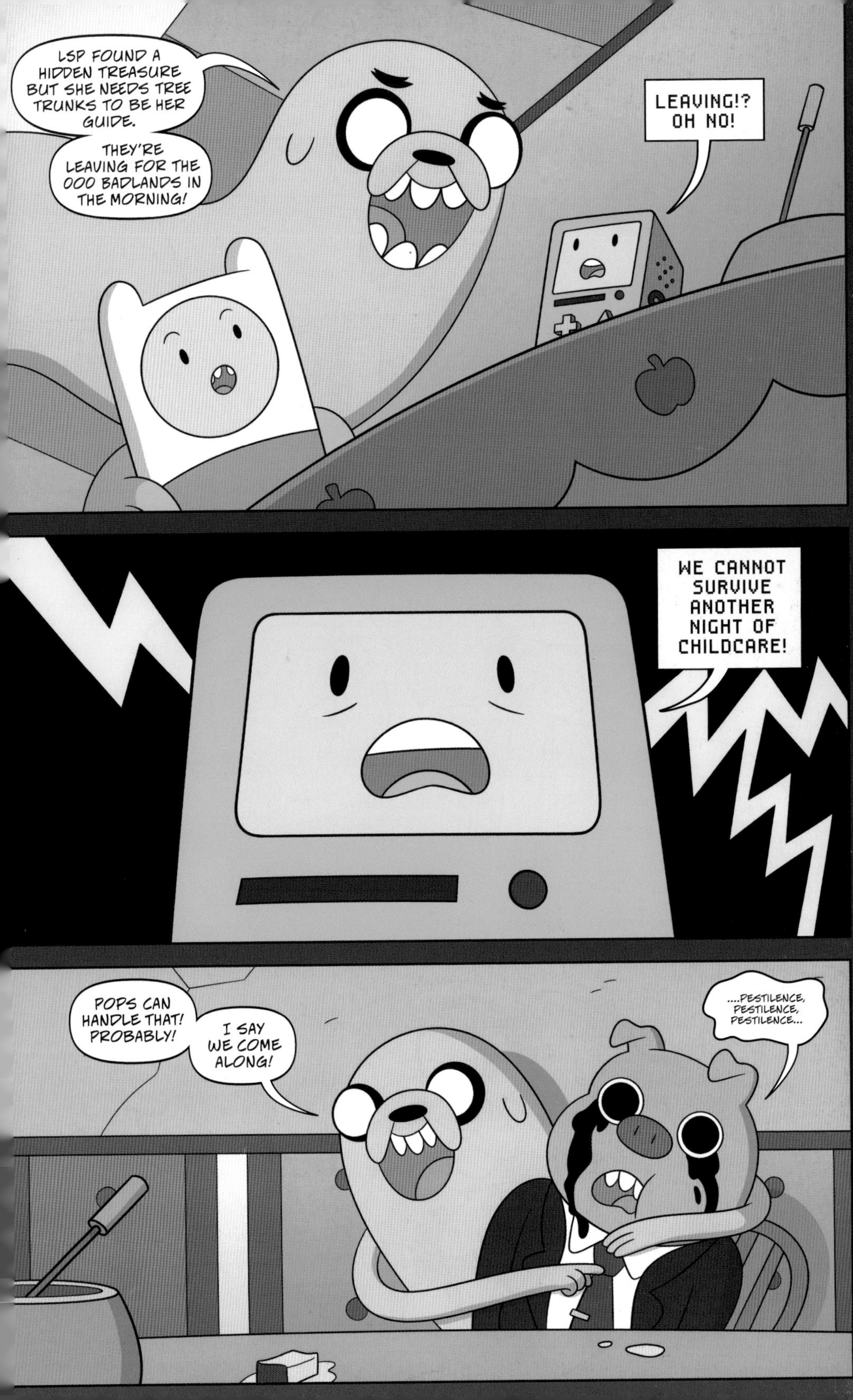
LSP FOUND A HIDDEN TREASURE BUT SHE NEEDS TREE TRUNKS TO BE HER GUIDE.
THEY'RE LEAVING FOR THE OOO BADLANDS IN THE MORNING!
LEAVING!? OH NO!
WE CANNOT SURVIVE ANOTHER NIGHT OF CHILDCARE!
POPS CAN HANDLE THAT! PROBABLY!
I SAY WE COME ALONG!
....PESTILENCE, PESTILENCE, PESTILENCE...

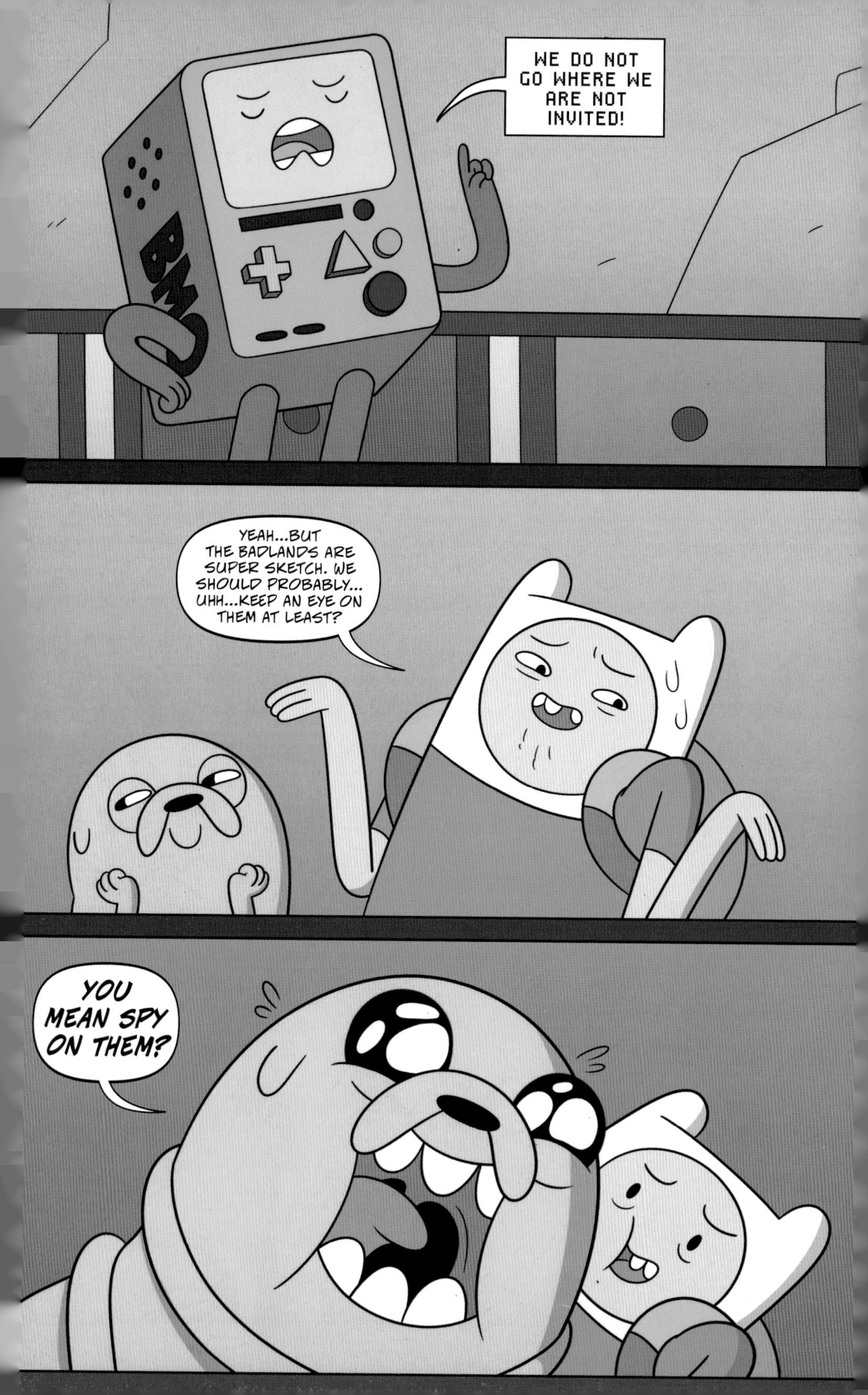
WE DO NOT GO WHERE WE ARE NOT INVITED!
BMO
YEAH...BUT THE BADLANDS ARE SUPER SKETCH. WE SHOULD PROBABLY... UHH...KEEP AN EYE ON THEM AT LEAST?
YOU MEAN SPY ON THEM?

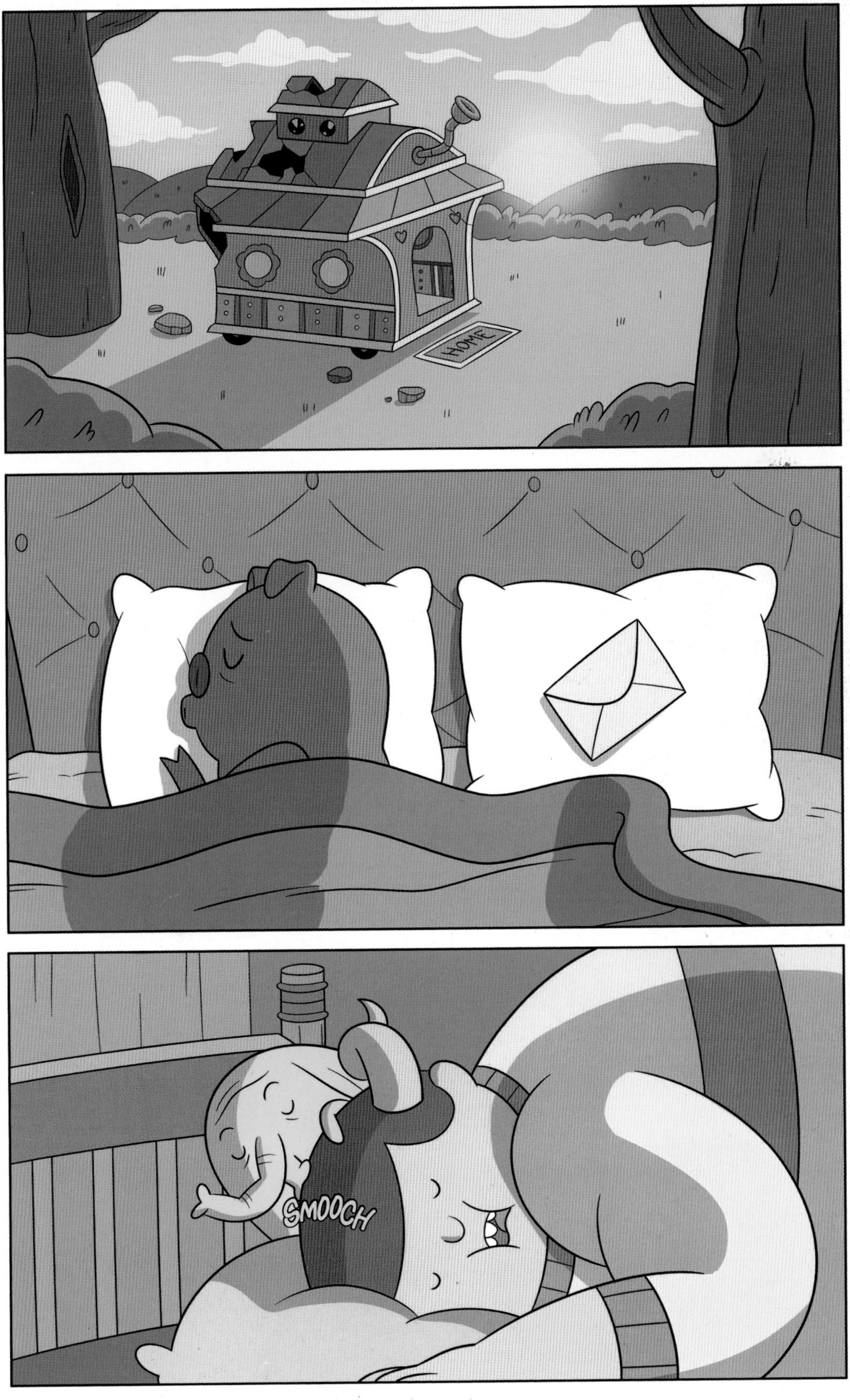
HOME
SMOOCH

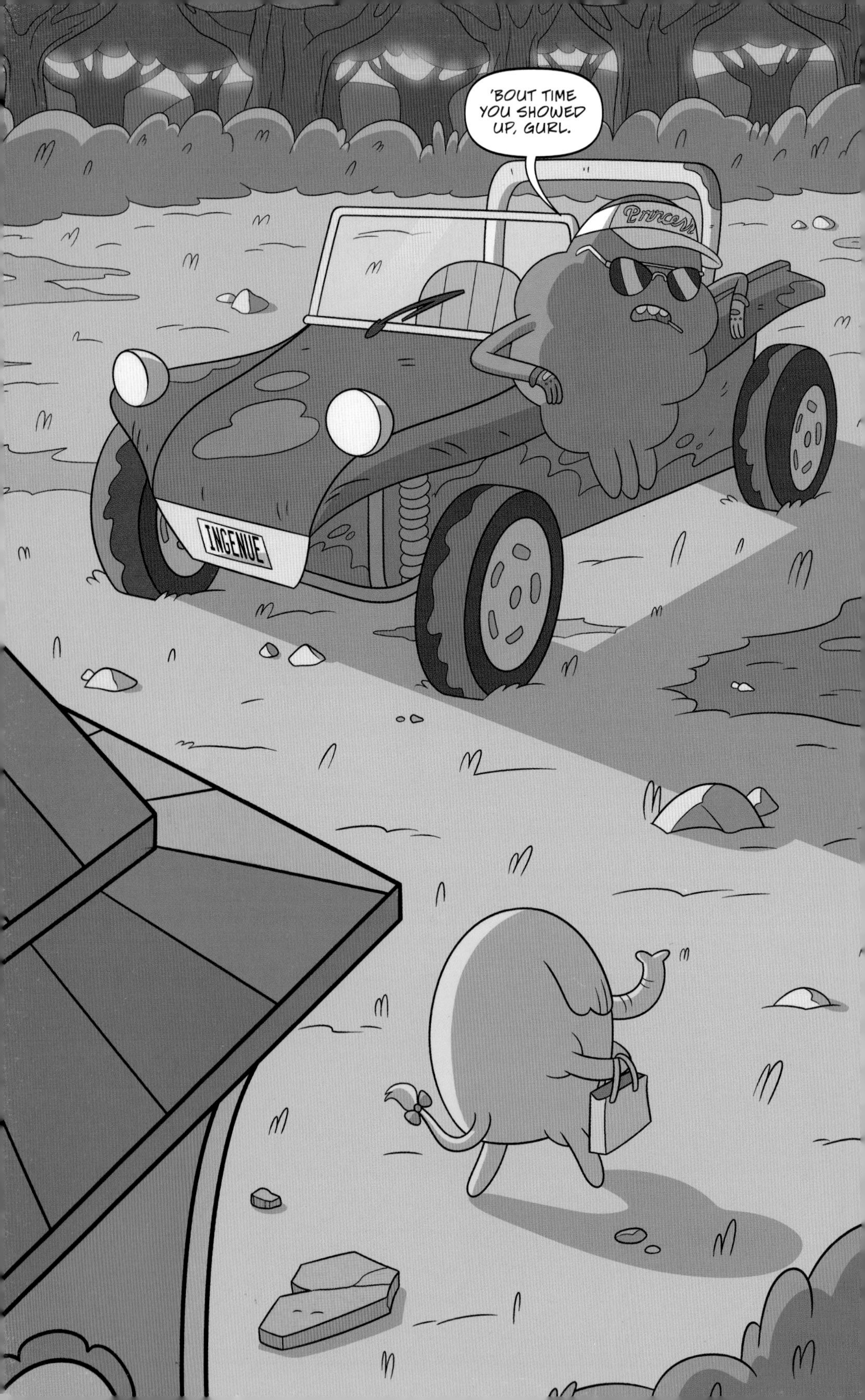
'BOUT TIME YOU SHOWED UP, GURL.
INGENUE

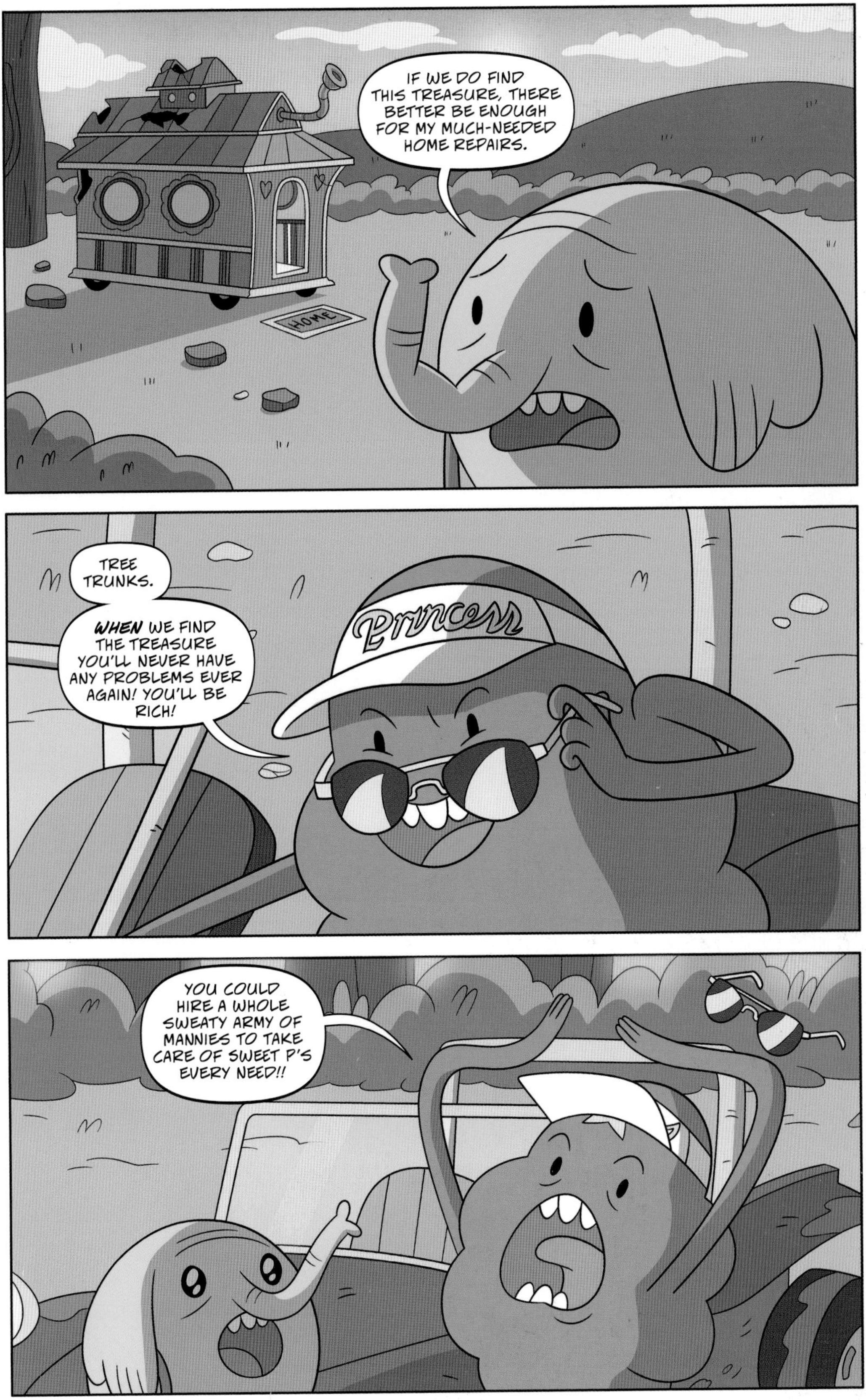
IF WE DO FIND THIS TREASURE, THERE BETTER BE ENOUGH FOR MY MUCH-NEEDED HOME REPAIRS.
HOME
TREE TRUNKS.
WHEN WE FIND THE TREASURE YOU'LL NEVER HAVE ANY PROBLEMS EVER AGAIN! YOU'LL BE RICH!
Princess
YOU COULD HIRE A WHOLE SWEATY ARMY OF MANNIES TO TAKE CARE OF SWEET P'S EVERY NEED!!

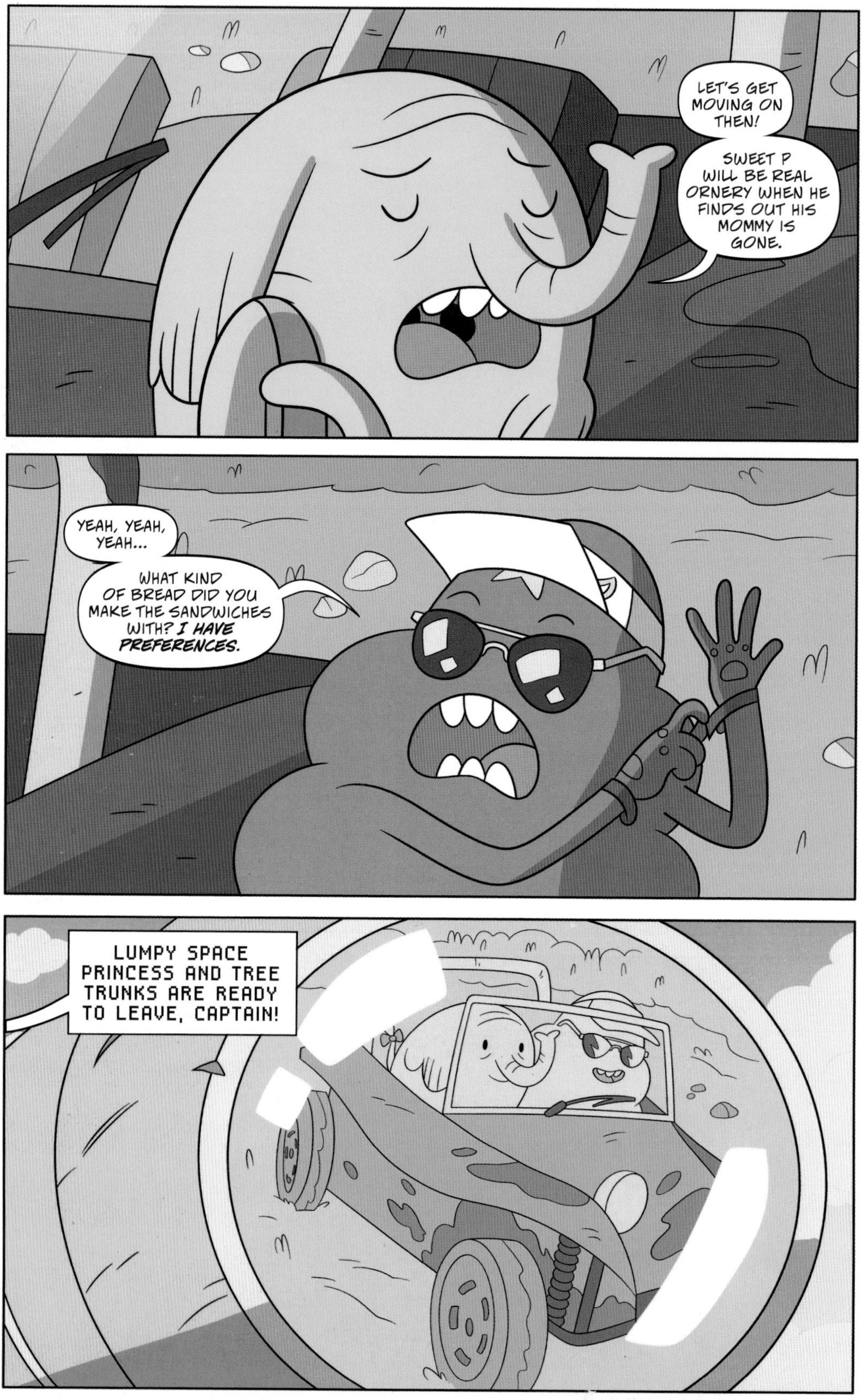
LET'S GET MOVING ON THEN!
SWEET P WILL BE REAL ORNERY WHEN HE FINDS OUT HIS MOMMY IS GONE.
YEAH, YEAH, YEAH...
WHAT KIND OF BREAD DID YOU MAKE THE SANDWICHES WITH? *I HAVE PREFERENCES.*
LUMPY SPACE PRINCESS AND TREE TRUNKS ARE READY TO LEAVE, CAPTAIN!

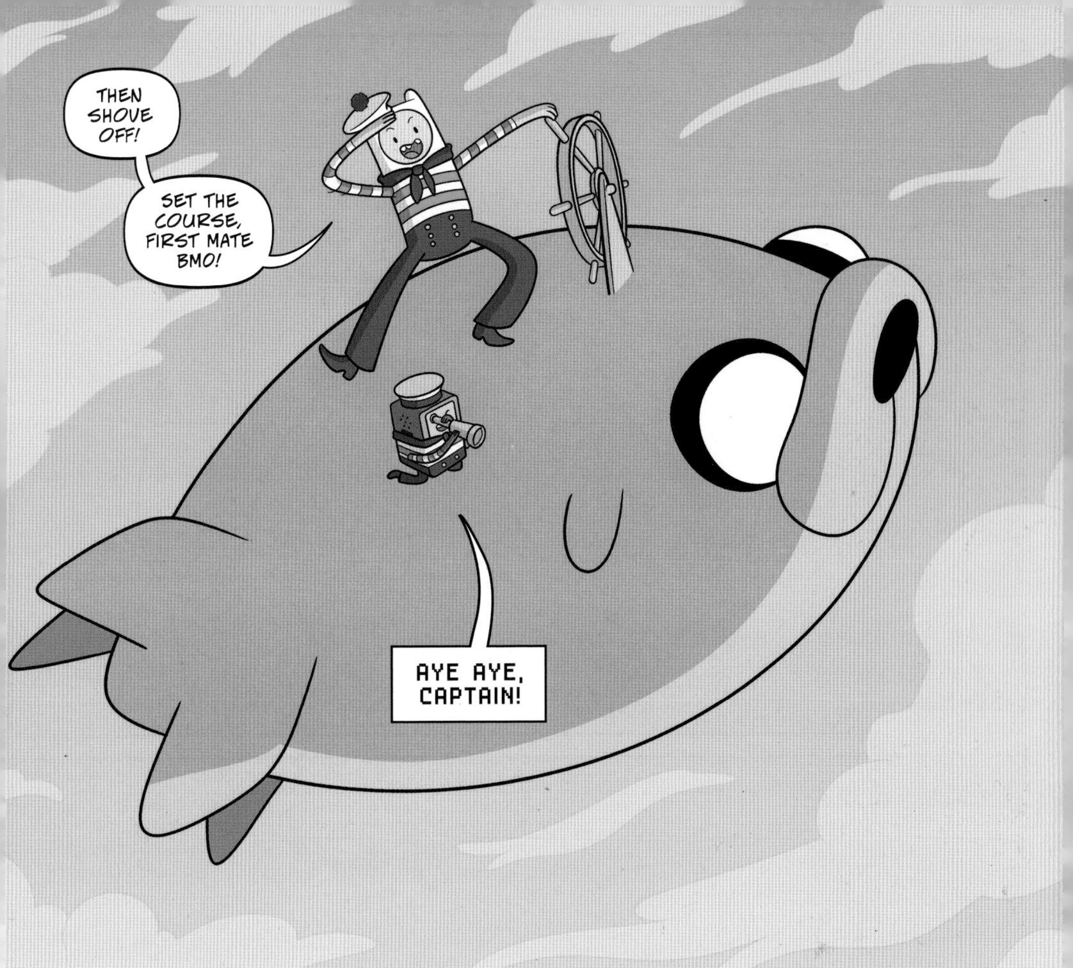
THEN SHOVE OFF!
SET THE COURSE, FIRST MATE BMO!
AYE AYE, CAPTAIN!

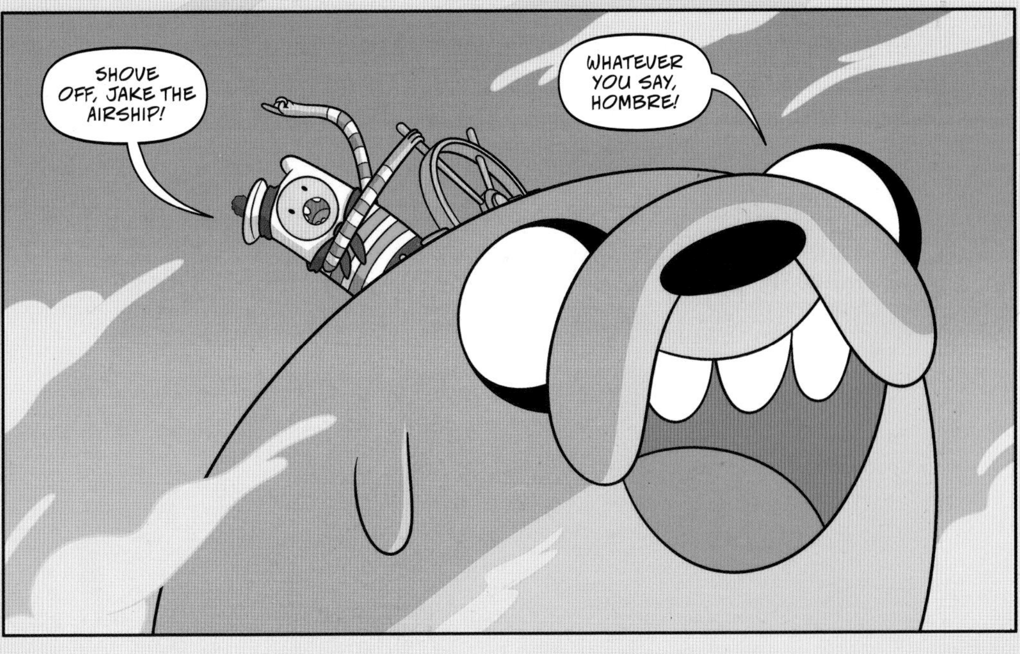
SHOVE OFF, JAKE THE AIRSHIP!
WHATEVER YOU SAY, HOMBRE!

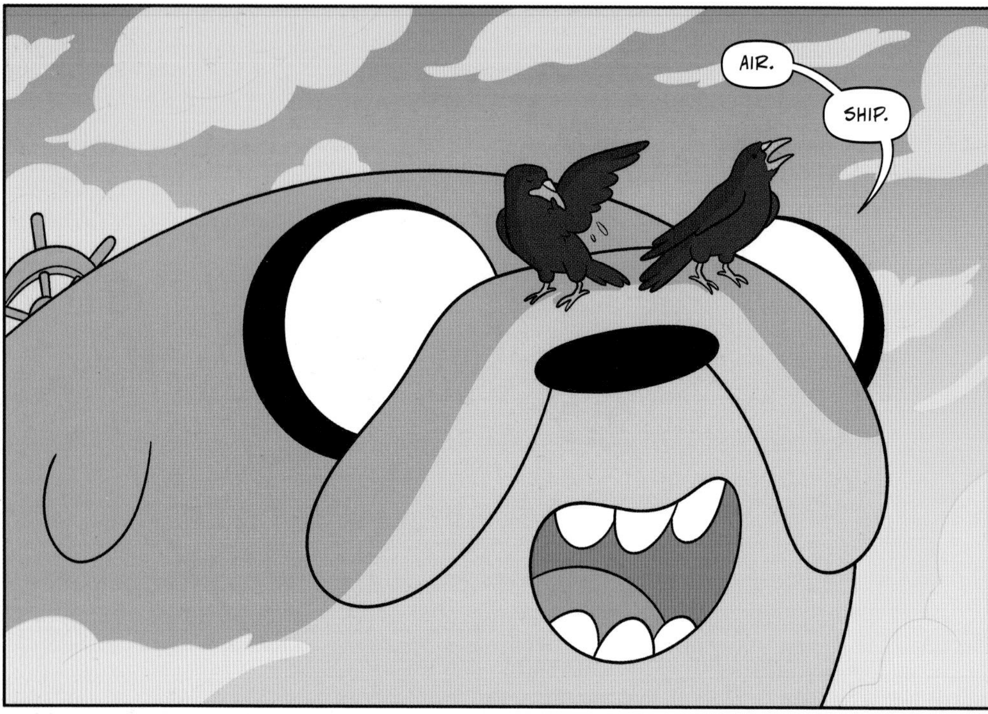
AIR.
SHIP.
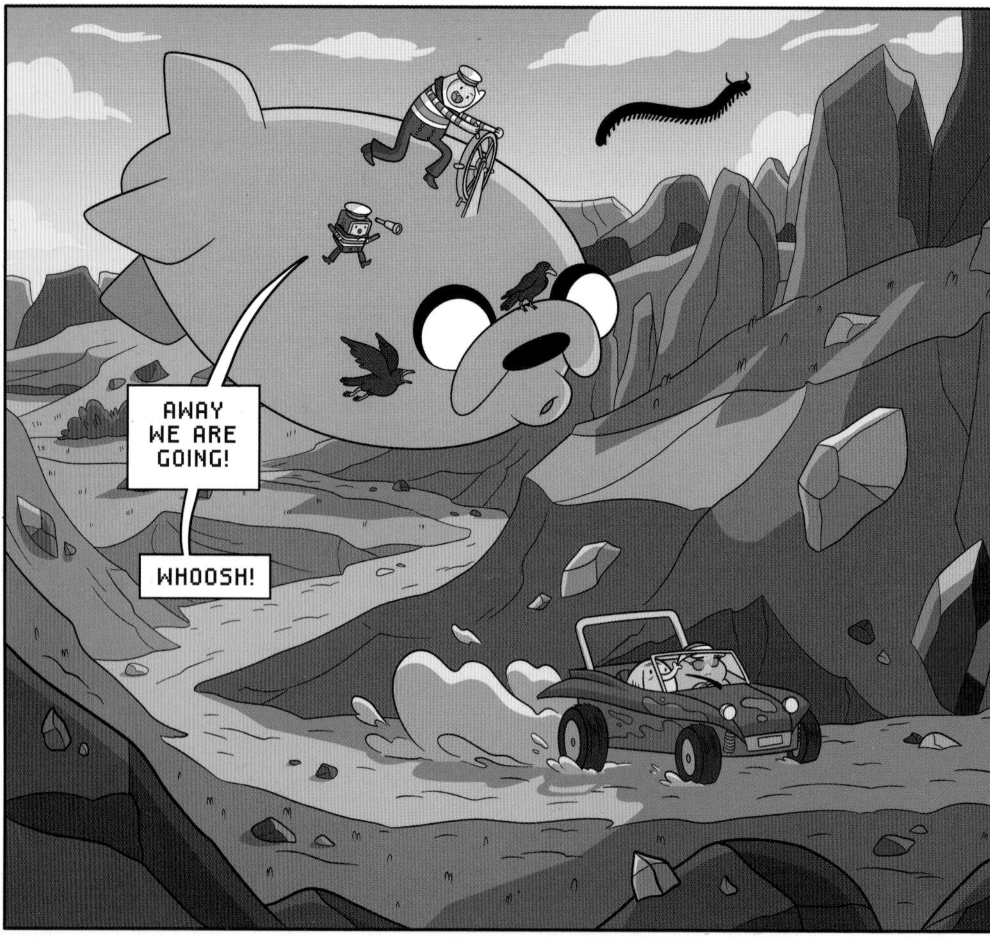
AWAY WE ARE GOING!
WHOOSH!

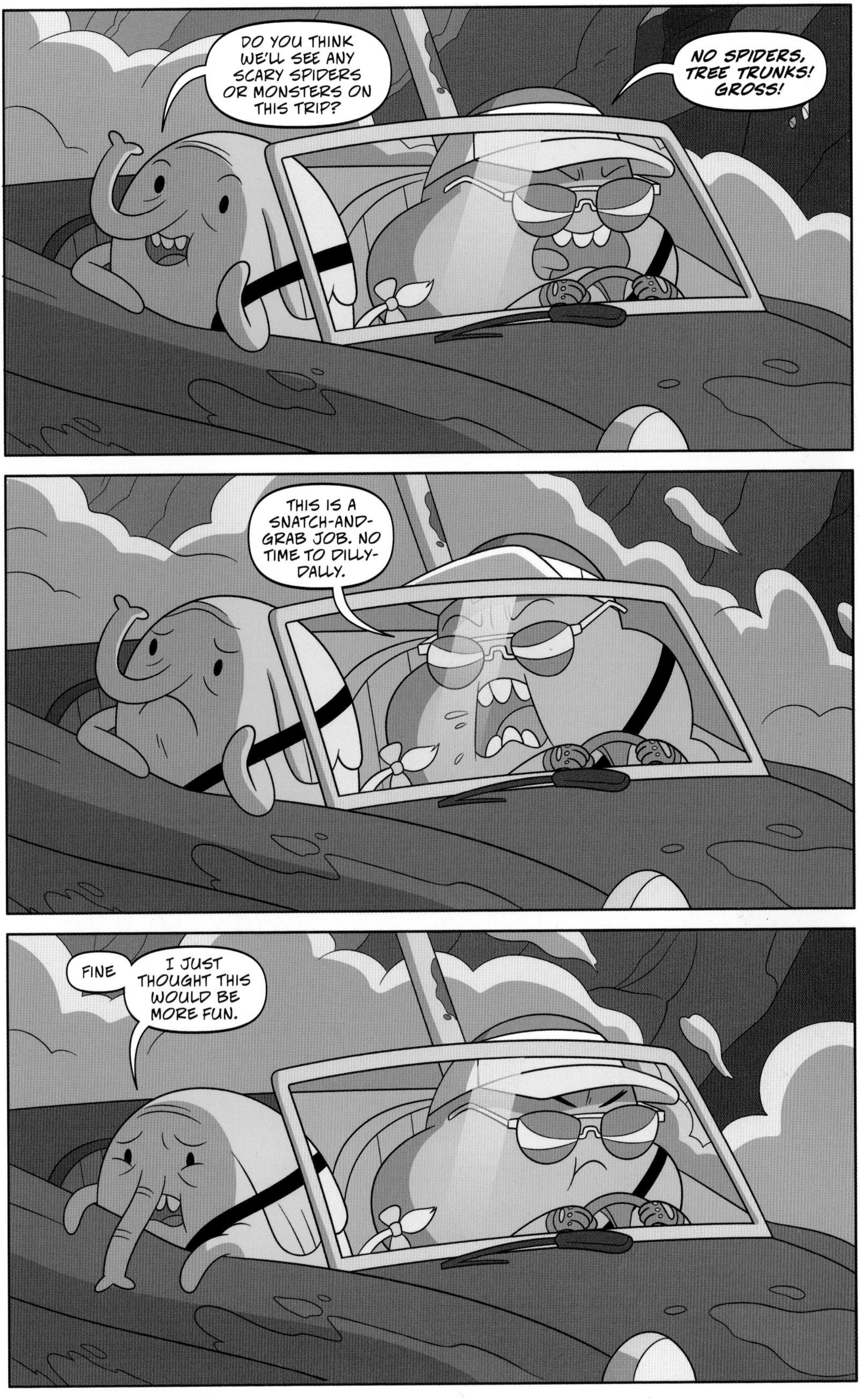
DO YOU THINK WE'LL SEE ANY SCARY SPIDERS OR MONSTERS ON THIS TRIP?
NO SPIDERS, TREE TRUNKS! GROSS!
THIS IS A SNATCH-AND-GRAB JOB. NO TIME TO DILLY-DALLY.
FINE
I JUST THOUGHT THIS WOULD BE MORE FUN.

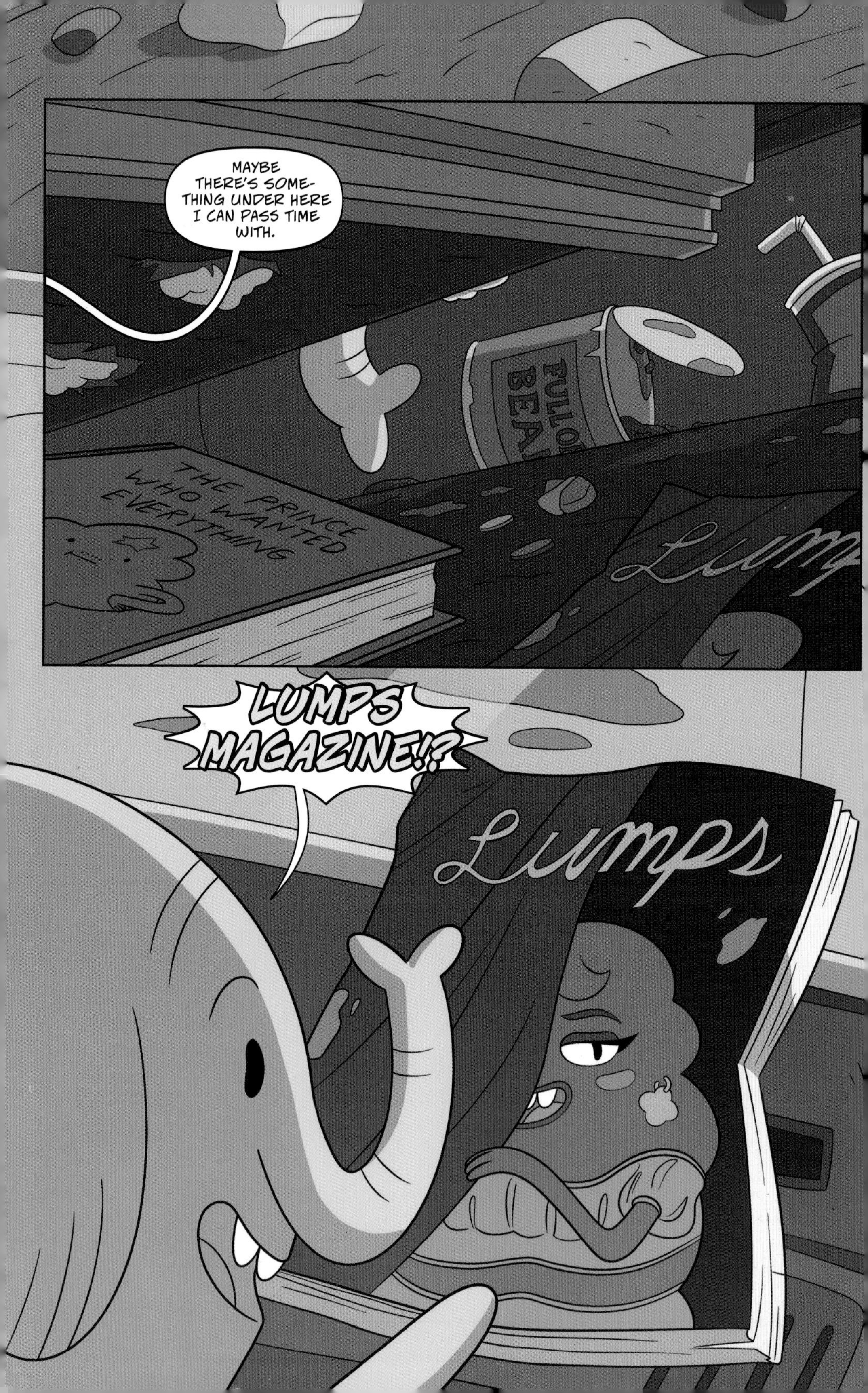
MAYBE THERE'S SOME-THING UNDER HERE I CAN PASS TIME WITH.
THE PRINCE WHO WANTED EVERYTHING
Lumps
LUMPS MAGAZINE!?
Lumps

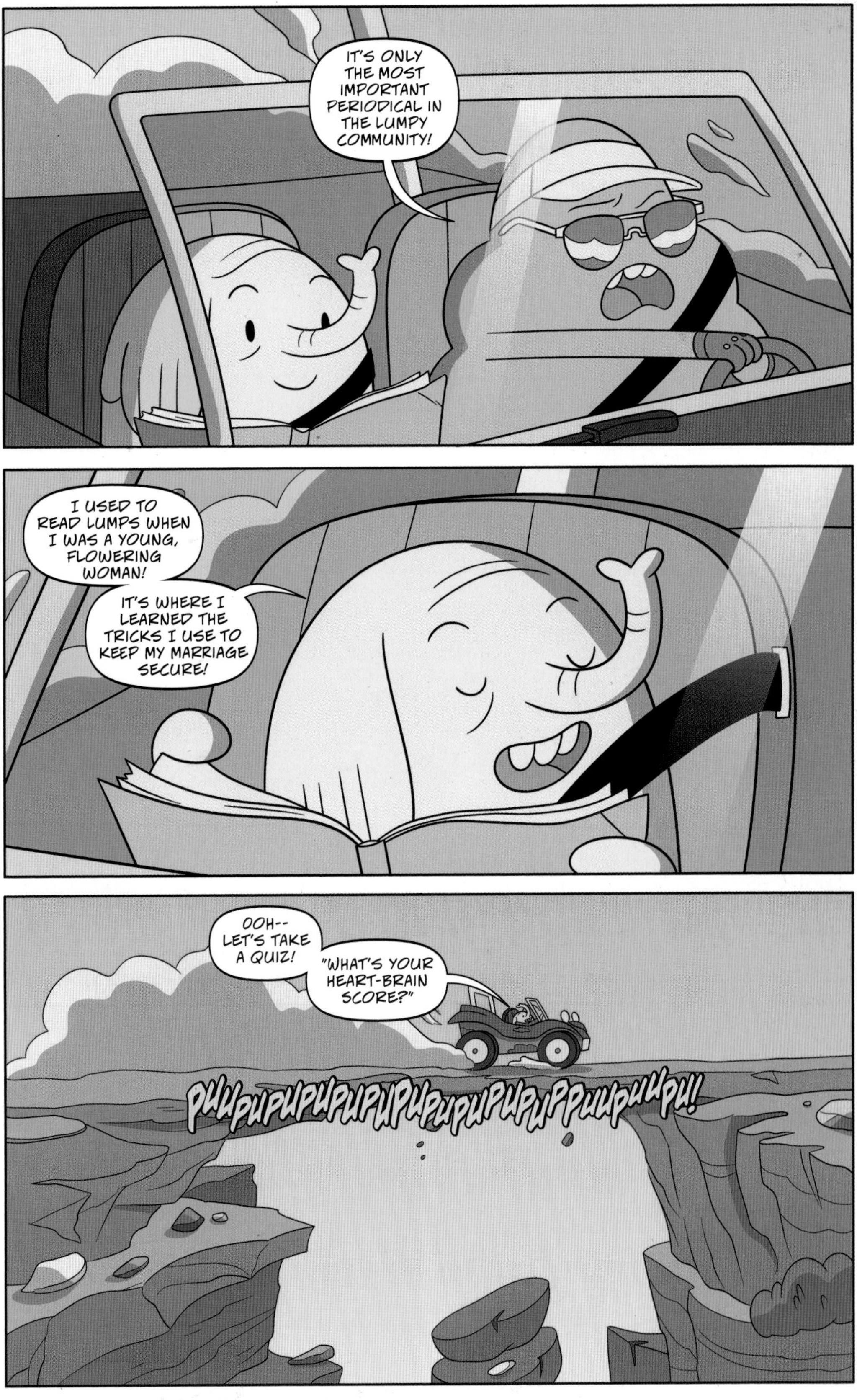
IT'S ONLY THE MOST IMPORTANT PERIODICAL IN THE LUMPY COMMUNITY!
I USED TO READ LUMPS WHEN I WAS A YOUNG, FLOWERING WOMAN!
IT'S WHERE I LEARNED THE TRICKS I USE TO KEEP MY MARRIAGE SECURE!
OOH-- LET'S TAKE A QUIZ!
"WHAT'S YOUR HEART-BRAIN SCORE?"
PUUPUPUPUPUPUPUPUPUPUPUPUPUPPUUPUUPU!

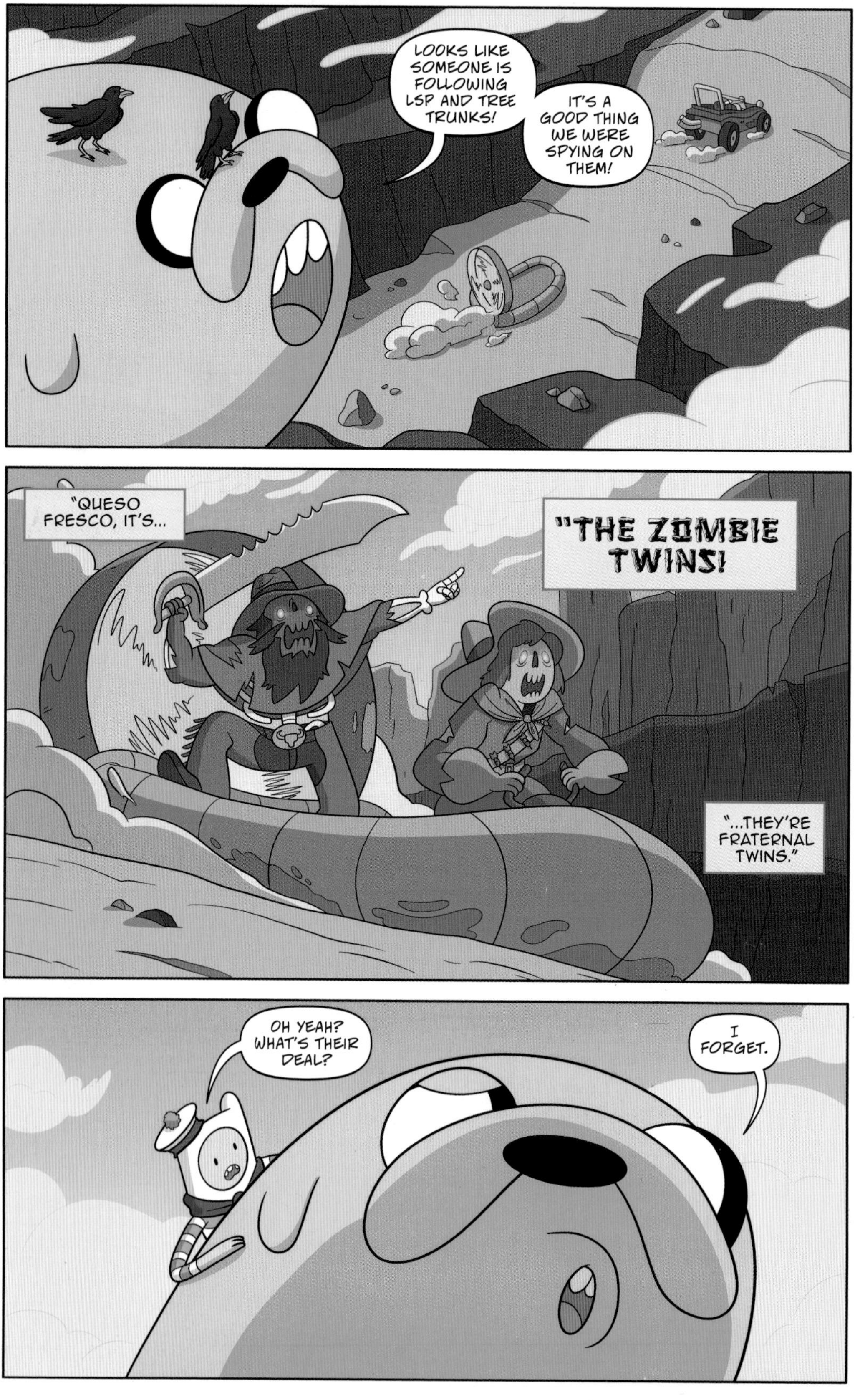
LOOKS LIKE SOMEONE IS FOLLOWING LSP AND TREE TRUNKS!
IT'S A GOOD THING WE WERE SPYING ON THEM!
"QUESO FRESCO, IT'S...
"THE ZOMBIE TWINS!
"...THEY'RE FRATERNAL TWINS."
OH YEAH? WHAT'S THEIR DEAL?
I FORGET.

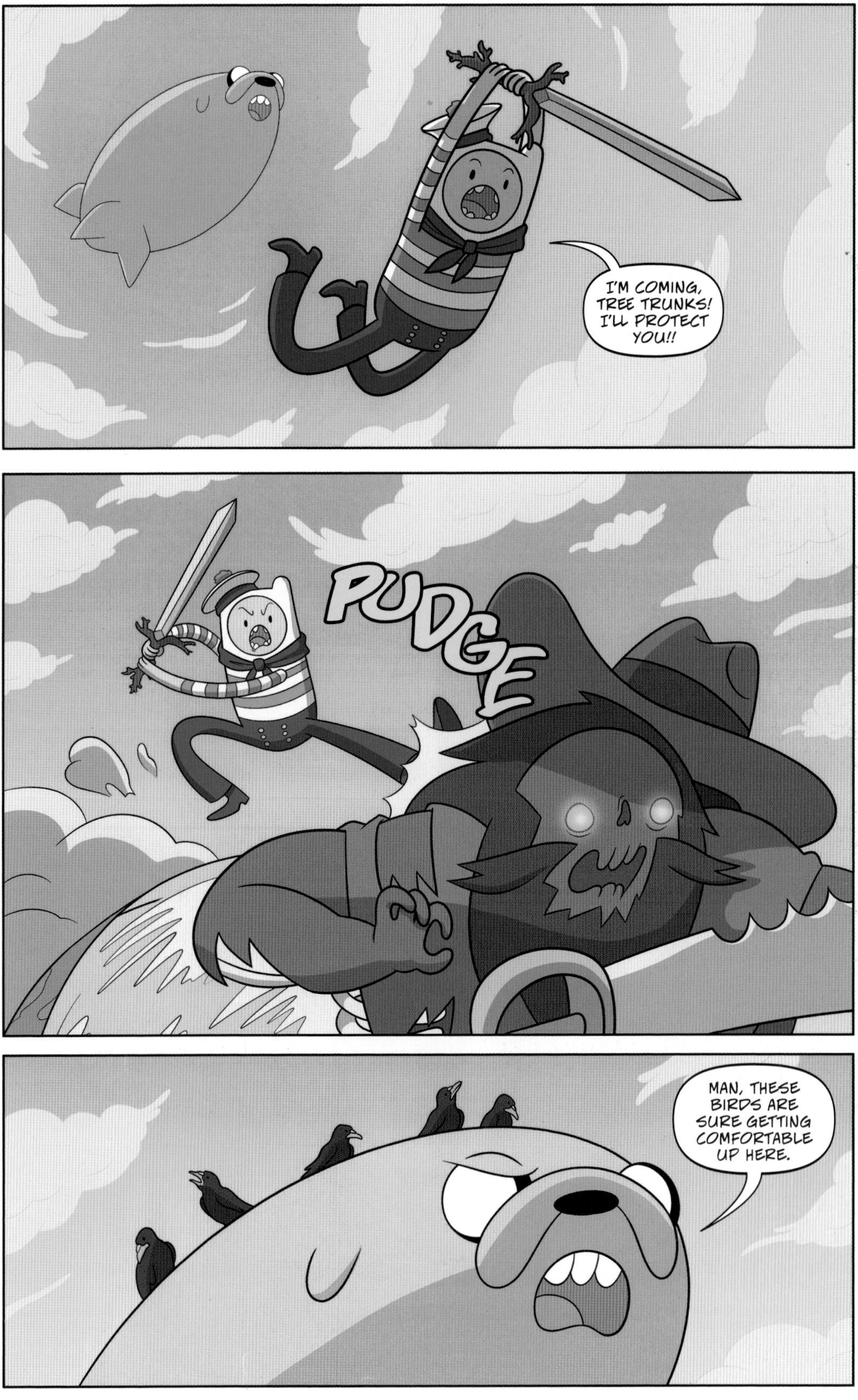
I'M COMING, TREE TRUNKS! I'LL PROTECT YOU!!
PUDGE
MAN, THESE BIRDS ARE SURE GETTING COMFORTABLE UP HERE.

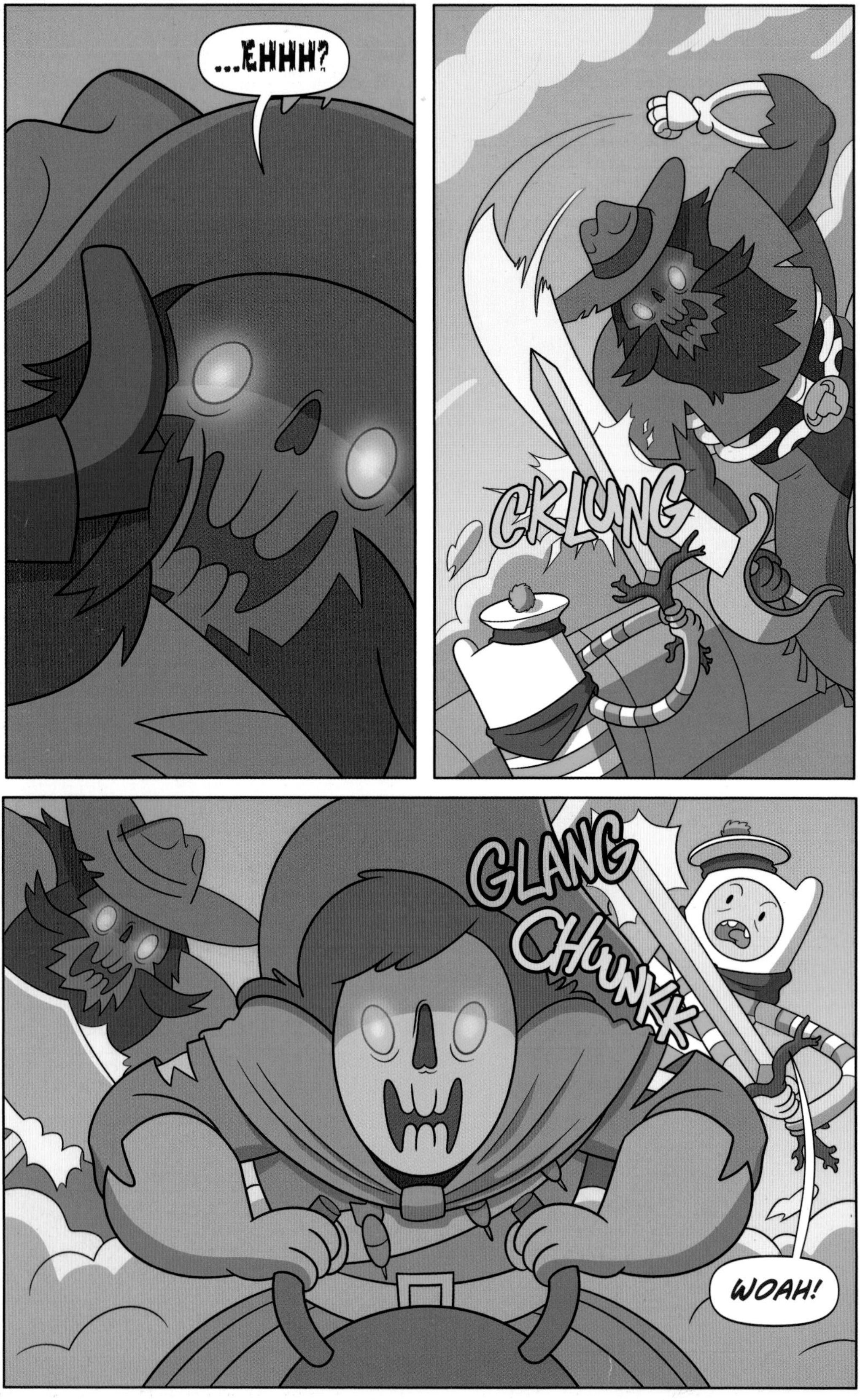
...EHHH?
CKLUNG
GLANG
CHUNKK
WOAH!

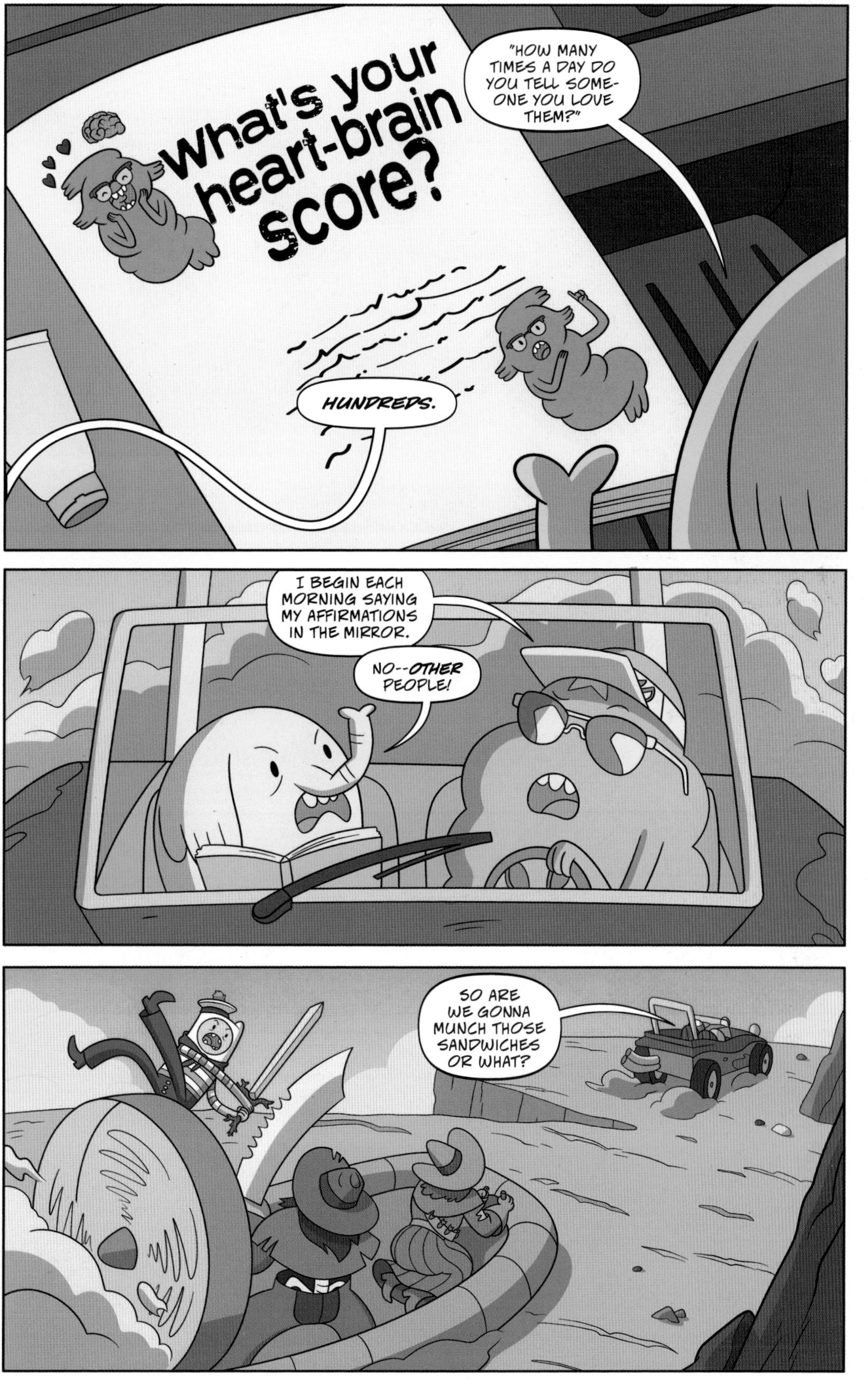
What's your heart-brain score?
"HOW MANY TIMES A DAY DO YOU TELL SOME-ONE YOU LOVE THEM?"
HUNDREDS.
I BEGIN EACH MORNING SAYING MY AFFIRMATIONS IN THE MIRROR.
NO--OTHER PEOPLE!
SO ARE WE GONNA MUNCH THOSE SANDWICHES OR WHAT?

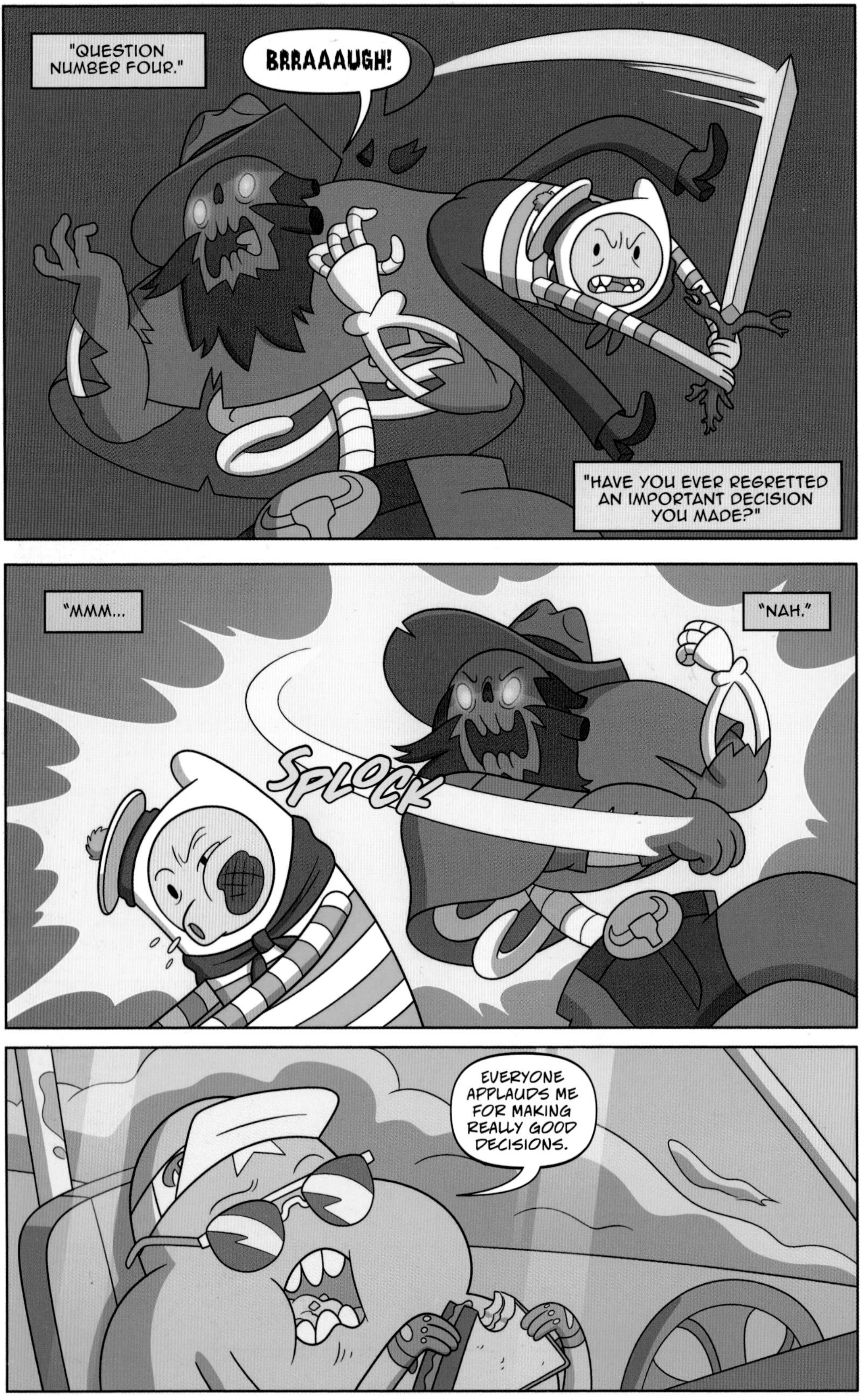
"QUESTION NUMBER FOUR."
BRRAAAUGH!
"HAVE YOU EVER REGRETTED AN IMPORTANT DECISION YOU MADE?"
"MMM...
"NAH."
SPLOCK
EVERYONE APPLAUDS ME FOR MAKING REALLY GOOD DECISIONS.

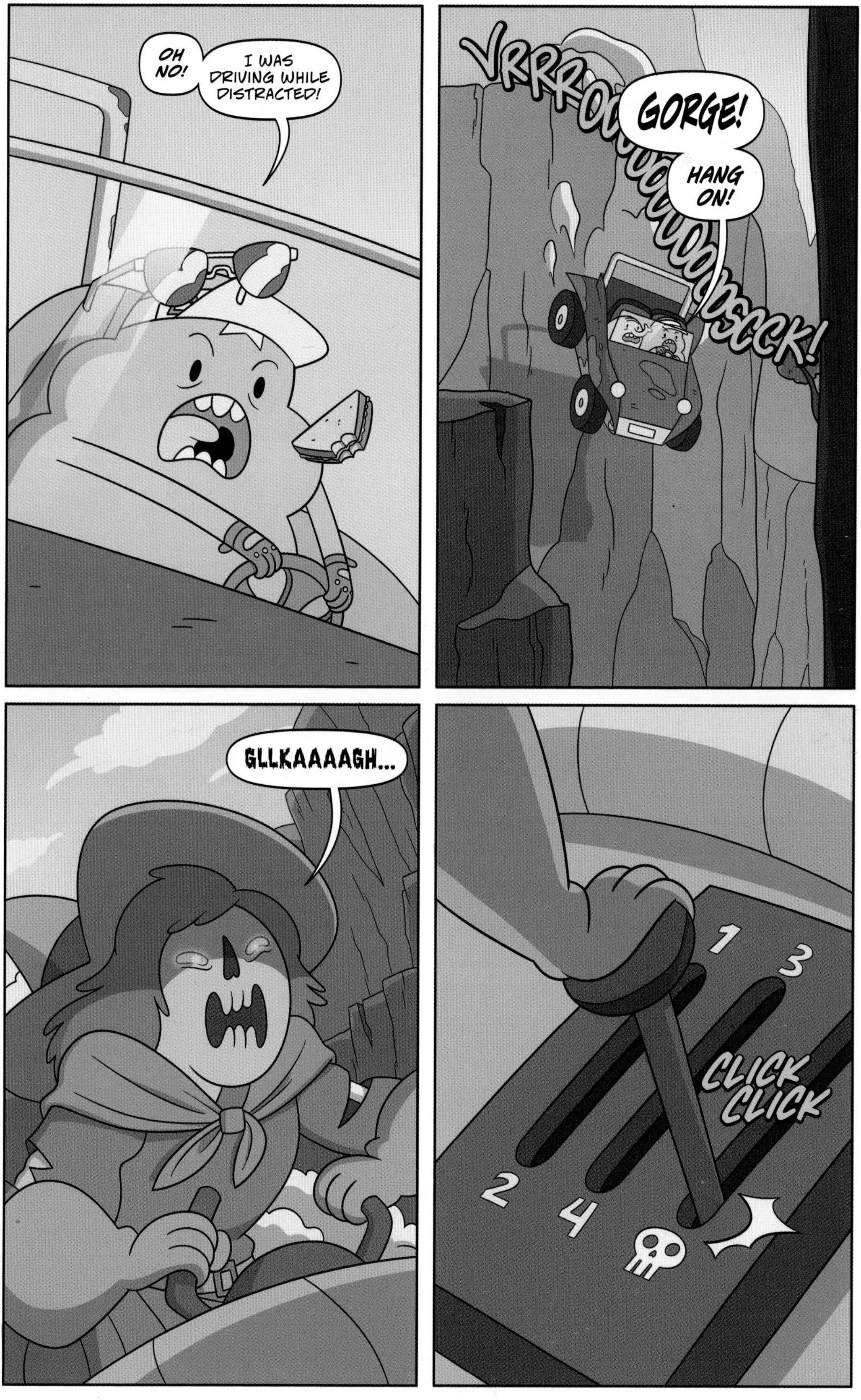
OH NO!
I WAS DRIVING WHILE DISTRACTED!
VRRROOOOOOOOOOOSCCK!
GORGE!
HANG ON!
GLLKAAAAGH...
1
3
CLICK CLICK
2
4

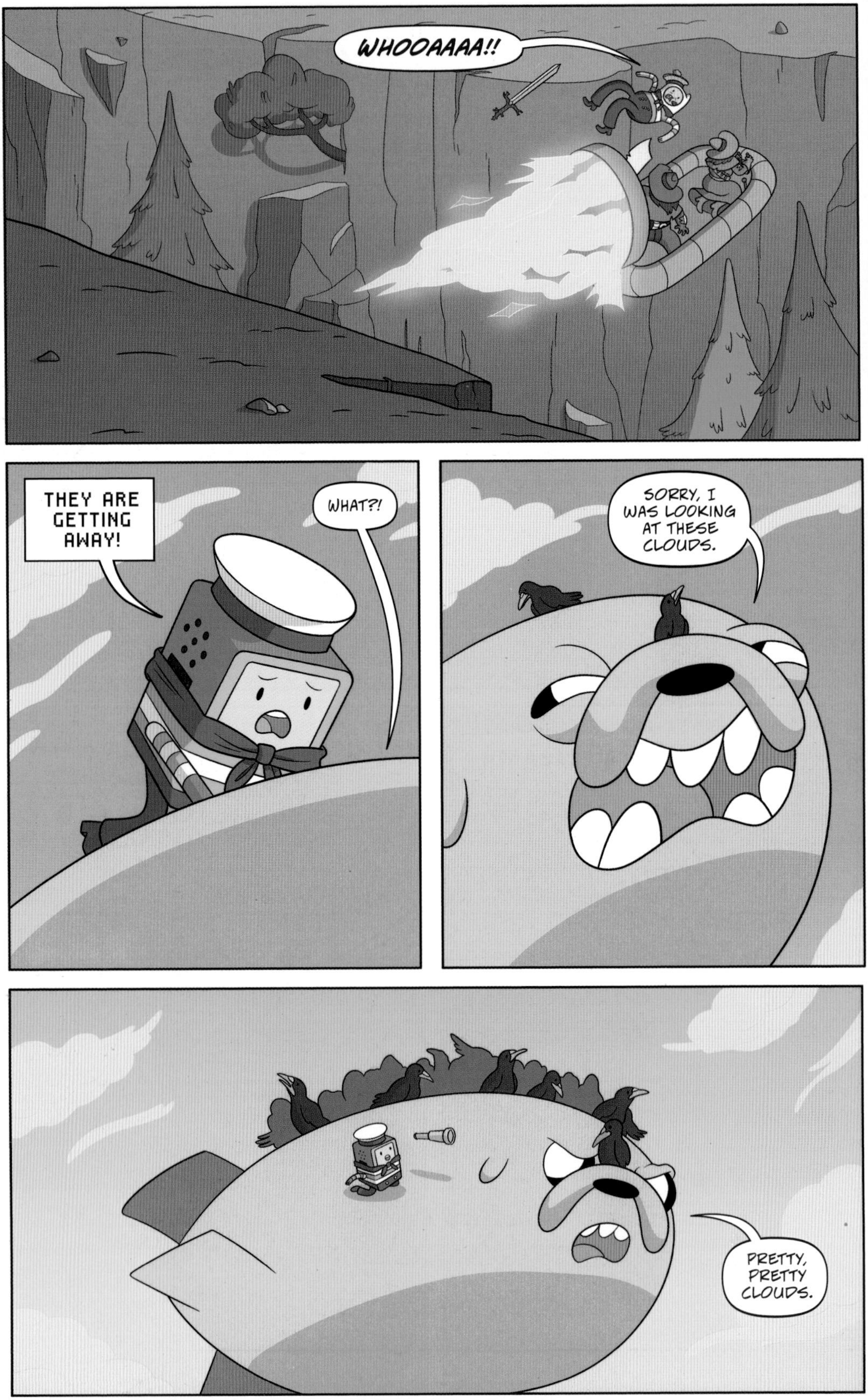
WHOOAAAA!!
THEY ARE GETTING AWAY!
WHAT?!
SORRY, I WAS LOOKING AT THESE CLOUDS.
PRETTY, PRETTY CLOUDS.

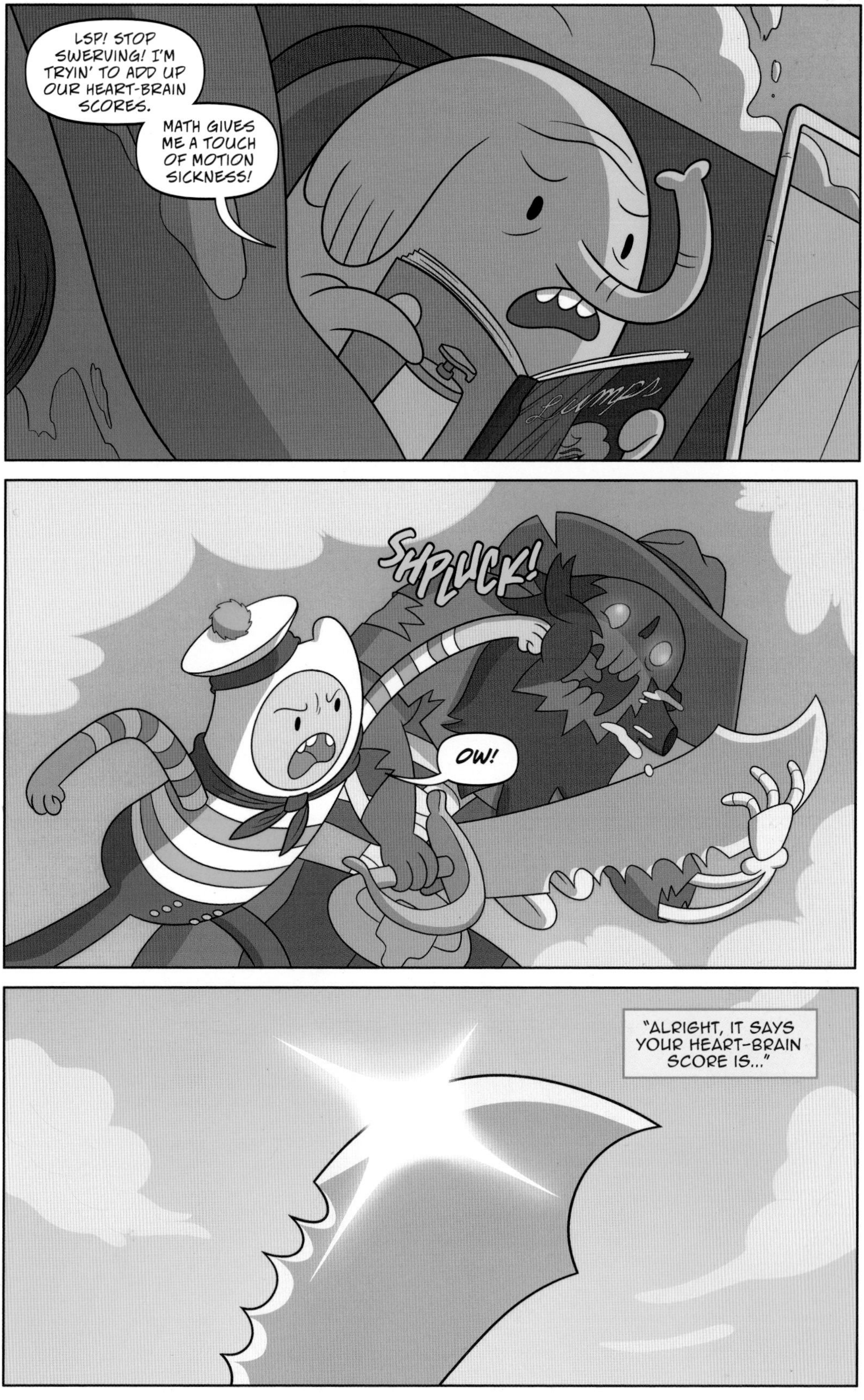
LSP! STOP SWERVING! I'M TRYIN' TO ADD UP OUR HEART-BRAIN SCORES.
MATH GIVES ME A TOUCH OF MOTION SICKNESS!
SHPLUCK!
OW!
"ALRIGHT, IT SAYS YOUR HEART-BRAIN SCORE IS..."

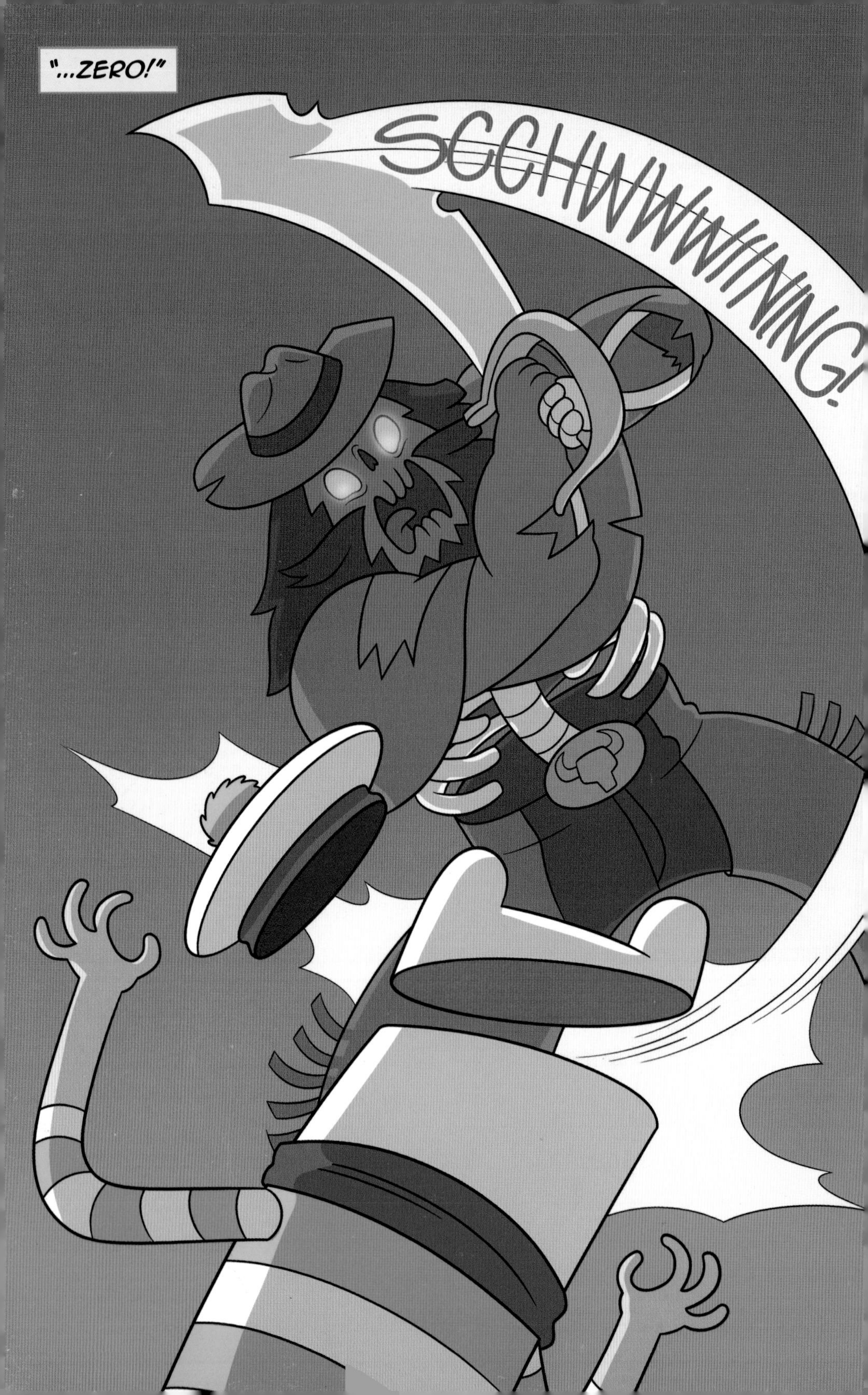
"...ZERO!"
SCCHWWWWING!

BRRROUUUGN?

HISSSS...

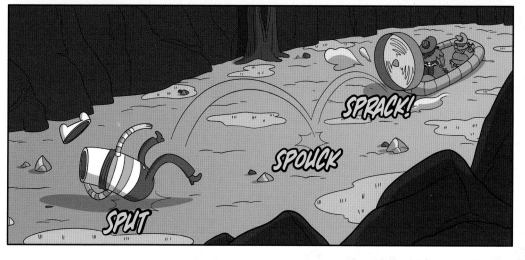

SPRACK!

SPOUCK

SPUT

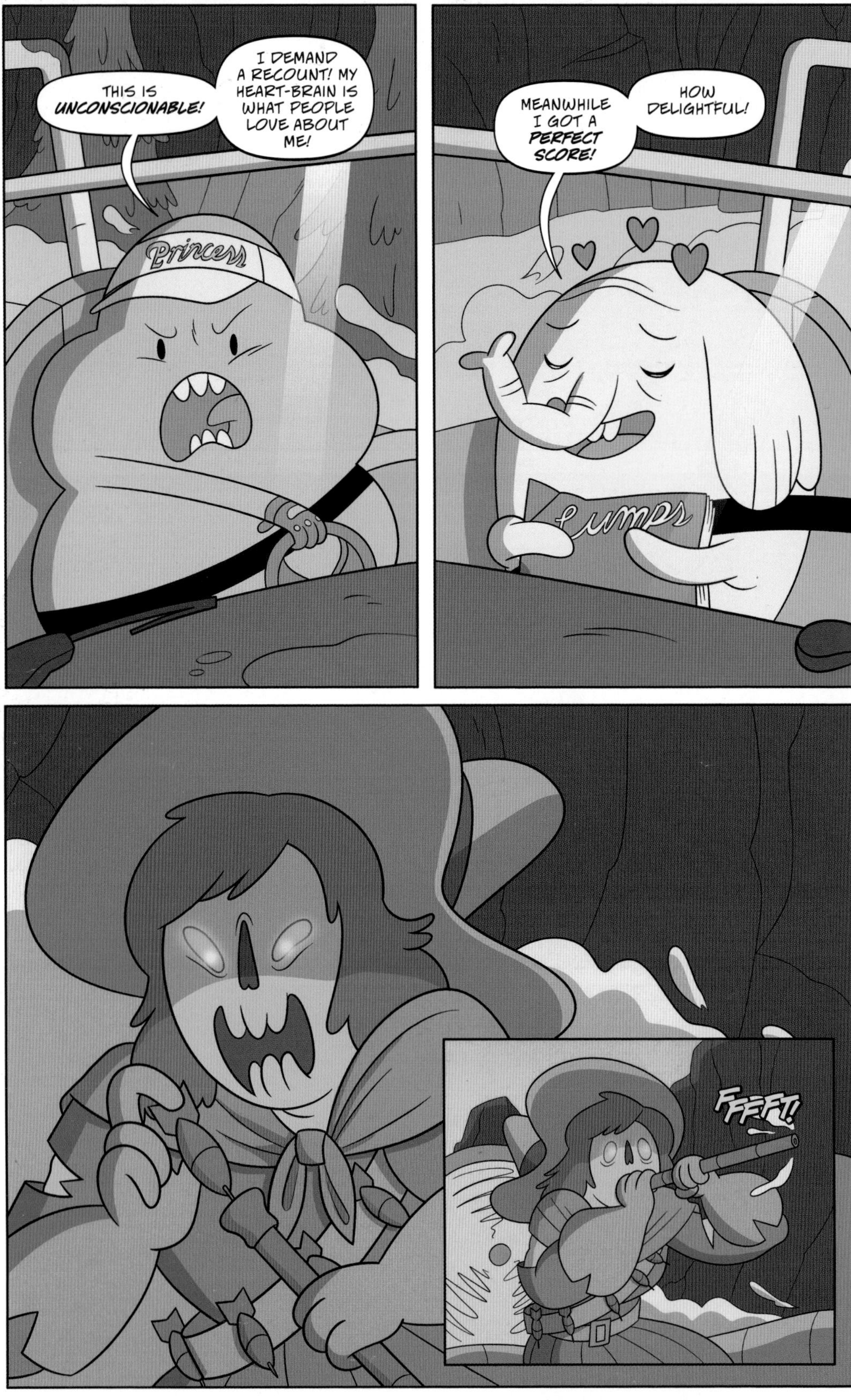
THIS IS UNCONSCIONABLE!
I DEMAND A RECOUNT! MY HEART-BRAIN IS WHAT PEOPLE LOVE ABOUT ME!
Princess
MEANWHILE I GOT A PERFECT SCORE!
HOW DELIGHTFUL!
Lumps
FFFFT!

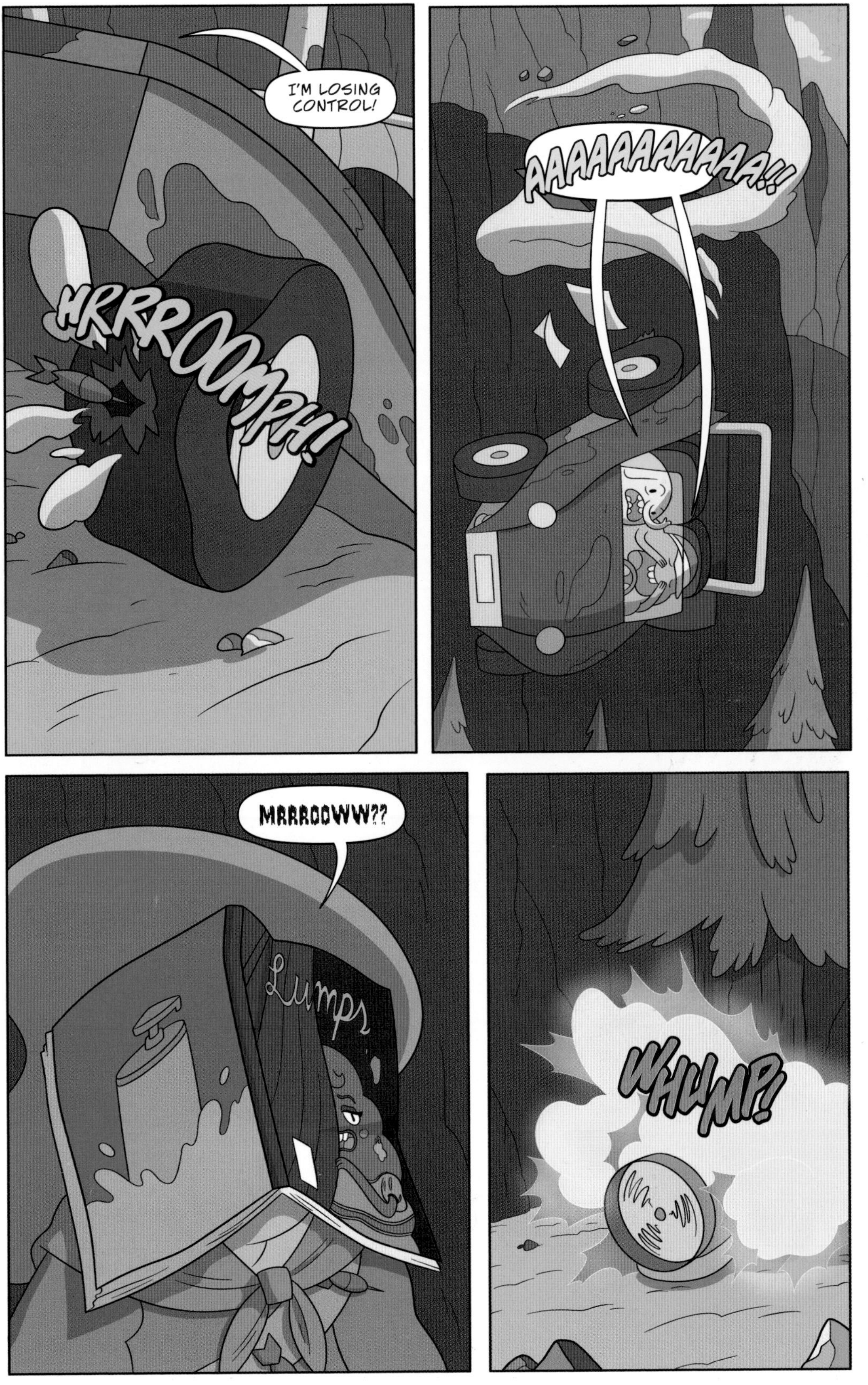
I'M LOSING CONTROL!
HRRROOMPH!
AAAAAAAAAAA!!
MRRROOWW??
Lumps
WHUMP!

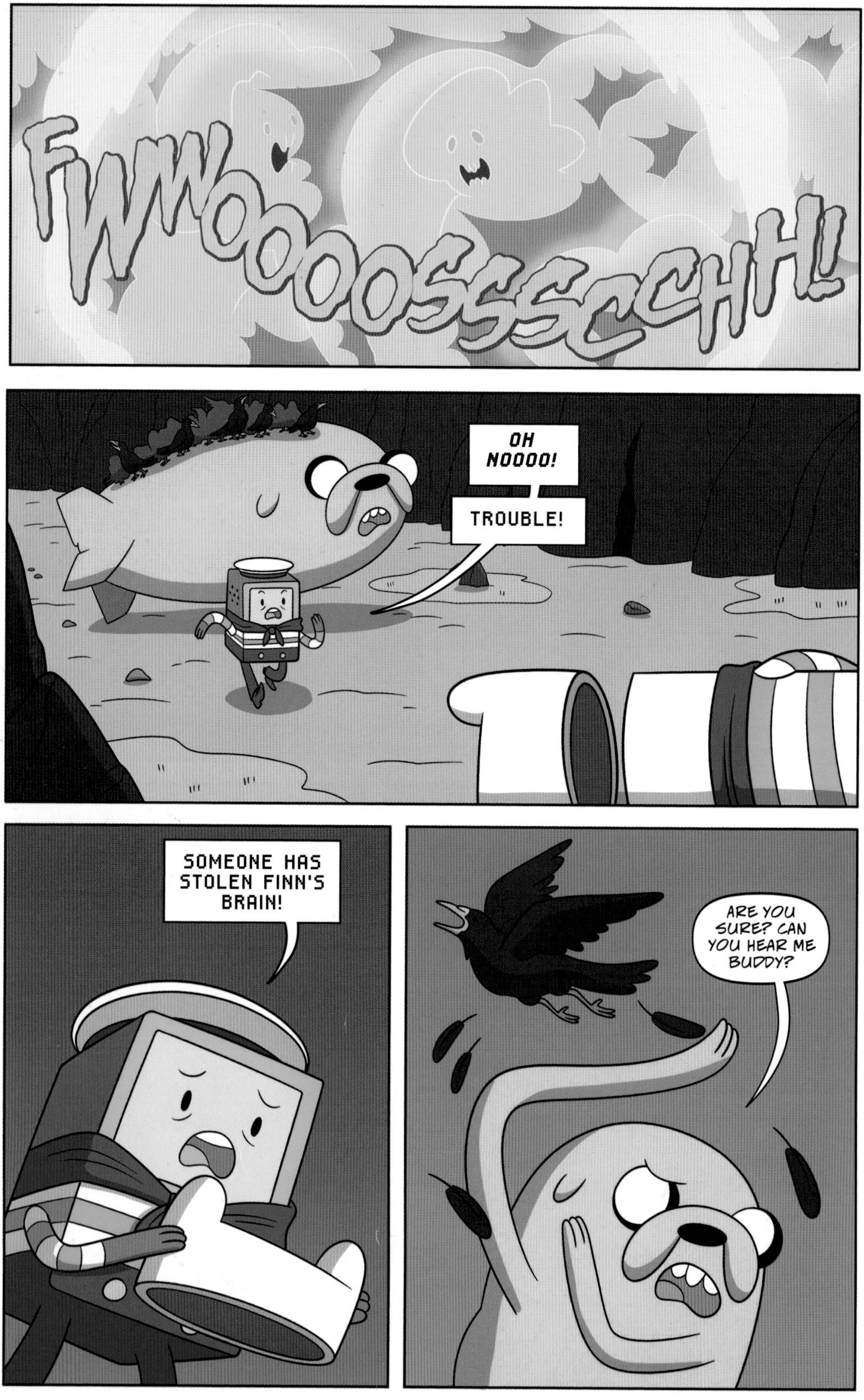
FWWOOOOOSSSCCHH!!
OH NOOOO!
TROUBLE!
SOMEONE HAS STOLEN FINN'S BRAIN!
ARE YOU SURE? CAN YOU HEAR ME BUDDY?

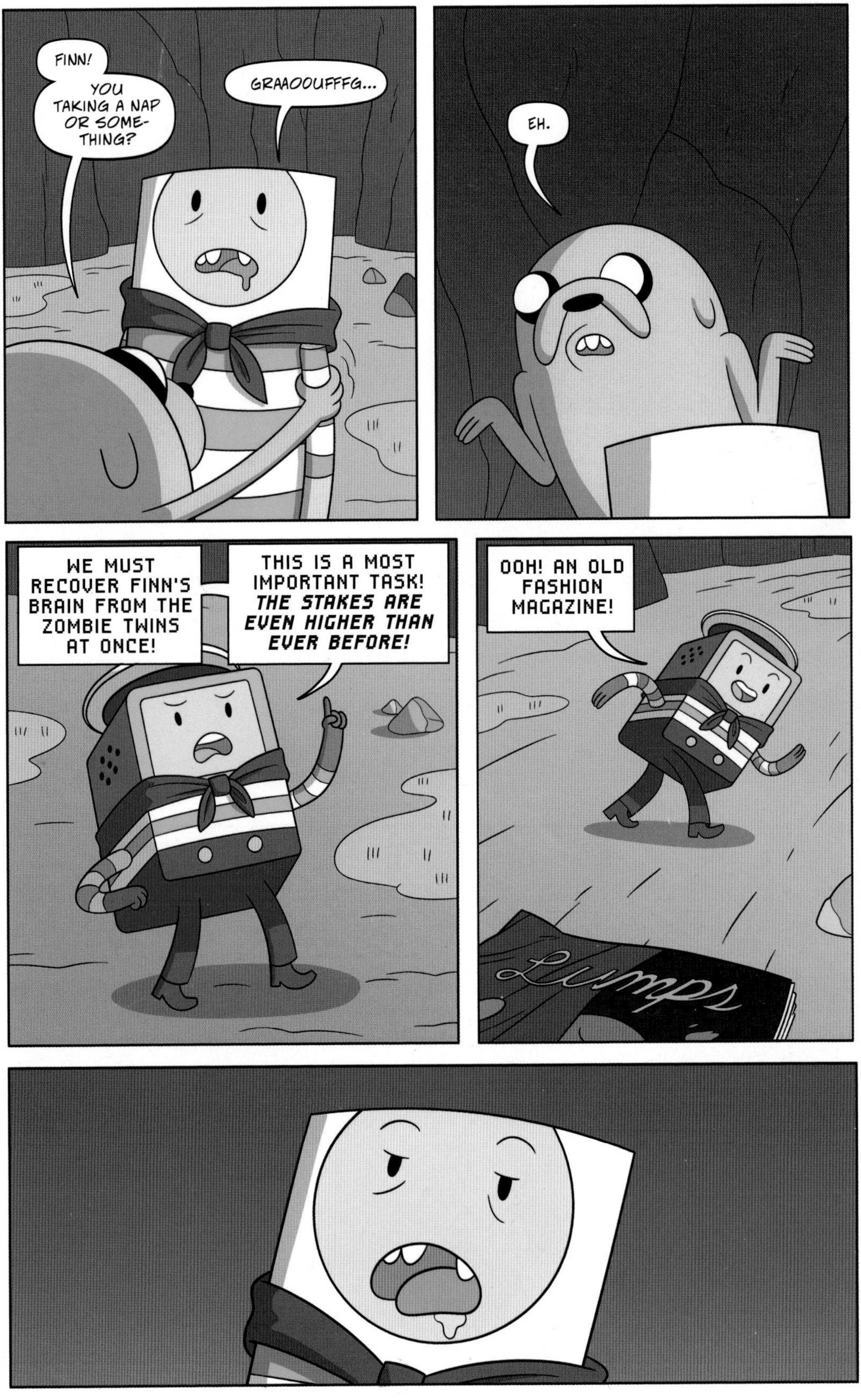
FINN!
YOU TAKING A NAP OR SOME-THING?
GRAAOOUFFFG...
EH.
WE MUST RECOVER FINN'S BRAIN FROM THE ZOMBIE TWINS AT ONCE!
THIS IS A MOST IMPORTANT TASK! *THE STAKES ARE EVEN HIGHER THAN EVER BEFORE!*
OOH! AN OLD FASHION MAGAZINE!
Lumps

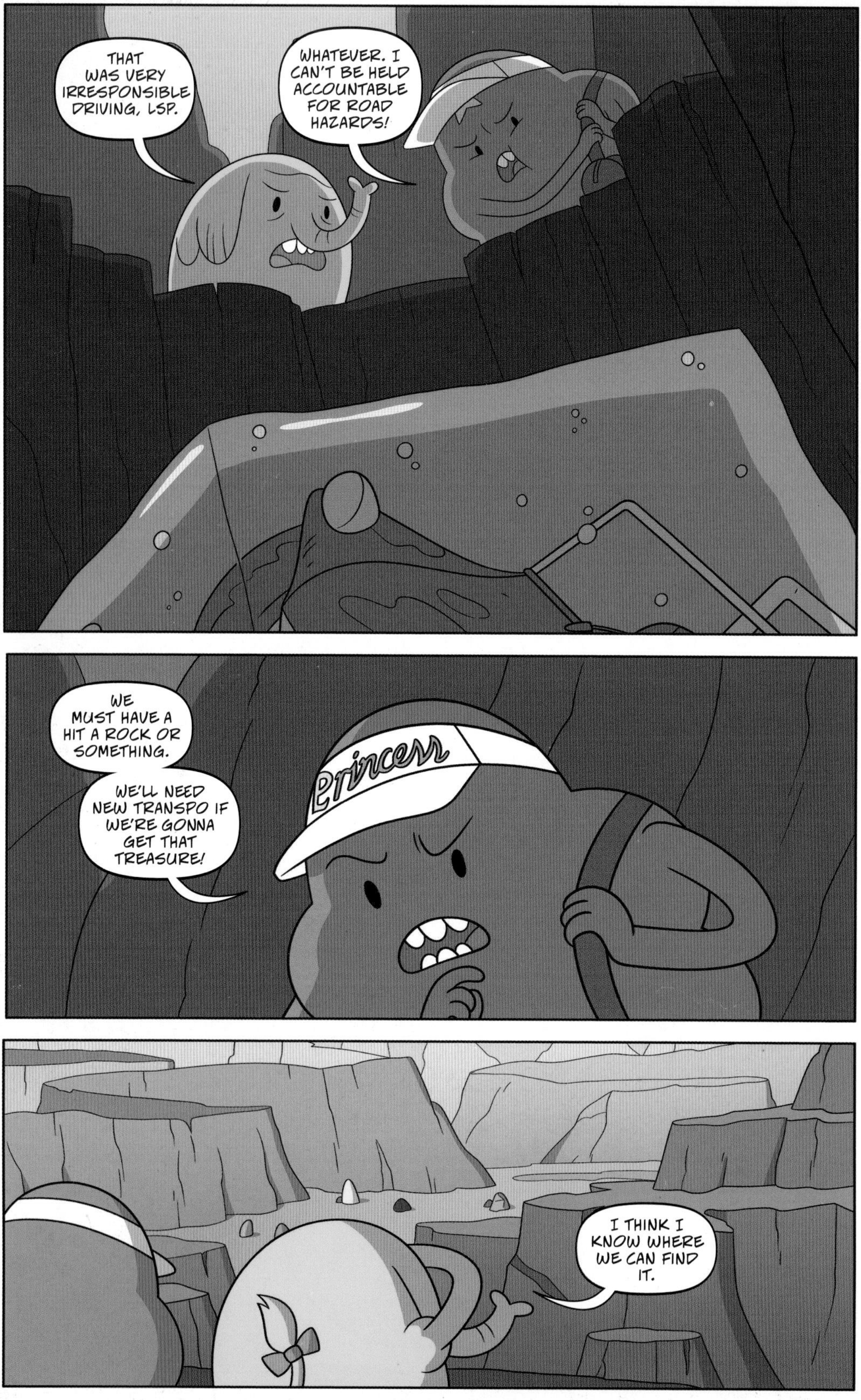
THAT WAS VERY IRRESPONSIBLE DRIVING, LSP.
WHATEVER. I CAN'T BE HELD ACCOUNTABLE FOR ROAD HAZARDS!
WE MUST HAVE A HIT A ROCK OR SOMETHING.
WE'LL NEED NEW TRANSPO IF WE'RE GONNA GET THAT TREASURE!
Princess
I THINK I KNOW WHERE WE CAN FIND IT.

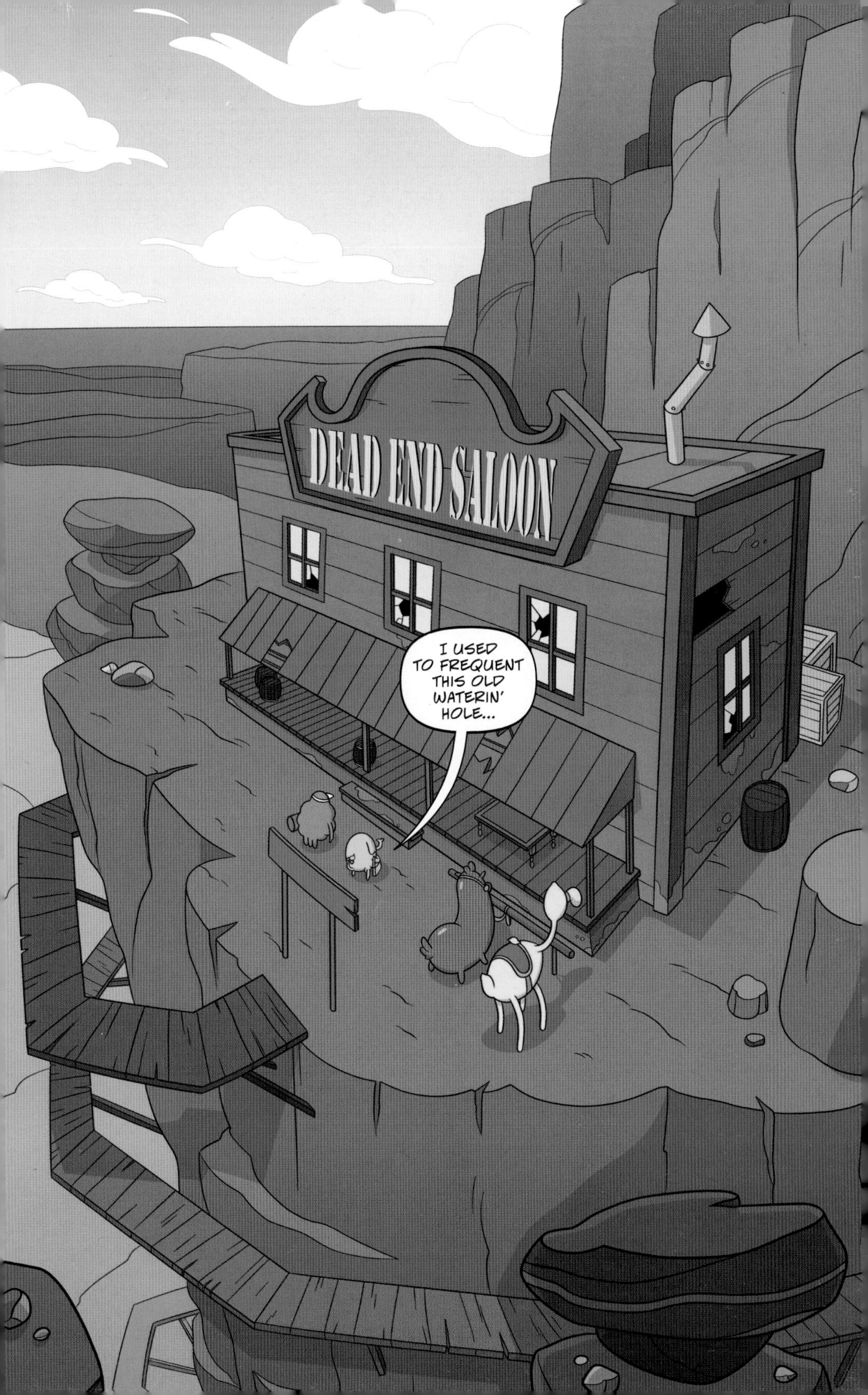
DEAD END SALOON
I USED TO FREQUENT THIS OLD WATERIN' HOLE...

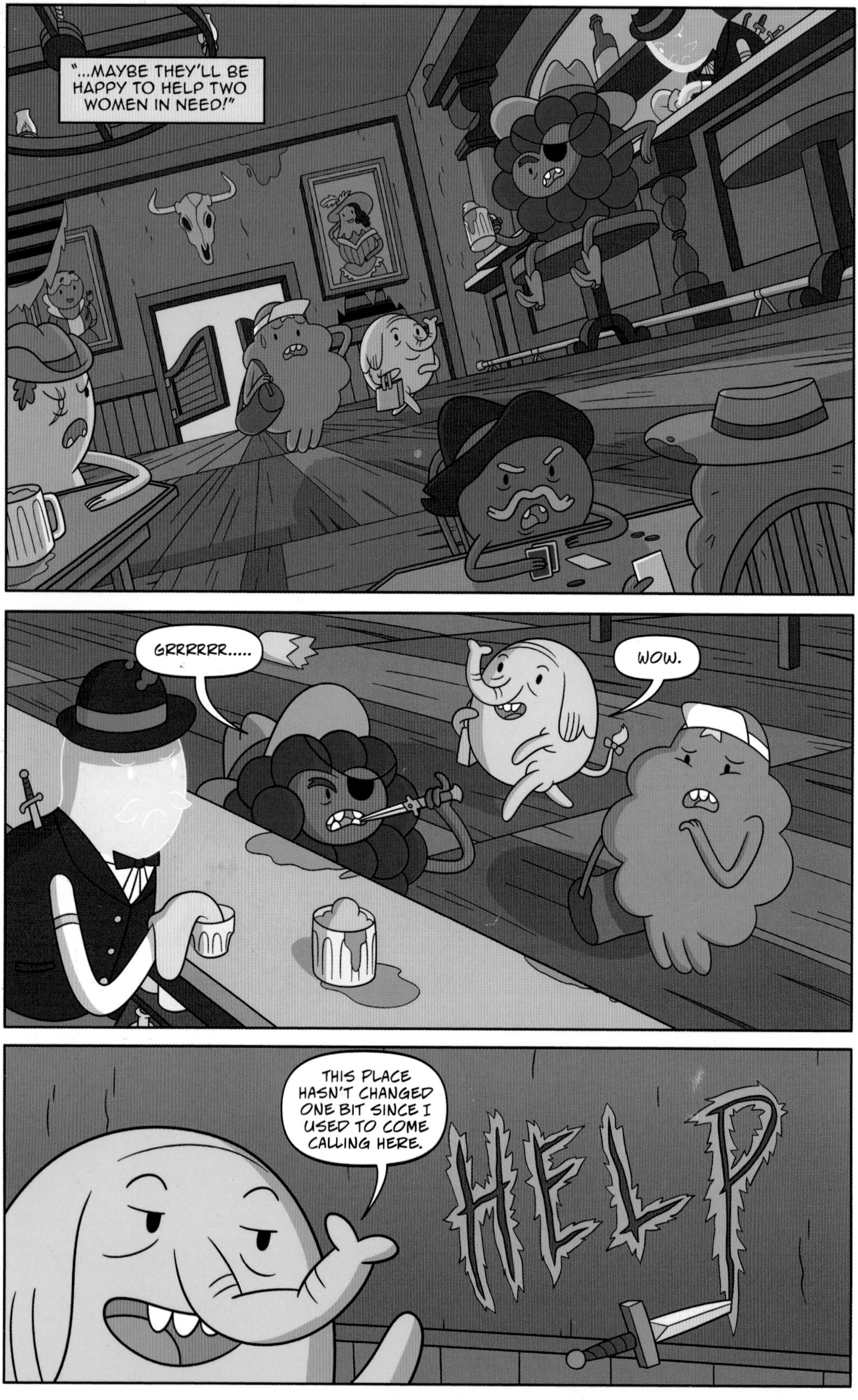
"...MAYBE THEY'LL BE HAPPY TO HELP TWO WOMEN IN NEED!"
GRRRRRR.....
WOW.
THIS PLACE HASN'T CHANGED ONE BIT SINCE I USED TO COME CALLING HERE.
HELP

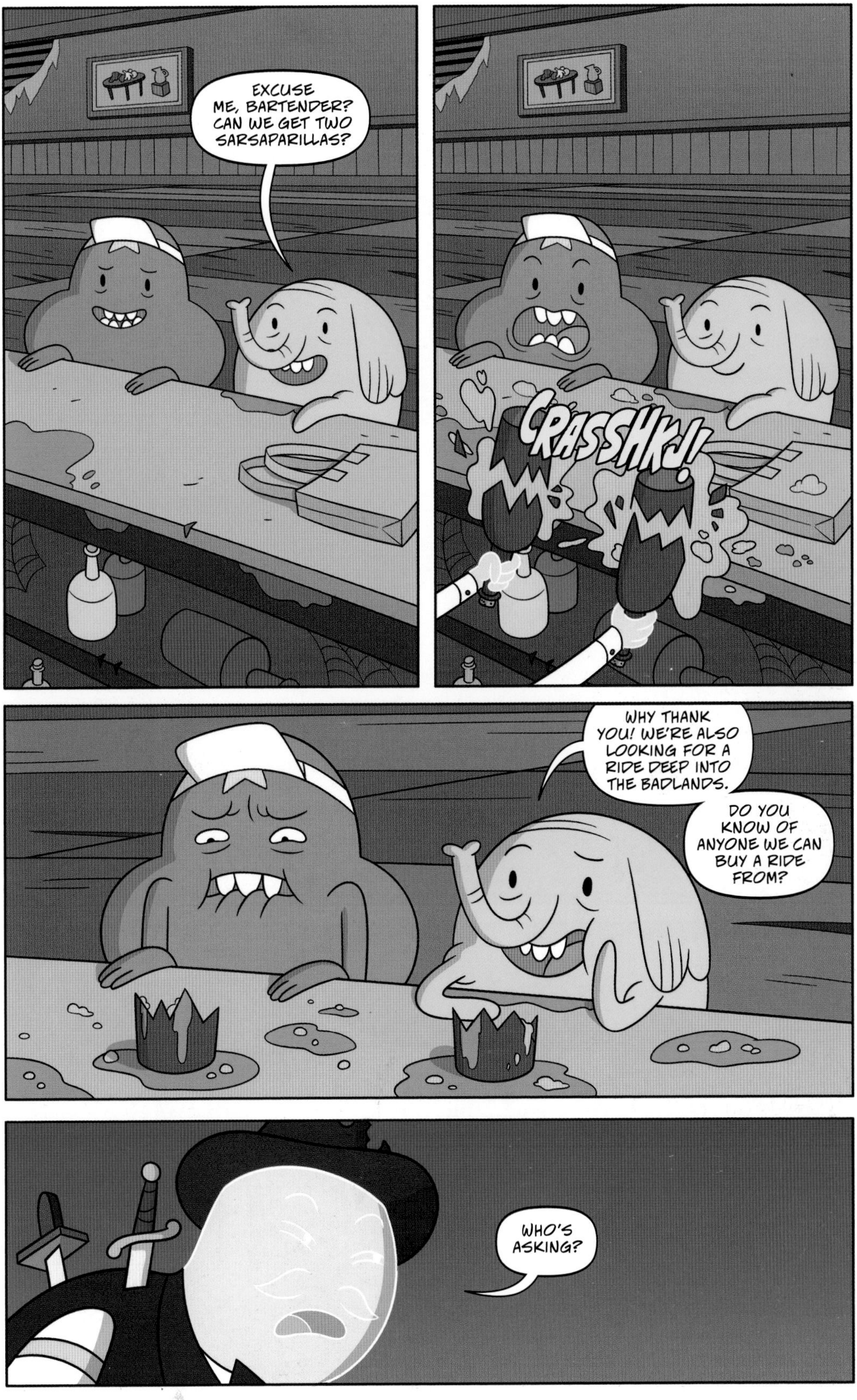
EXCUSE ME, BARTENDER? CAN WE GET TWO SARSAPARILLAS?
CRASSHKJ!
WHY THANK YOU! WE'RE ALSO LOOKING FOR A RIDE DEEP INTO THE BADLANDS.
DO YOU KNOW OF ANYONE WE CAN BUY A RIDE FROM?
WHO'S ASKING?

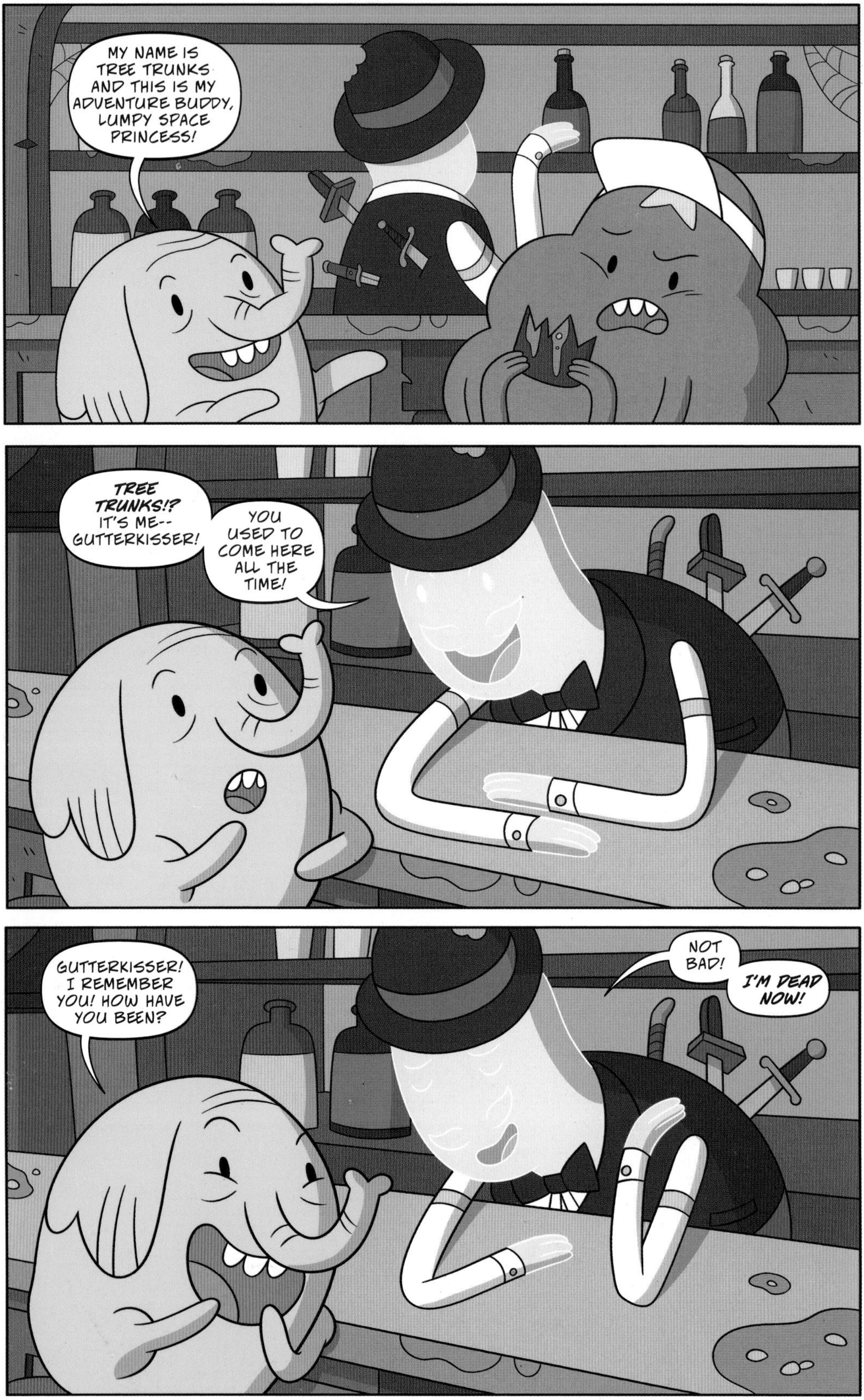
MY NAME IS TREE TRUNKS AND THIS IS MY ADVENTURE BUDDY, LUMPY SPACE PRINCESS!
TREE TRUNKS!? IT'S ME-- GUTTERKISSER!
YOU USED TO COME HERE ALL THE TIME!
GUTTERKISSER! I REMEMBER YOU! HOW HAVE YOU BEEN?
NOT BAD!
I'M DEAD NOW!

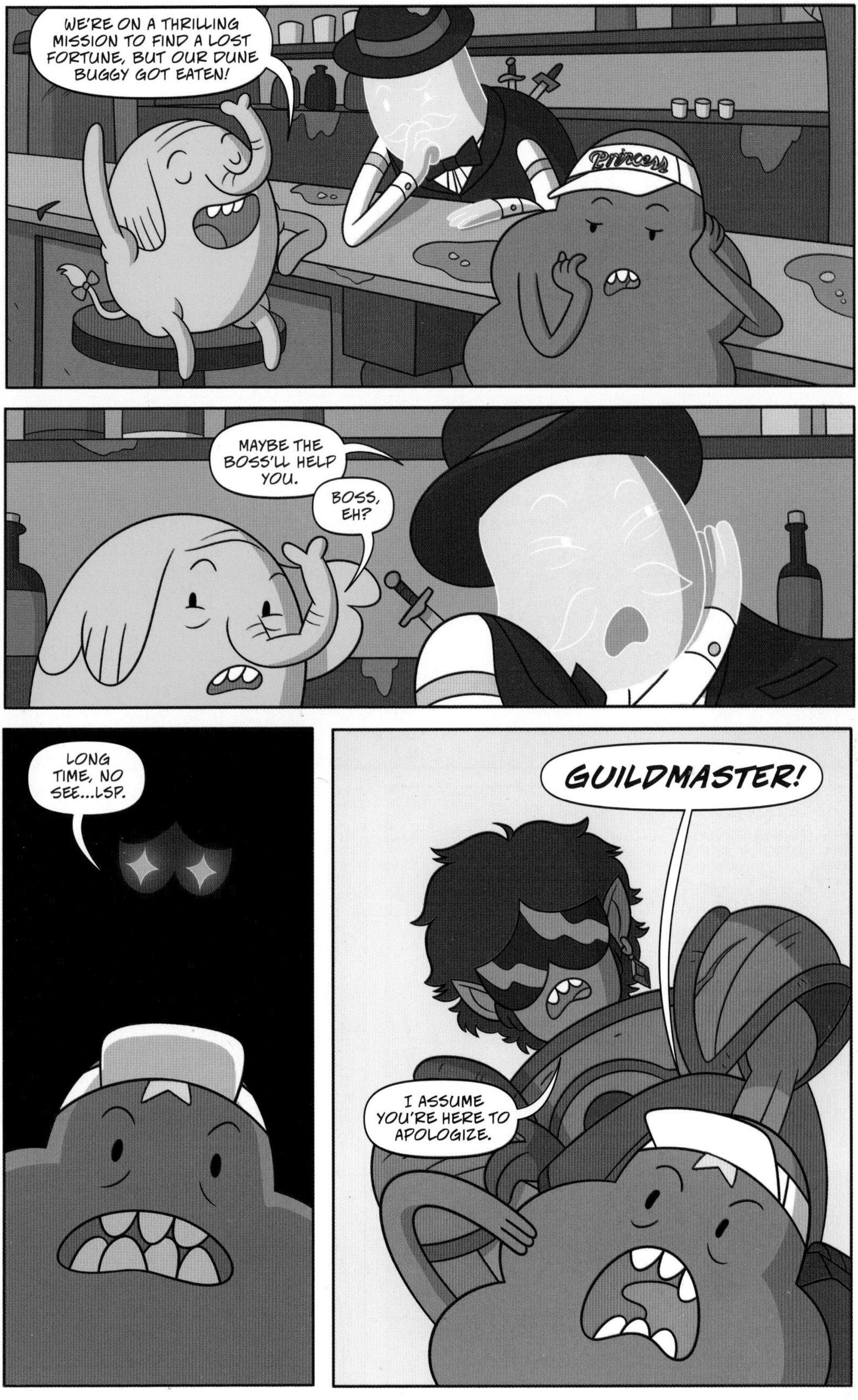
WE'RE ON A THRILLING MISSION TO FIND A LOST FORTUNE, BUT OUR DUNE BUGGY GOT EATEN!
Princess
MAYBE THE BOSS'LL HELP YOU.
BOSS, EH?
LONG TIME, NO SEE...LSP.
GUILDMASTER!
I ASSUME YOU'RE HERE TO APOLOGIZE.

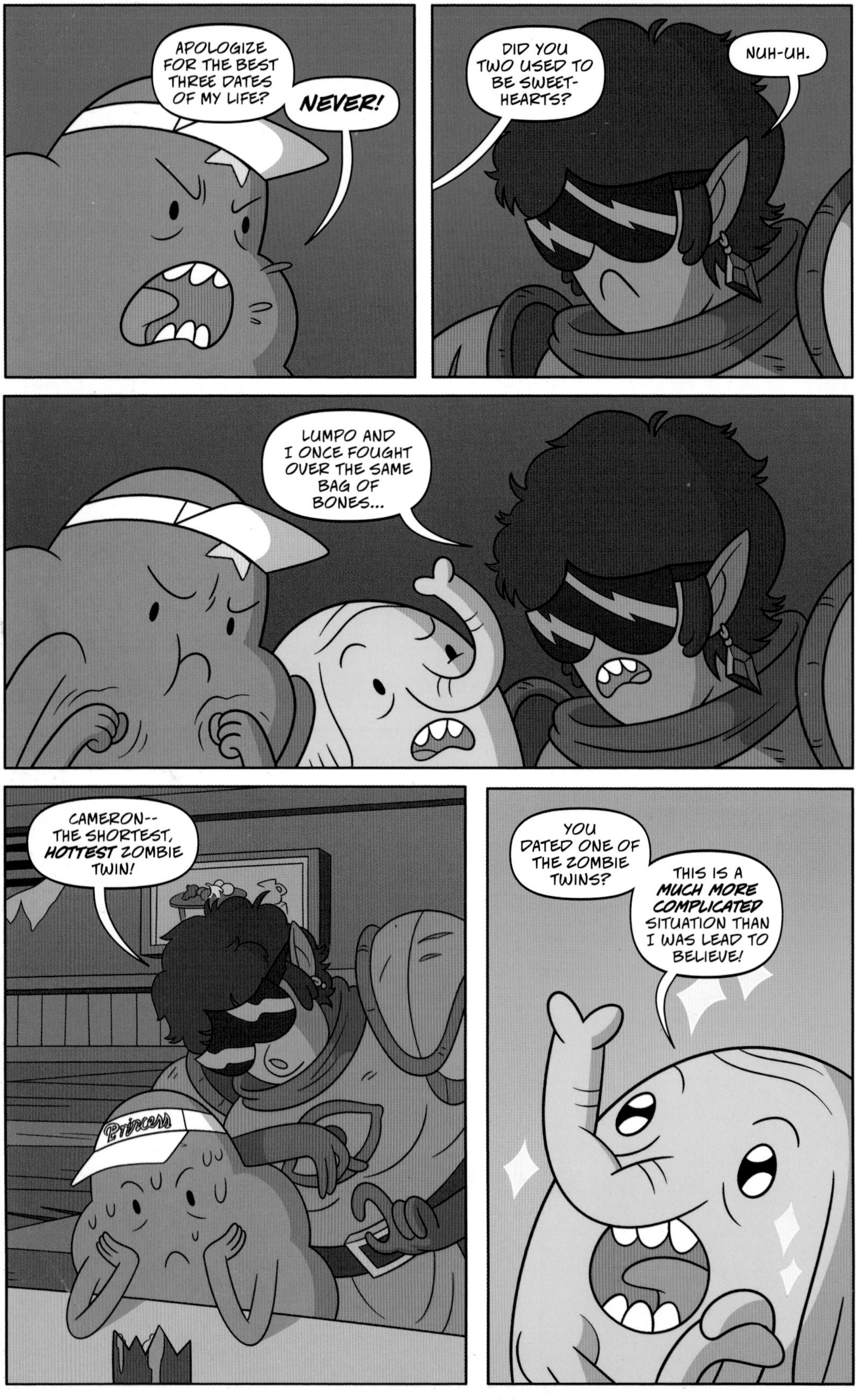
APOLOGIZE FOR THE BEST THREE DATES OF MY LIFE?
NEVER!
DID YOU TWO USED TO BE SWEET-HEARTS?
NUH-UH.
LUMPO AND I ONCE FOUGHT OVER THE SAME BAG OF BONES...
CAMERON-- THE SHORTEST, HOTTEST ZOMBIE TWIN!
Princess
YOU DATED ONE OF THE ZOMBIE TWINS?
THIS IS A MUCH MORE COMPLICATED SITUATION THAN I WAS LEAD TO BELIEVE!

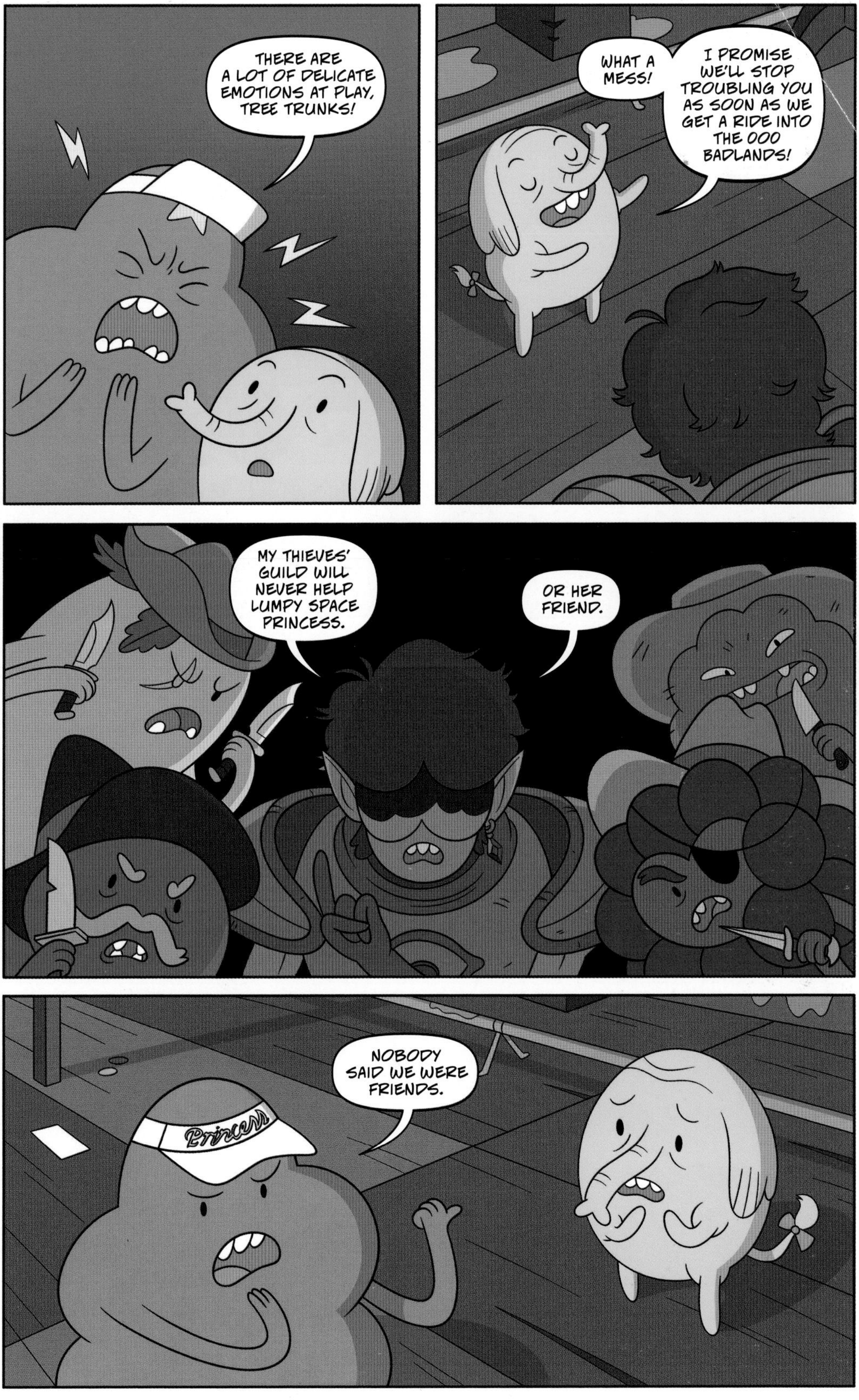
THERE ARE A LOT OF DELICATE EMOTIONS AT PLAY, TREE TRUNKS!
WHAT A MESS!
I PROMISE WE'LL STOP TROUBLING YOU AS SOON AS WE GET A RIDE INTO THE OOO BADLANDS!
MY THIEVES' GUILD WILL NEVER HELP LUMPY SPACE PRINCESS.
OR HER FRIEND.
NOBODY SAID WE WERE FRIENDS.
Princess

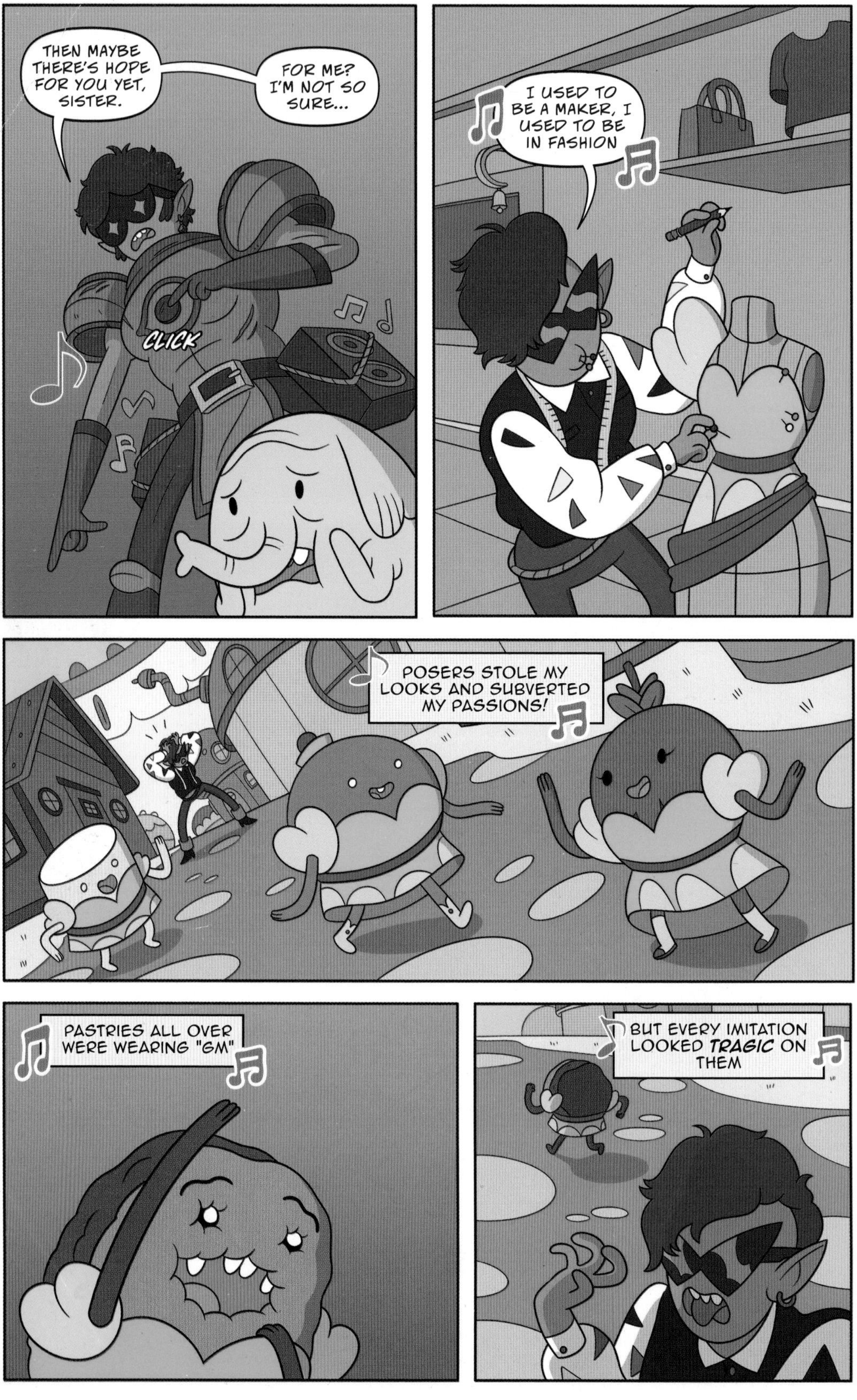
THEN MAYBE THERE'S HOPE FOR YOU YET, SISTER.
FOR ME? I'M NOT SO SURE...
CLICK
I USED TO BE A MAKER, I USED TO BE IN FASHION
POSERS STOLE MY LOOKS AND SUBVERTED MY PASSIONS!
PASTRIES ALL OVER WERE WEARING "GM"
BUT EVERY IMITATION LOOKED *TRAGIC* ON THEM

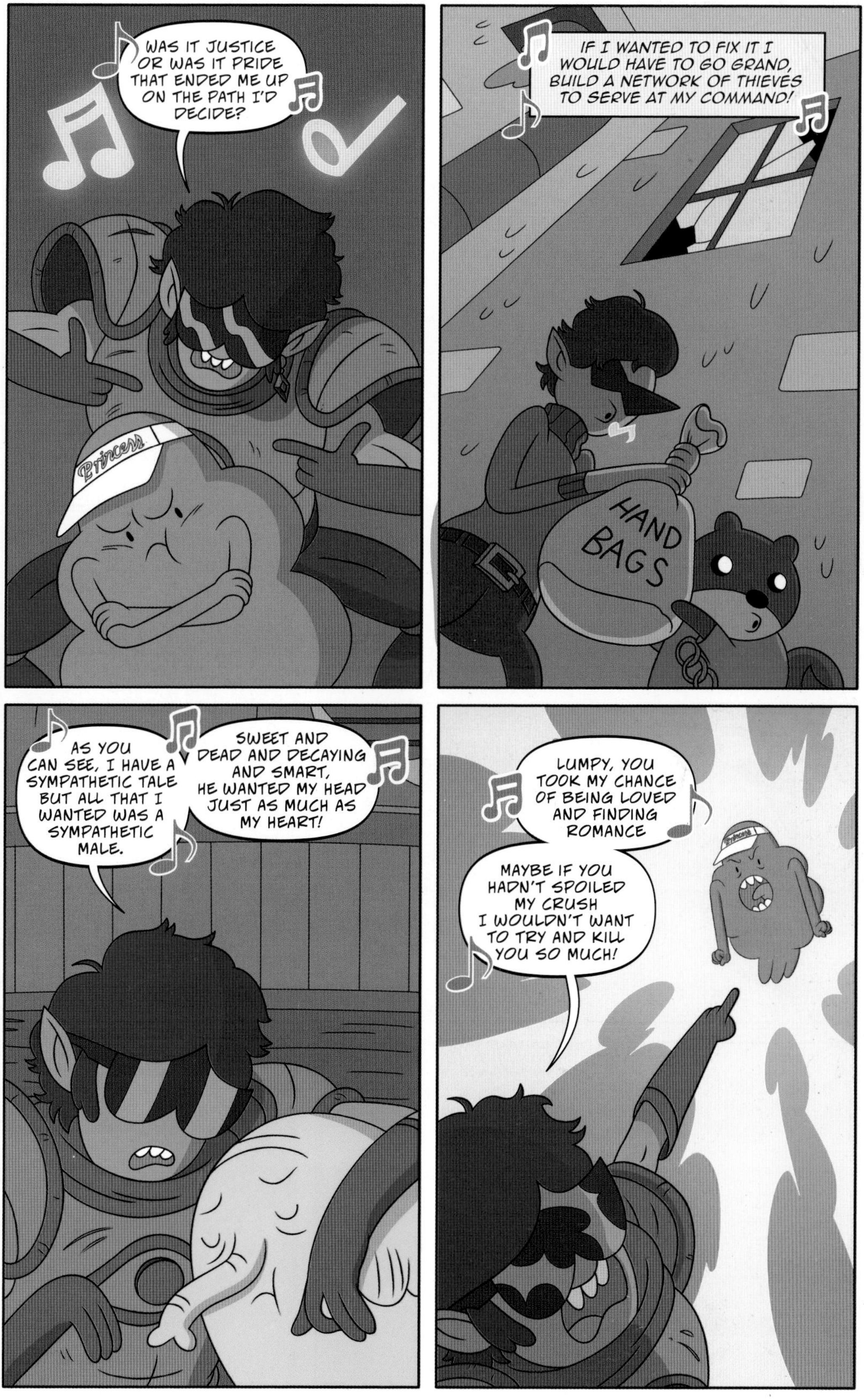
WAS IT JUSTICE OR WAS IT PRIDE THAT ENDED ME UP ON THE PATH I'D DECIDE?
IF I WANTED TO FIX IT I WOULD HAVE TO GO GRAND, BUILD A NETWORK OF THIEVES TO SERVE AT MY COMMAND!
HAND BAGS
AS YOU CAN SEE, I HAVE A SYMPATHETIC TALE BUT ALL THAT I WANTED WAS A SYMPATHETIC MALE.
SWEET AND DEAD AND DECAYING AND SMART, HE WANTED MY HEAD JUST AS MUCH AS MY HEART!
LUMPY, YOU TOOK MY CHANCE OF BEING LOVED AND FINDING ROMANCE
MAYBE IF YOU HADN'T SPOILED MY CRUSH I WOULDN'T WANT TO TRY AND KILL YOU SO MUCH!

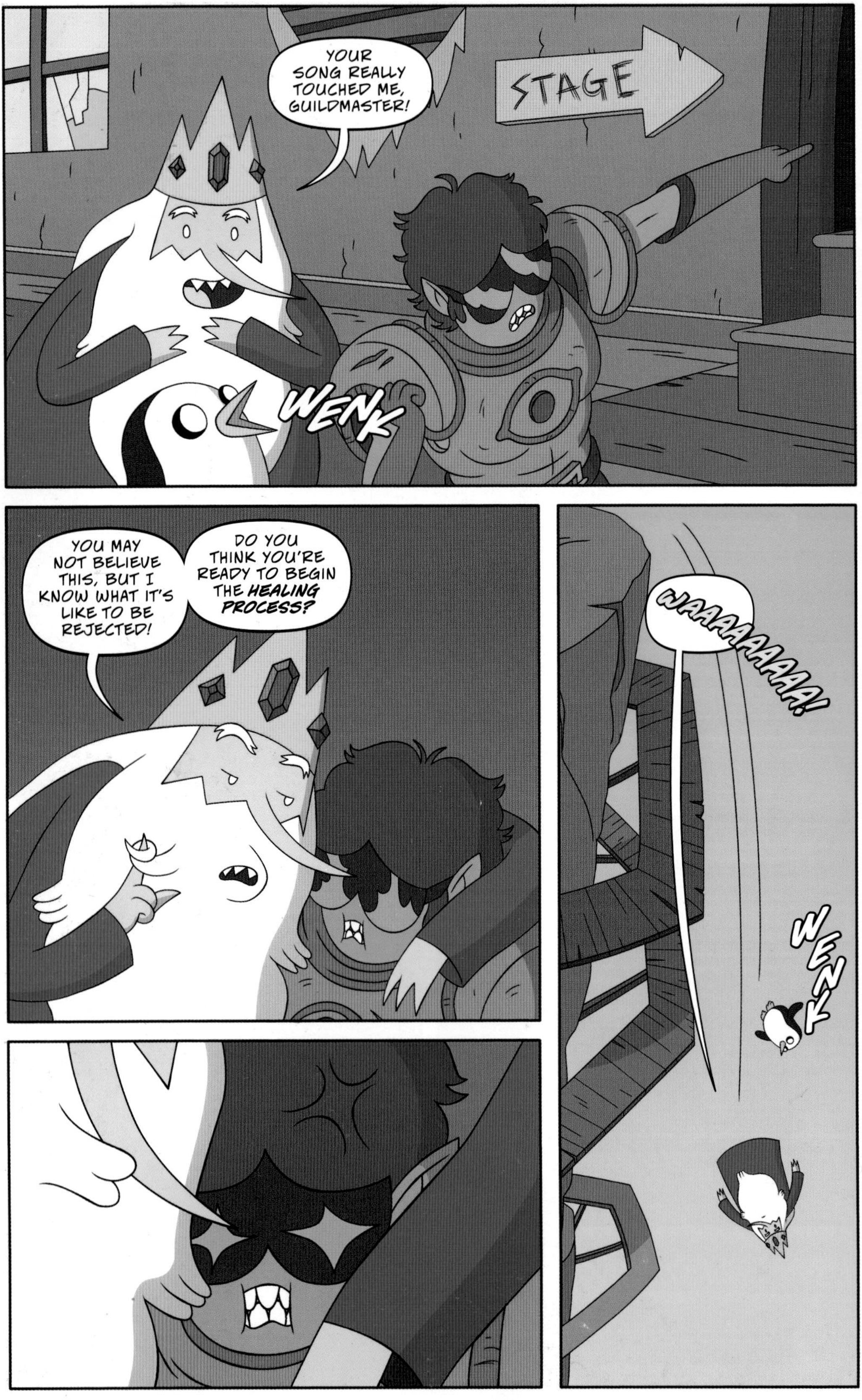

YOUR SONG REALLY TOUCHED ME, GUILDMASTER!
STAGE
WENK
YOU MAY NOT BELIEVE THIS, BUT I KNOW WHAT IT'S LIKE TO BE REJECTED!
DO YOU THINK YOU'RE READY TO BEGIN THE HEALING PROCESS?
WAAAAAAAAA!
WENK

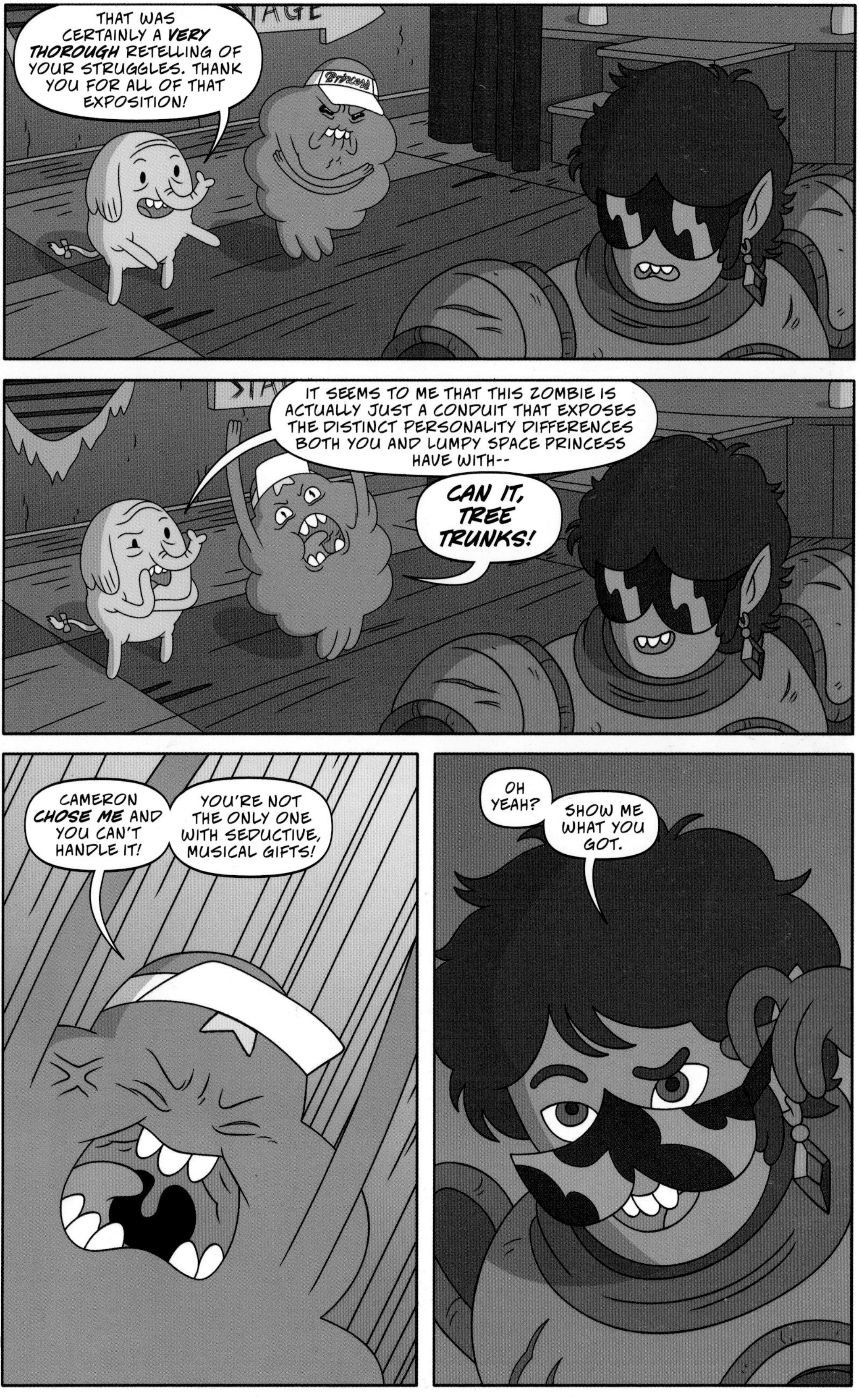
THAT WAS CERTAINLY A VERY THOROUGH RETELLING OF YOUR STRUGGLES. THANK YOU FOR ALL OF THAT EXPOSITION!
IT SEEMS TO ME THAT THIS ZOMBIE IS ACTUALLY JUST A CONDUIT THAT EXPOSES THE DISTINCT PERSONALITY DIFFERENCES BOTH YOU AND LUMPY SPACE PRINCESS HAVE WITH--
CAN IT, TREE TRUNKS!
CAMERON CHOSE ME AND YOU CAN'T HANDLE IT!
YOU'RE NOT THE ONLY ONE WITH SEDUCTIVE, MUSICAL GIFTS!
OH YEAH?
SHOW ME WHAT YOU GOT.

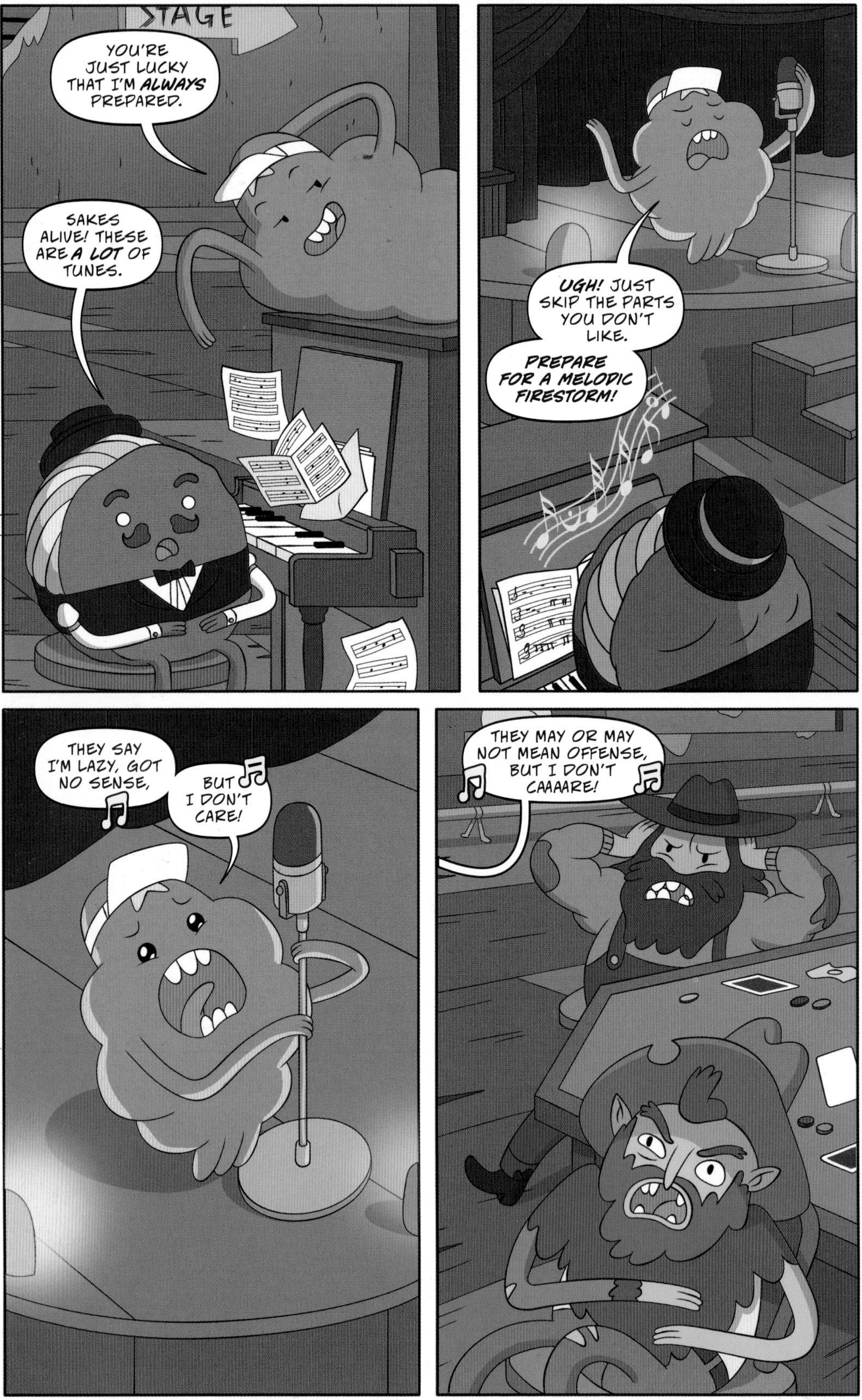
STAGE
YOU'RE JUST LUCKY THAT I'M ALWAYS PREPARED.
SAKES ALIVE! THESE ARE A LOT OF TUNES.
UGH! JUST SKIP THE PARTS YOU DON'T LIKE.
PREPARE FOR A MELODIC FIRESTORM!
THEY SAY I'M LAZY, GOT NO SENSE,
BUT I DON'T CARE!
THEY MAY OR MAY NOT MEAN OFFENSE, BUT I DON'T CAAAARE!

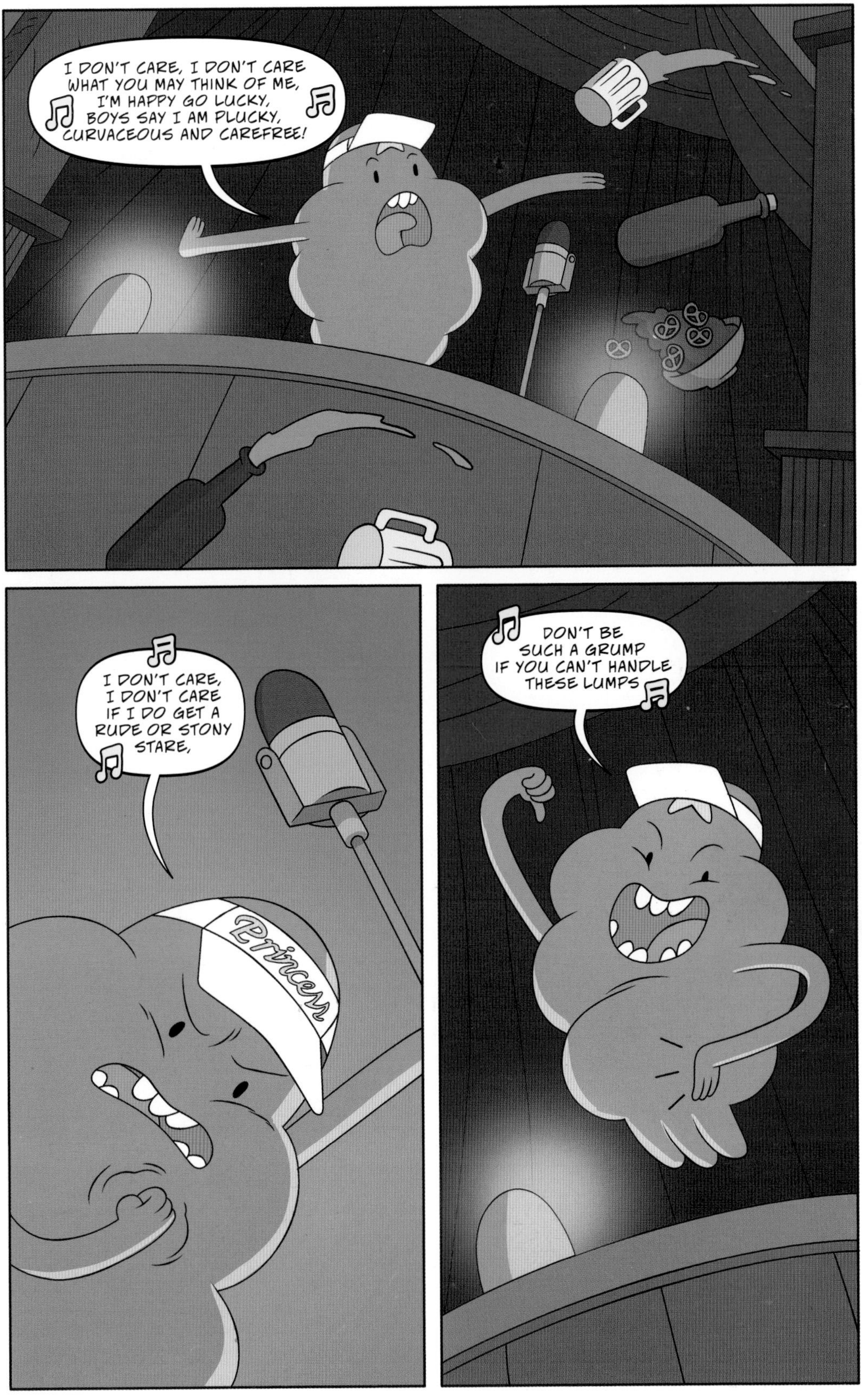
I DON'T CARE, I DON'T CARE WHAT YOU MAY THINK OF ME, I'M HAPPY GO LUCKY, BOYS SAY I AM PLUCKY, CURVACEOUS AND CAREFREE!
I DON'T CARE, I DON'T CARE IF I DO GET A RUDE OR STONY STARE,
Princess
DON'T BE SUCH A GRUMP IF YOU CAN'T HANDLE THESE LUMPS

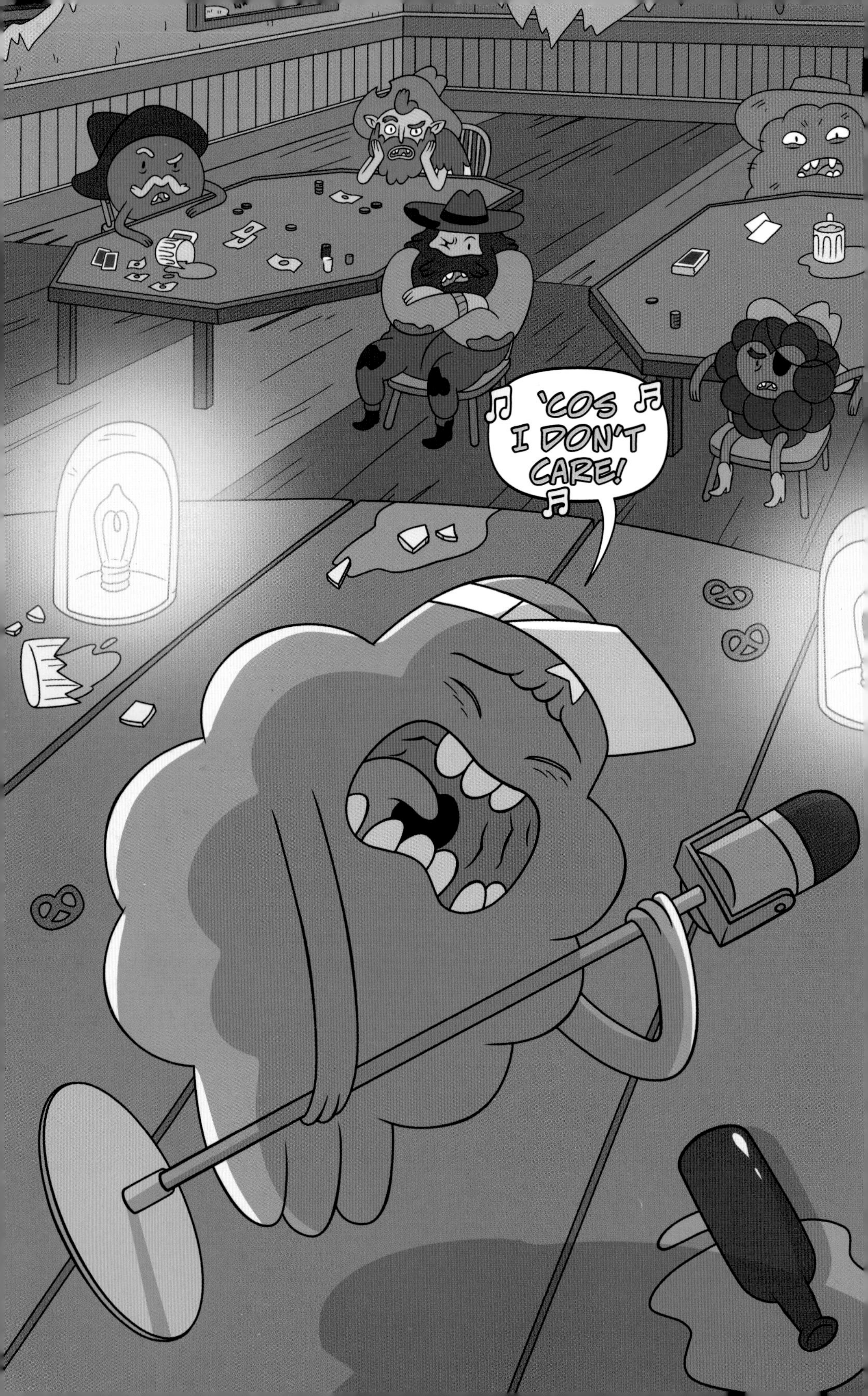
♫ 'COS I DON'T CARE! ♫

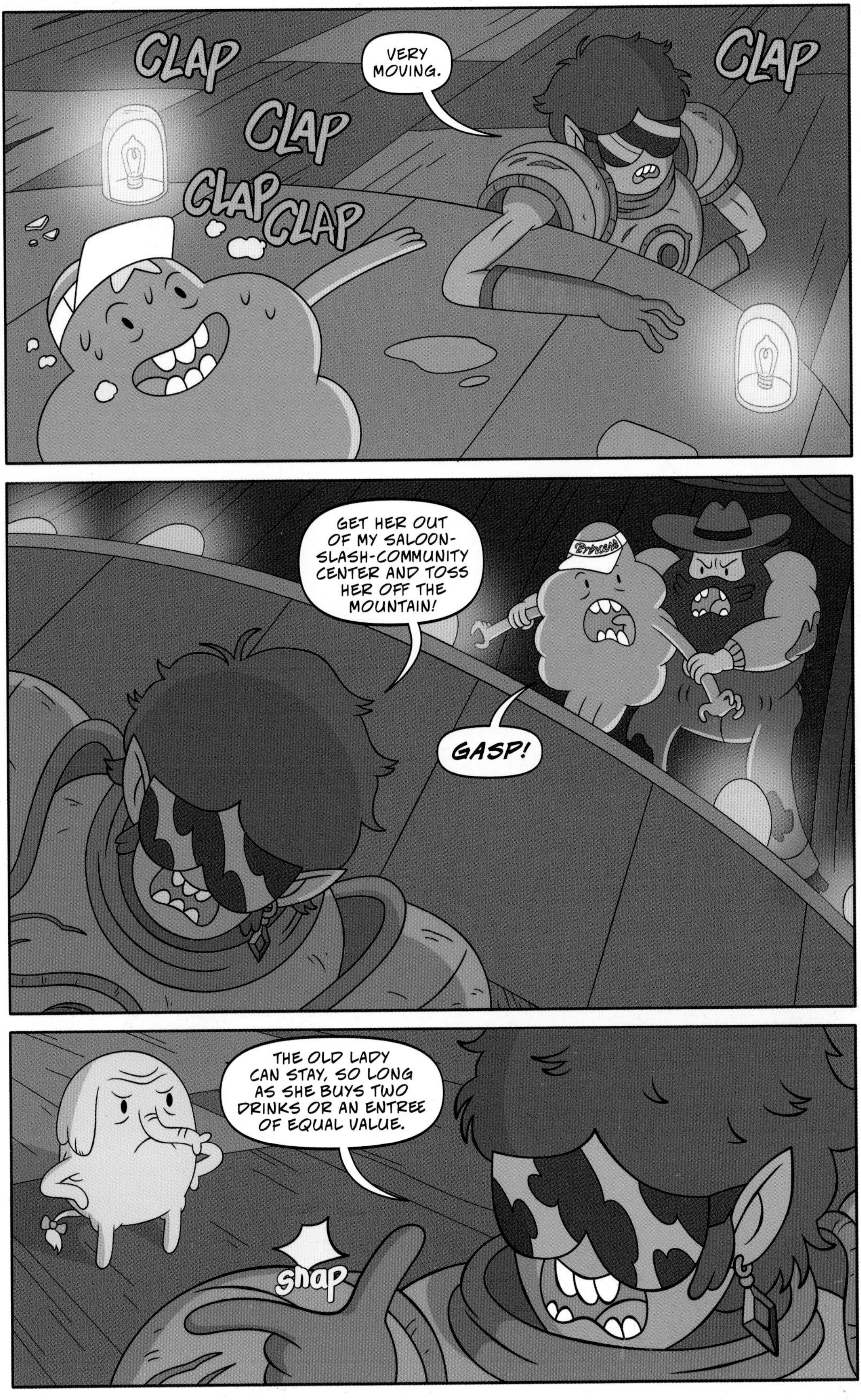
CLAP
VERY MOVING.
CLAP
CLAP
CLAP CLAP
GET HER OUT OF MY SALOON-SLASH-COMMUNITY CENTER AND TOSS HER OFF THE MOUNTAIN!
Princess
GASP!
THE OLD LADY CAN STAY, SO LONG AS SHE BUYS TWO DRINKS OR AN ENTREE OF EQUAL VALUE.
snap

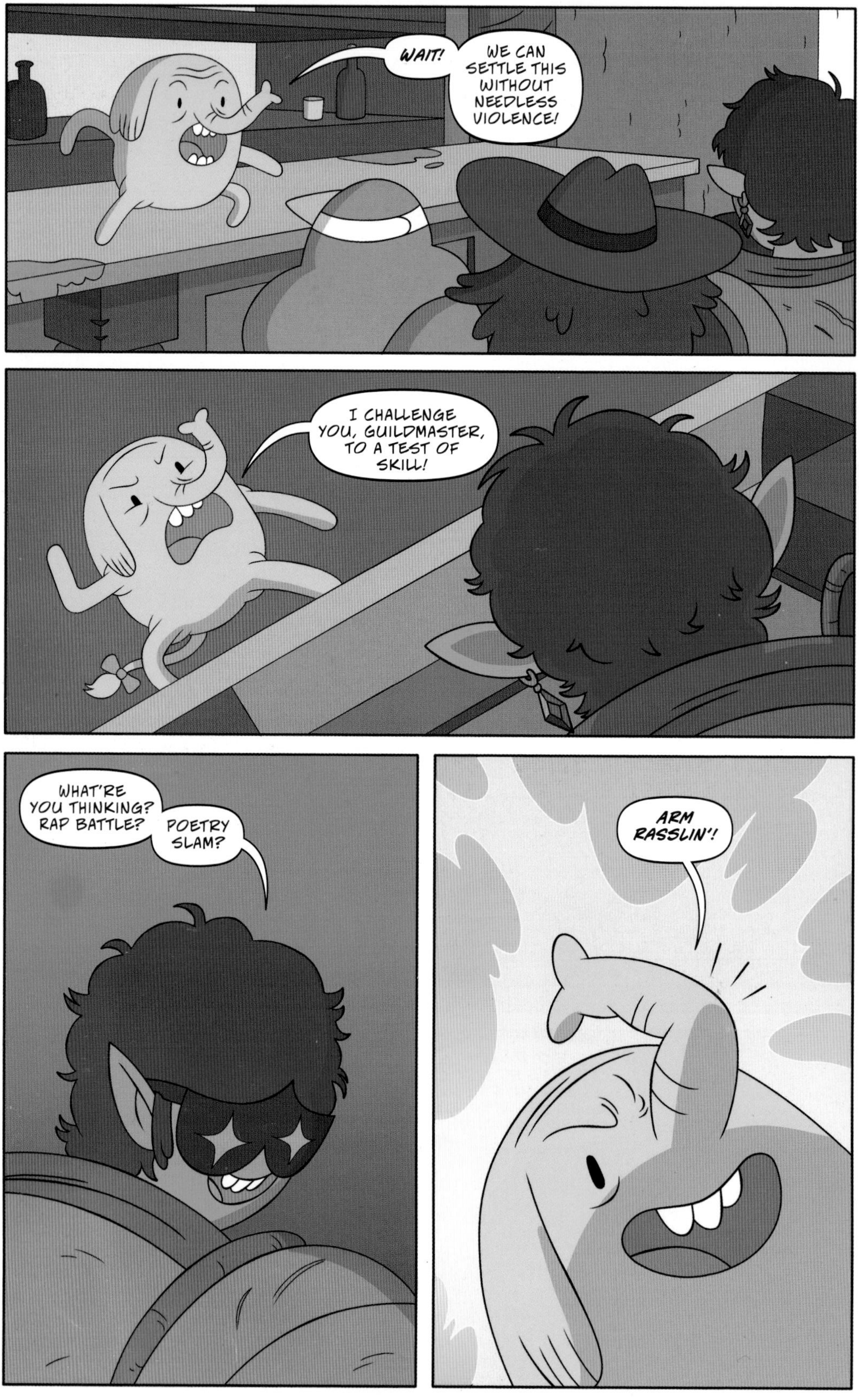
WAIT!
WE CAN SETTLE THIS WITHOUT NEEDLESS VIOLENCE!
I CHALLENGE YOU, GUILDMASTER, TO A TEST OF SKILL!
WHAT'RE YOU THINKING? RAP BATTLE?
POETRY SLAM?
ARM RASSLIN'!

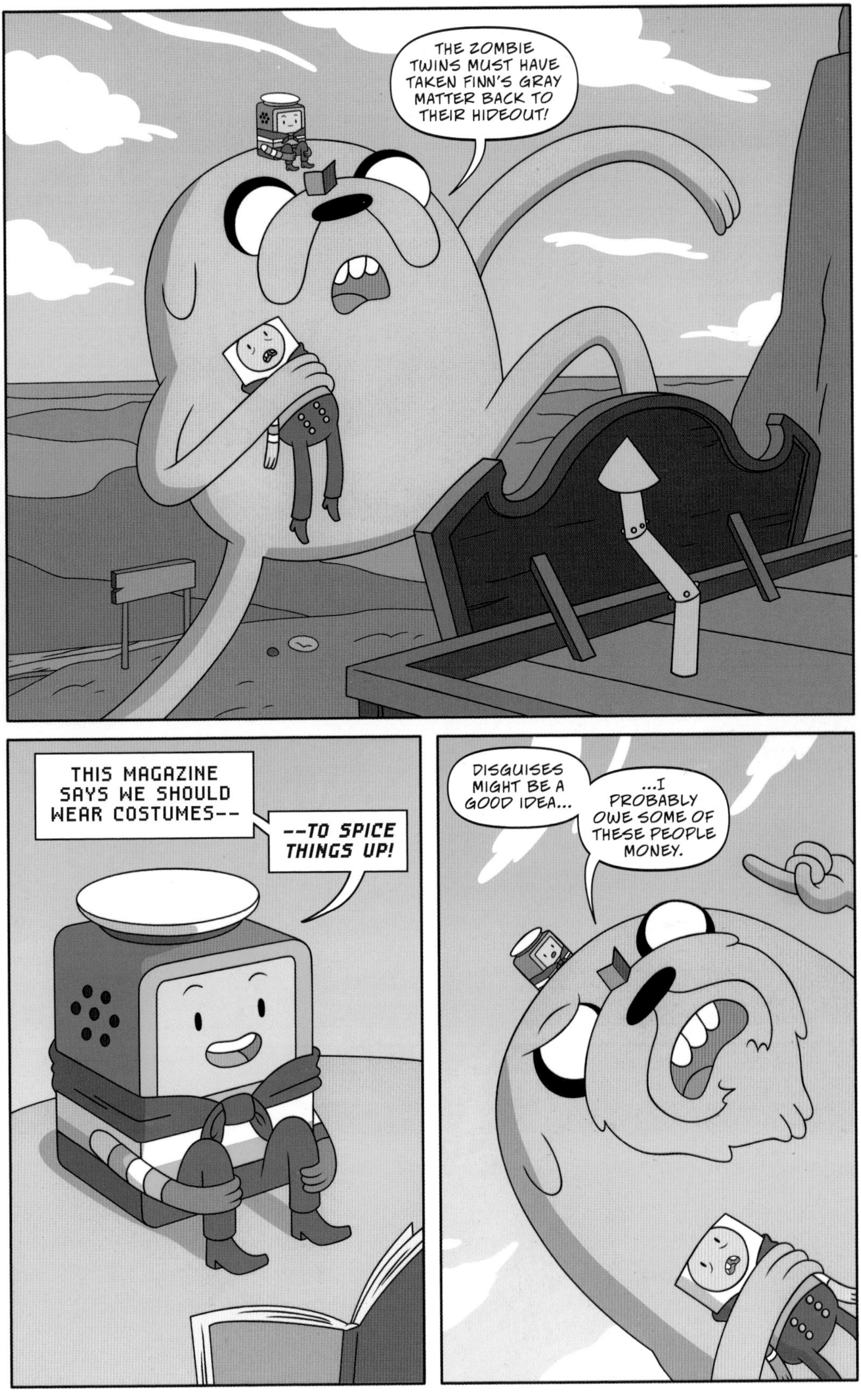
THE ZOMBIE TWINS MUST HAVE TAKEN FINN'S GRAY MATTER BACK TO THEIR HIDEOUT!
THIS MAGAZINE SAYS WE SHOULD WEAR COSTUMES--
--TO SPICE THINGS UP!
DISGUISES MIGHT BE A GOOD IDEA...
...I PROBABLY OWE SOME OF THESE PEOPLE MONEY.

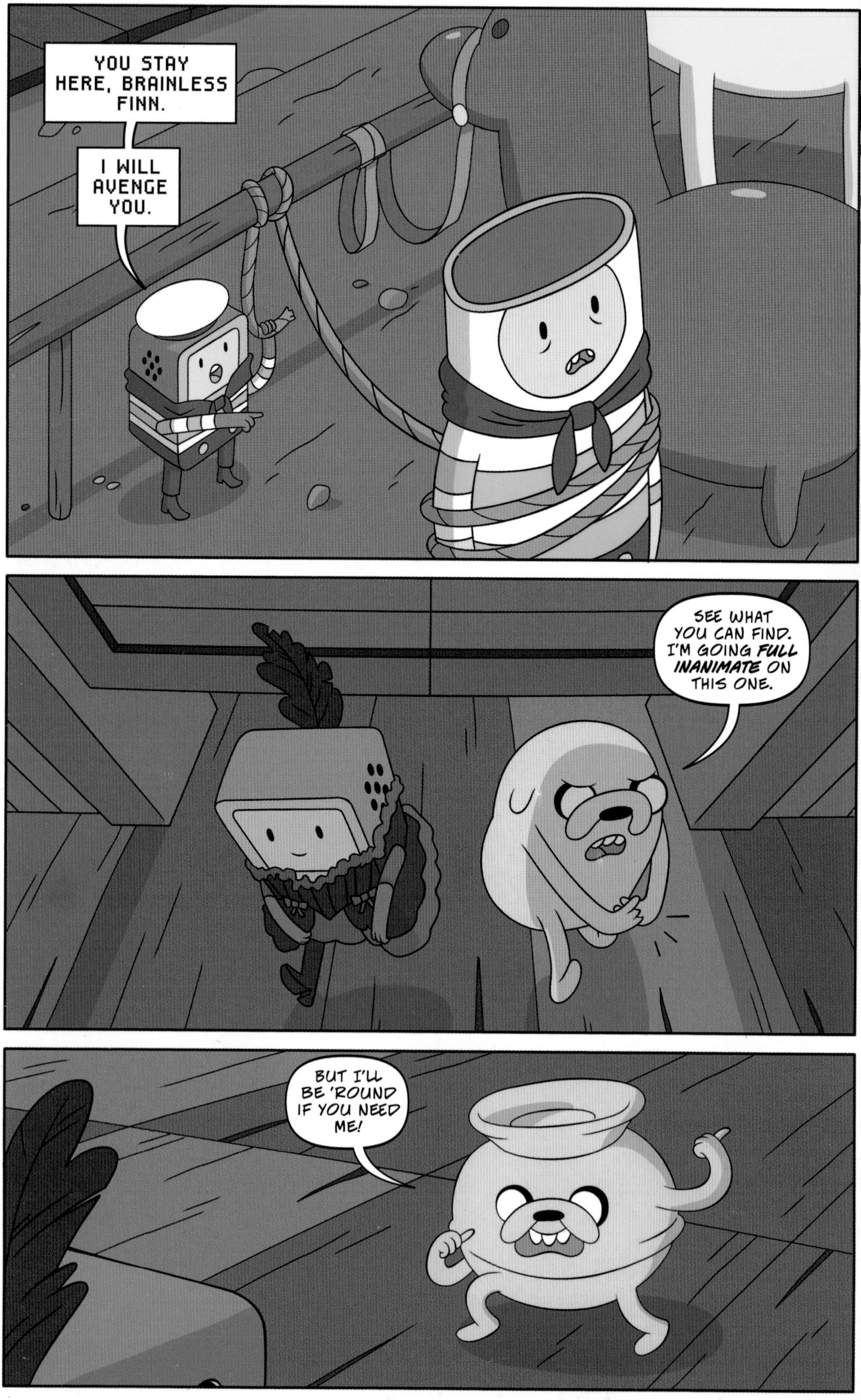
YOU STAY HERE, BRAINLESS FINN.
I WILL AVENGE YOU.
SEE WHAT YOU CAN FIND. I'M GOING **FULL INANIMATE** ON THIS ONE.
BUT I'LL BE 'ROUND IF YOU NEED ME!

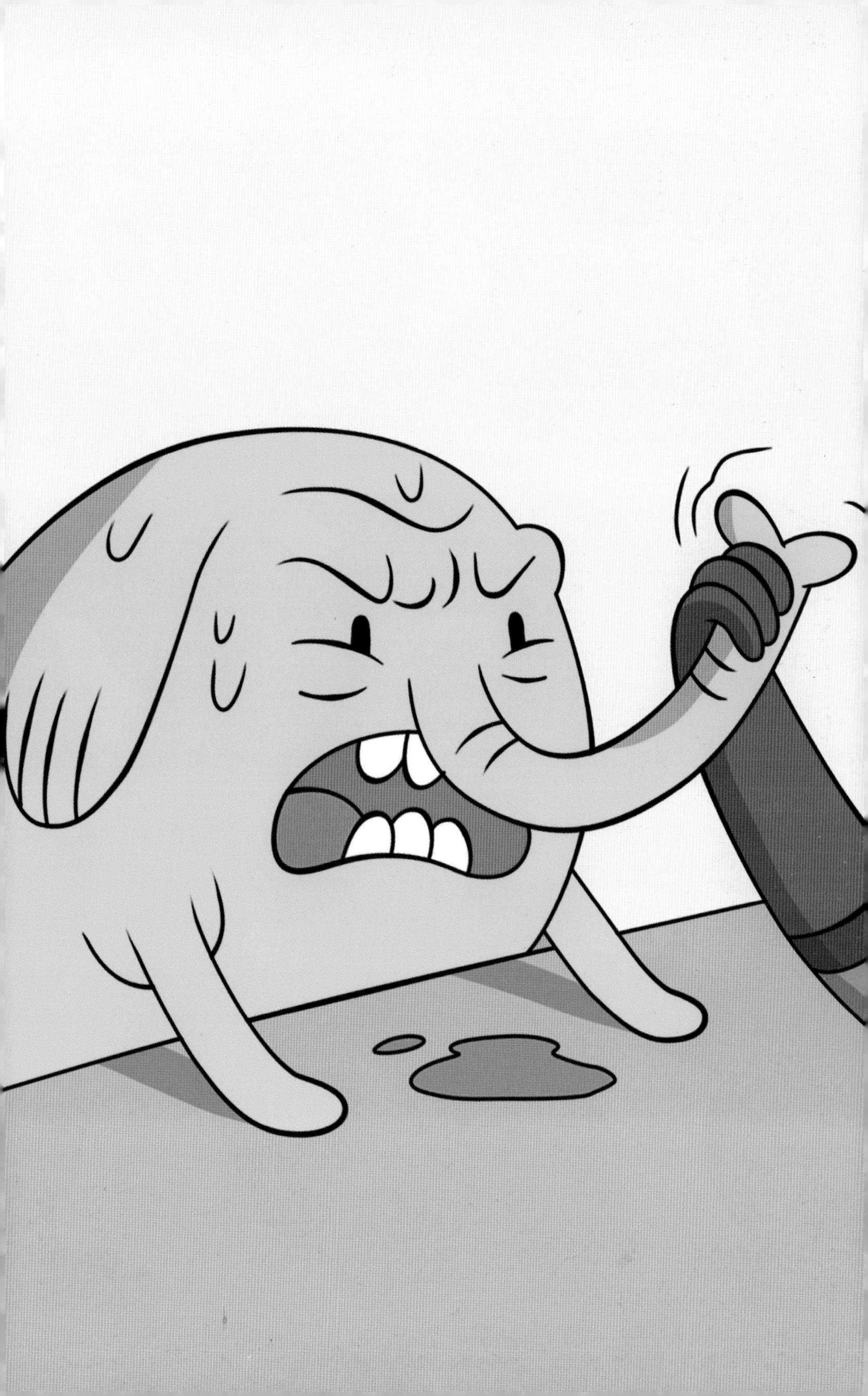

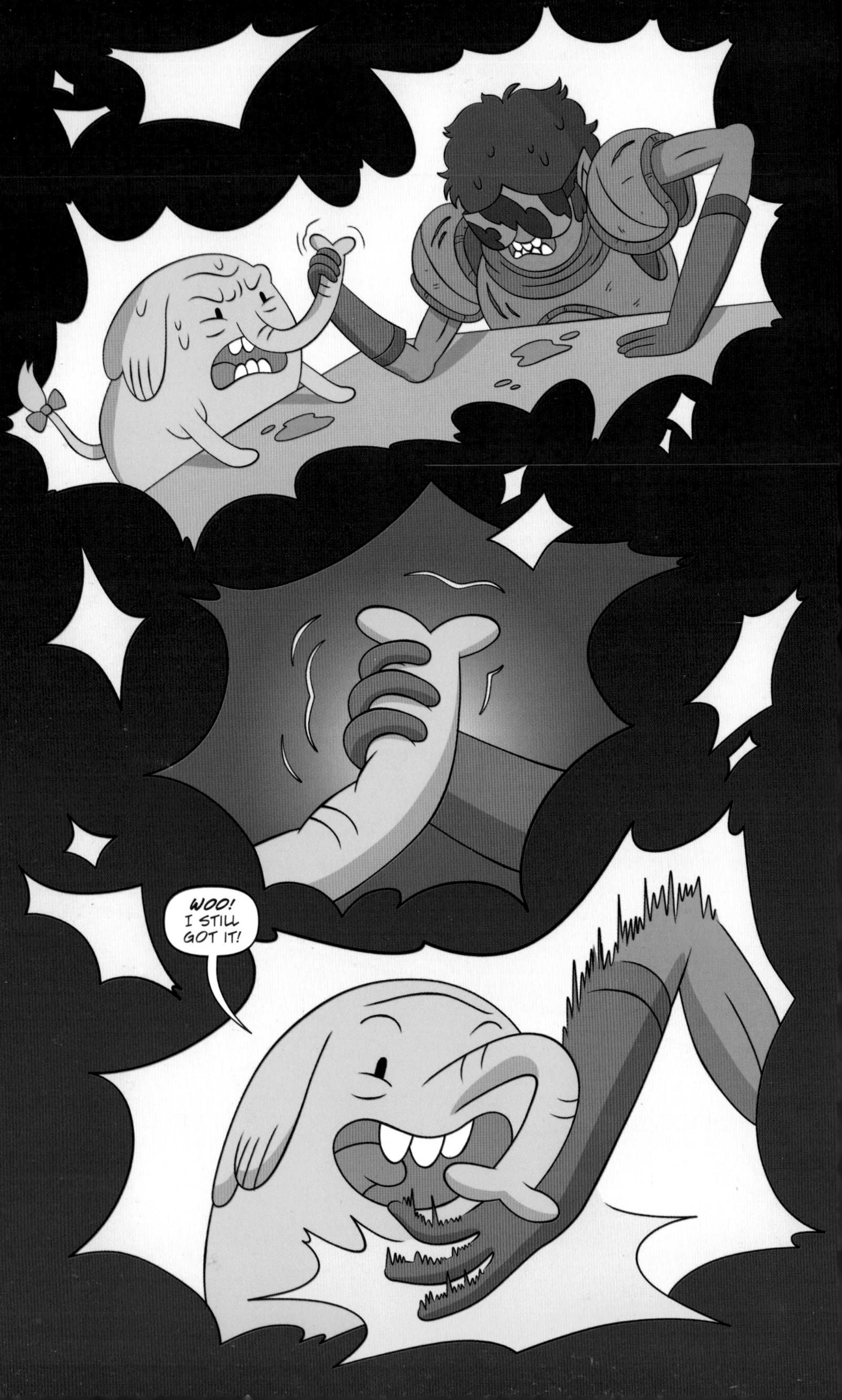
WOO! I STILL GOT IT!

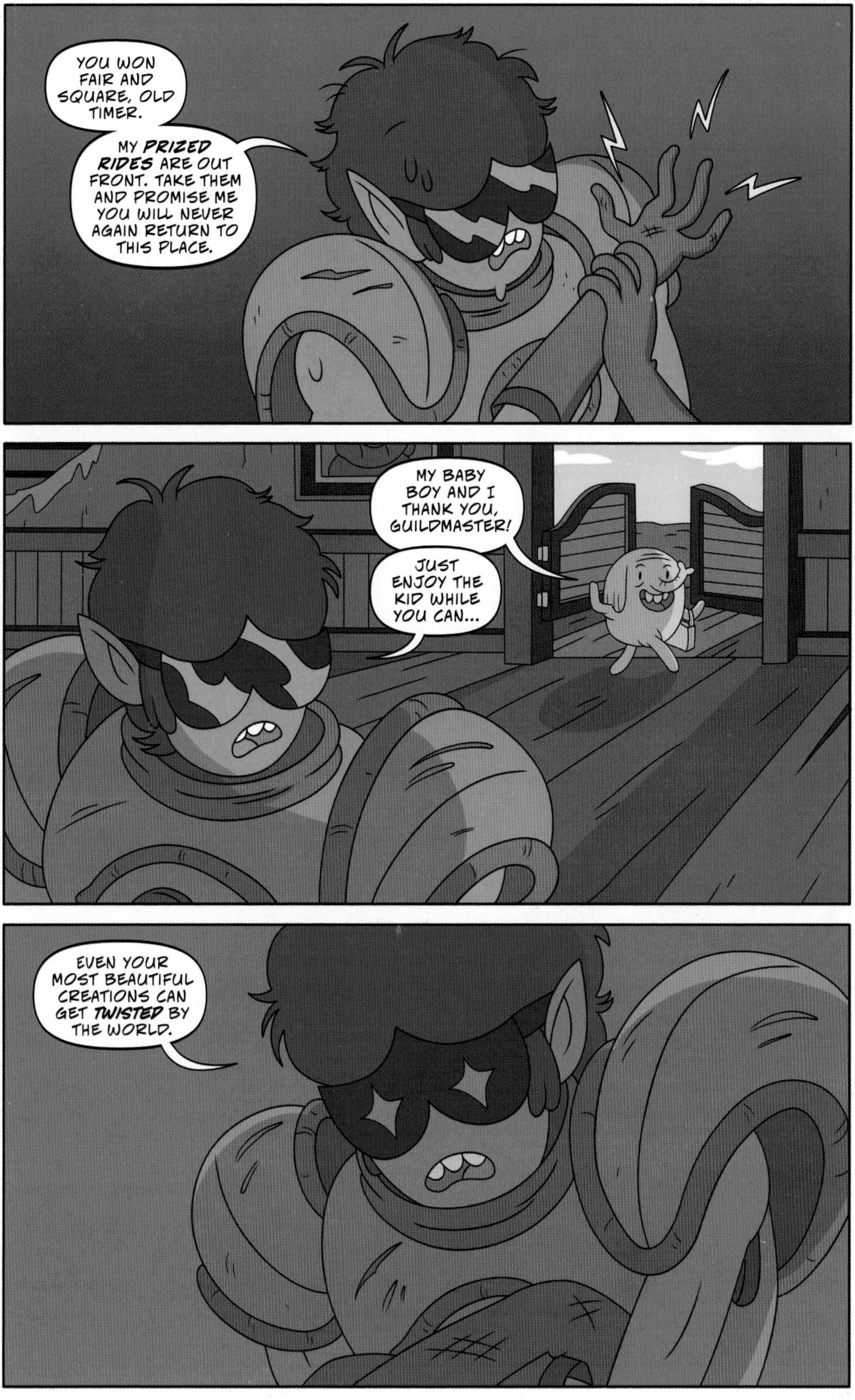
YOU WON FAIR AND SQUARE, OLD TIMER.
MY **PRIZED RIDES** ARE OUT FRONT. TAKE THEM AND PROMISE ME YOU WILL NEVER AGAIN RETURN TO THIS PLACE.
MY BABY BOY AND I THANK YOU, GUILDMASTER!
JUST ENJOY THE KID WHILE YOU CAN...
EVEN YOUR MOST BEAUTIFUL CREATIONS CAN GET ***TWISTED*** BY THE WORLD.

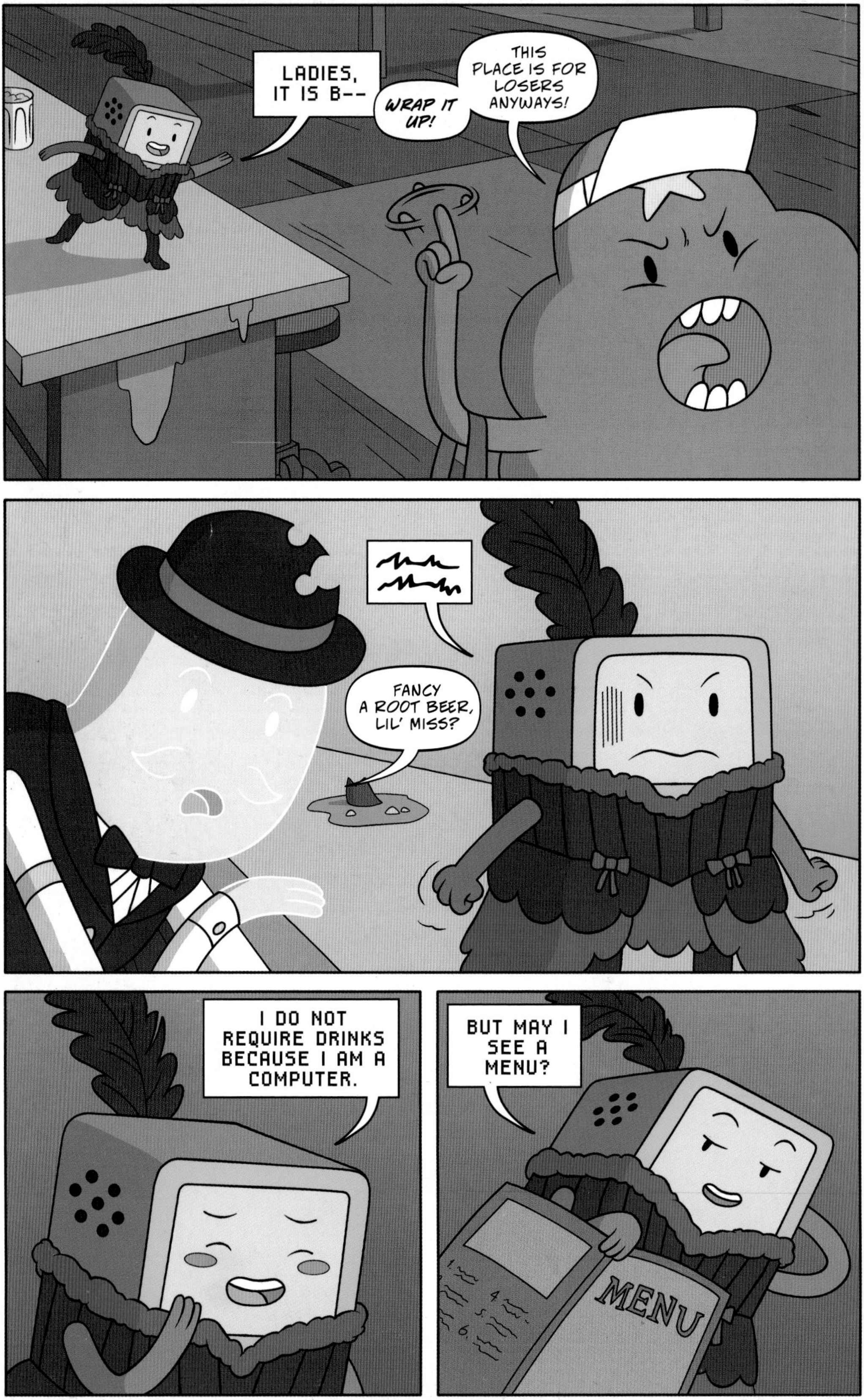
LADIES, IT IS B--
WRAP IT UP!
THIS PLACE IS FOR LOSERS ANYWAYS!
FANCY A ROOT BEER, LIL' MISS?
I DO NOT REQUIRE DRINKS BECAUSE I AM A COMPUTER.
BUT MAY I SEE A MENU?
MENU

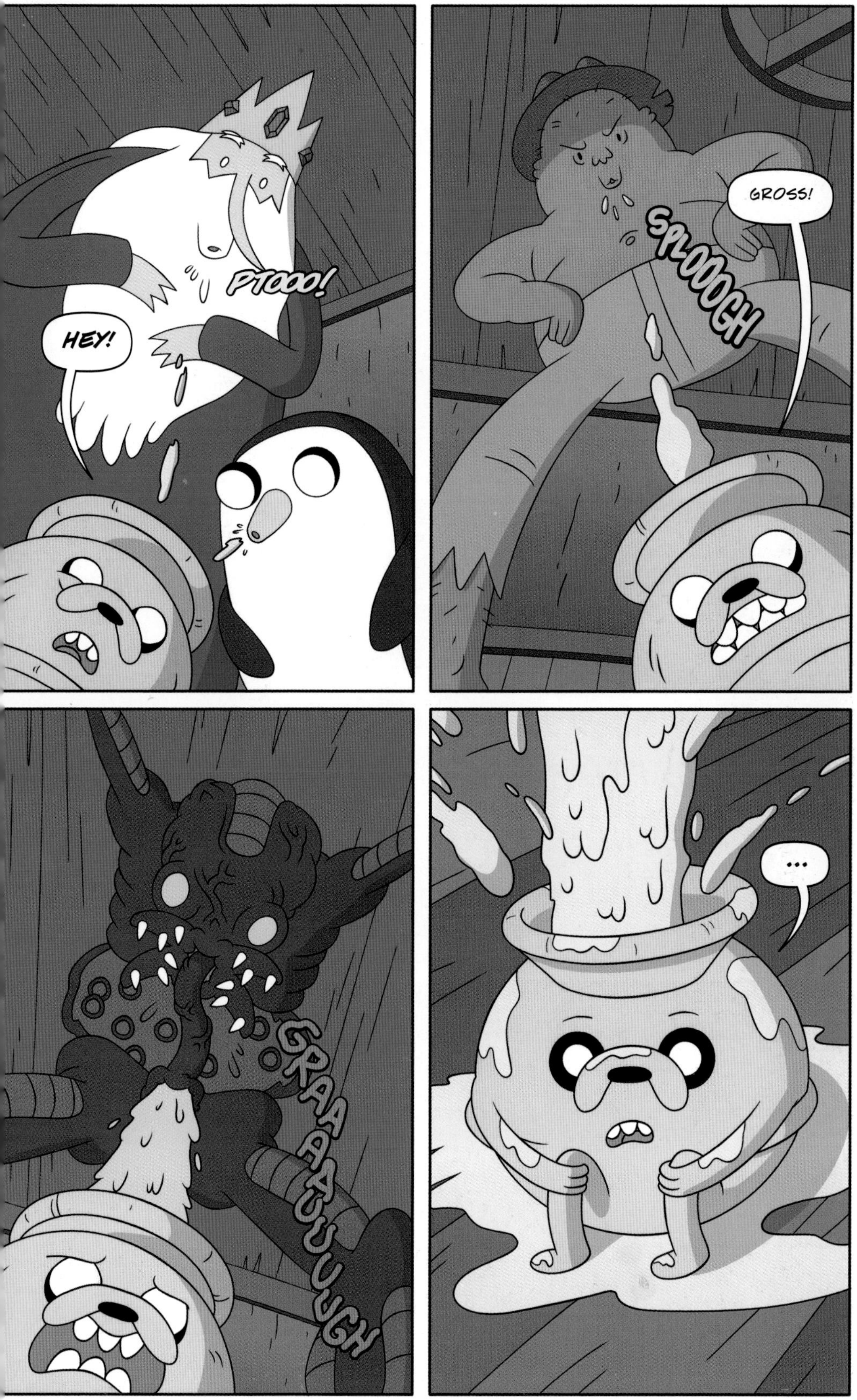
PTOOO!
HEY!
SPLOOOCH
GROSS!
GRAAAUUUGH
...

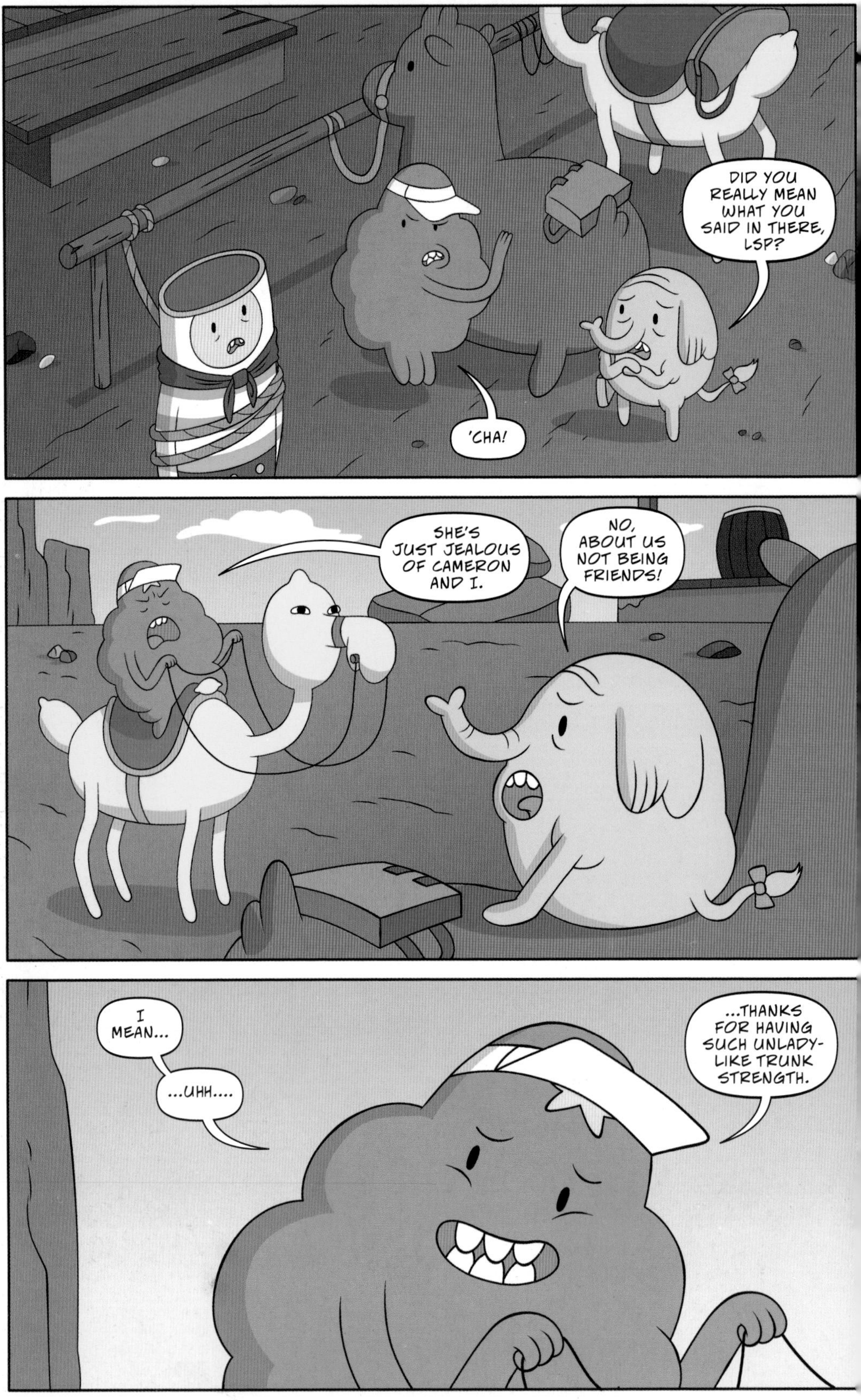
DID YOU REALLY MEAN WHAT YOU SAID IN THERE, LSP?
'CHA!
SHE'S JUST JEALOUS OF CAMERON AND I.
NO, ABOUT US NOT BEING FRIENDS!
I MEAN...
...UHH....
...THANKS FOR HAVING SUCH UNLADY-LIKE TRUNK STRENGTH.

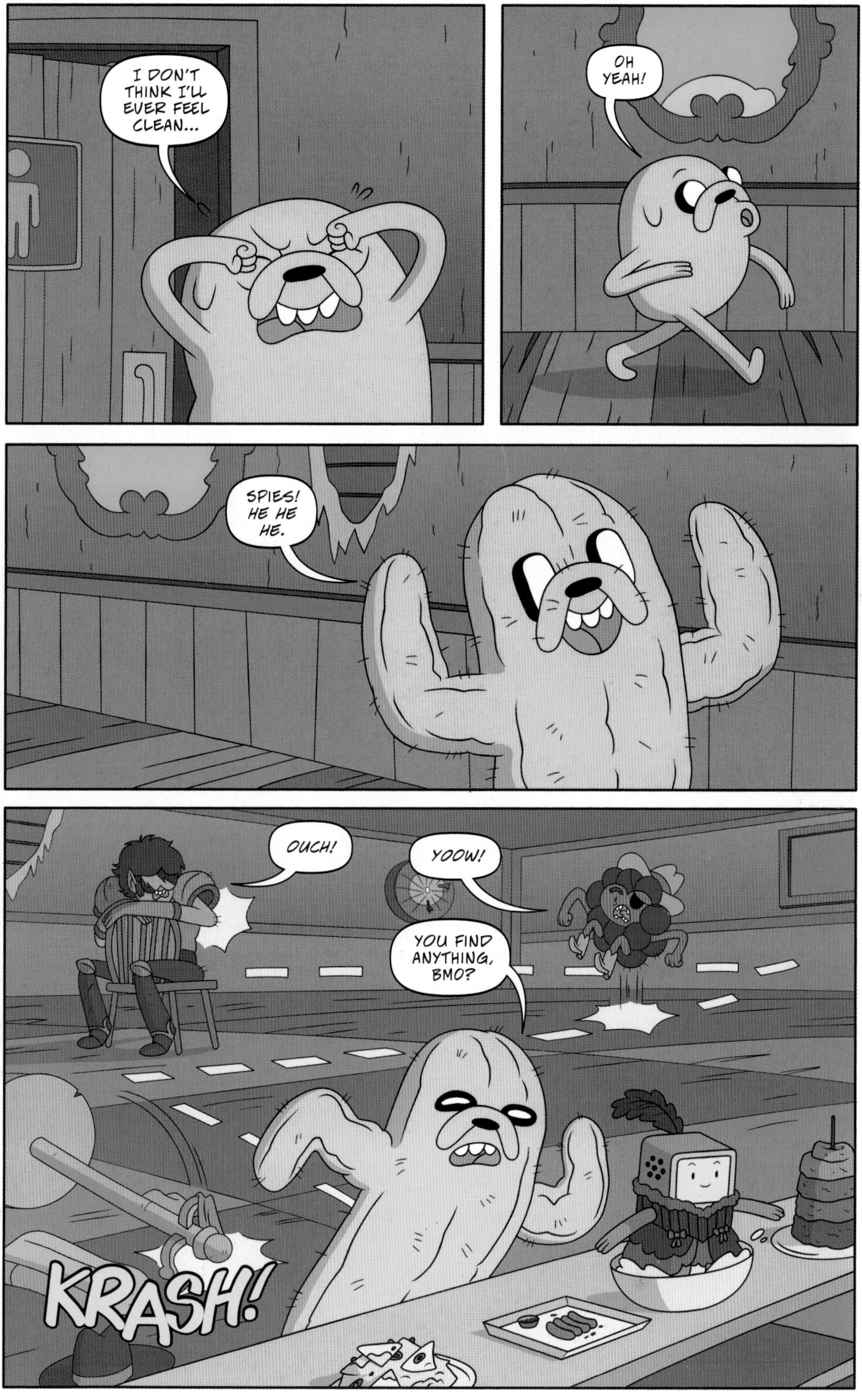
I DON'T THINK I'LL EVER FEEL CLEAN...
OH YEAH!
SPIES! HE HE HE.
OUCH!
YOOW!
YOU FIND ANYTHING, BMO?
KRASH!

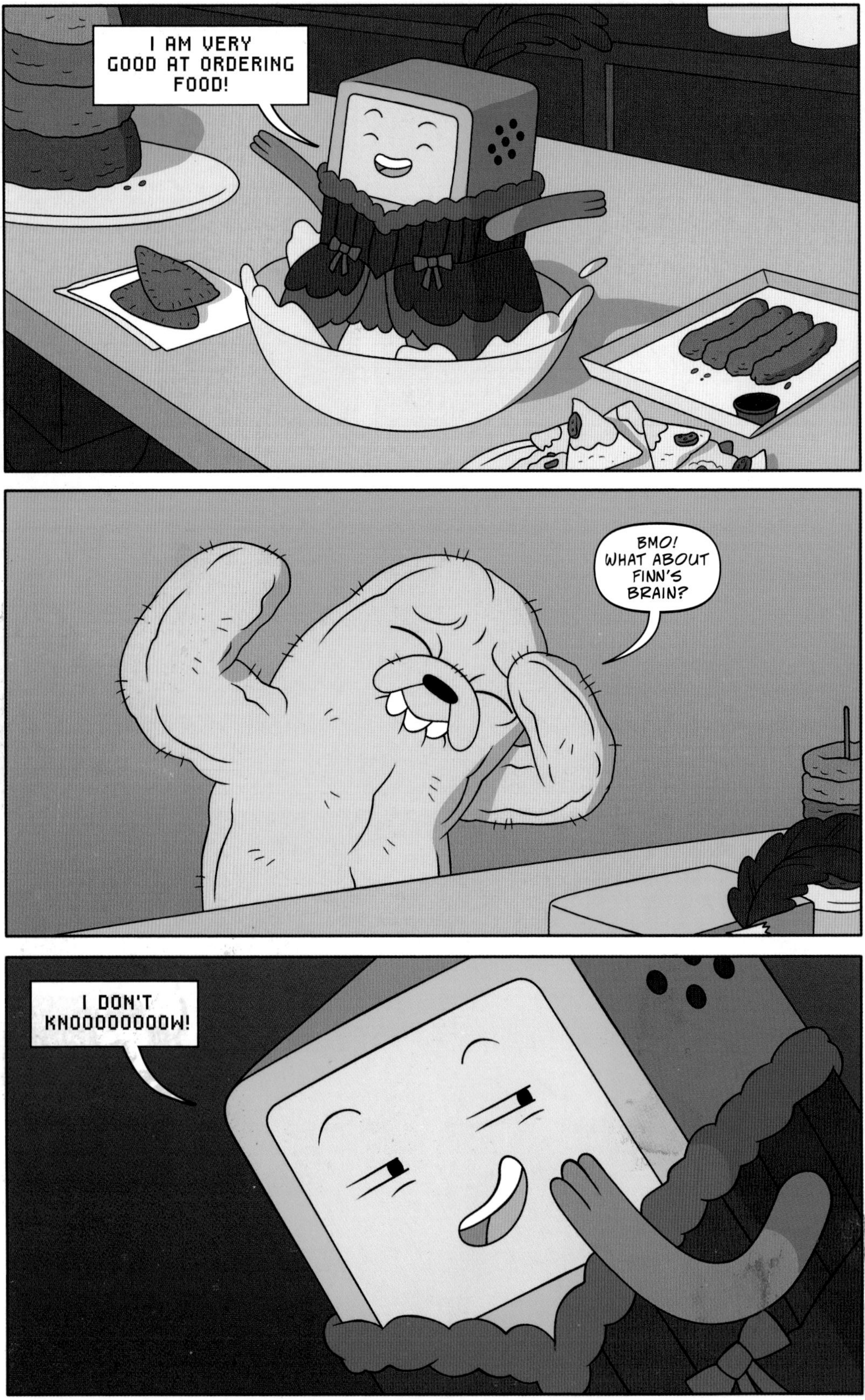
I AM VERY GOOD AT ORDERING FOOD!
BMO! WHAT ABOUT FINN'S BRAIN?
I DON'T KNOOOOOOOOW!

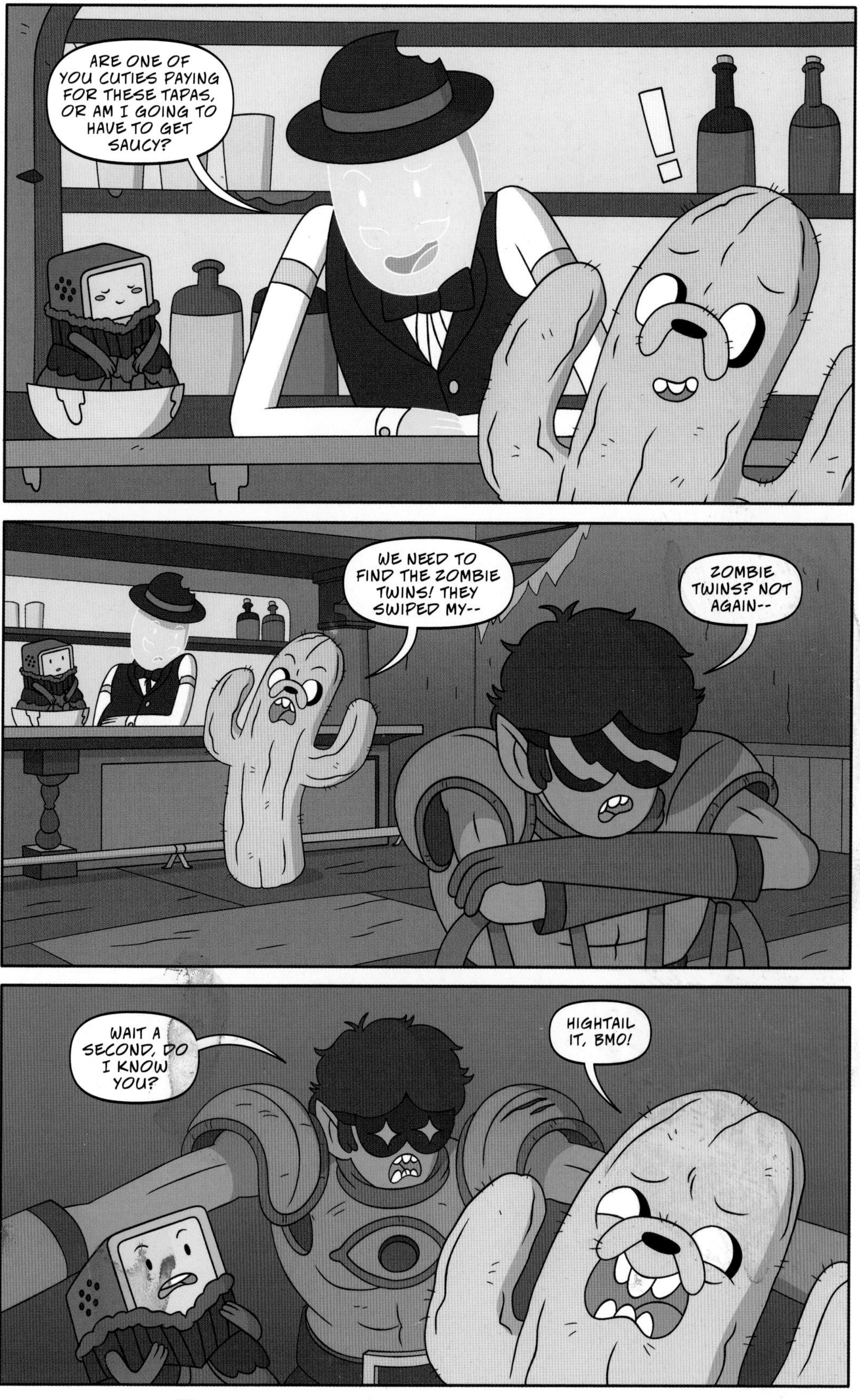
ARE ONE OF YOU CUTIES PAYING FOR THESE TAPAS, OR AM I GOING TO HAVE TO GET SAUCY?
!
WE NEED TO FIND THE ZOMBIE TWINS! THEY SWIPED MY--
ZOMBIE TWINS? NOT AGAIN--
WAIT A SECOND, DO I KNOW YOU?
HIGHTAIL IT, BMO!

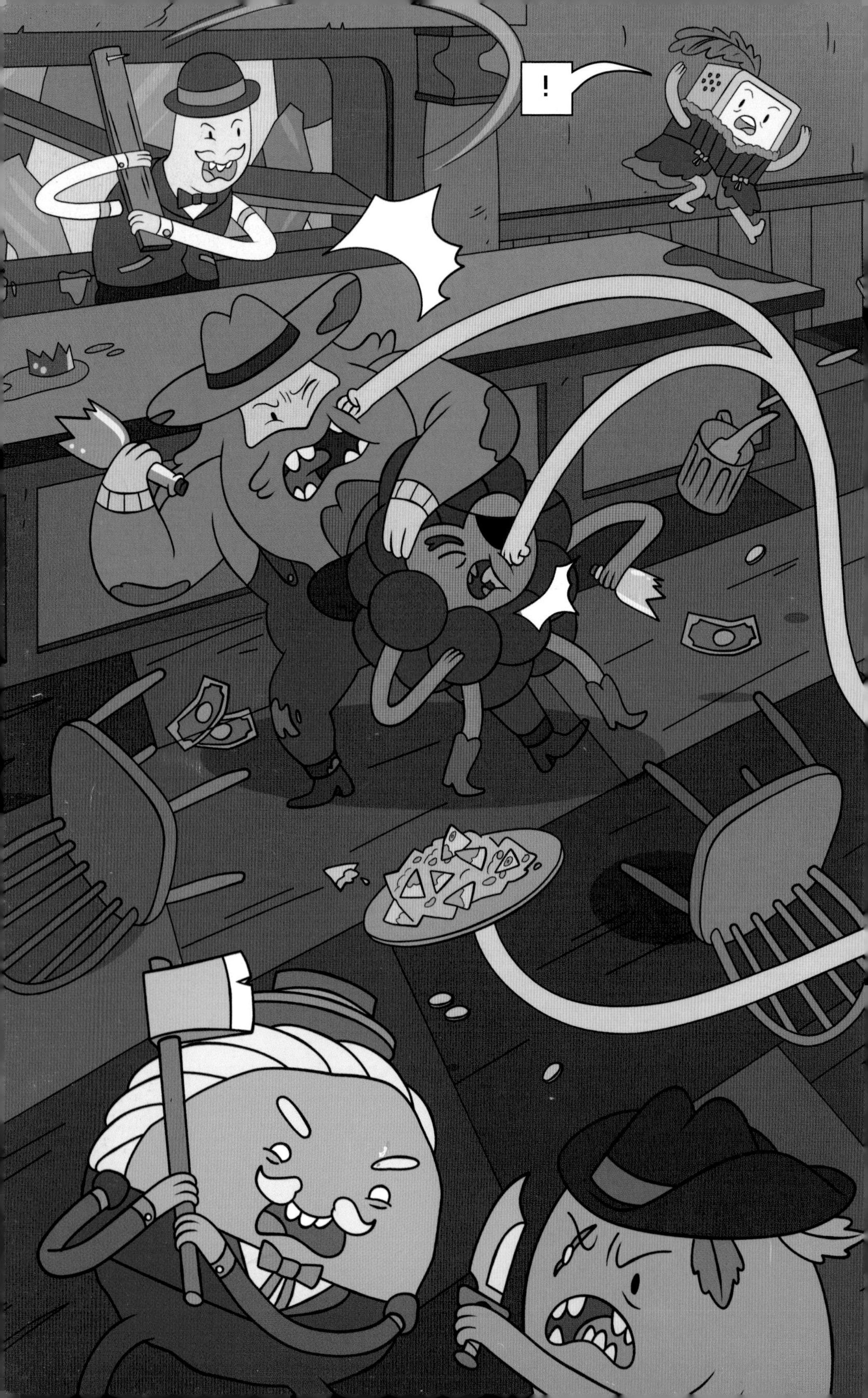
!

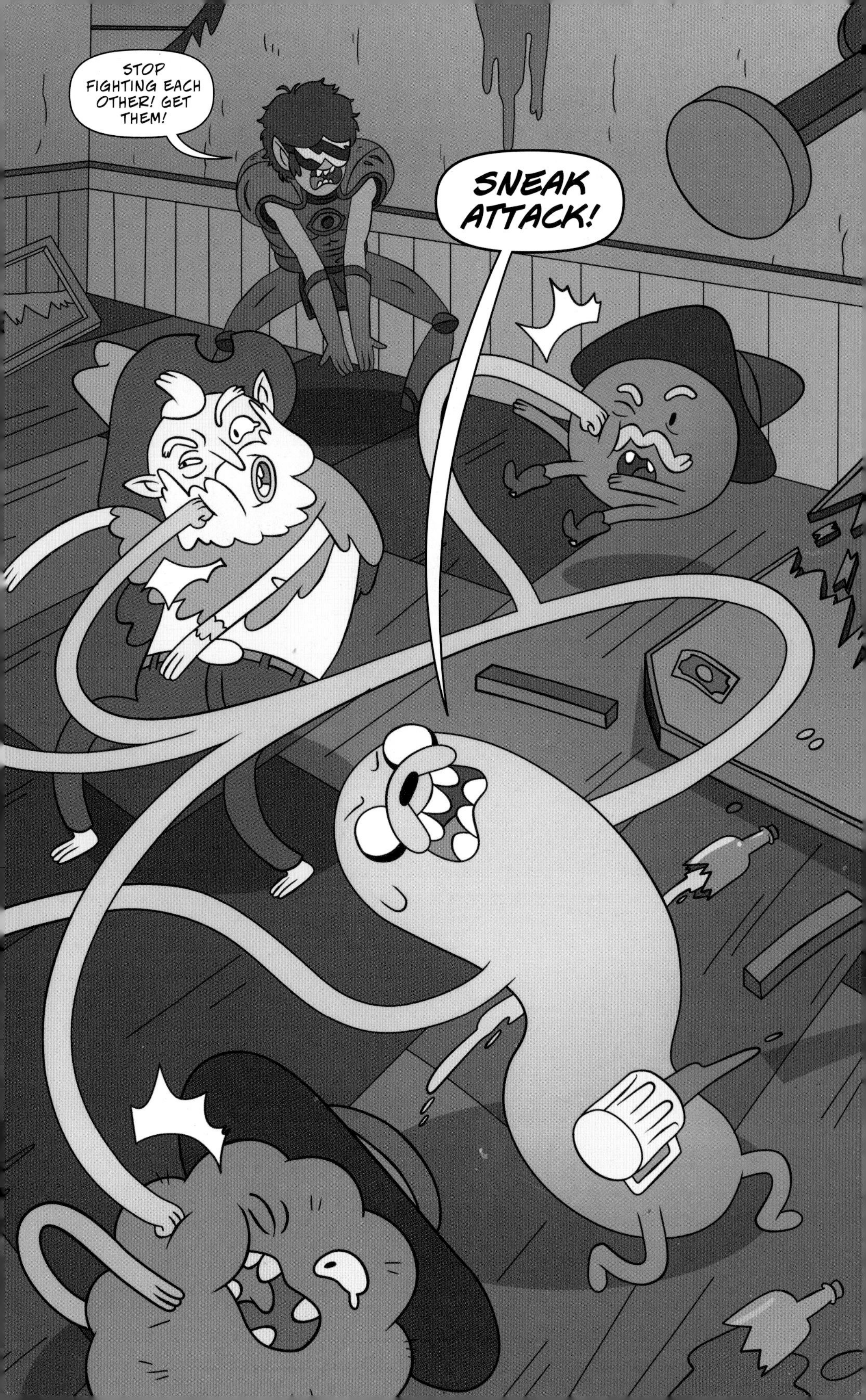
STOP FIGHTING EACH OTHER! GET THEM!
SNEAK ATTACK!

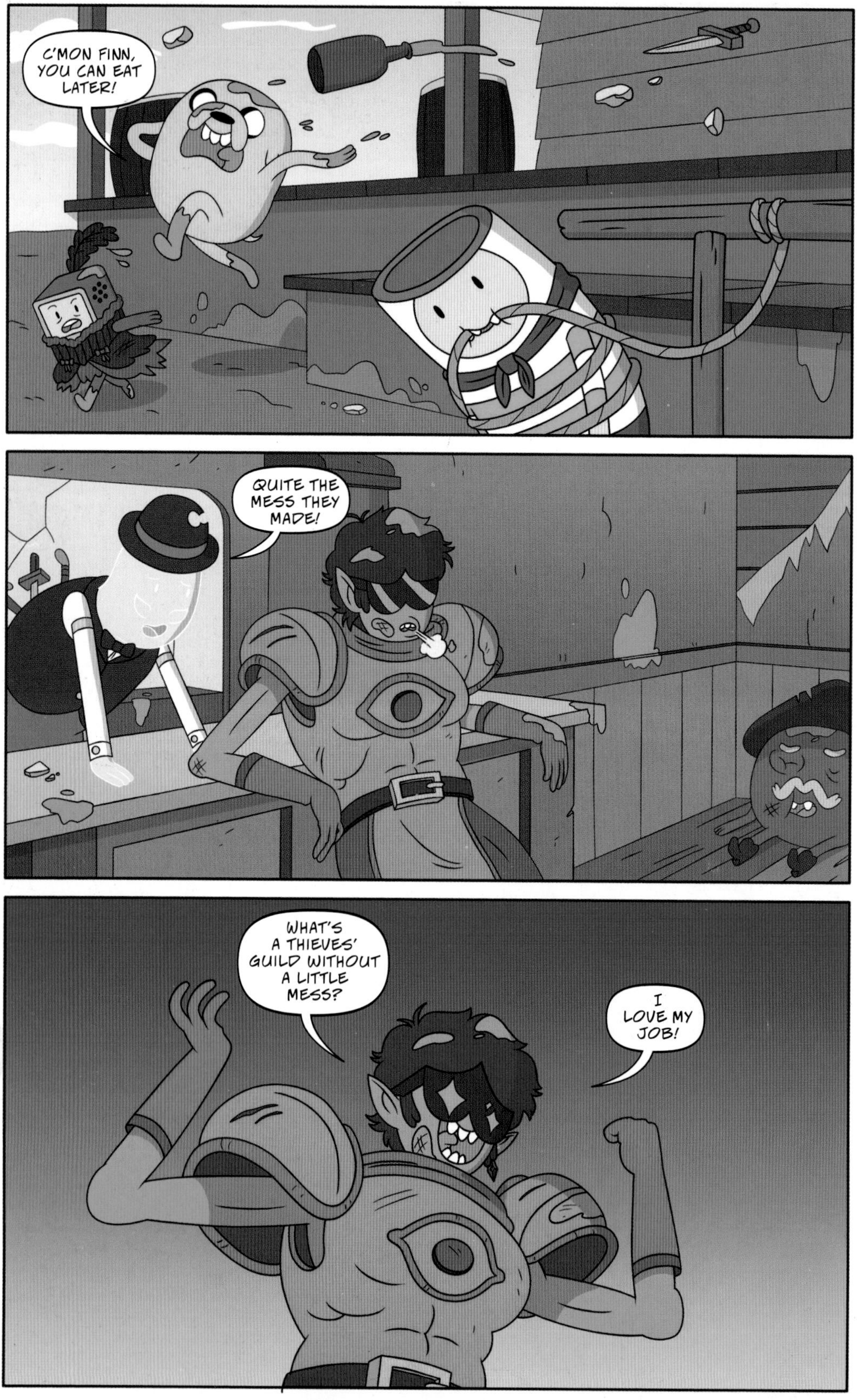
C'MON FINN, YOU CAN EAT LATER!
QUITE THE MESS THEY MADE!
WHAT'S A THIEVES' GUILD WITHOUT A LITTLE MESS?
I LOVE MY JOB!

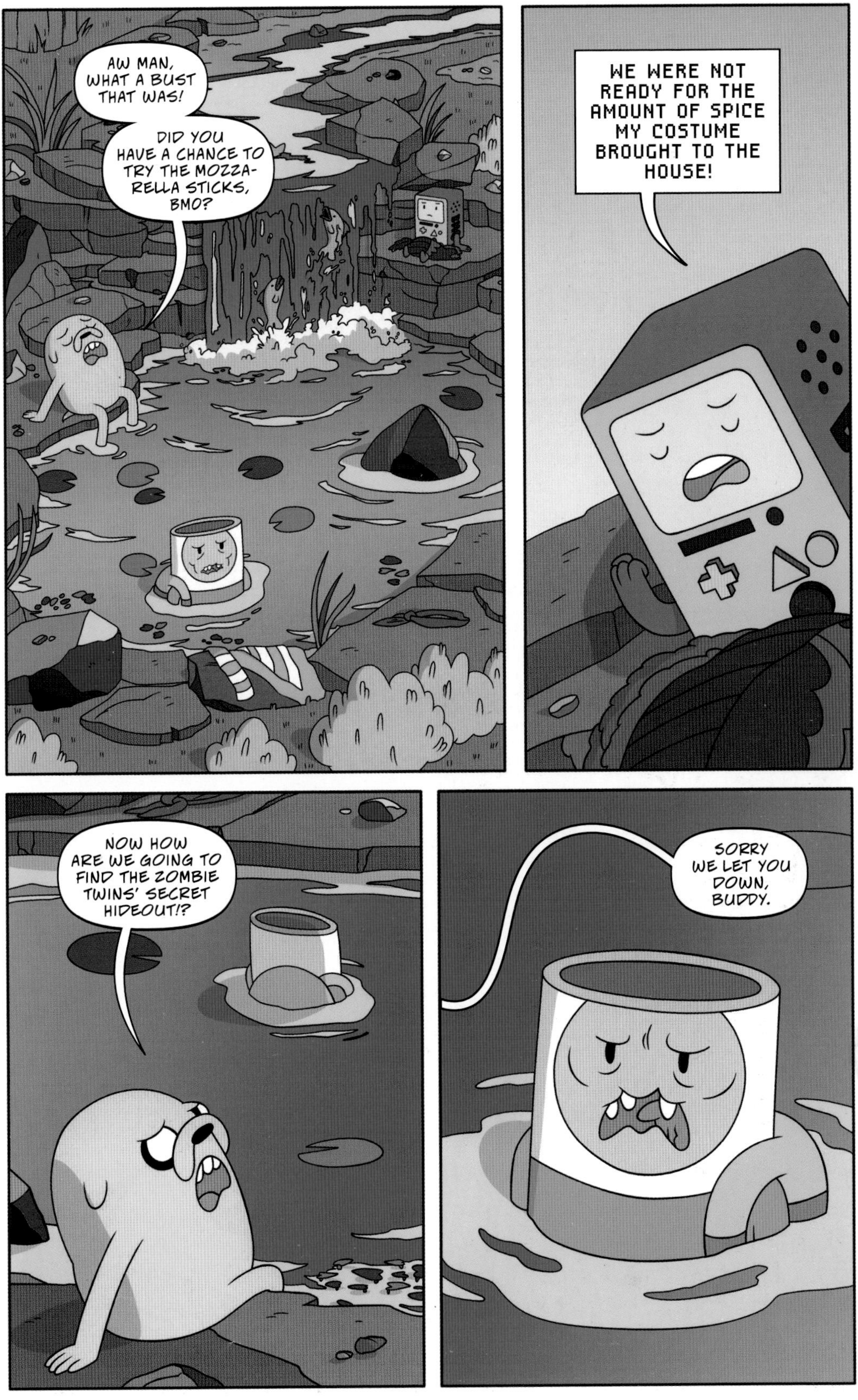
AW MAN, WHAT A BUST THAT WAS!
DID YOU HAVE A CHANCE TO TRY THE MOZZA-RELLA STICKS, BMO?
WE WERE NOT READY FOR THE AMOUNT OF SPICE MY COSTUME BROUGHT TO THE HOUSE!
NOW HOW ARE WE GOING TO FIND THE ZOMBIE TWINS' SECRET HIDEOUT!?
SORRY WE LET YOU DOWN, BUDDY.

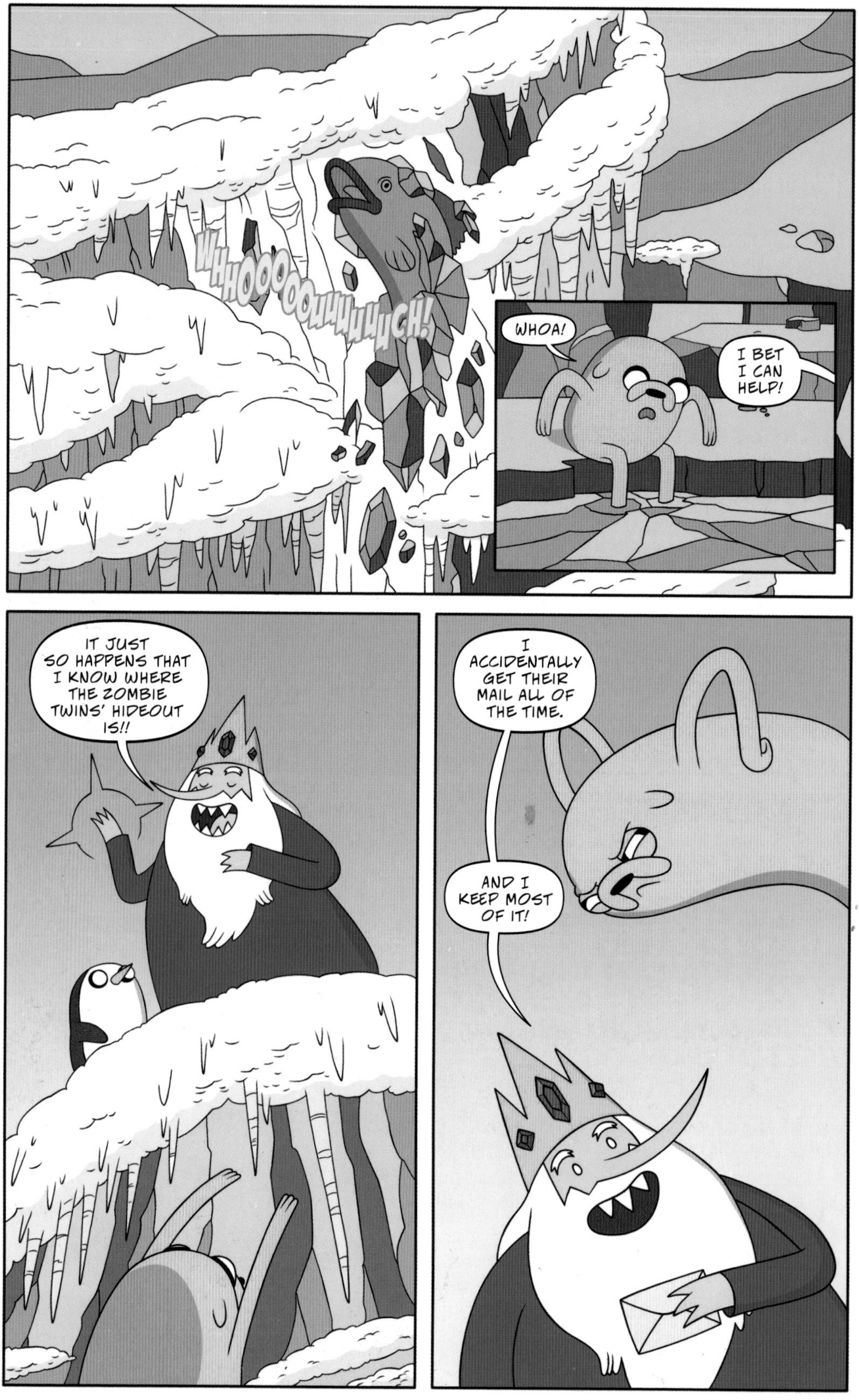
WHHOOOOOUUUUUUCH!
WHOA!
I BET I CAN HELP!
IT JUST SO HAPPENS THAT I KNOW WHERE THE ZOMBIE TWINS' HIDEOUT IS!!
I ACCIDENTALLY GET THEIR MAIL ALL OF THE TIME.
AND I KEEP MOST OF IT!

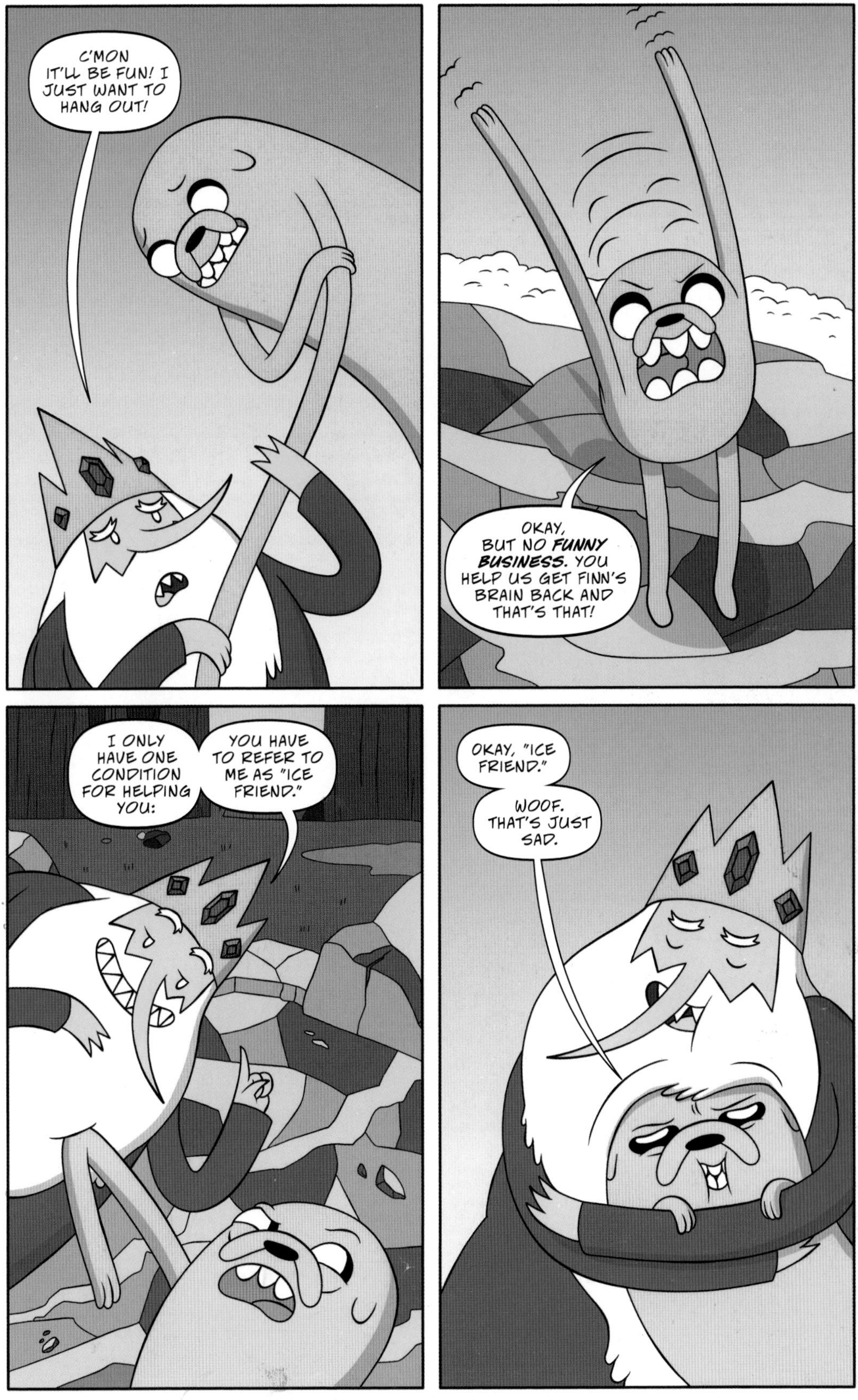
C'MON IT'LL BE FUN! I JUST WANT TO HANG OUT!
OKAY, BUT NO FUNNY BUSINESS. YOU HELP US GET FINN'S BRAIN BACK AND THAT'S THAT!
I ONLY HAVE ONE CONDITION FOR HELPING YOU:
YOU HAVE TO REFER TO ME AS "ICE FRIEND."
OKAY, "ICE FRIEND."
WOOF. THAT'S JUST SAD.

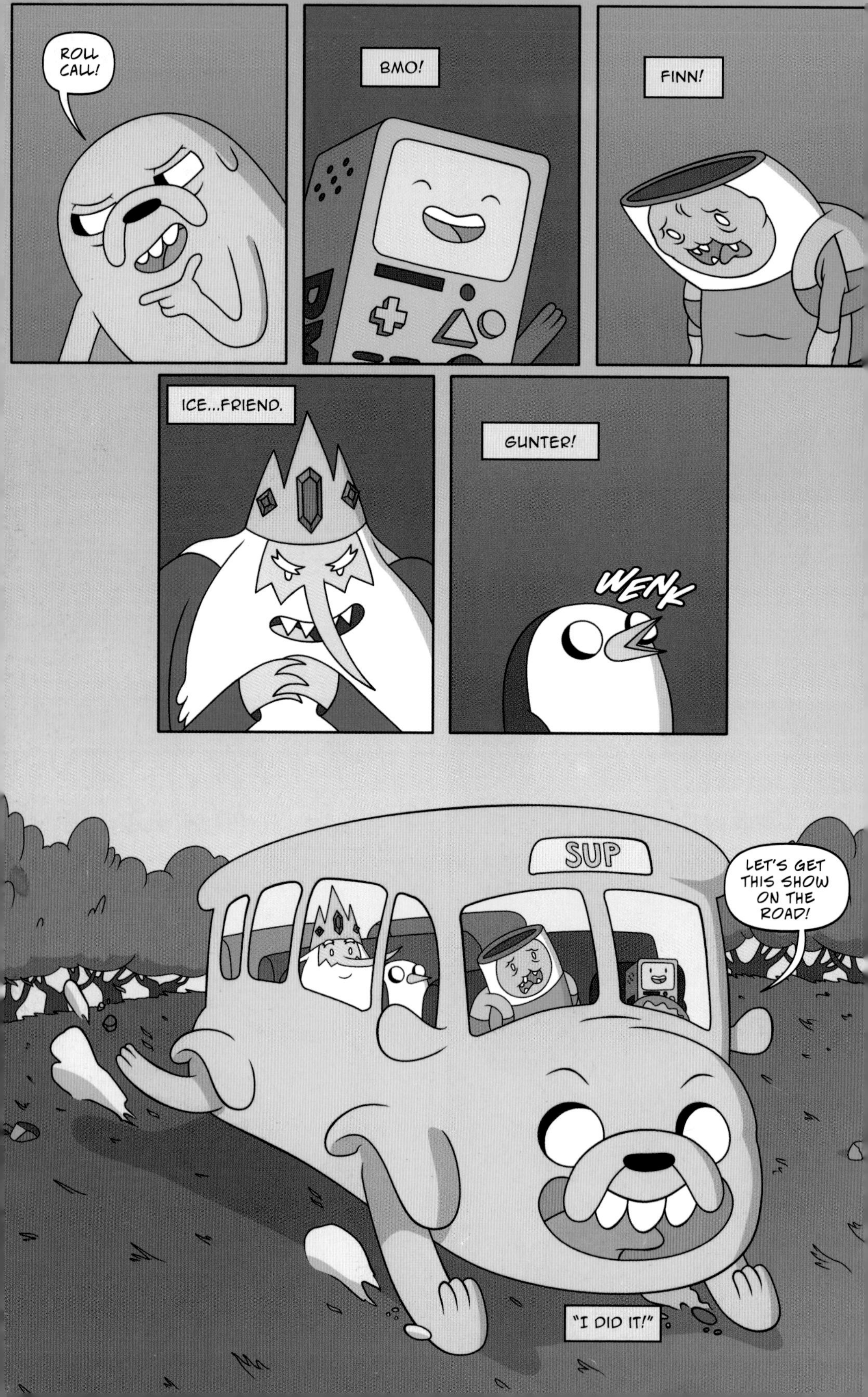
ROLL CALL!
BMO!
FINN!
ICE...FRIEND.
GUNTER!
WENK
SUP
LET'S GET THIS SHOW ON THE ROAD!
"I DID IT!"

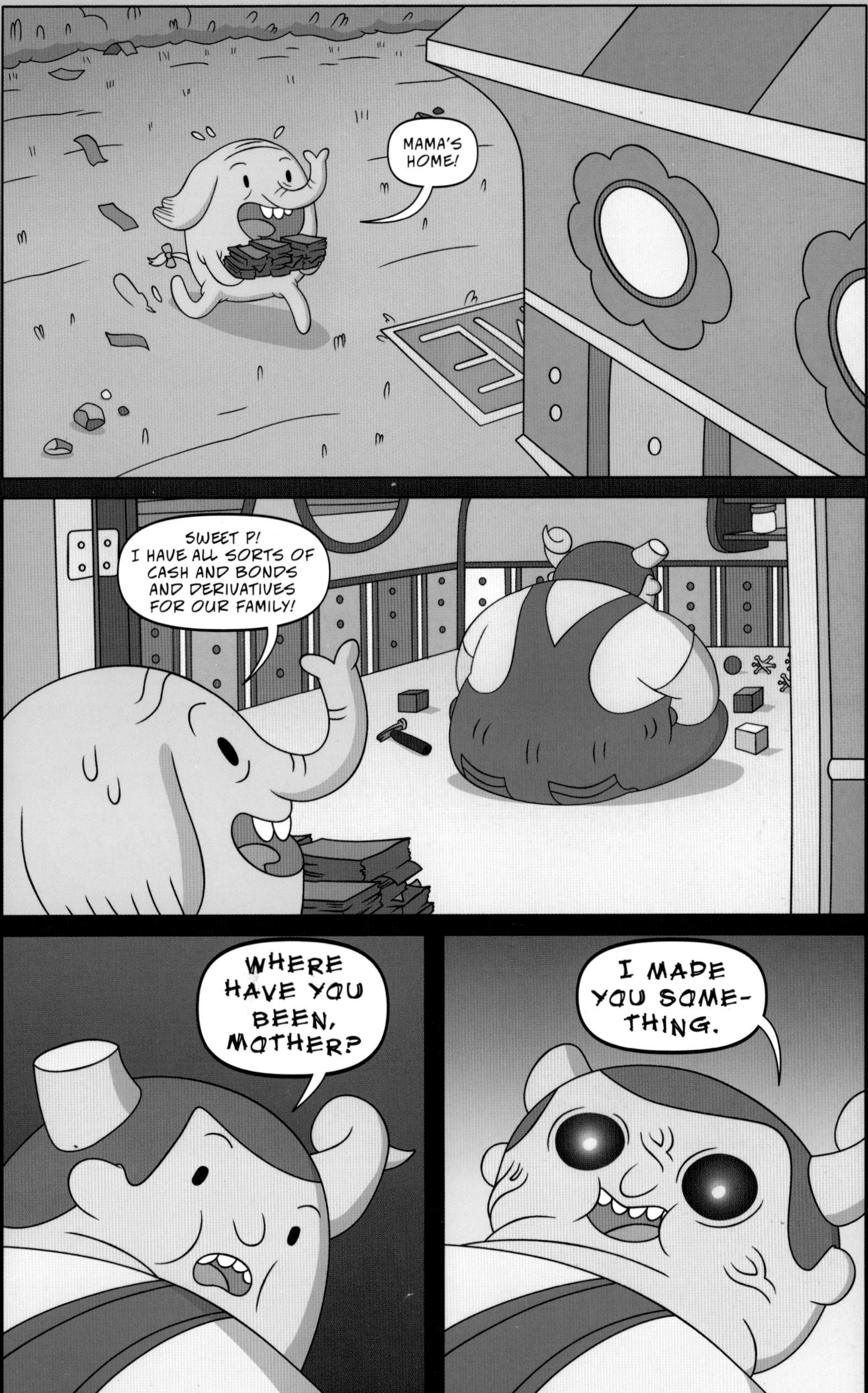
MAMA'S HOME!
SWEET P! I HAVE ALL SORTS OF CASH AND BONDS AND DERIVATIVES FOR OUR FAMILY!
WHERE HAVE YOU BEEN, MOTHER?
I MADE YOU SOME-THING.

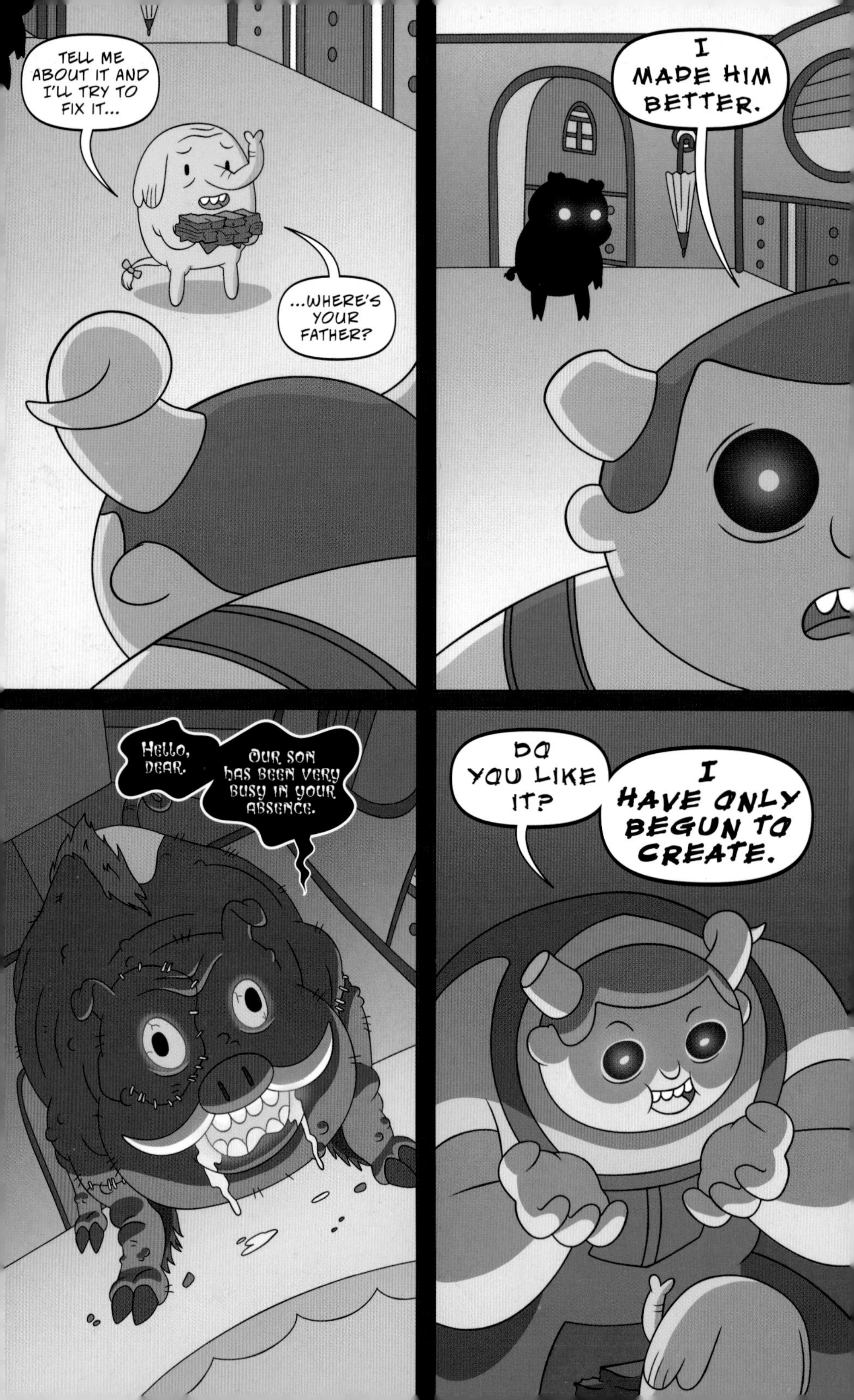
TELL ME ABOUT IT AND I'LL TRY TO FIX IT...
...WHERE'S YOUR FATHER?
I MADE HIM BETTER.
Hello, dear.
Our son has been very busy in your absence.
DO YOU LIKE IT?
I HAVE ONLY BEGUN TO CREATE.

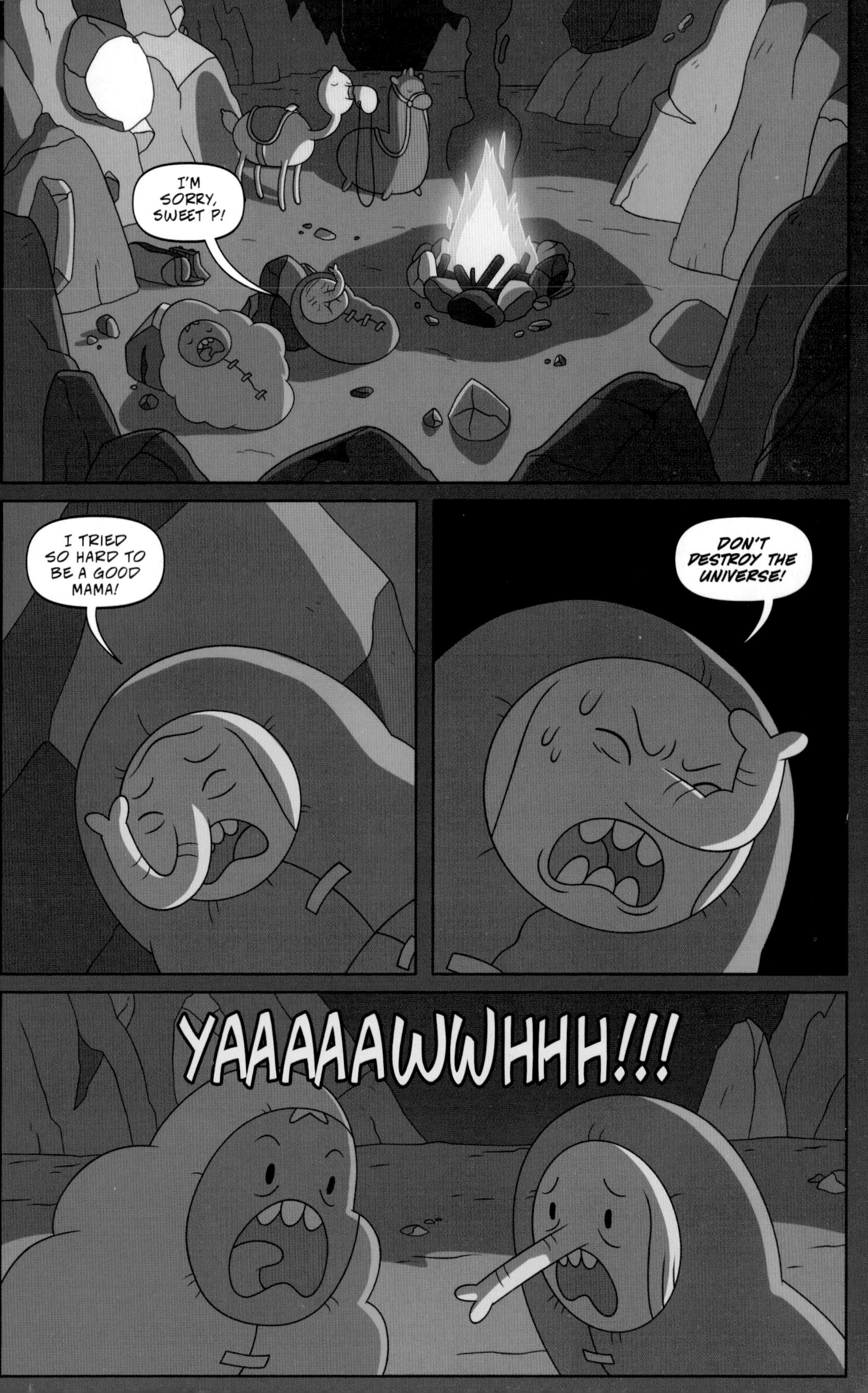
I'M SORRY, SWEET P!
I TRIED SO HARD TO BE A GOOD MAMA!
DON'T DESTROY THE UNIVERSE!
YAAAAAWWHHH!!!

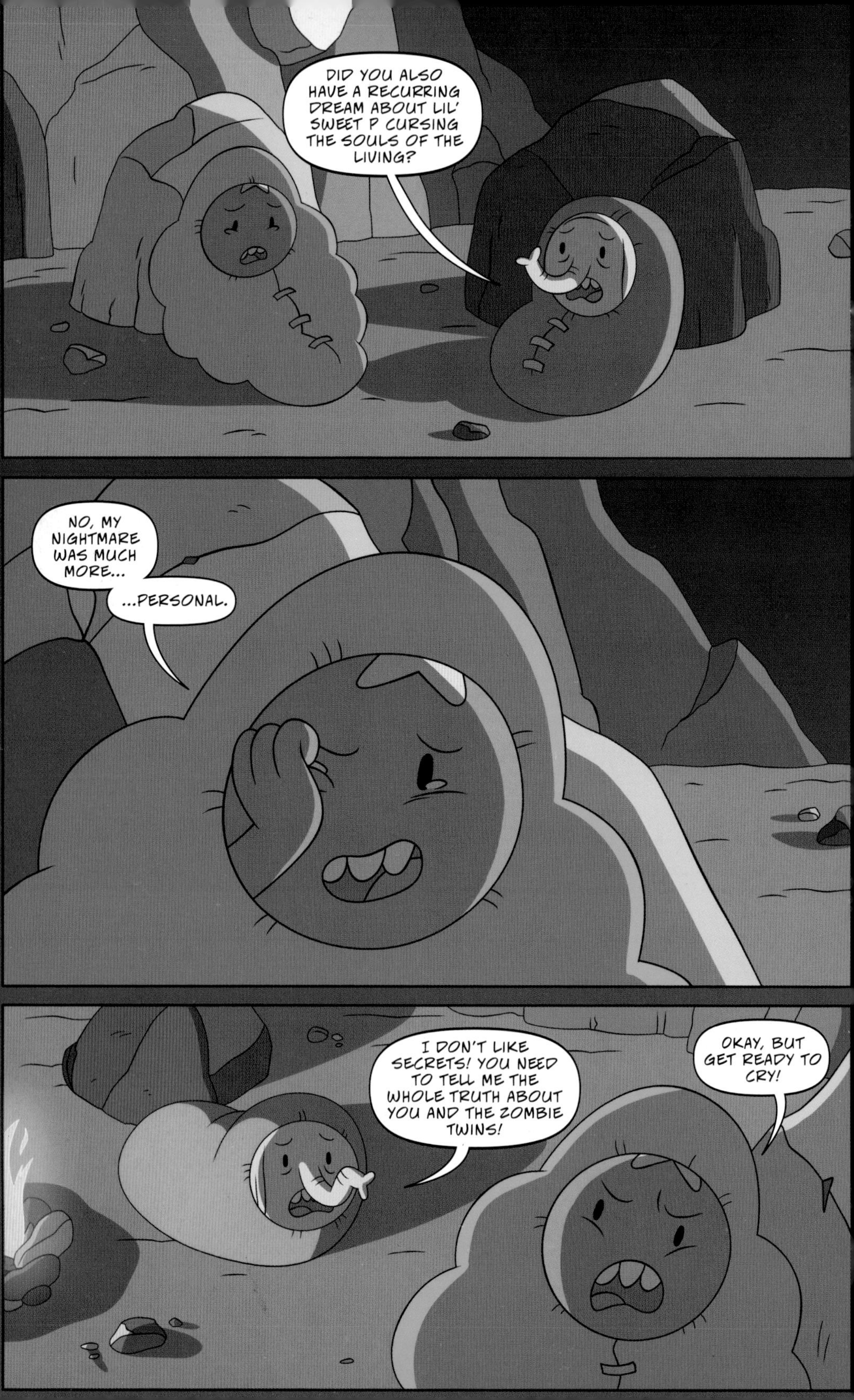
DID YOU ALSO HAVE A RECURRING DREAM ABOUT LIL' SWEET P CURSING THE SOULS OF THE LIVING?
NO, MY NIGHTMARE WAS MUCH MORE...
...PERSONAL.
I DON'T LIKE SECRETS! YOU NEED TO TELL ME THE WHOLE TRUTH ABOUT YOU AND THE ZOMBIE TWINS!
OKAY, BUT GET READY TO CRY!

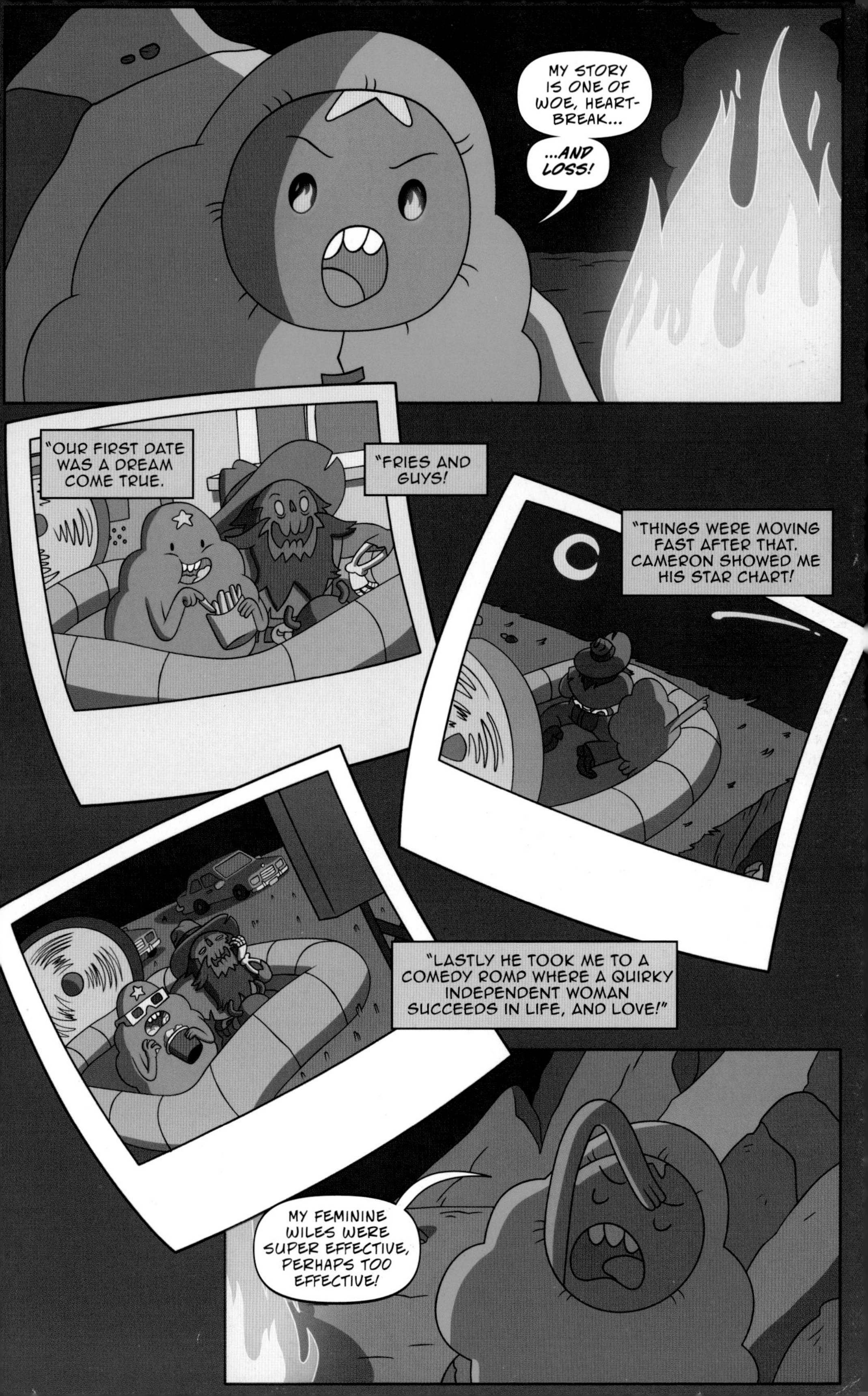

MY STORY IS ONE OF WOE, HEART-BREAK...
...AND LOSS!
"OUR FIRST DATE WAS A DREAM COME TRUE.
"FRIES AND GUYS!
"THINGS WERE MOVING FAST AFTER THAT. CAMERON SHOWED ME HIS STAR CHART!
"LASTLY HE TOOK ME TO A COMEDY ROMP WHERE A QUIRKY INDEPENDENT WOMAN SUCCEEDS IN LIFE, AND LOVE!"
MY FEMININE WILES WERE SUPER EFFECTIVE, PERHAPS TOO EFFECTIVE!

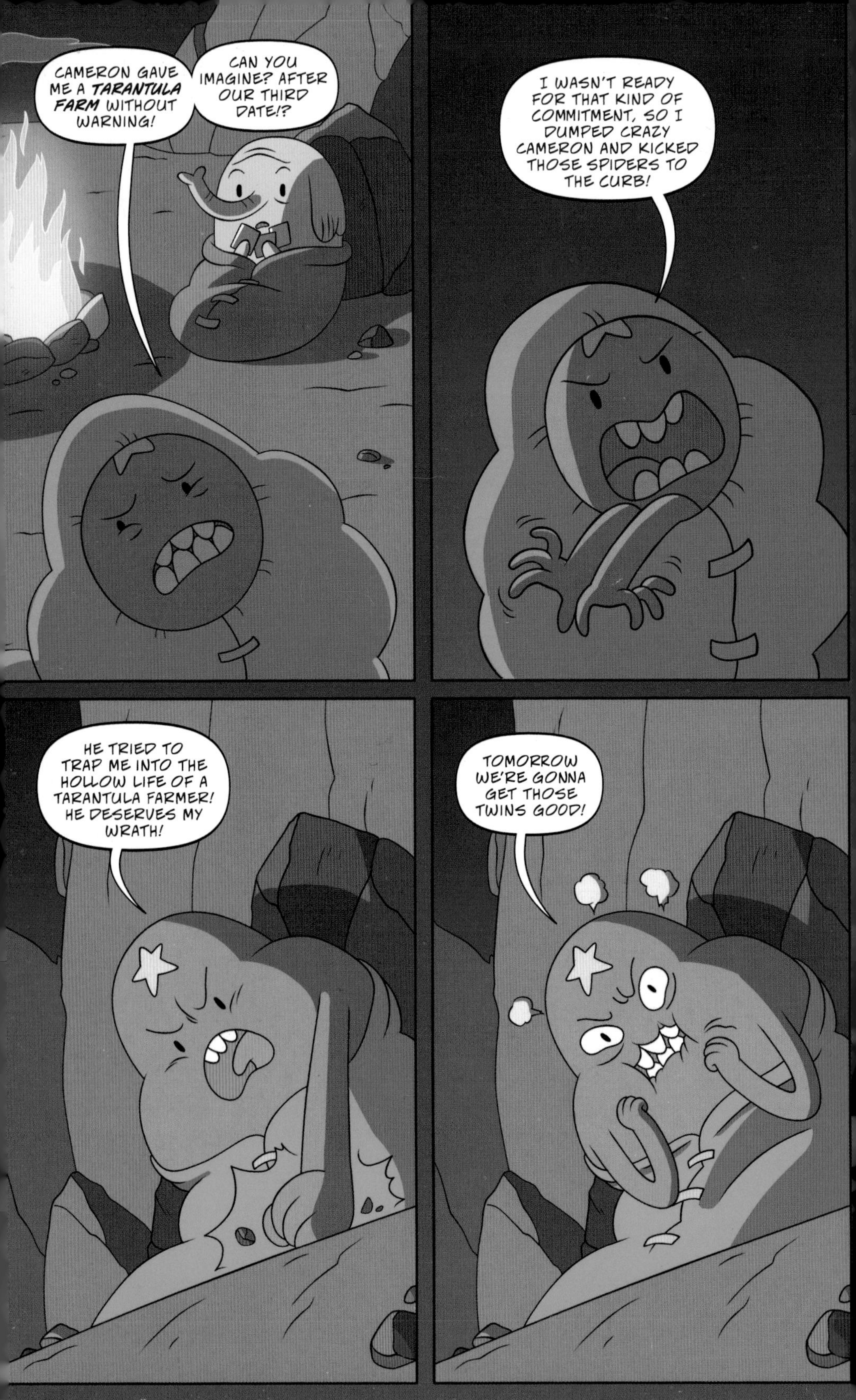
CAMERON GAVE ME A **TARANTULA FARM** WITHOUT WARNING!
CAN YOU IMAGINE? AFTER OUR THIRD DATE!?
I WASN'T READY FOR THAT KIND OF COMMITMENT, SO I DUMPED CRAZY CAMERON AND KICKED THOSE SPIDERS TO THE CURB!
HE TRIED TO TRAP ME INTO THE HOLLOW LIFE OF A TARANTULA FARMER! HE DESERVES MY WRATH!
TOMORROW WE'RE GONNA GET THOSE TWINS GOOD!

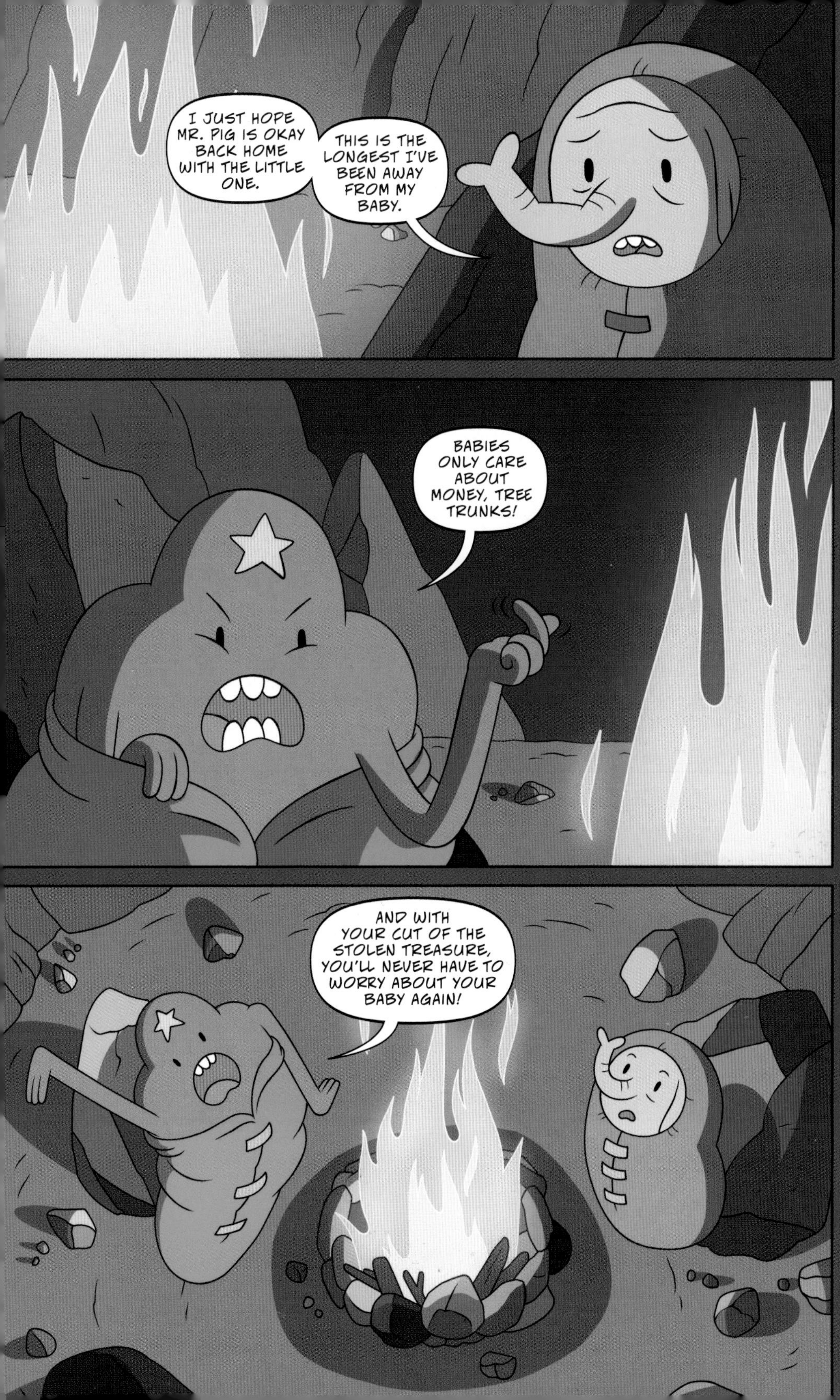
I JUST HOPE MR. PIG IS OKAY BACK HOME WITH THE LITTLE ONE.
THIS IS THE LONGEST I'VE BEEN AWAY FROM MY BABY.
BABIES ONLY CARE ABOUT MONEY, TREE TRUNKS!
AND WITH YOUR CUT OF THE STOLEN TREASURE, YOU'LL NEVER HAVE TO WORRY ABOUT YOUR BABY AGAIN!

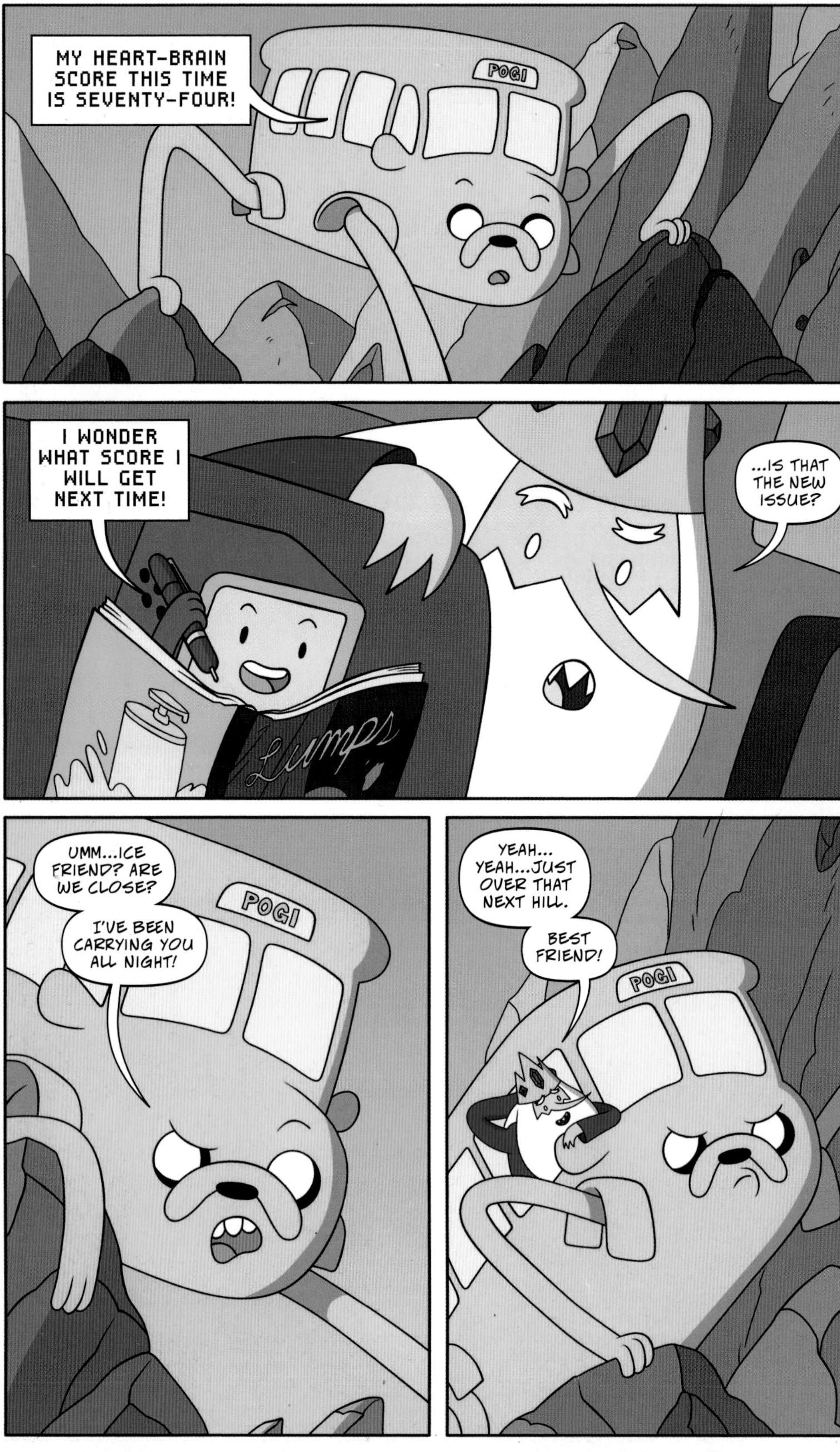
MY HEART-BRAIN SCORE THIS TIME IS SEVENTY-FOUR!
POGI
I WONDER WHAT SCORE I WILL GET NEXT TIME!
...IS THAT THE NEW ISSUE?
Lumps
UMM...ICE FRIEND? ARE WE CLOSE?
I'VE BEEN CARRYING YOU ALL NIGHT!
POGI
YEAH... YEAH...JUST OVER THAT NEXT HILL.
BEST FRIEND!
POGI

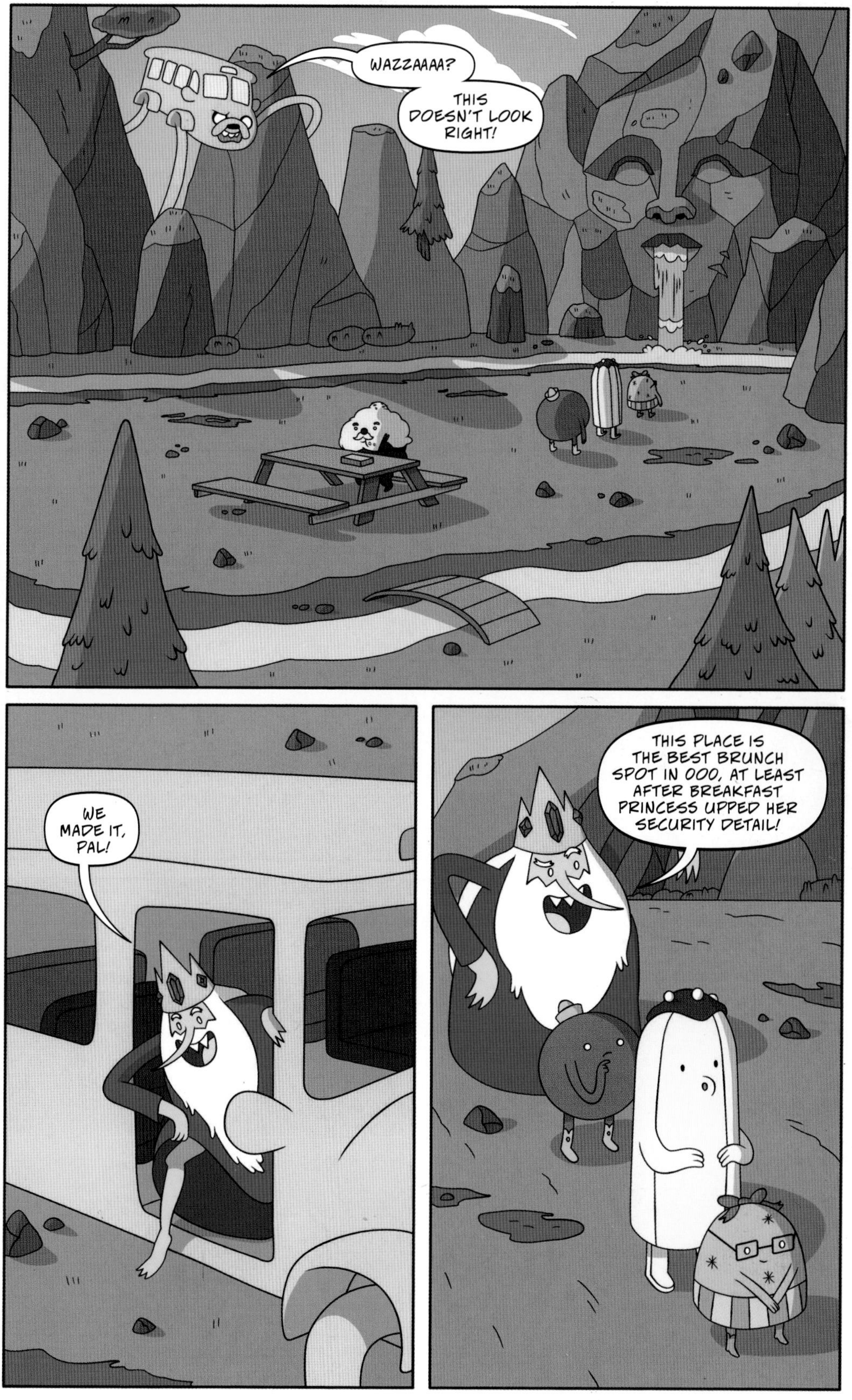
WAZZAAAA?
THIS DOESN'T LOOK RIGHT!
WE MADE IT, PAL!
THIS PLACE IS THE BEST BRUNCH SPOT IN OOO, AT LEAST AFTER BREAKFAST PRINCESS UPPED HER SECURITY DETAIL!

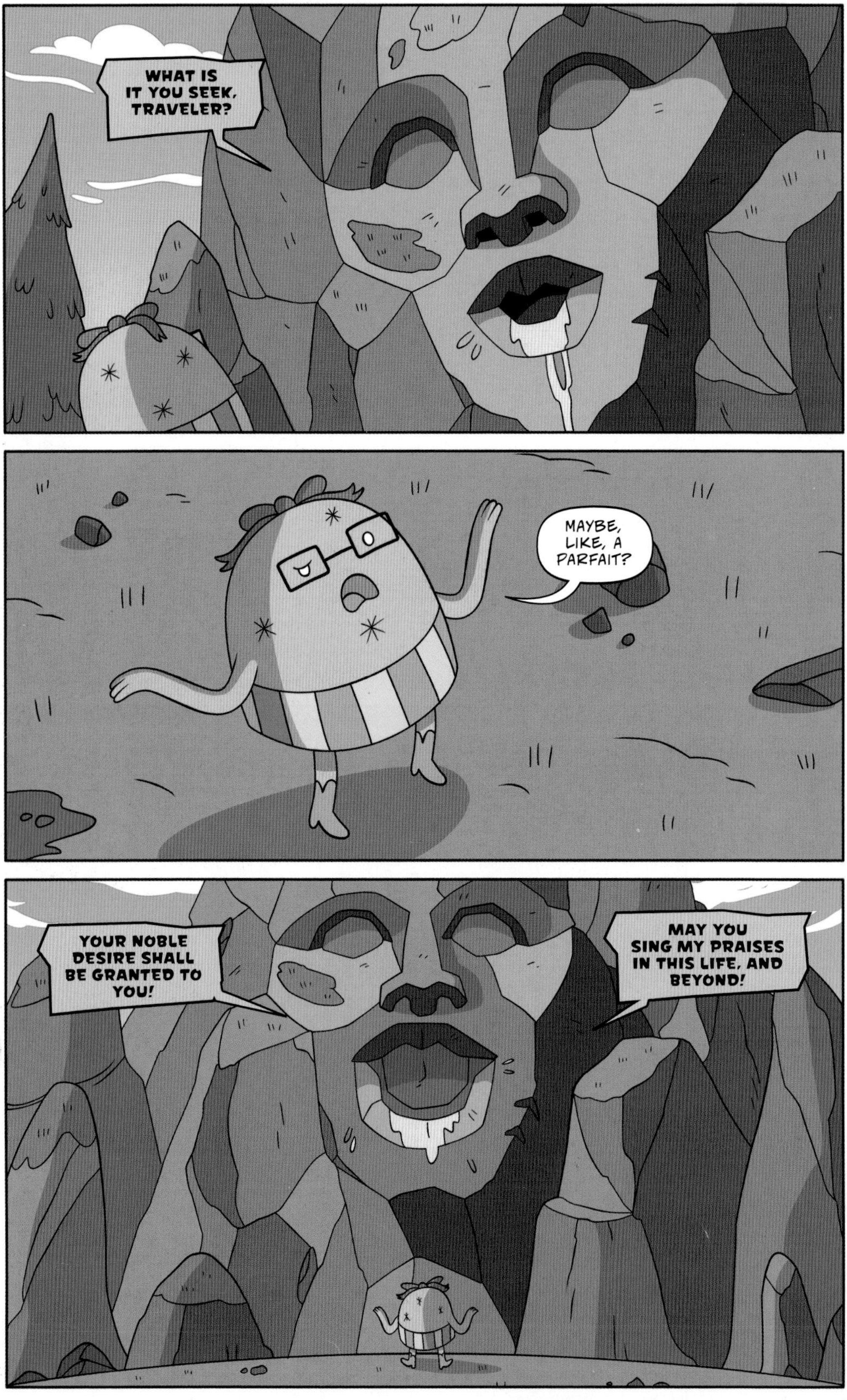
WHAT IS IT YOU SEEK, TRAVELER?
MAYBE, LIKE, A PARFAIT?
YOUR NOBLE DESIRE SHALL BE GRANTED TO YOU!
MAY YOU SING MY PRAISES IN THIS LIFE, AND BEYOND!

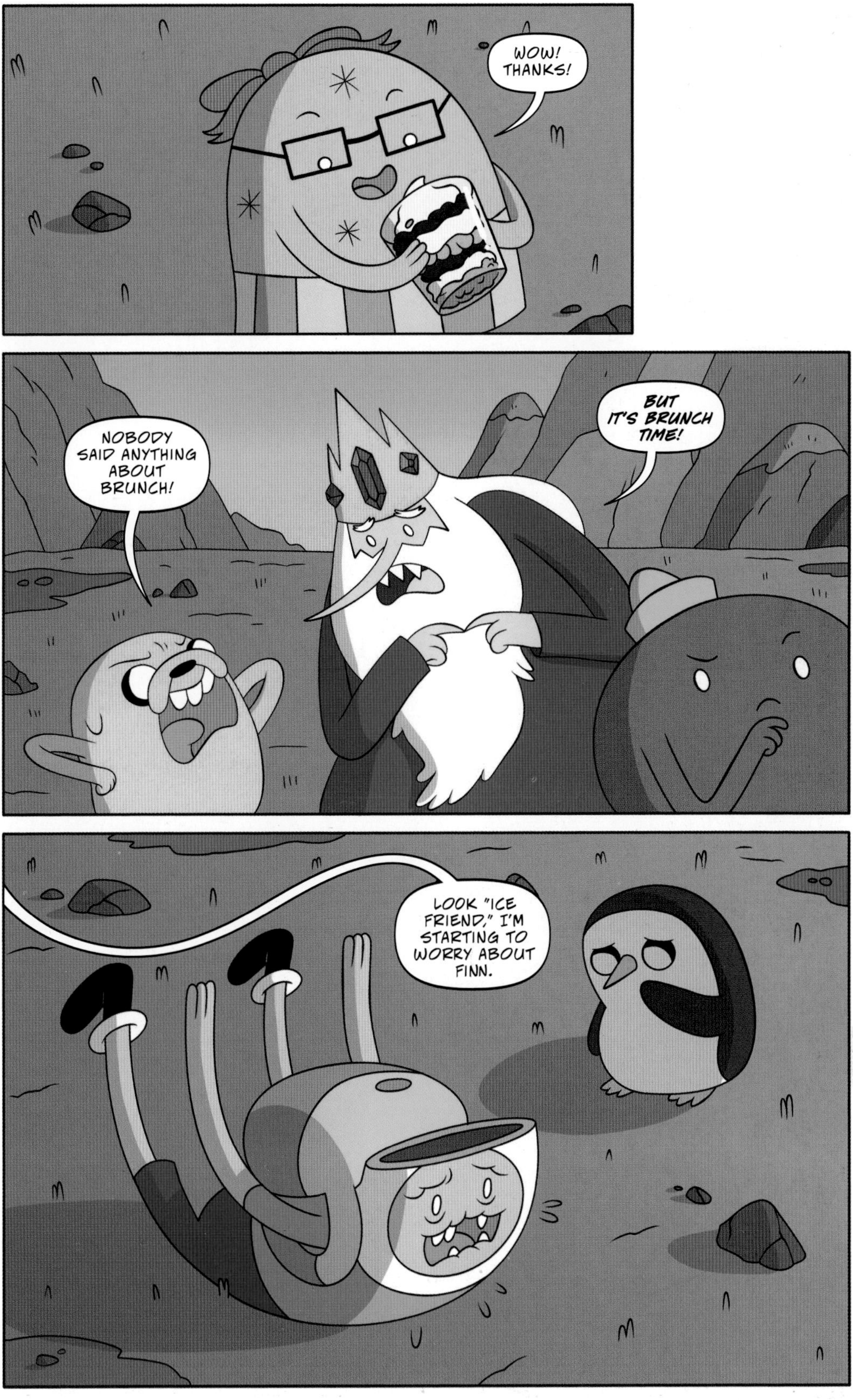
WOW! THANKS!
NOBODY SAID ANYTHING ABOUT BRUNCH!
BUT IT'S BRUNCH TIME!
LOOK "ICE FRIEND," I'M STARTING TO WORRY ABOUT FINN.

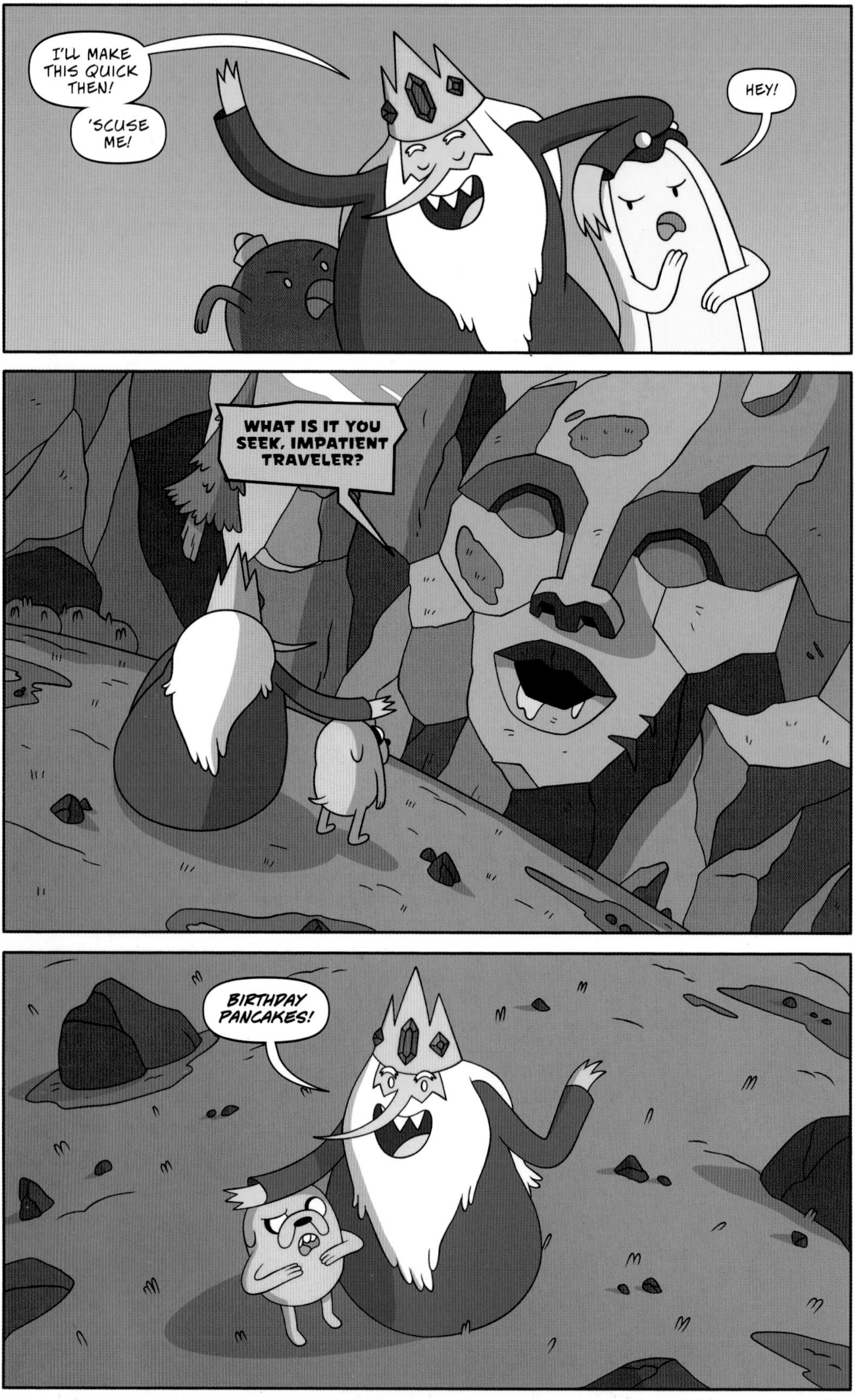
I'LL MAKE THIS QUICK THEN!
'SCUSE ME!
HEY!
WHAT IS IT YOU SEEK, IMPATIENT TRAVELER?
BIRTHDAY PANCAKES!

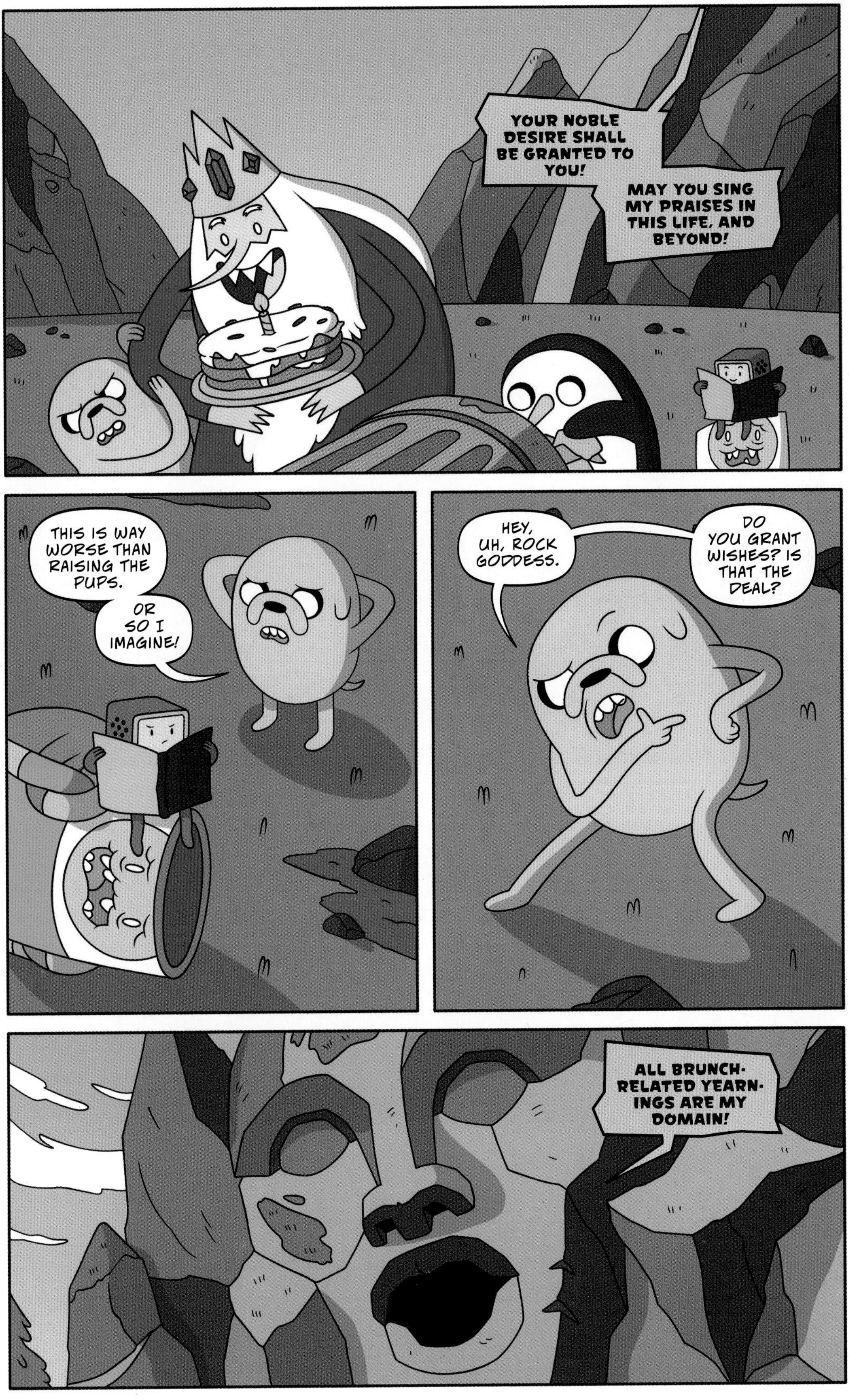
YOUR NOBLE DESIRE SHALL BE GRANTED TO YOU!
MAY YOU SING MY PRAISES IN THIS LIFE, AND BEYOND!
THIS IS WAY WORSE THAN RAISING THE PUPS.
OR SO I IMAGINE!
HEY, UH, ROCK GODDESS.
DO YOU GRANT WISHES? IS THAT THE DEAL?
ALL BRUNCH-RELATED YEARN-INGS ARE MY DOMAIN!

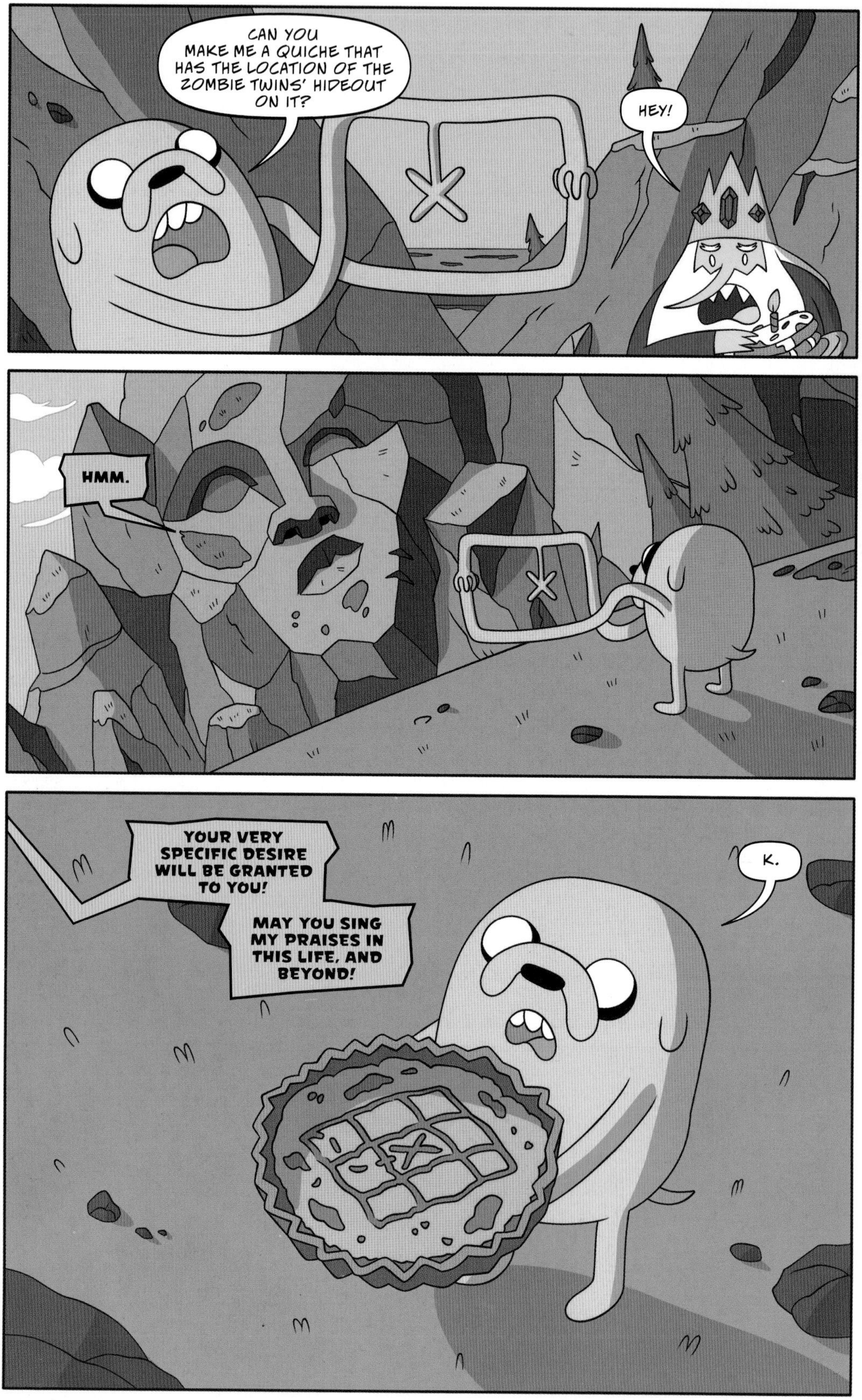
CAN YOU MAKE ME A QUICHE THAT HAS THE LOCATION OF THE ZOMBIE TWINS' HIDEOUT ON IT?
HEY!
HMM.
YOUR VERY SPECIFIC DESIRE WILL BE GRANTED TO YOU!
MAY YOU SING MY PRAISES IN THIS LIFE, AND BEYOND!
K.

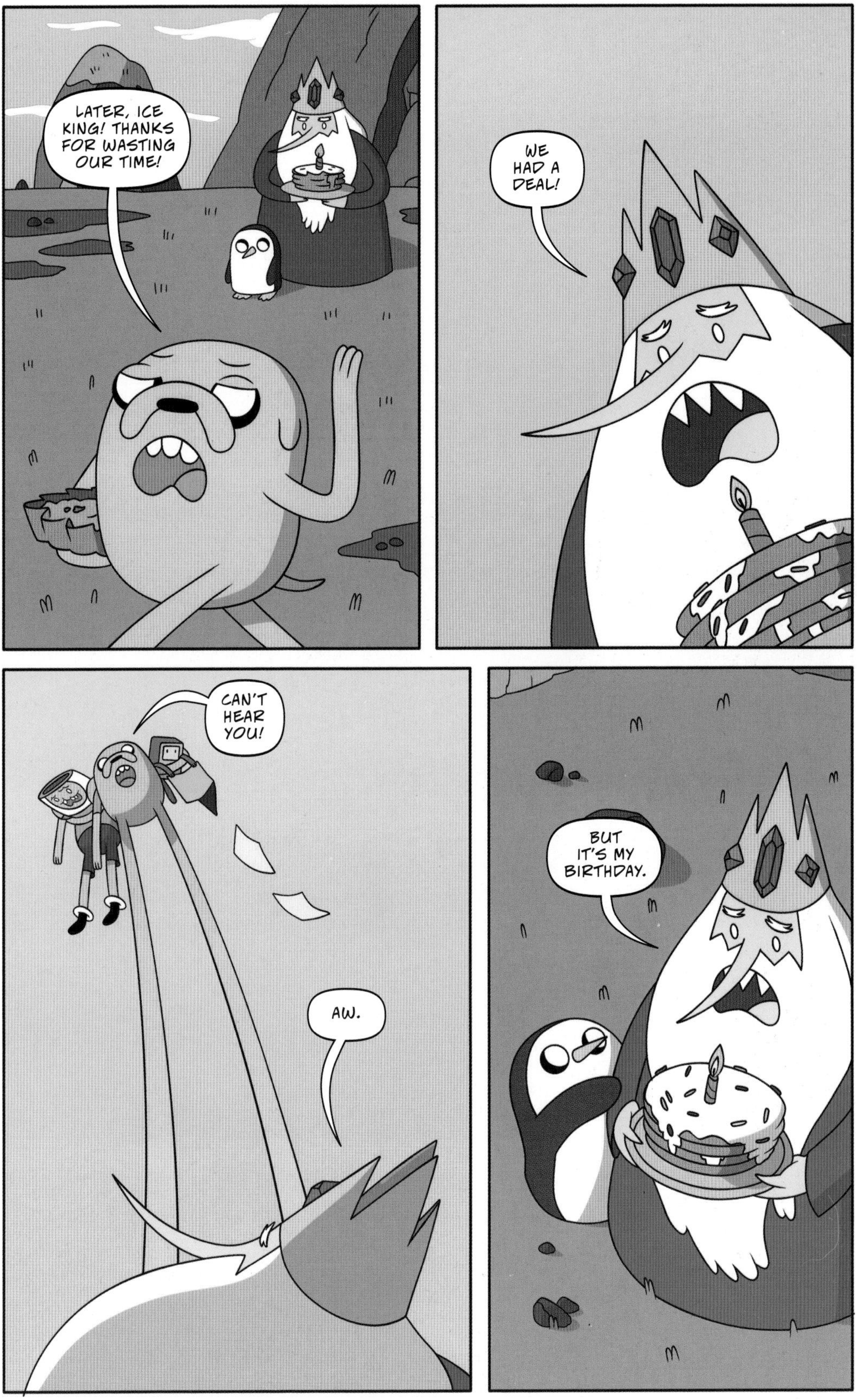
LATER, ICE KING! THANKS FOR WASTING OUR TIME!
WE HAD A DEAL!
CAN'T HEAR YOU!
AW.
BUT IT'S MY BIRTHDAY.

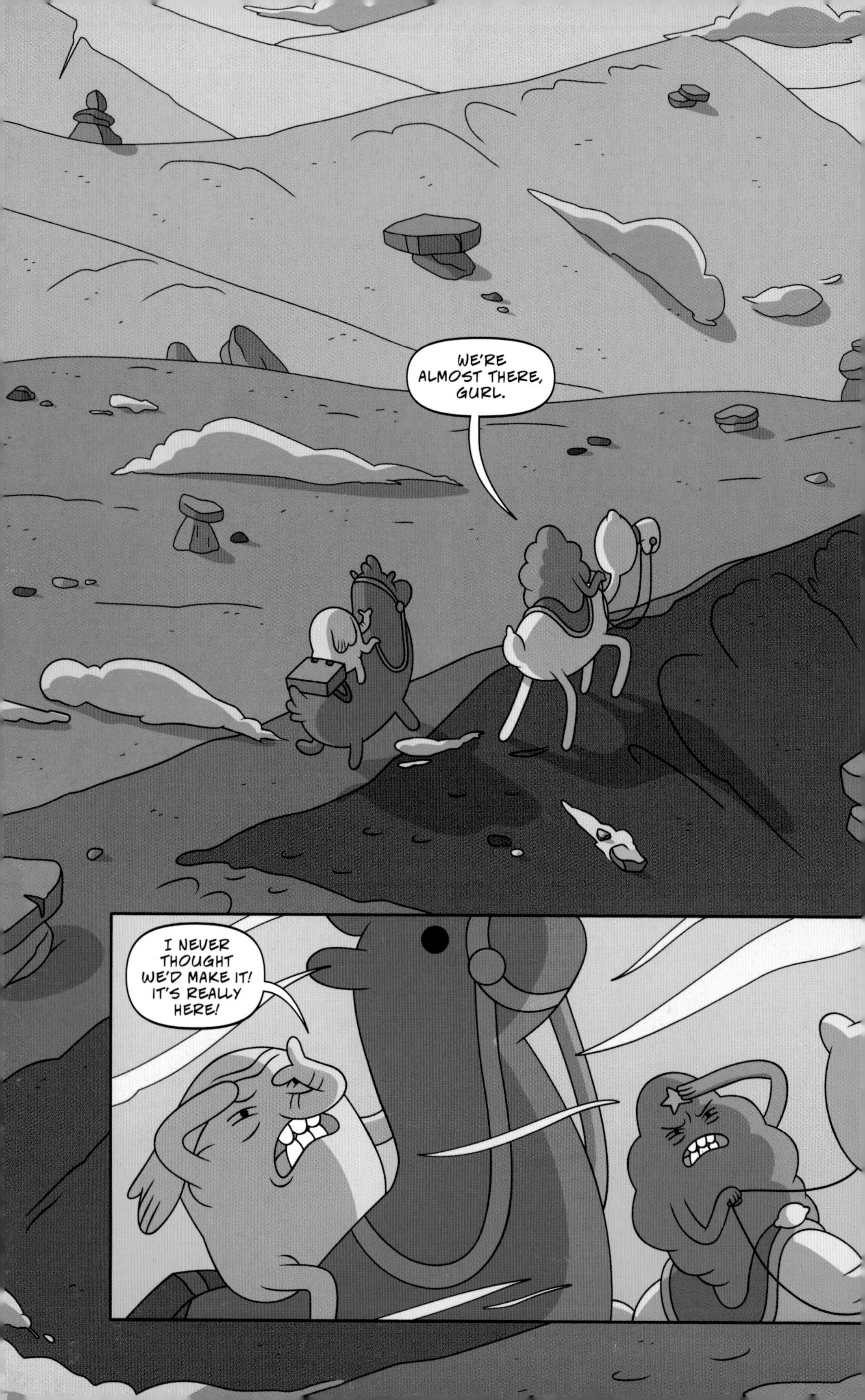
WE'RE ALMOST THERE, GURL.
I NEVER THOUGHT WE'D MAKE IT! IT'S REALLY HERE!

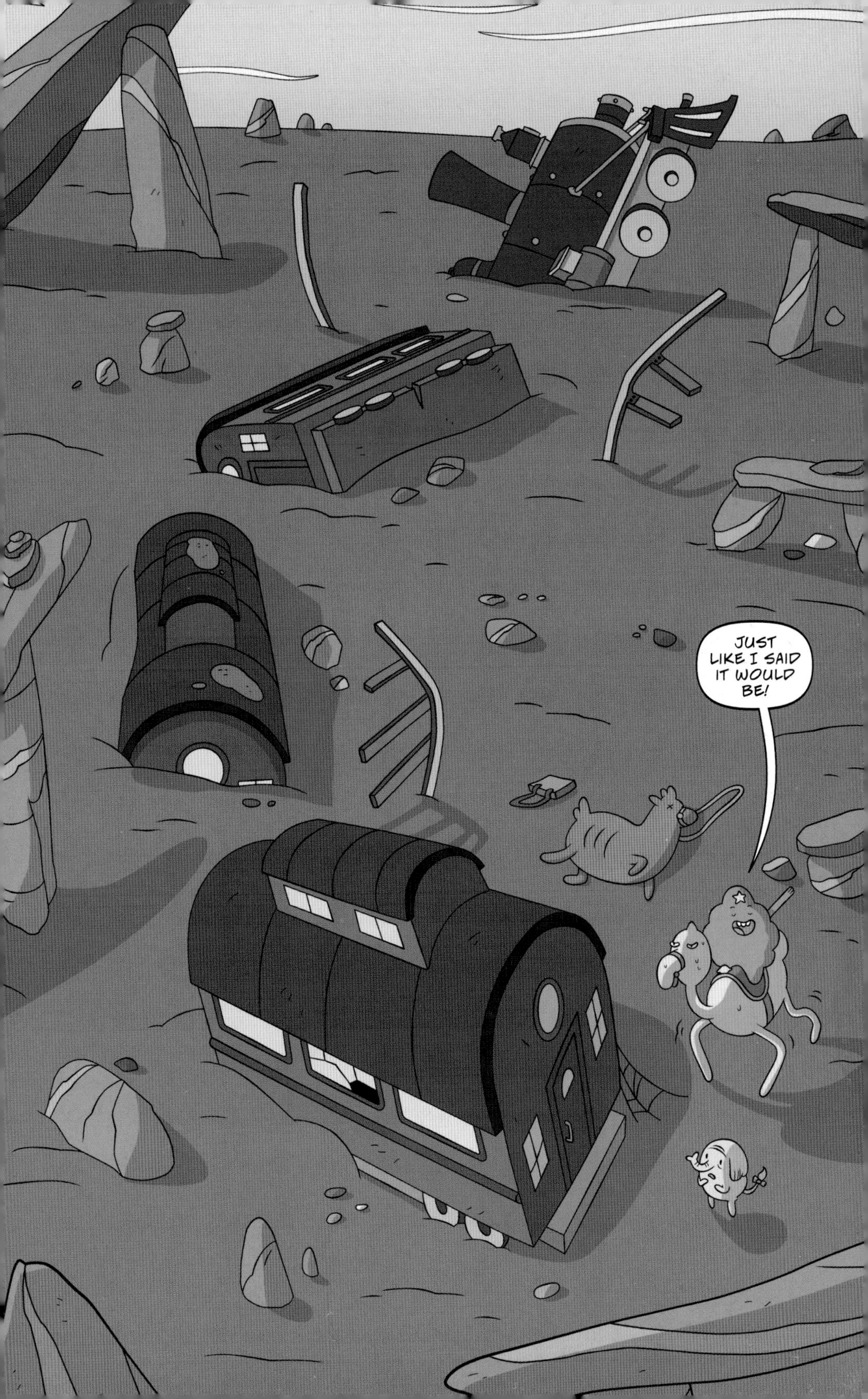
JUST LIKE I SAID IT WOULD BE!

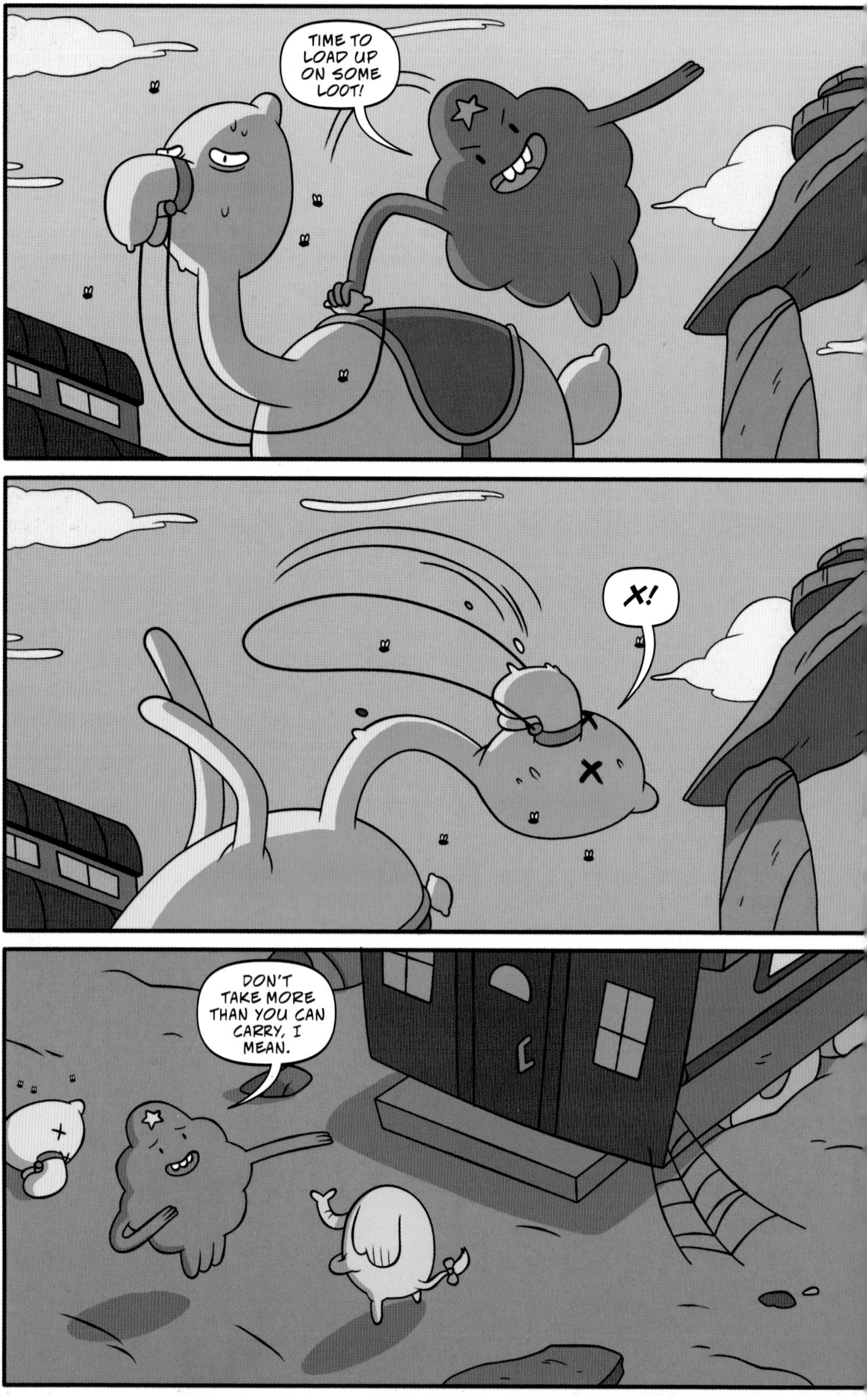
TIME TO LOAD UP ON SOME LOOT!
X!
DON'T TAKE MORE THAN YOU CAN CARRY, I MEAN.

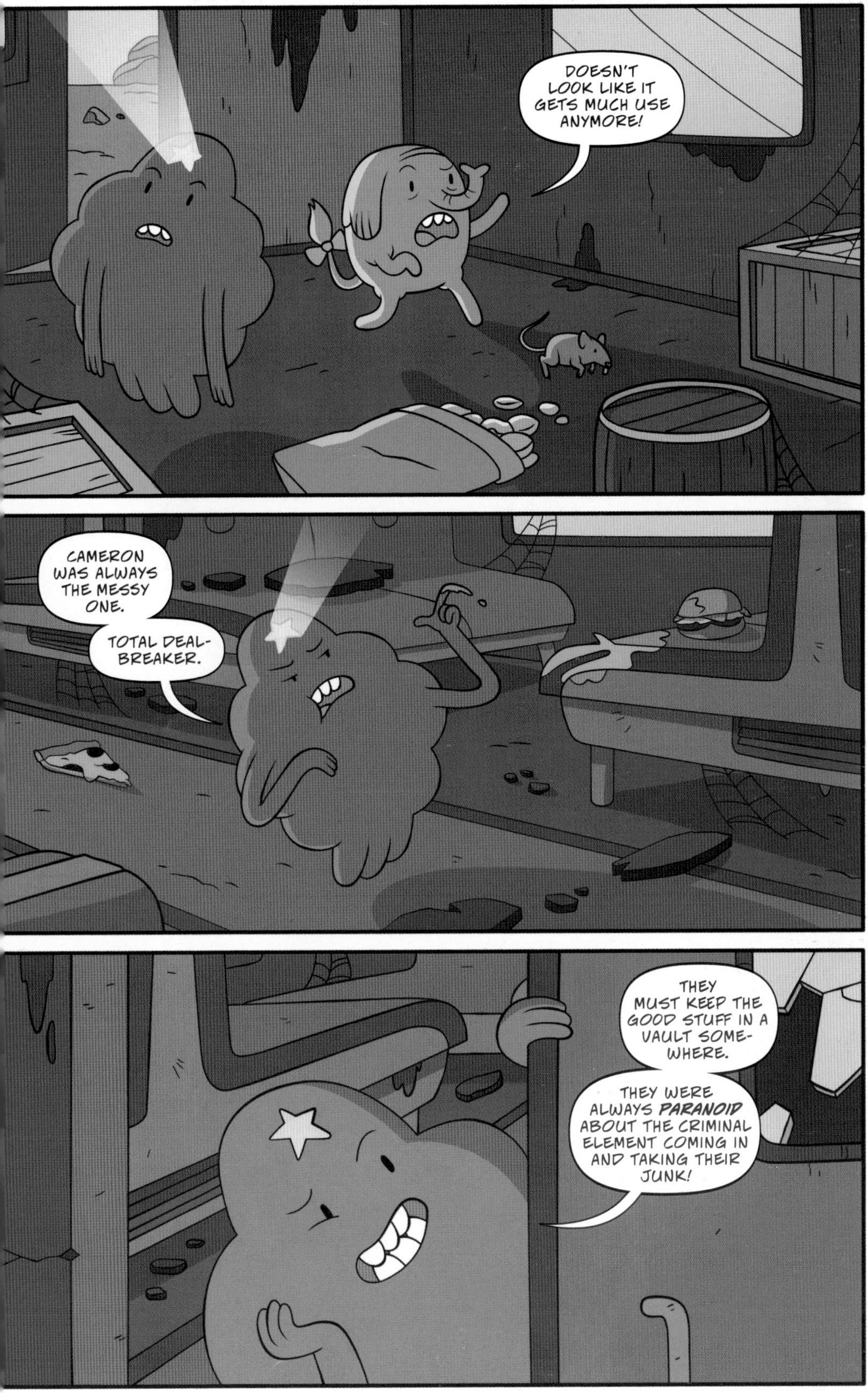
DOESN'T LOOK LIKE IT GETS MUCH USE ANYMORE!
CAMERON WAS ALWAYS THE MESSY ONE.
TOTAL DEAL-BREAKER.
THEY MUST KEEP THE GOOD STUFF IN A VAULT SOME-WHERE.
THEY WERE ALWAYS *PARANOID* ABOUT THE CRIMINAL ELEMENT COMING IN AND TAKING THEIR JUNK!

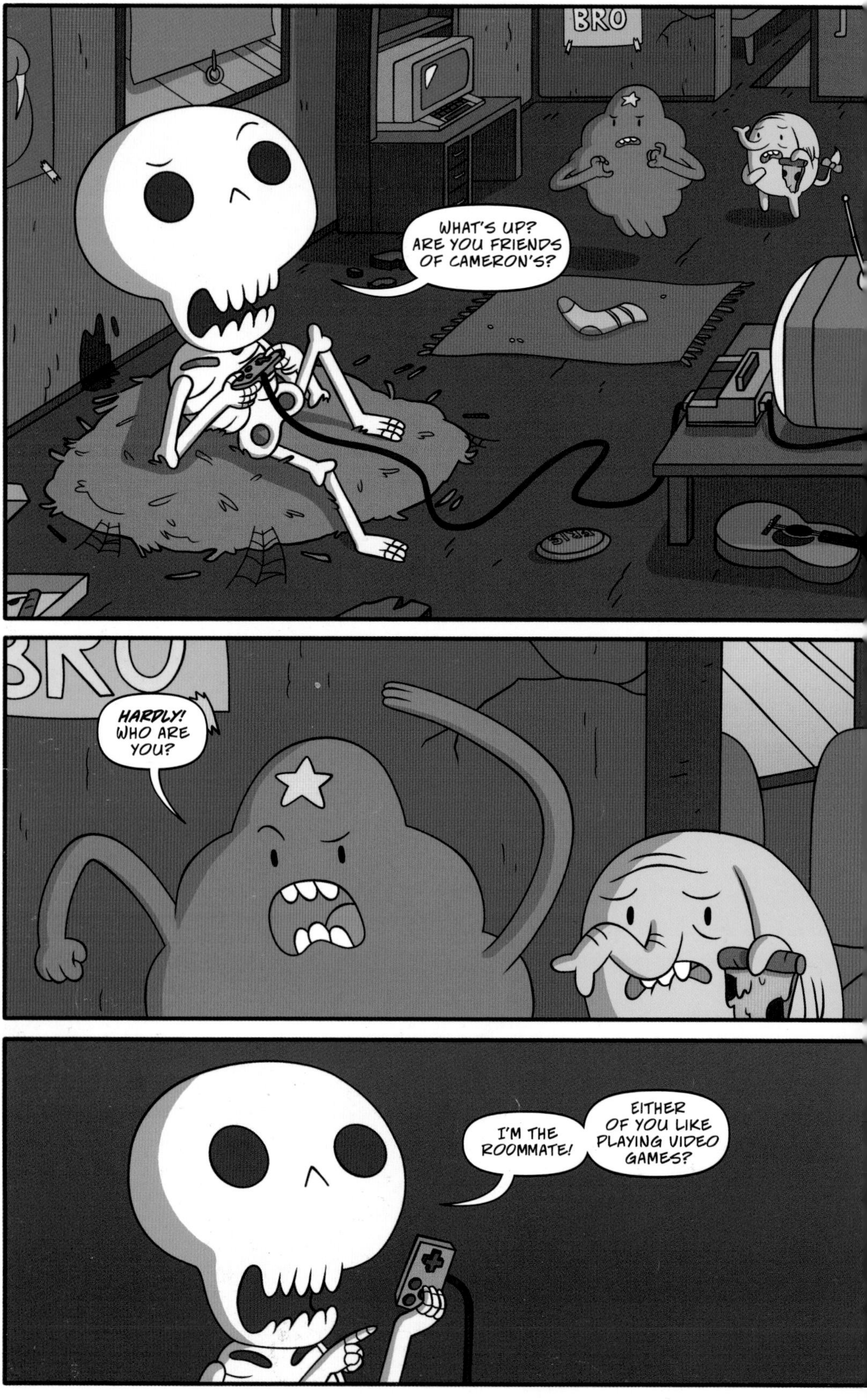
BRO
WHAT'S UP? ARE YOU FRIENDS OF CAMERON'S?
BRO
HARDLY! WHO ARE YOU?
I'M THE ROOMMATE!
EITHER OF YOU LIKE PLAYING VIDEO GAMES?

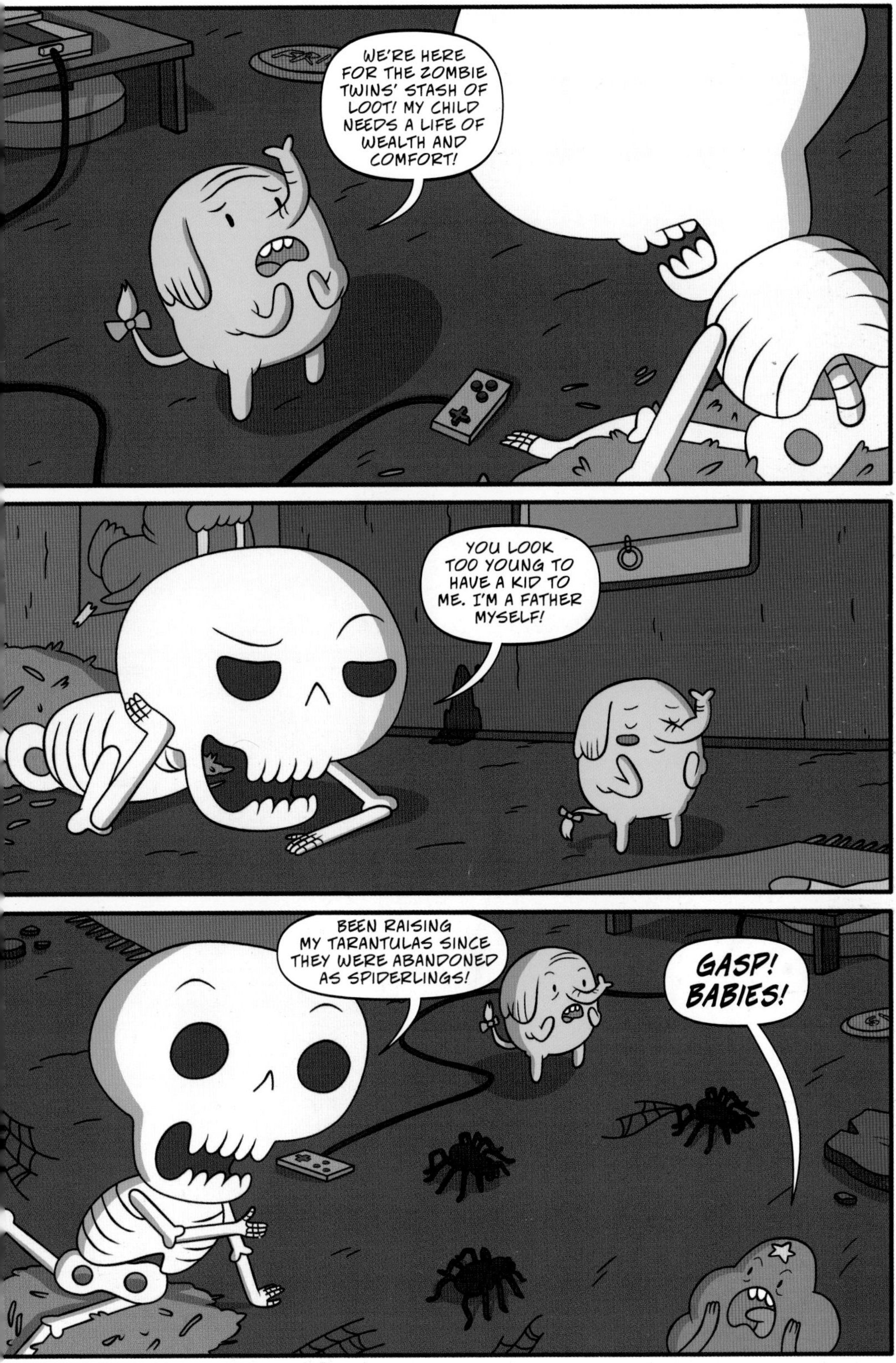
WE'RE HERE FOR THE ZOMBIE TWINS' STASH OF LOOT! MY CHILD NEEDS A LIFE OF WEALTH AND COMFORT!
YOU LOOK TOO YOUNG TO HAVE A KID TO ME. I'M A FATHER MYSELF!
BEEN RAISING MY TARANTULAS SINCE THEY WERE ABANDONED AS SPIDERLINGS!
GASP! BABIES!

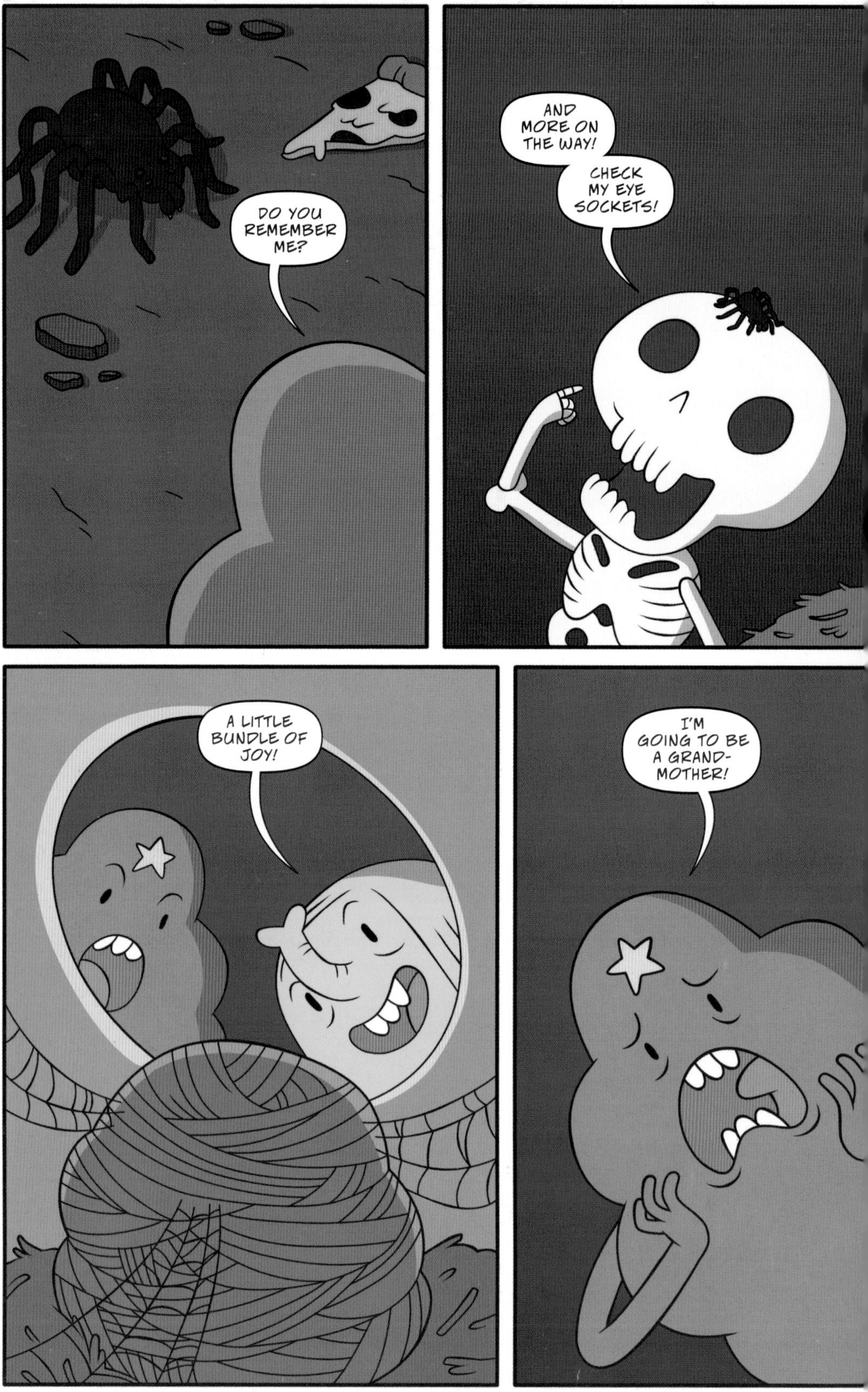
DO YOU REMEMBER ME?
AND MORE ON THE WAY!
CHECK MY EYE SOCKETS!
A LITTLE BUNDLE OF JOY!
I'M GOING TO BE A GRAND-MOTHER!

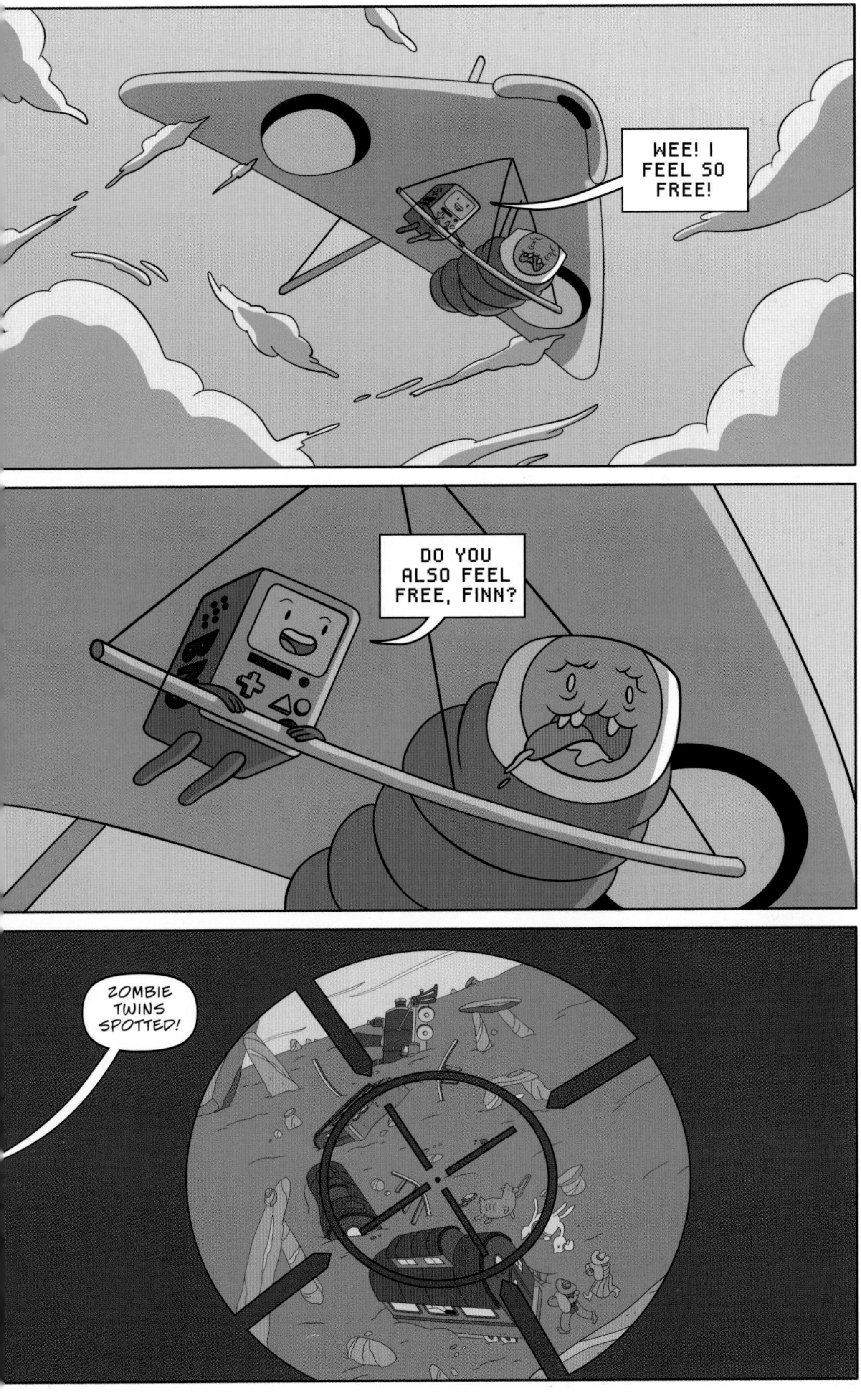
WEE! I FEEL SO FREE!
DO YOU ALSO FEEL FREE, FINN?
ZOMBIE TWINS SPOTTED!

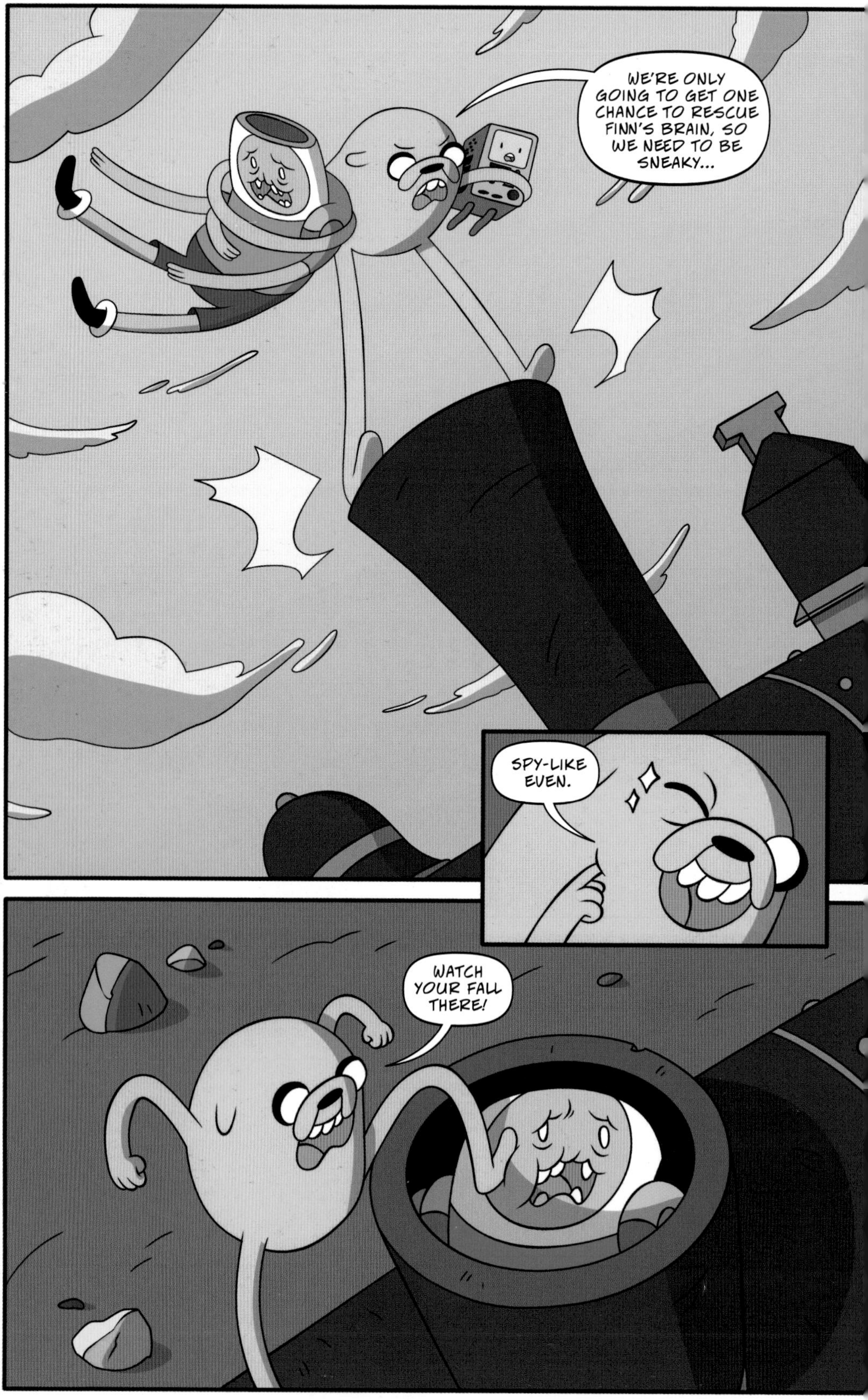
WE'RE ONLY GOING TO GET ONE CHANCE TO RESCUE FINN'S BRAIN, SO WE NEED TO BE SNEAKY...
SPY-LIKE EVEN.
WATCH YOUR FALL THERE!

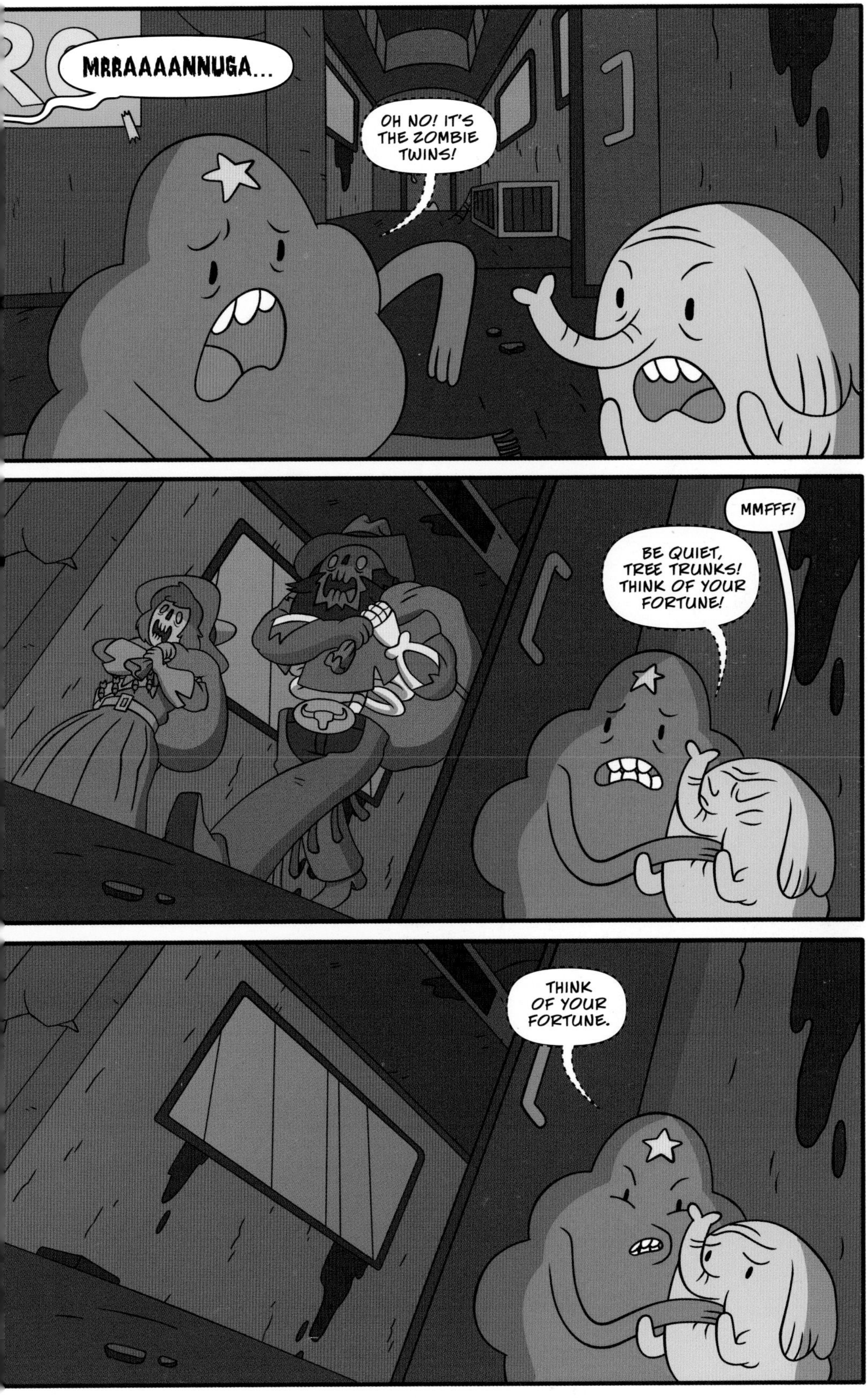
MRRAAAANNUGA...
OH NO! IT'S THE ZOMBIE TWINS!
MMFFF!
BE QUIET, TREE TRUNKS! THINK OF YOUR FORTUNE!
THINK OF YOUR FORTUNE.

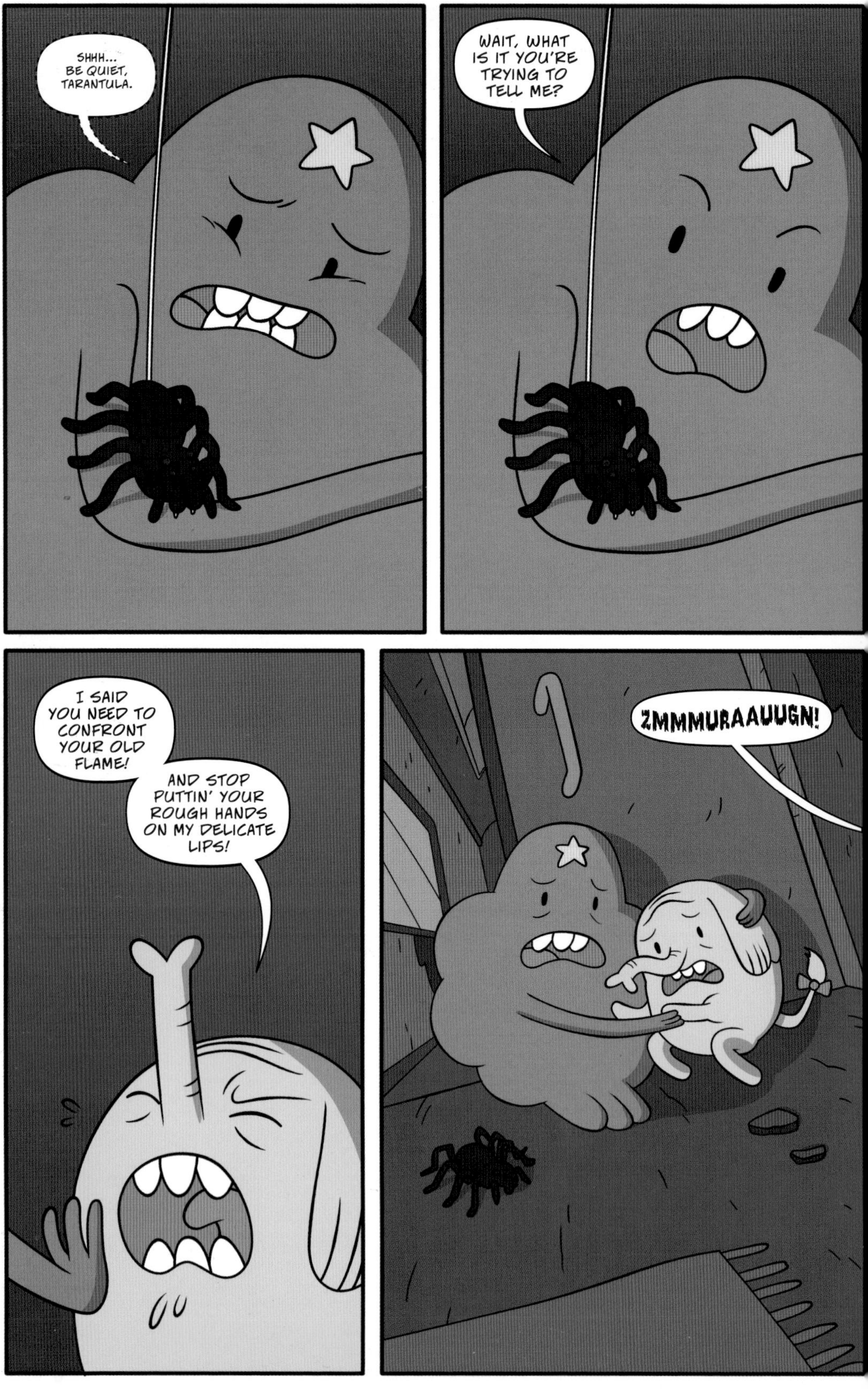
SHHH... BE QUIET, TARANTULA.
WAIT, WHAT IS IT YOU'RE TRYING TO TELL ME?
I SAID YOU NEED TO CONFRONT YOUR OLD FLAME!
AND STOP PUTTIN' YOUR ROUGH HANDS ON MY DELICATE LIPS!
ZMMMURAAUUGN!

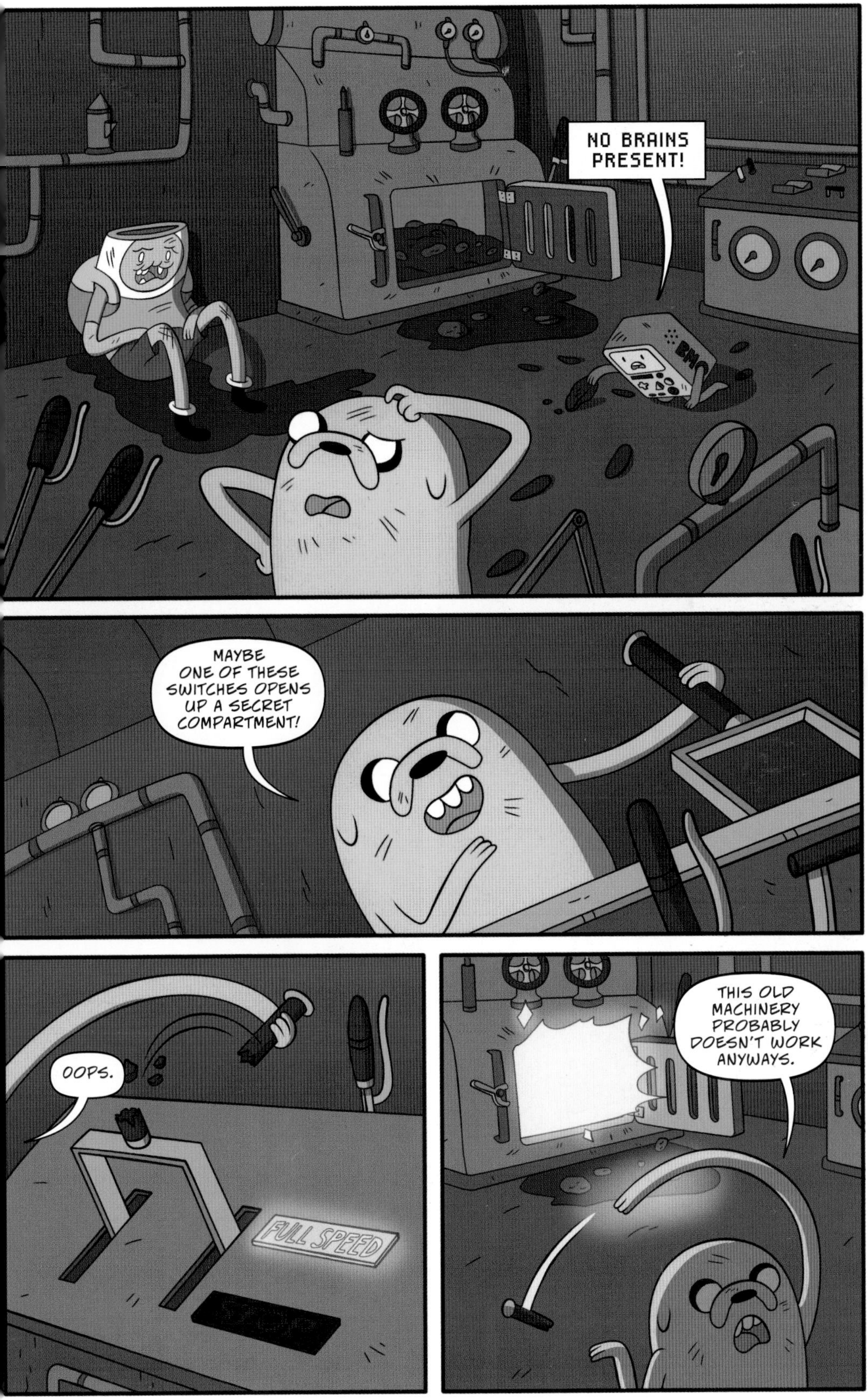
NO BRAINS PRESENT!
MAYBE ONE OF THESE SWITCHES OPENS UP A SECRET COMPARTMENT!
OOPS.
FULL SPEED
THIS OLD MACHINERY PROBABLY DOESN'T WORK ANYWAYS.

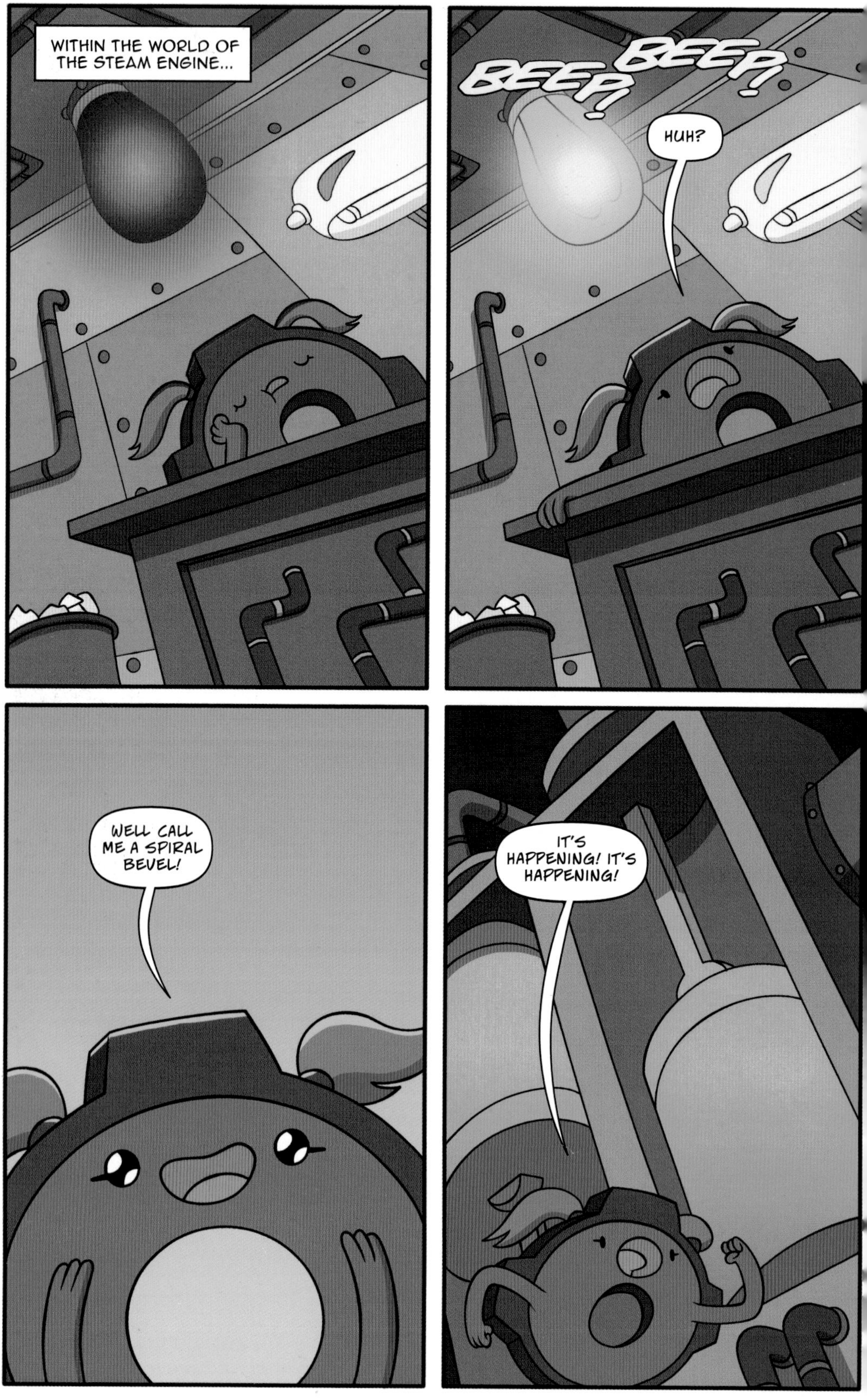
WITHIN THE WORLD OF THE STEAM ENGINE...
BEEP! BEEP!
HUH?
WELL CALL ME A SPIRAL BEVEL!
IT'S HAPPENING! IT'S HAPPENING!

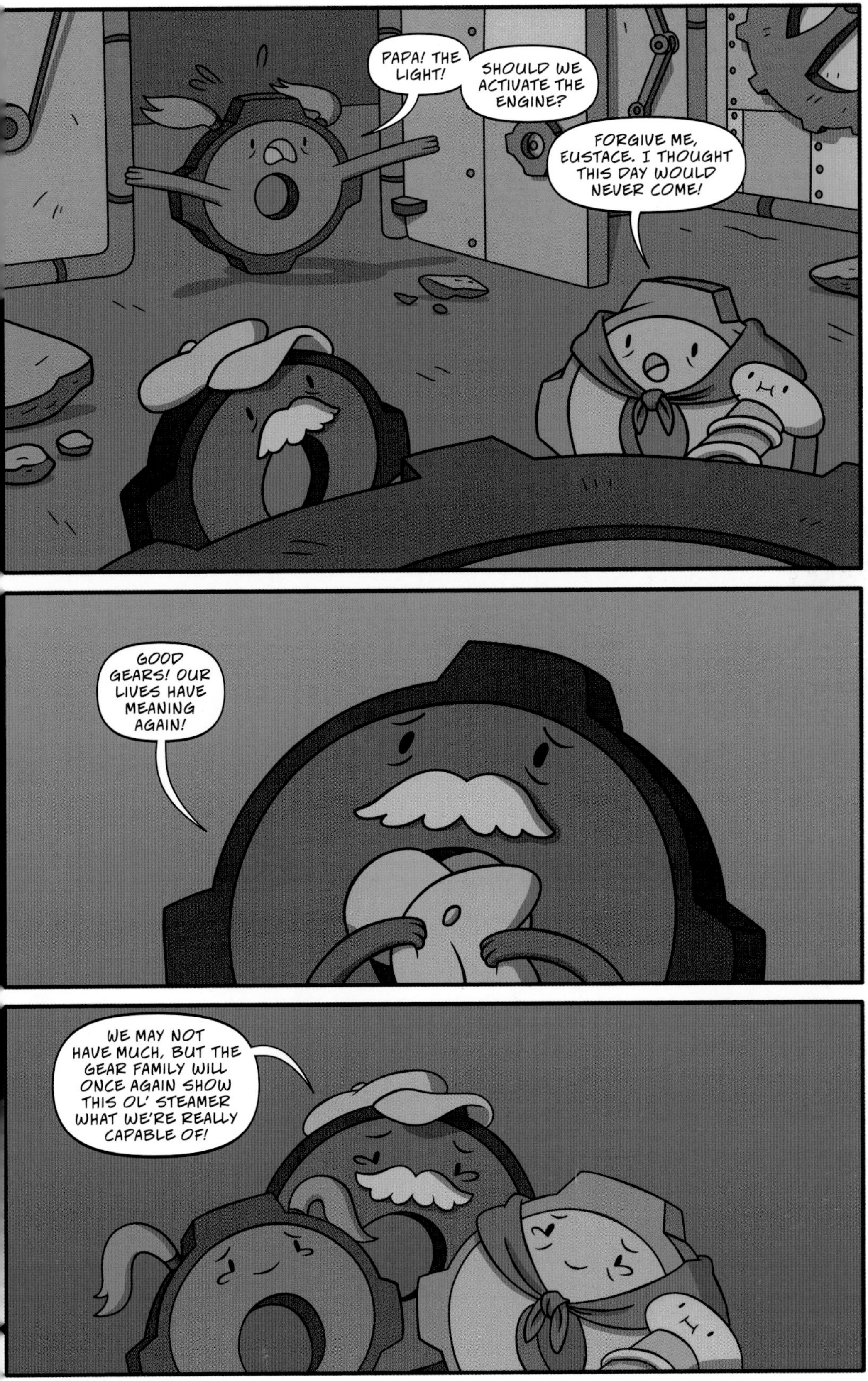
PAPA! THE LIGHT!
SHOULD WE ACTIVATE THE ENGINE?
FORGIVE ME, EUSTACE. I THOUGHT THIS DAY WOULD NEVER COME!
GOOD GEARS! OUR LIVES HAVE MEANING AGAIN!
WE MAY NOT HAVE MUCH, BUT THE GEAR FAMILY WILL ONCE AGAIN SHOW THIS OL' STEAMER WHAT WE'RE REALLY CAPABLE OF!

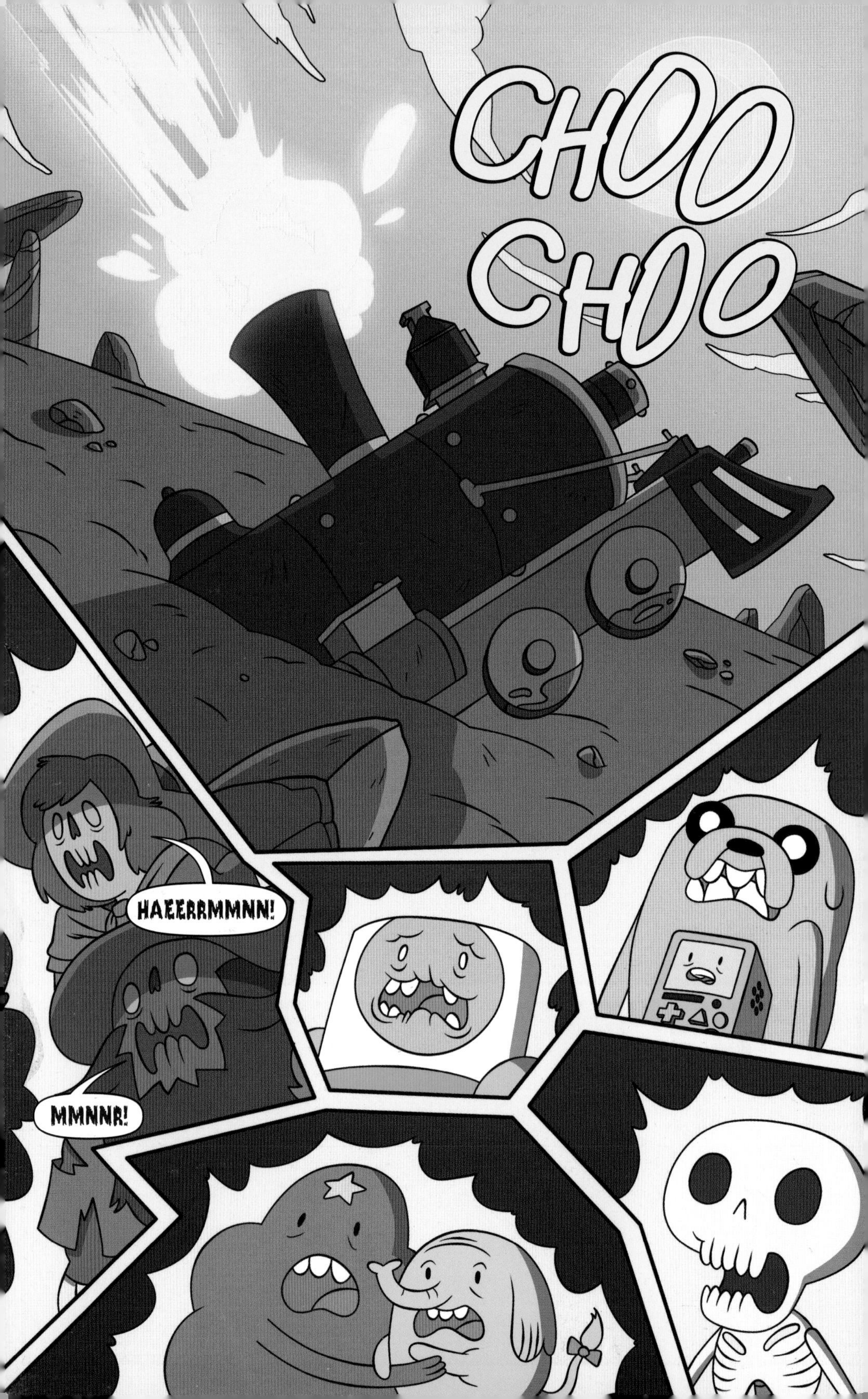
CHOO CHOO
HAEERRMMNN!
MMNNR!

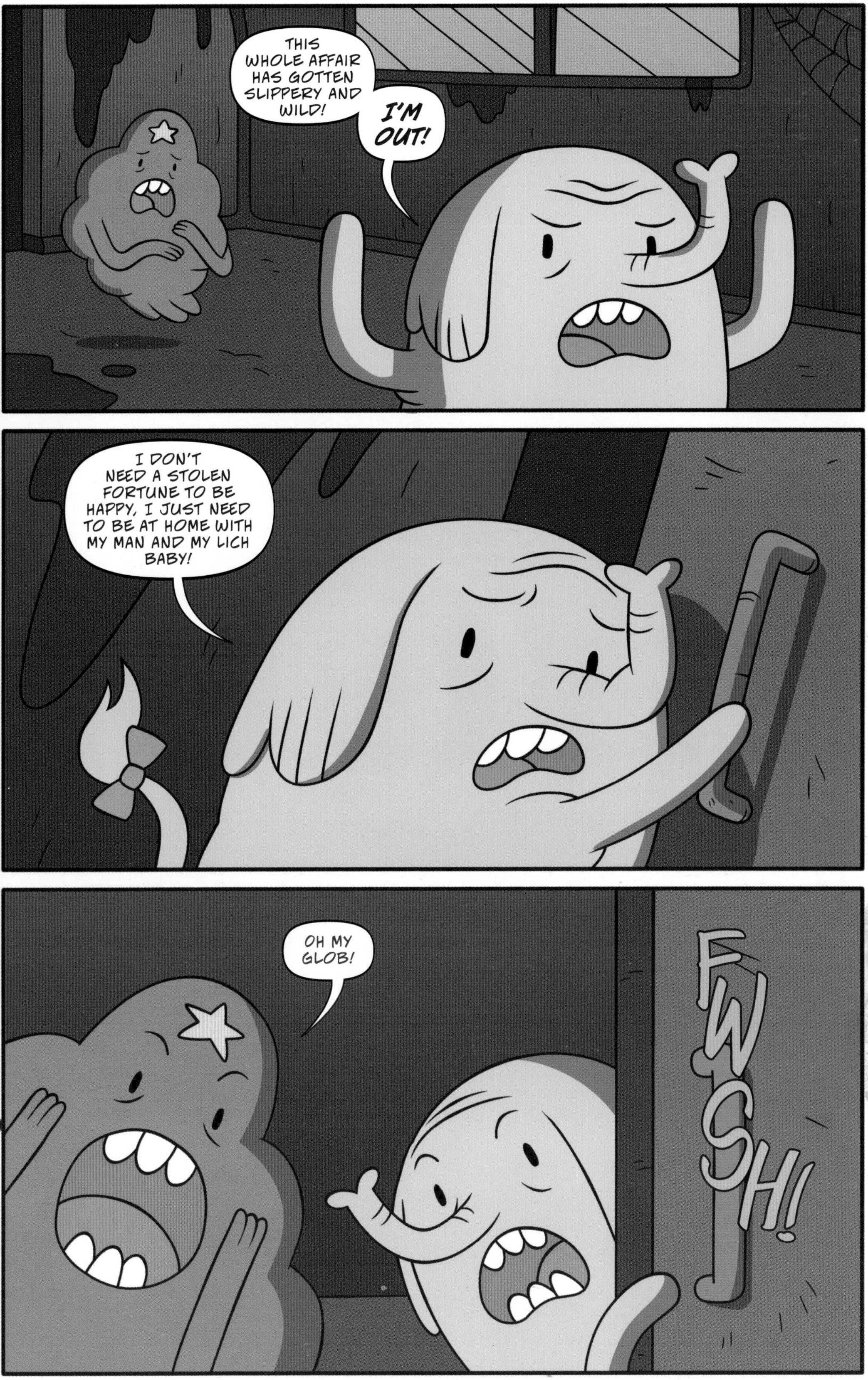
THIS WHOLE AFFAIR HAS GOTTEN SLIPPERY AND WILD!
I'M OUT!
I DON'T NEED A STOLEN FORTUNE TO BE HAPPY, I JUST NEED TO BE AT HOME WITH MY MAN AND MY LICH BABY!
OH MY GLOB!
FWSH!

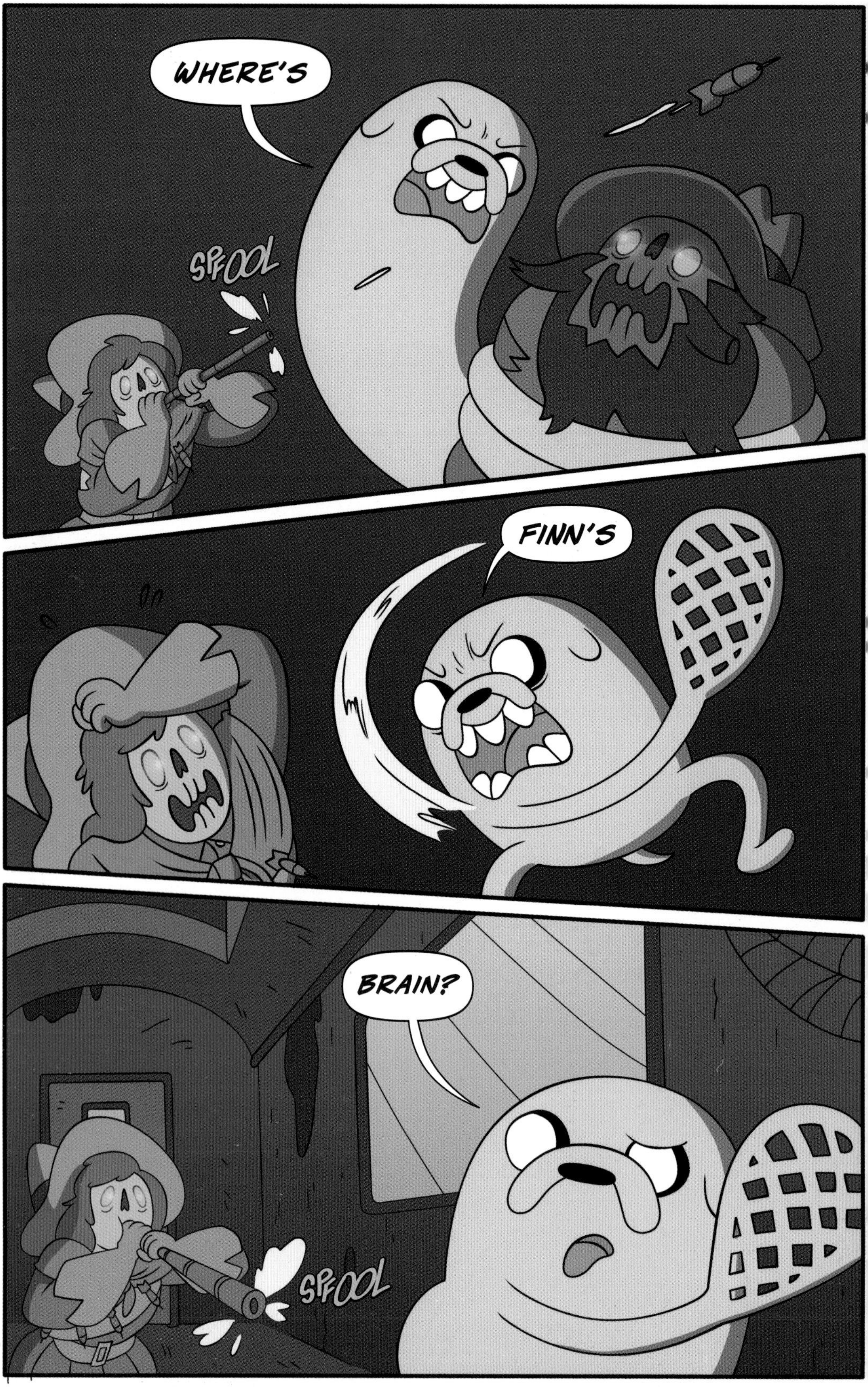
WHERE'S
SPFOOL
FINN'S
BRAIN?
SPFOOL

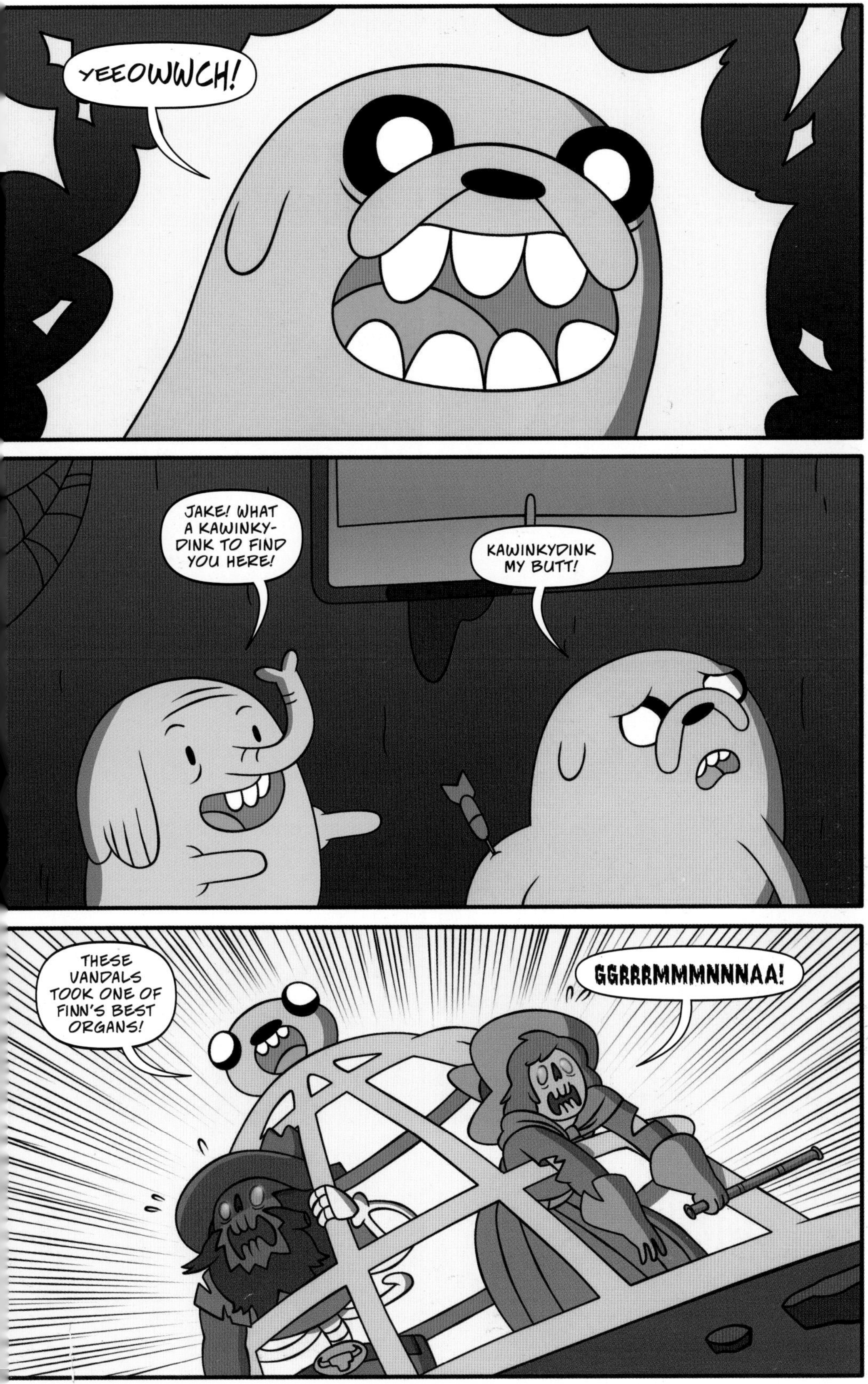

YEEOWWCH!
JAKE! WHAT A KAWINKY-DINK TO FIND YOU HERE!
KAWINKYDINK MY BUTT!
THESE VANDALS TOOK ONE OF FINN'S BEST ORGANS!
GGRRRMMMNNNAA!

HI, FINN!

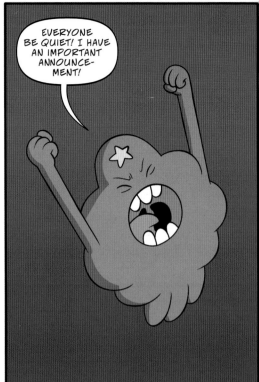

EVERYONE BE QUIET! I HAVE AN IMPORTANT ANNOUNCEMENT!

BE QUIET!

CAMERON, YOU WERE PUSHING ME TOO HARD FOR A LABEL AND IT SCARED ME AWAY.

I'M TOO MUCH OF A *FREE SPIRIT* TO FARM TARANTULAS WITH ANYONE!

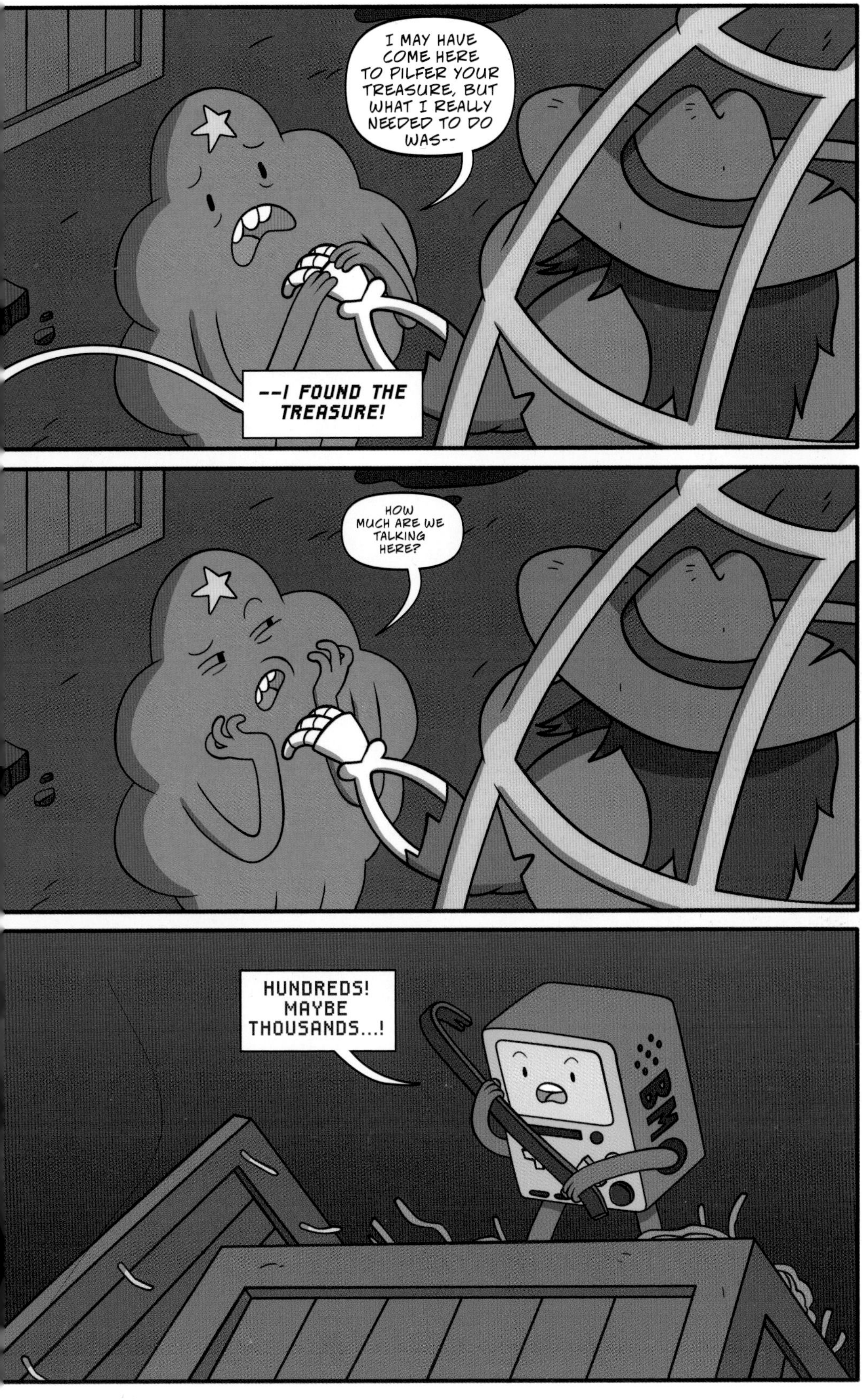
I MAY HAVE COME HERE TO PILFER YOUR TREASURE, BUT WHAT I REALLY NEEDED TO DO WAS--
--I FOUND THE TREASURE!
HOW MUCH ARE WE TALKING HERE?
HUNDREDS! MAYBE THOUSANDS...!
BMO

OF BRRAAAAAAAAAAAAAAIIIINS!!

LSP, DID YOU KNOW ABOUT THIS?

NO BUT I GUESS THE CLUES WERE THERE ALL ALONG!

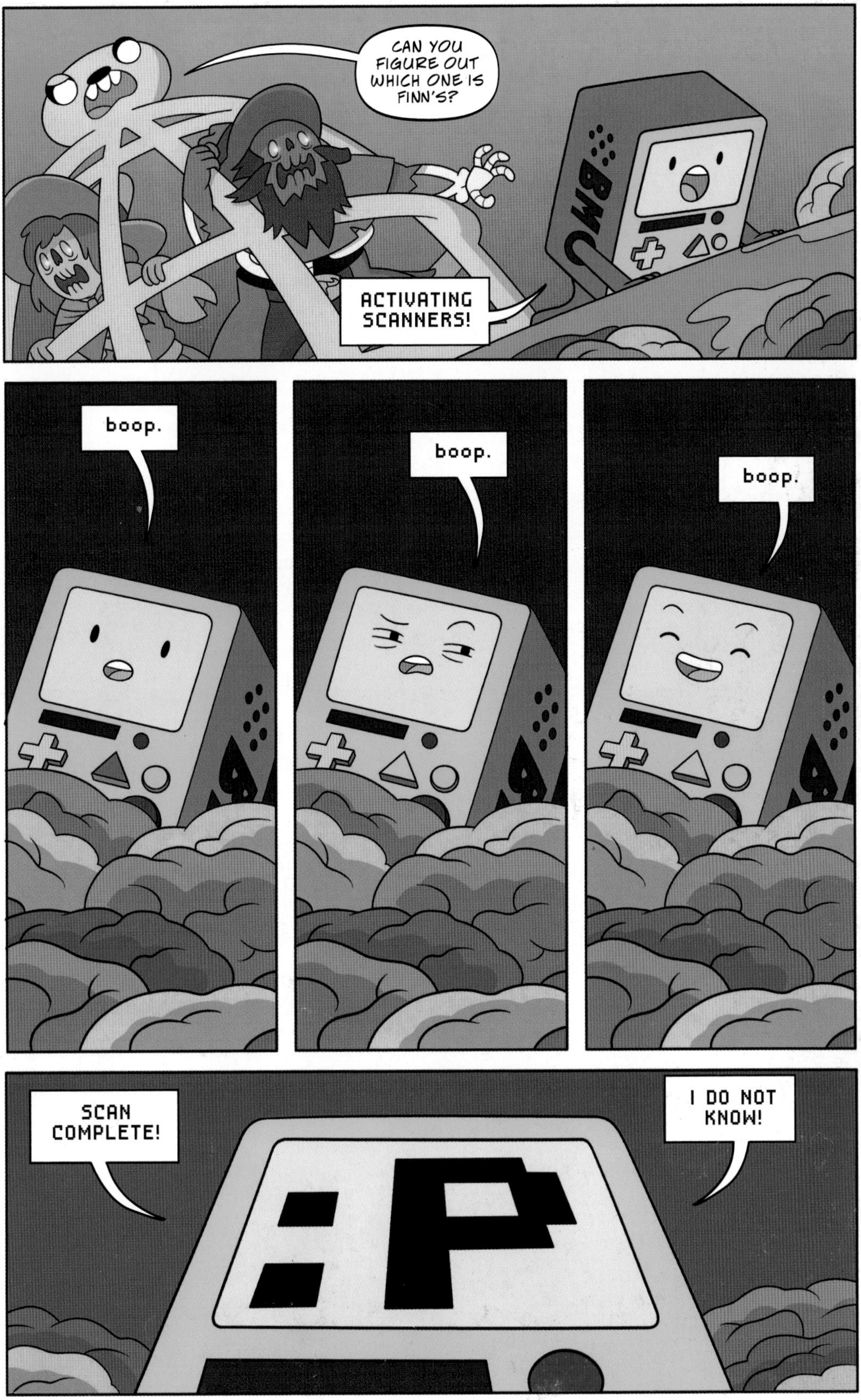
CAN YOU FIGURE OUT WHICH ONE IS FINN'S?
ACTIVATING SCANNERS!
boop.
boop.
boop.
SCAN COMPLETE!
I DO NOT KNOW!

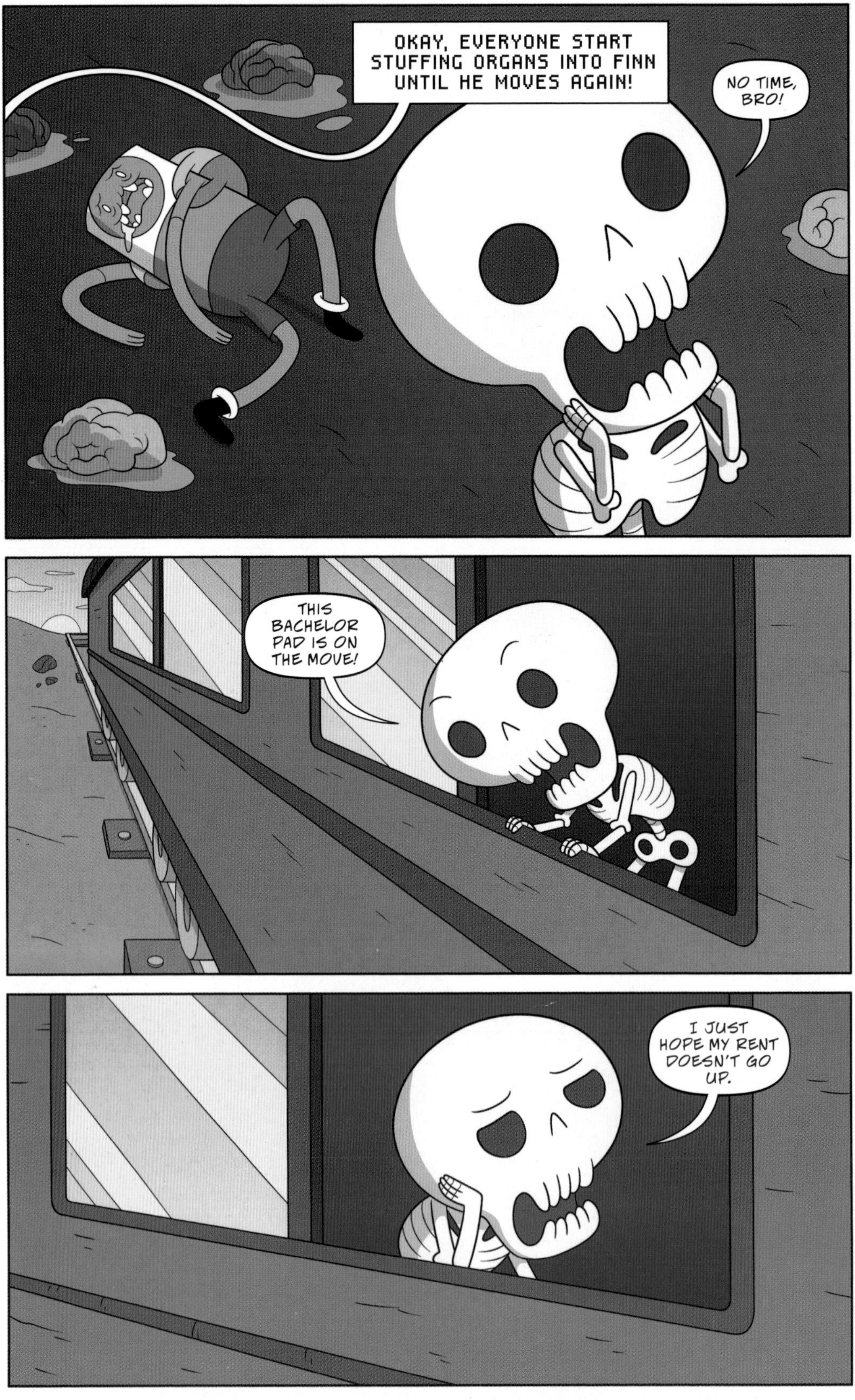
OKAY, EVERYONE START STUFFING ORGANS INTO FINN UNTIL HE MOVES AGAIN!
NO TIME, BRO!
THIS BACHELOR PAD IS ON THE MOVE!
I JUST HOPE MY RENT DOESN'T GO UP.

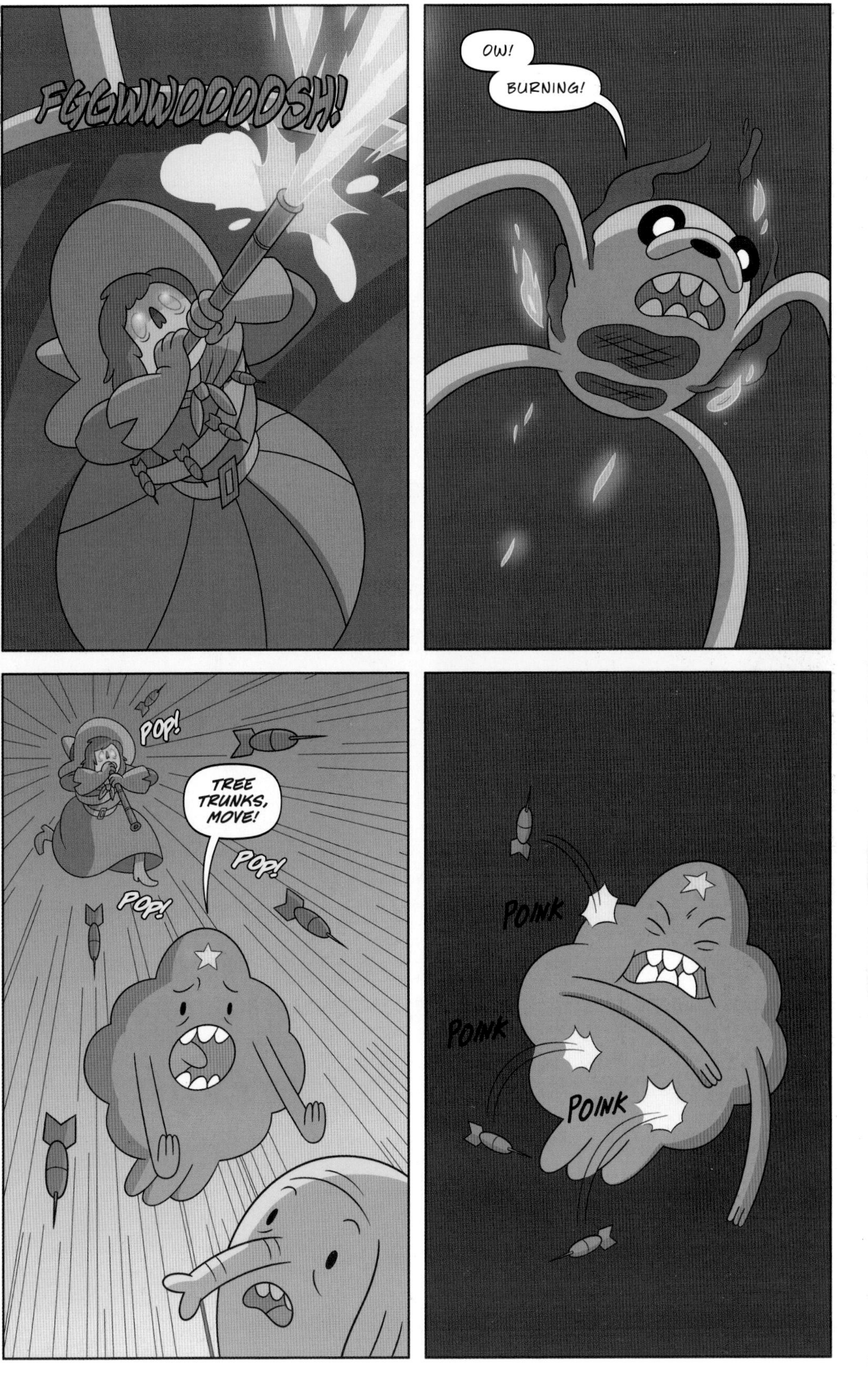
FGGWWOOOOSH!
OW!
BURNING!
POP!
TREE TRUNKS, MOVE!
POP!
POP!
POINK
POINK
POINK

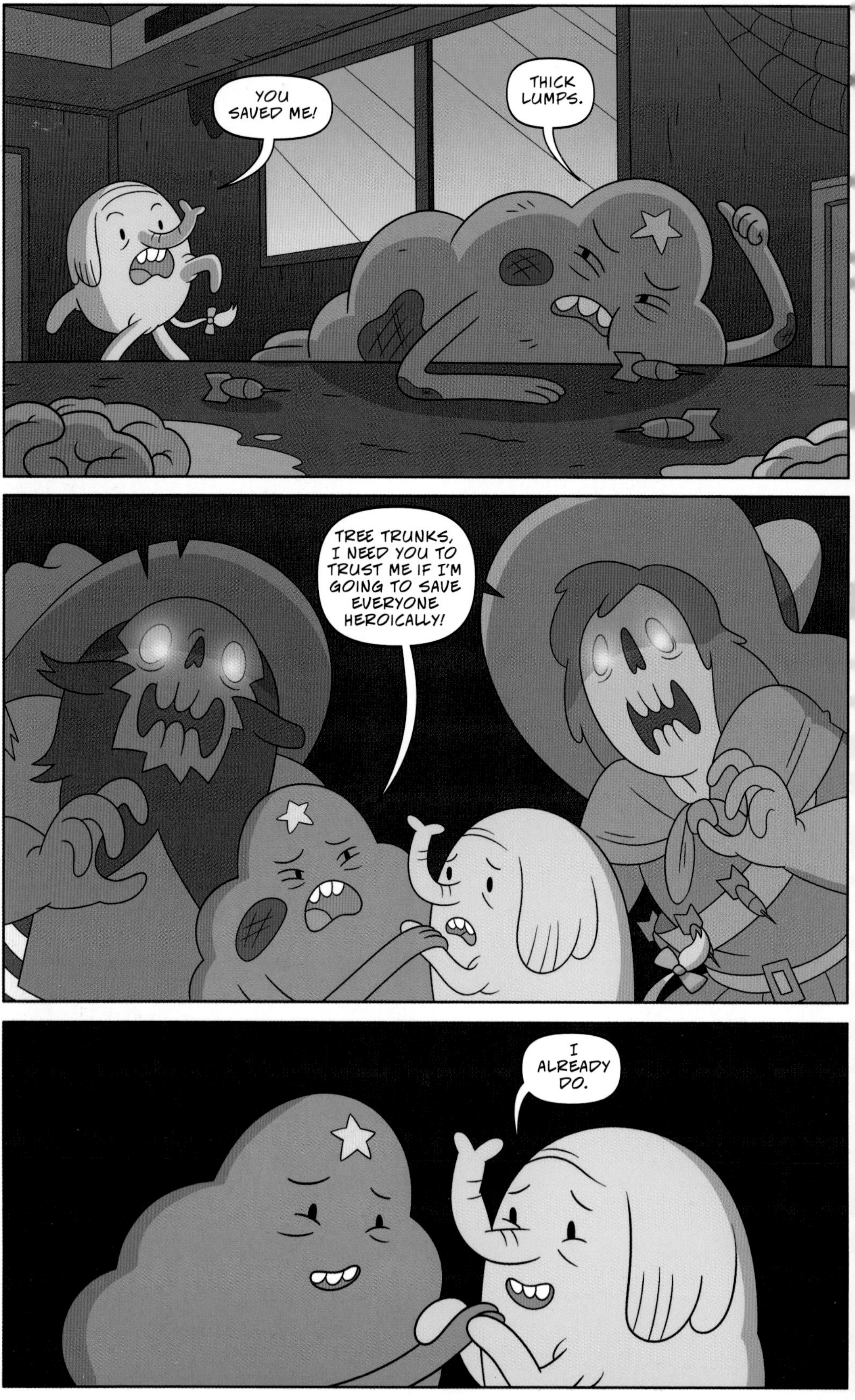
YOU SAVED ME!
THICK LUMPS.
TREE TRUNKS, I NEED YOU TO TRUST ME IF I'M GOING TO SAVE EVERYONE HEROICALLY!
I ALREADY DO.

STAY AWAY FROM MY FRIENDS!
WHOA!
SMASH!
WAAAAHHHH!
CRUNK!

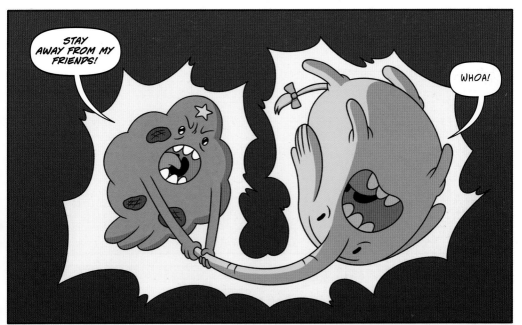

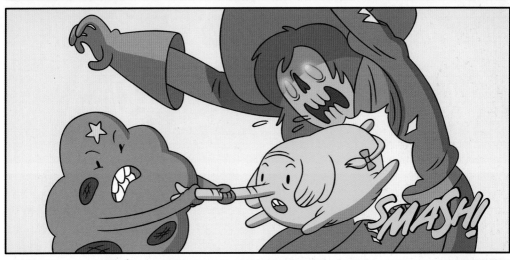

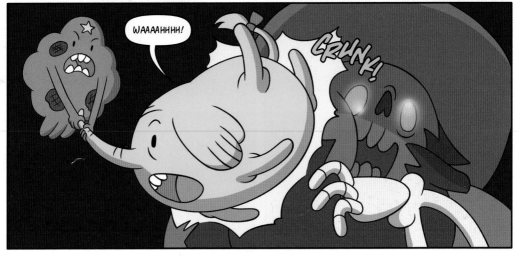

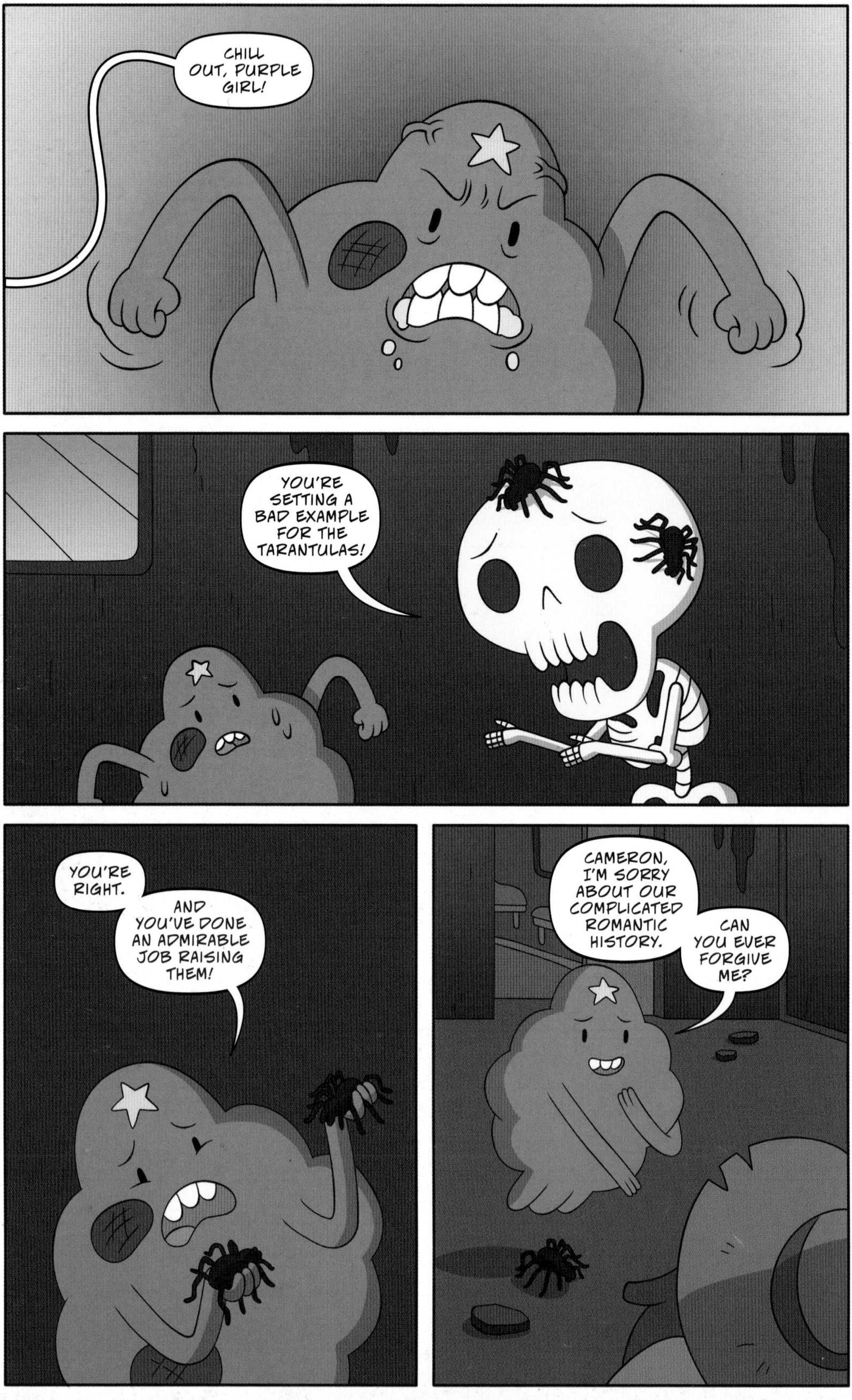
CHILL OUT, PURPLE GIRL!
YOU'RE SETTING A BAD EXAMPLE FOR THE TARANTULAS!
YOU'RE RIGHT.
AND YOU'VE DONE AN ADMIRABLE JOB RAISING THEM!
CAMERON, I'M SORRY ABOUT OUR COMPLICATED ROMANTIC HISTORY.
CAN YOU EVER FORGIVE ME?

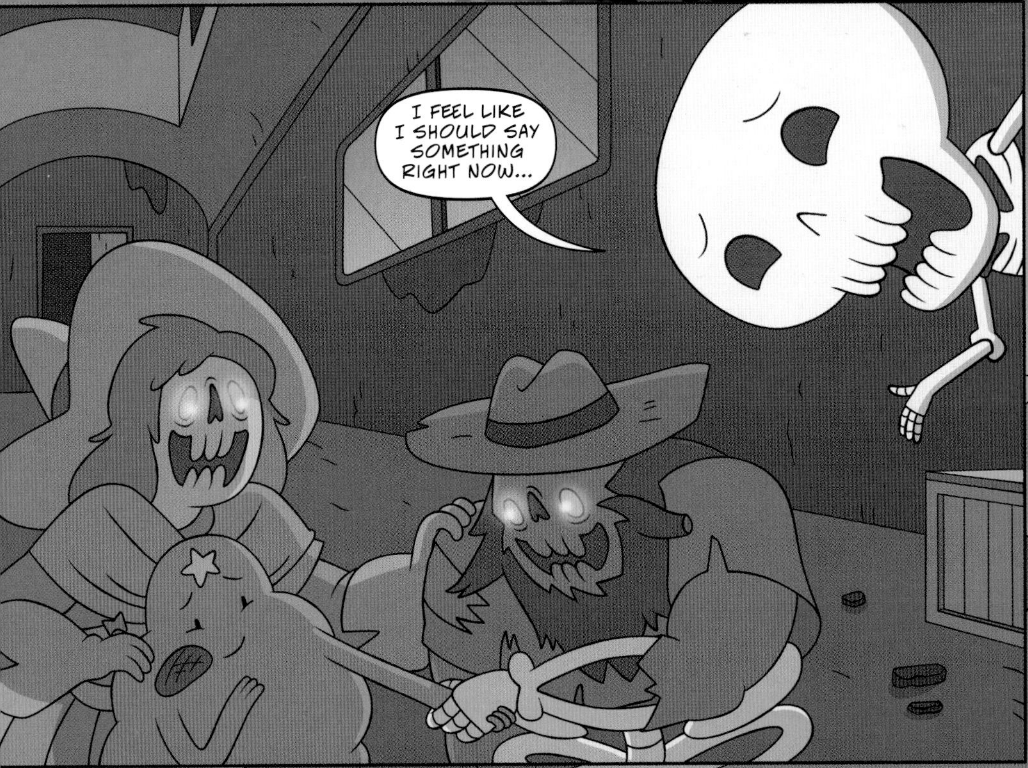
I FEEL LIKE I SHOULD SAY SOMETHING RIGHT NOW...

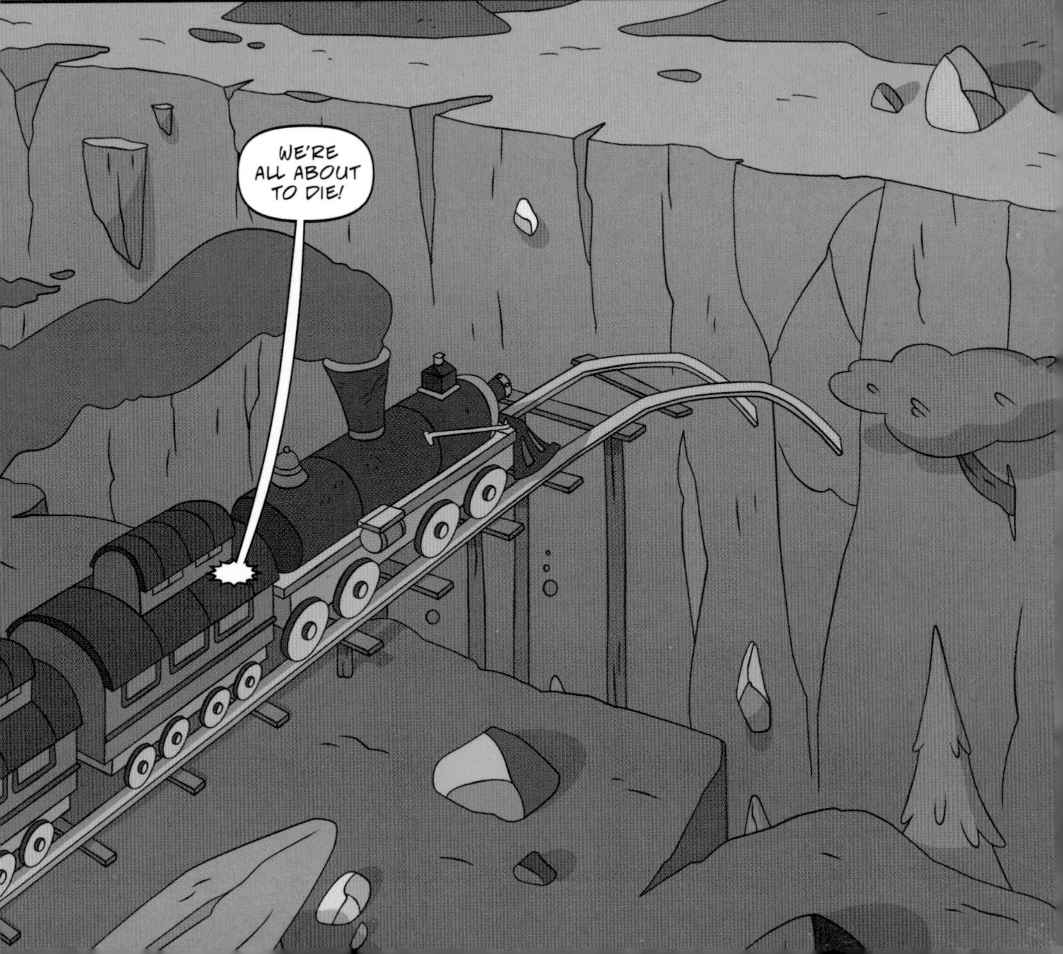
WE'RE ALL ABOUT TO DIE!

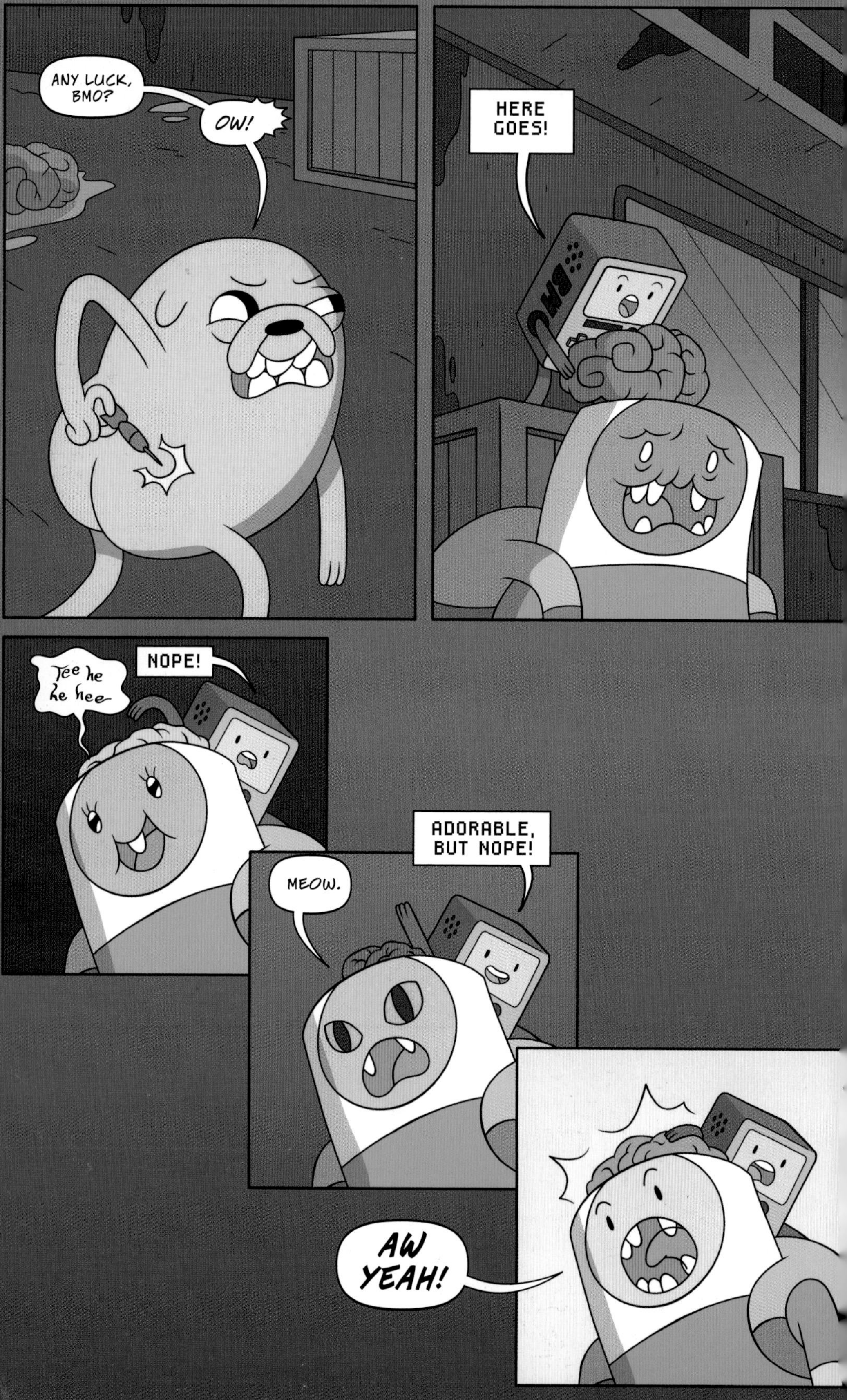
ANY LUCK, BMO?
OW!
HERE GOES!
NOPE!
Tee he he hee
ADORABLE, BUT NOPE!
MEOW.
AW YEAH!

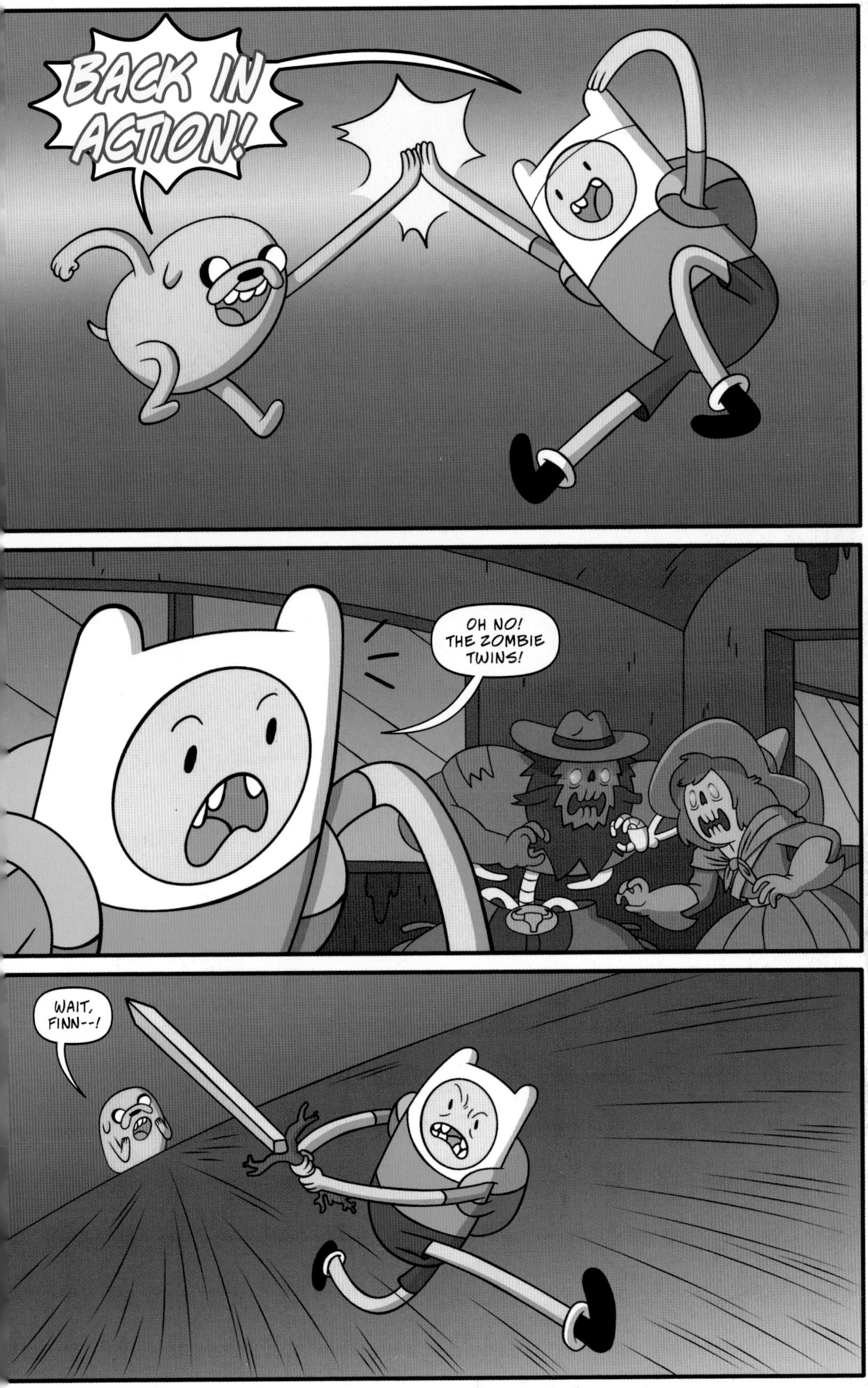
BACK IN ACTION!
OH NO! THE ZOMBIE TWINS!
WAIT, FINN--!

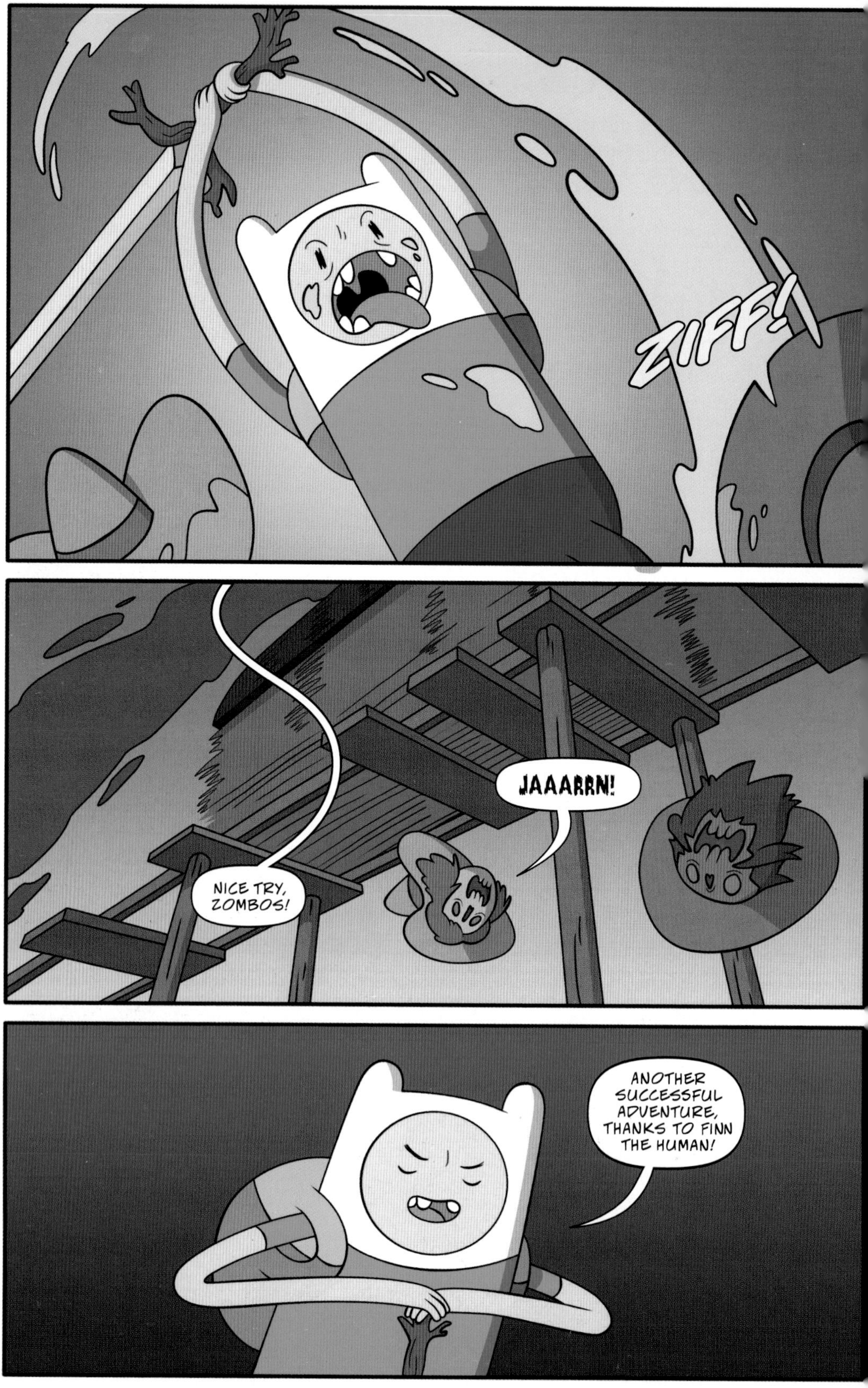
ZIFF!
NICE TRY, ZOMBOS!
JAAARRN!
ANOTHER SUCCESSFUL ADVENTURE, THANKS TO FINN THE HUMAN!

OH NO...
WHAT'D I DO?
TESS WAS THE ONLY ONE WHO KNEW HOW TO STOP THE TRAIN! HER PASSION WAS MECHANICAL ENGINEERING!
ABANDON SHIP!

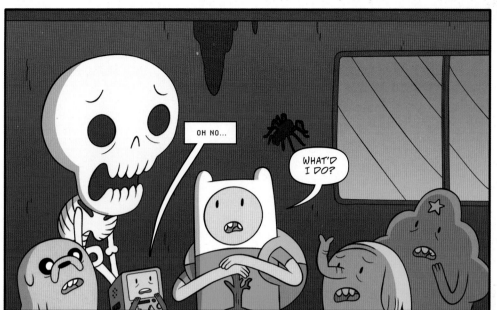

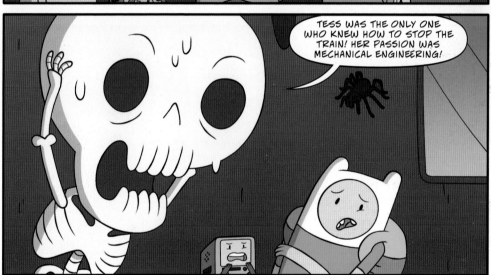

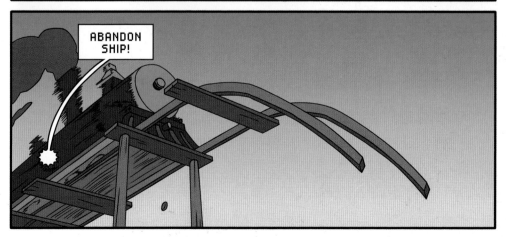

COME TO LUMPY!
THERE'S NO TIME!
WE'LL NEVER ALL MAKE IT! **THERE'S TOO MANY TARANTULAS!**
I WON'T LEAVE THEM AGAIN!
NOBODY IS GETTING LEFT BEHIND.
YOU'RE ALL MY RESPONSIBILITY!

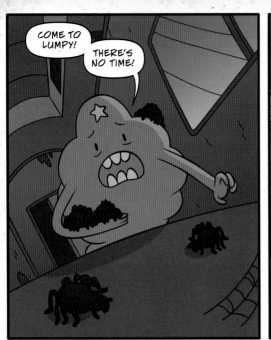

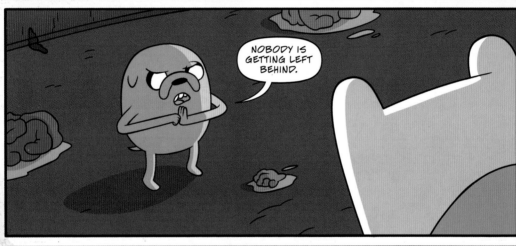

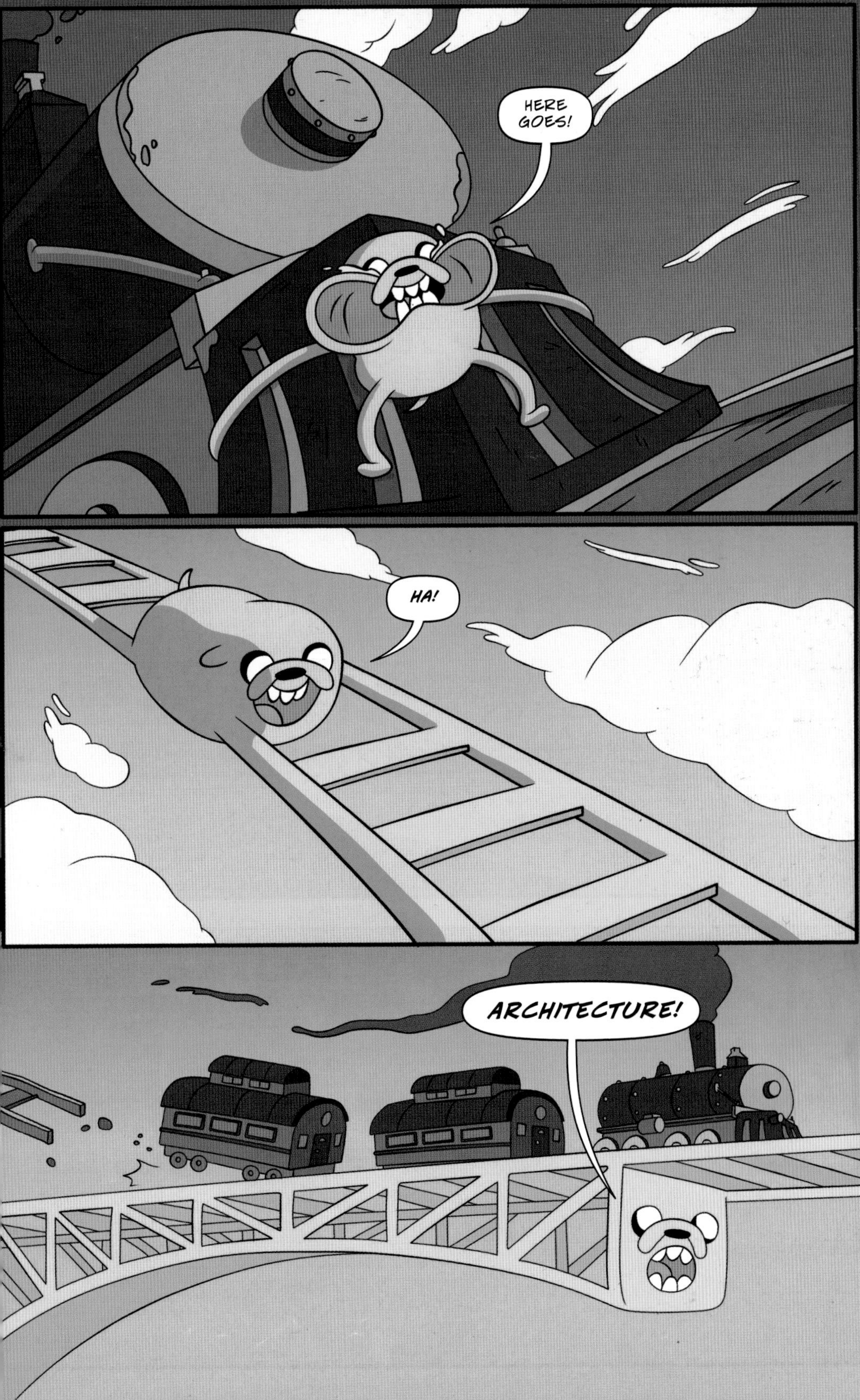
HERE GOES!
HA!
ARCHITECTURE!

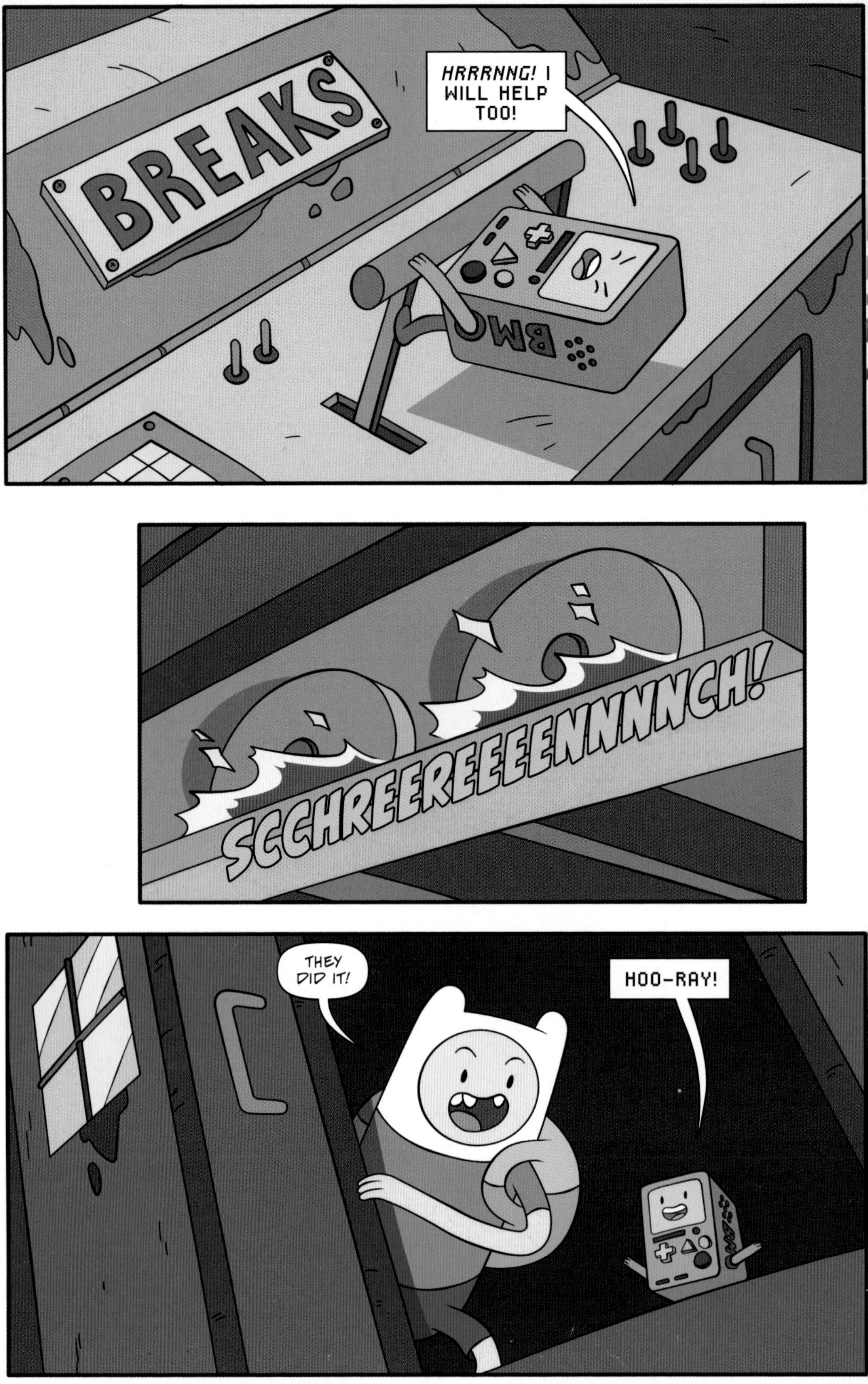
BREAKS
HRRRNNG! I WILL HELP TOO!
SCCHREEREEEENNNNNCH!
THEY DID IT!
HOO-RAY!

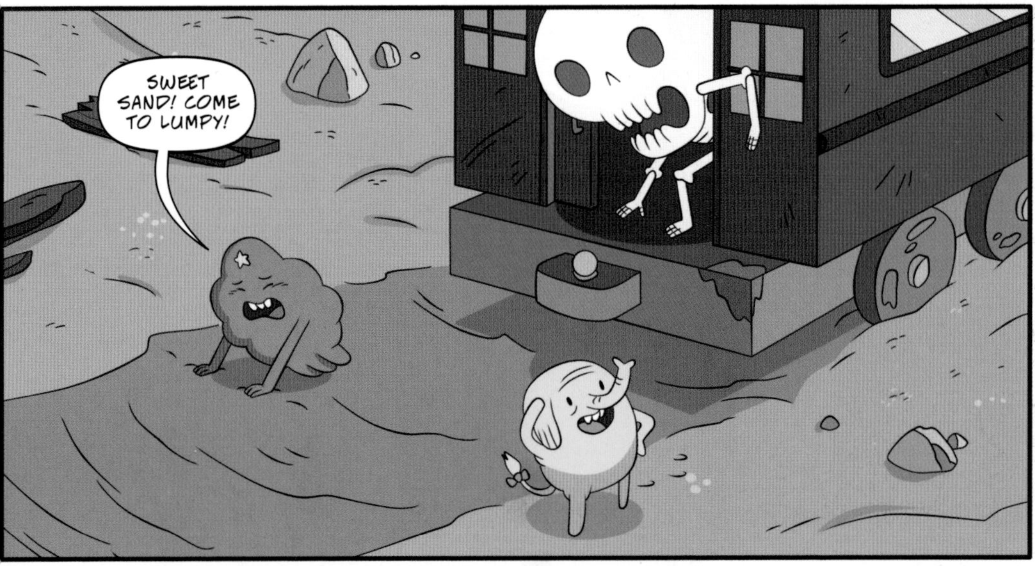
SWEET SAND! COME TO LUMPY!

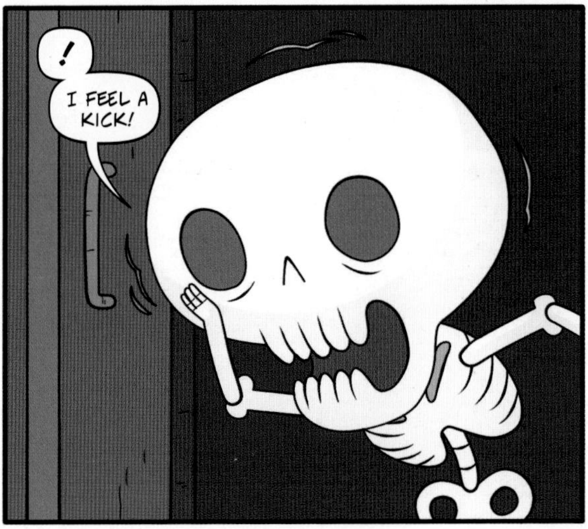
!
I FEEL A KICK!

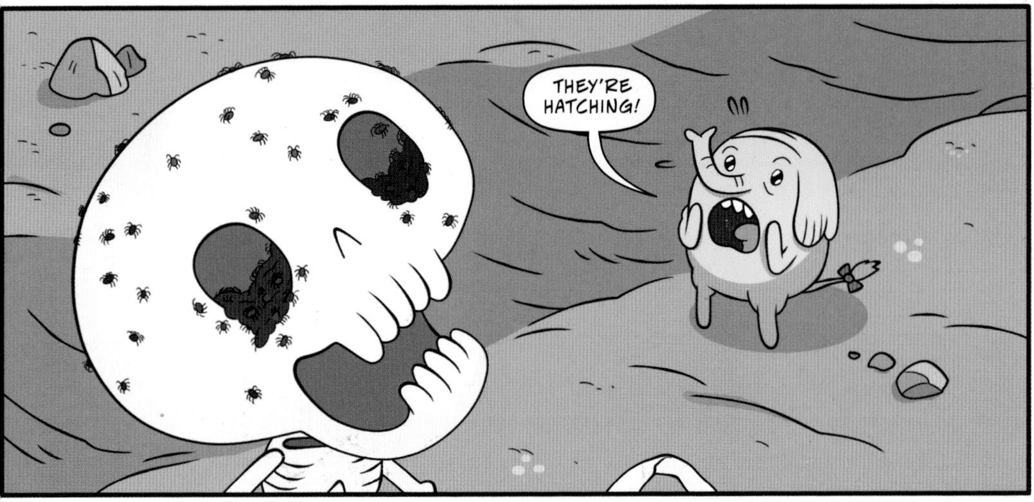
THEY'RE HATCHING!

NATURE IS BEAUTIFUL!

EVEN THOUGH YOUR FRIEND DECAPITATED MY ROOMMATES IT'S CLEAR HOW MUCH YOU CARE ABOUT THE SPIDERS.

THEY COULD USE A GOOD HOME!

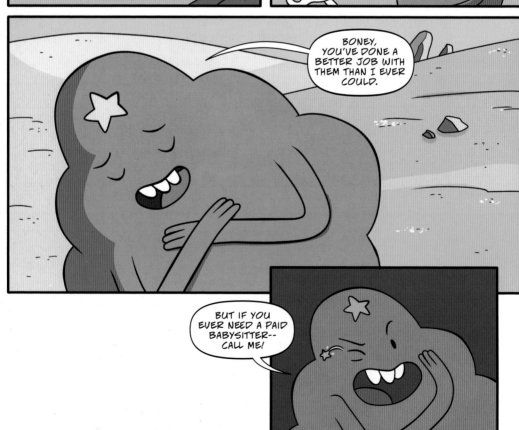

BONEY, YOU'VE DONE A BETTER JOB WITH THEM THAN I EVER COULD.

BUT IF YOU EVER NEED A PAID BABYSITTER-- CALL ME!

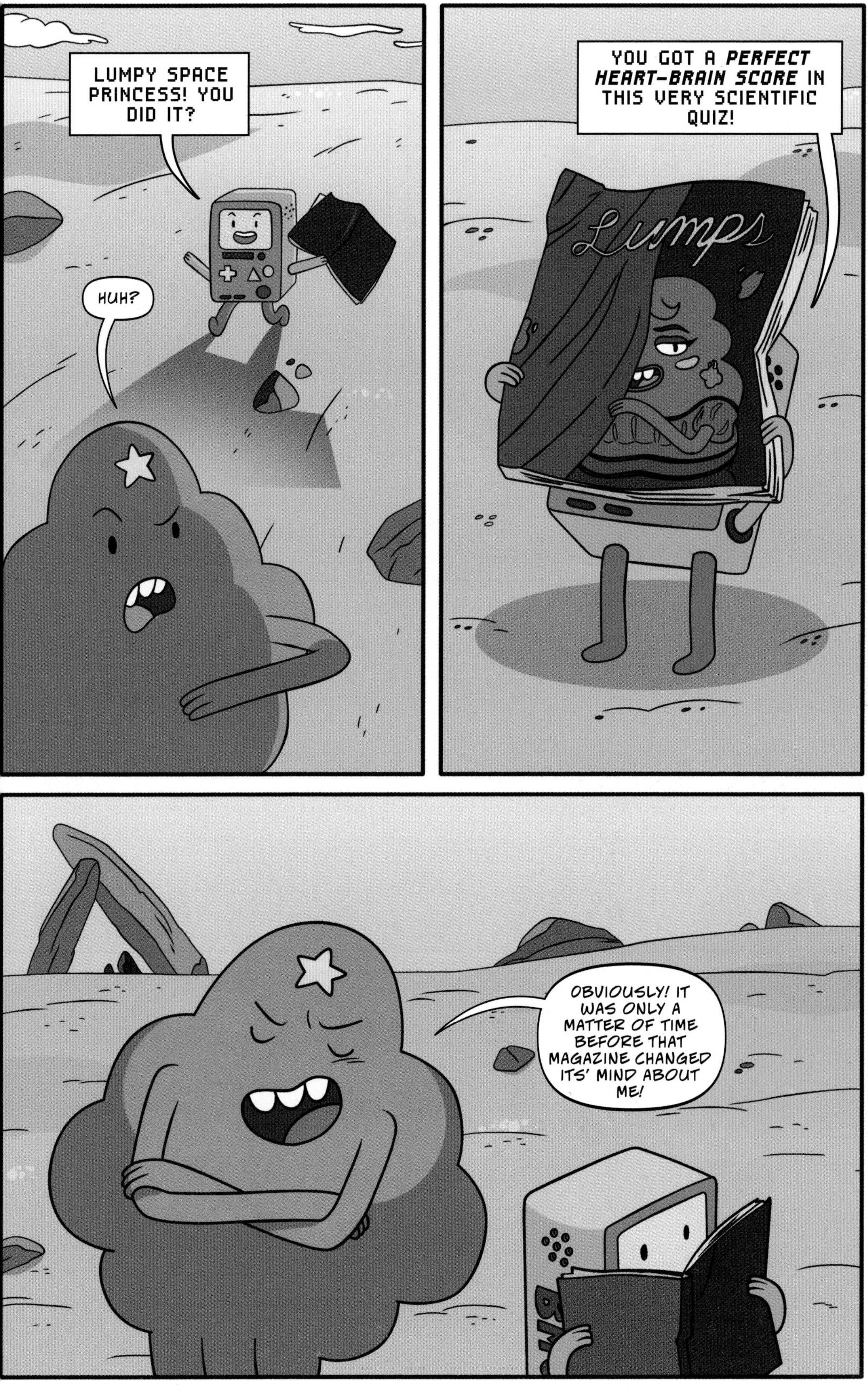
LUMPY SPACE PRINCESS! YOU DID IT?
HUH?
YOU GOT A *PERFECT HEART-BRAIN SCORE* IN THIS VERY SCIENTIFIC QUIZ!
Lumps
OBVIOUSLY! IT WAS ONLY A MATTER OF TIME BEFORE THAT MAGAZINE CHANGED ITS' MIND ABOUT ME!

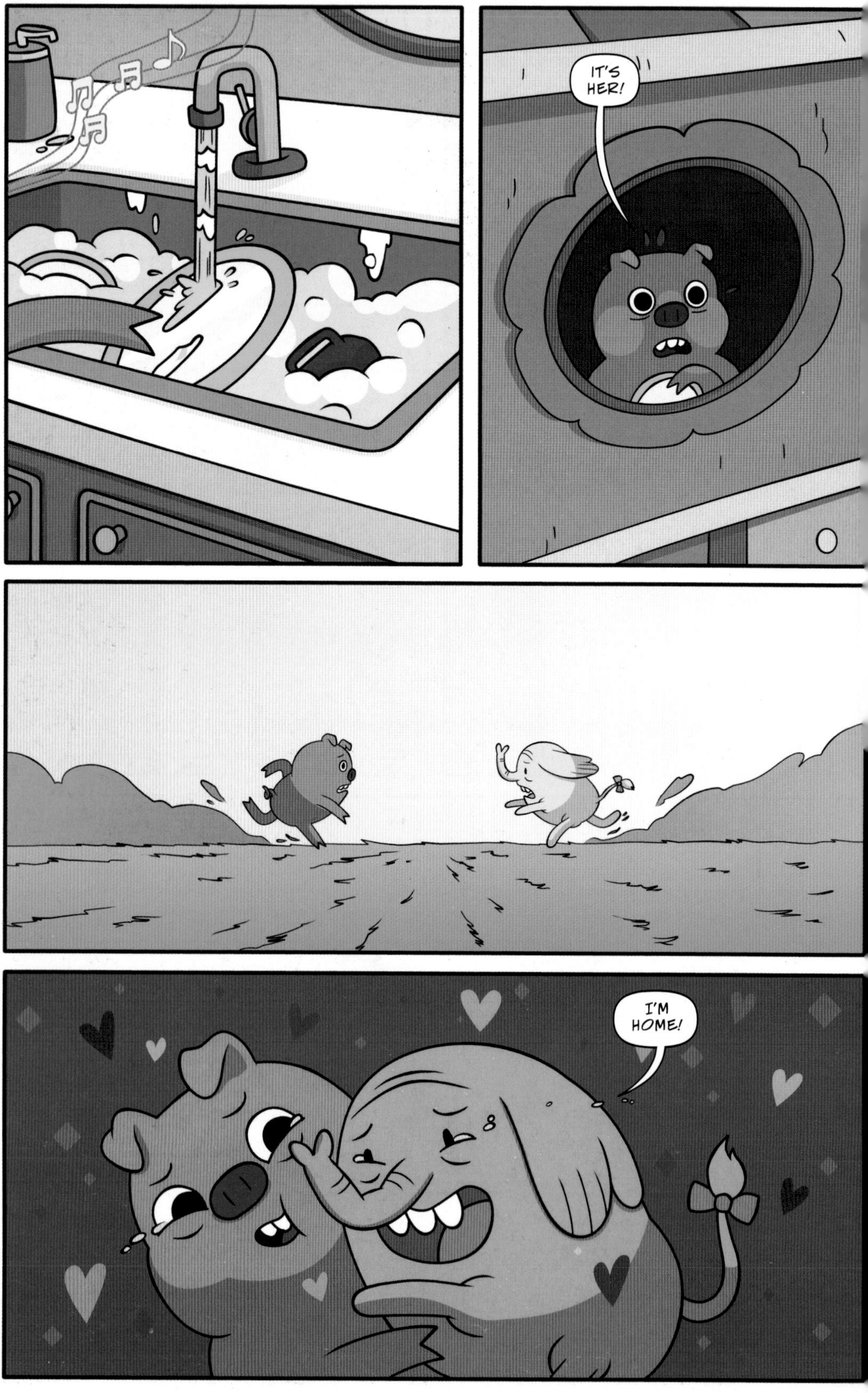
IT'S HER!
I'M HOME!

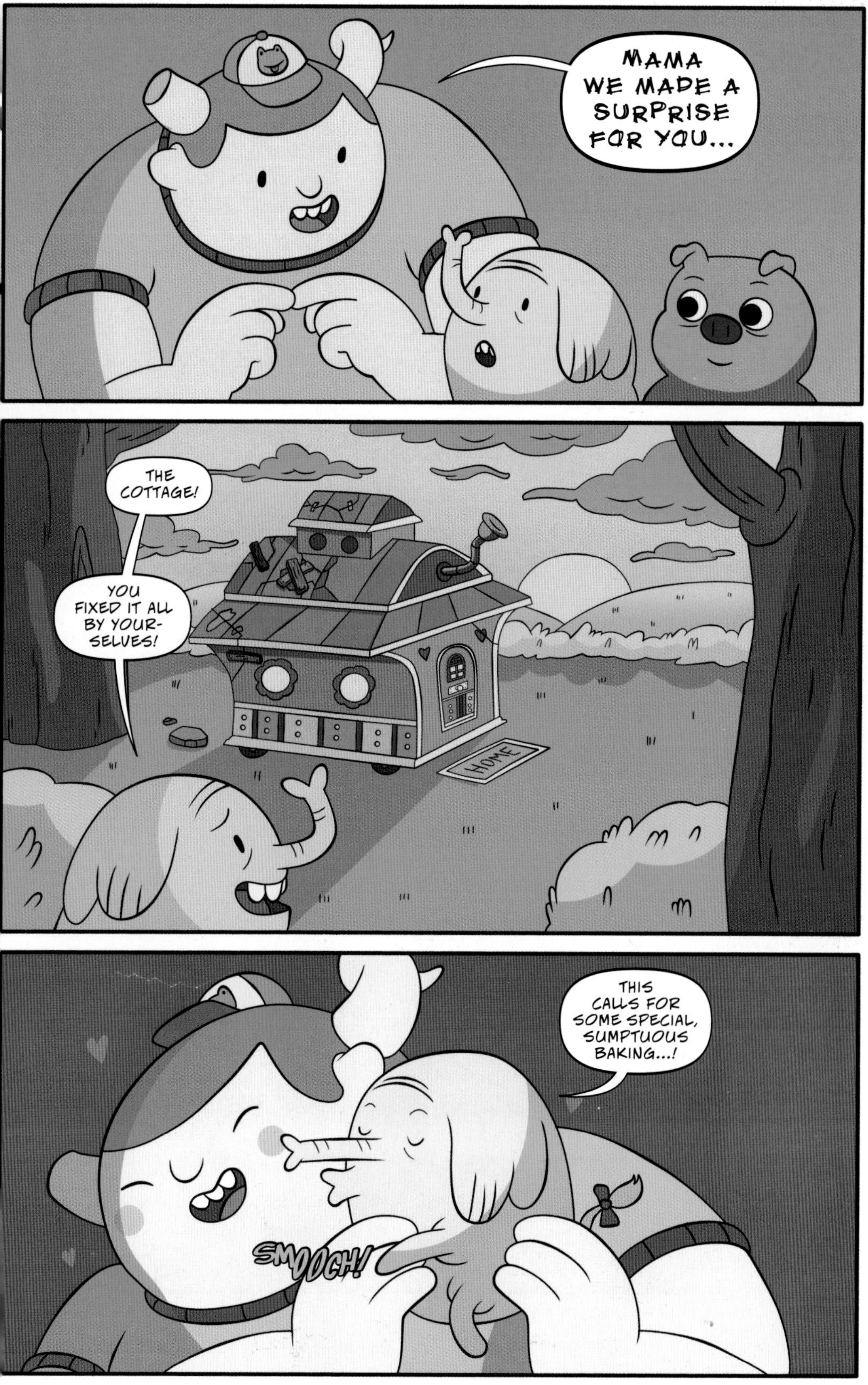
MAMA WE MADE A SURPRISE FOR YOU...
THE COTTAGE!
YOU FIXED IT ALL BY YOUR-SELVES!
HOME
THIS CALLS FOR SOME SPECIAL, SUMPTUOUS BAKING...!
SMOOCH!

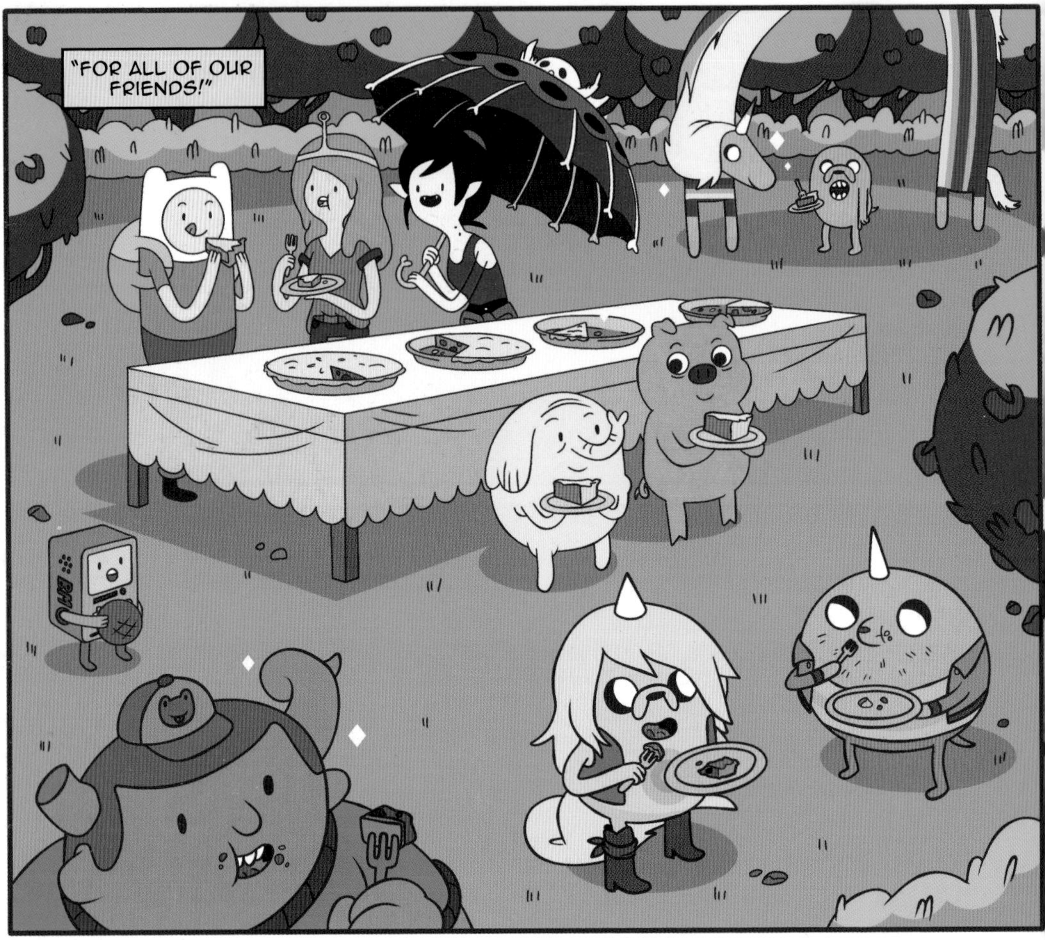
"FOR ALL OF OUR FRIENDS!"

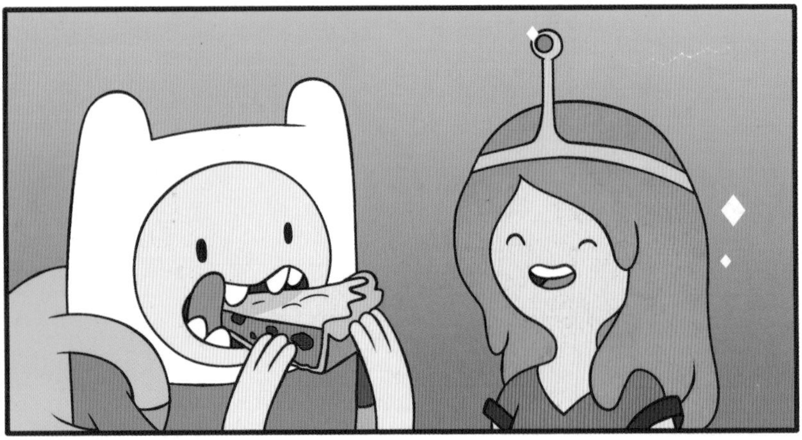

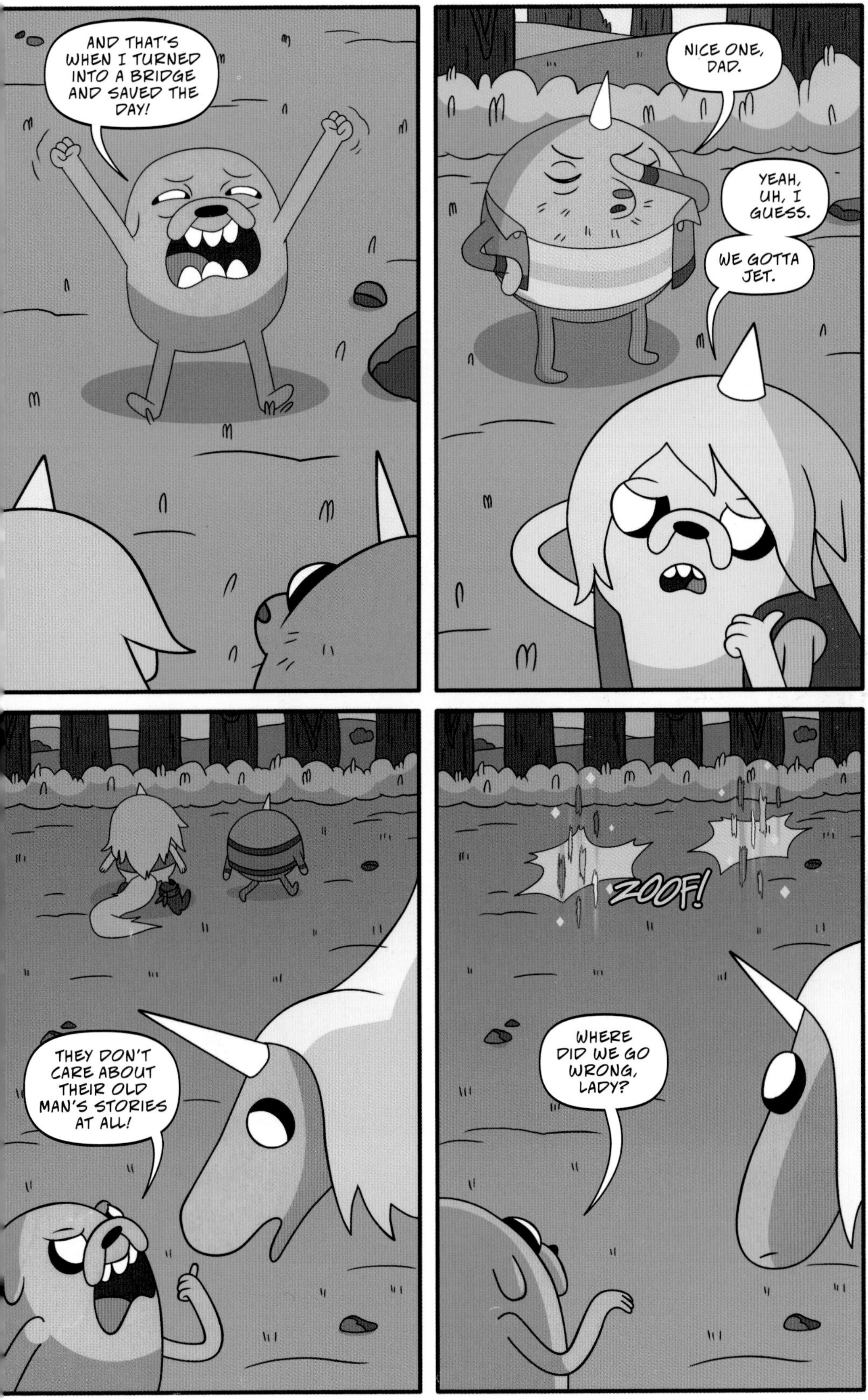
AND THAT'S WHEN I TURNED INTO A BRIDGE AND SAVED THE DAY!
NICE ONE, DAD.
YEAH, UH, I GUESS.
WE GOTTA JET.
THEY DON'T CARE ABOUT THEIR OLD MAN'S STORIES AT ALL!
ZOOF!
WHERE DID WE GO WRONG, LADY?

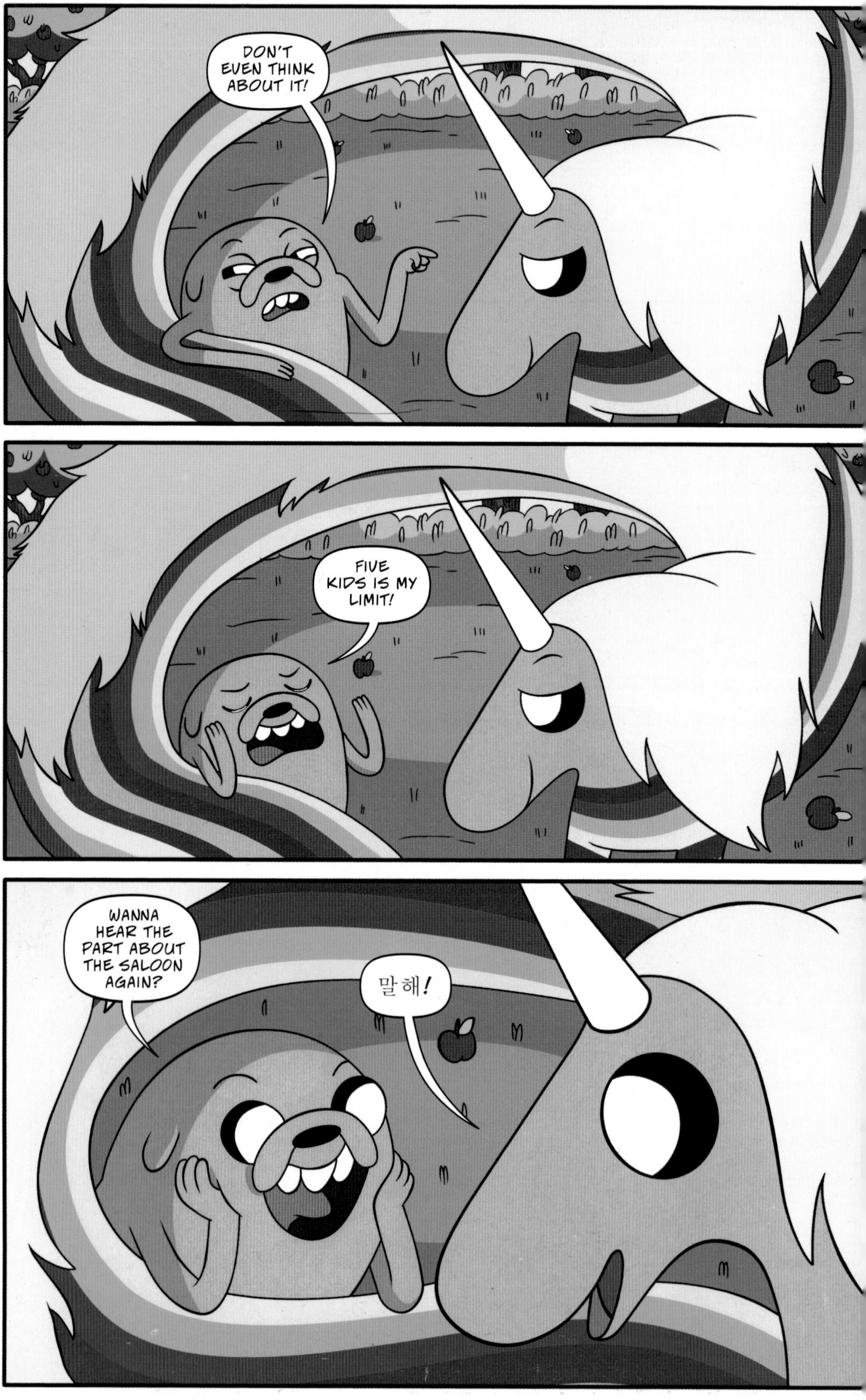
DON'T EVEN THINK ABOUT IT!
FIVE KIDS IS MY LIMIT!
WANNA HEAR THE PART ABOUT THE SALOON AGAIN?
말해!

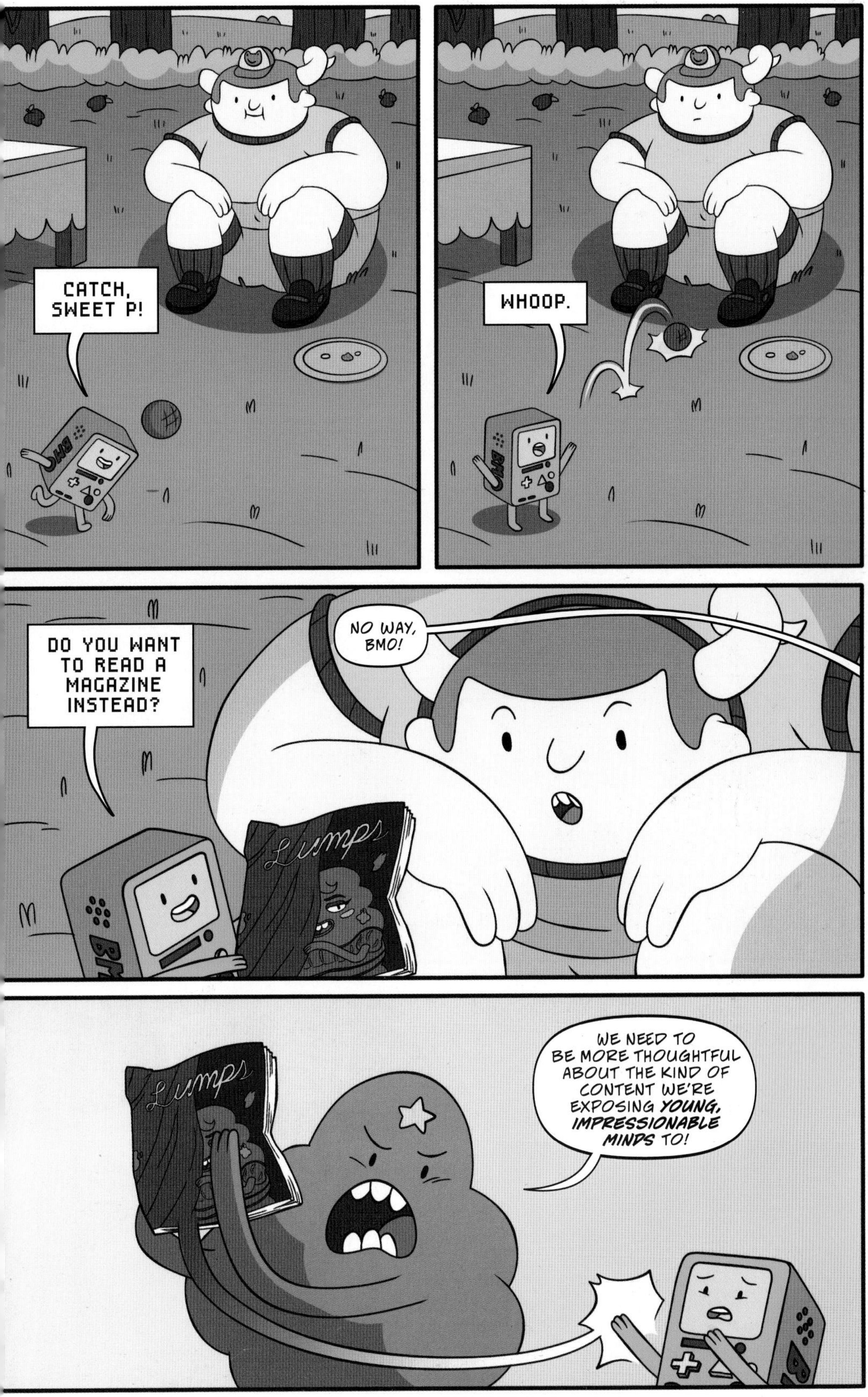
CATCH, SWEET P!
WHOOP.
DO YOU WANT TO READ A MAGAZINE INSTEAD?
NO WAY, BMO!
Lumps
WE NEED TO BE MORE THOUGHTFUL ABOUT THE KIND OF CONTENT WE'RE EXPOSING ***YOUNG, IMPRESSIONABLE MINDS*** TO!

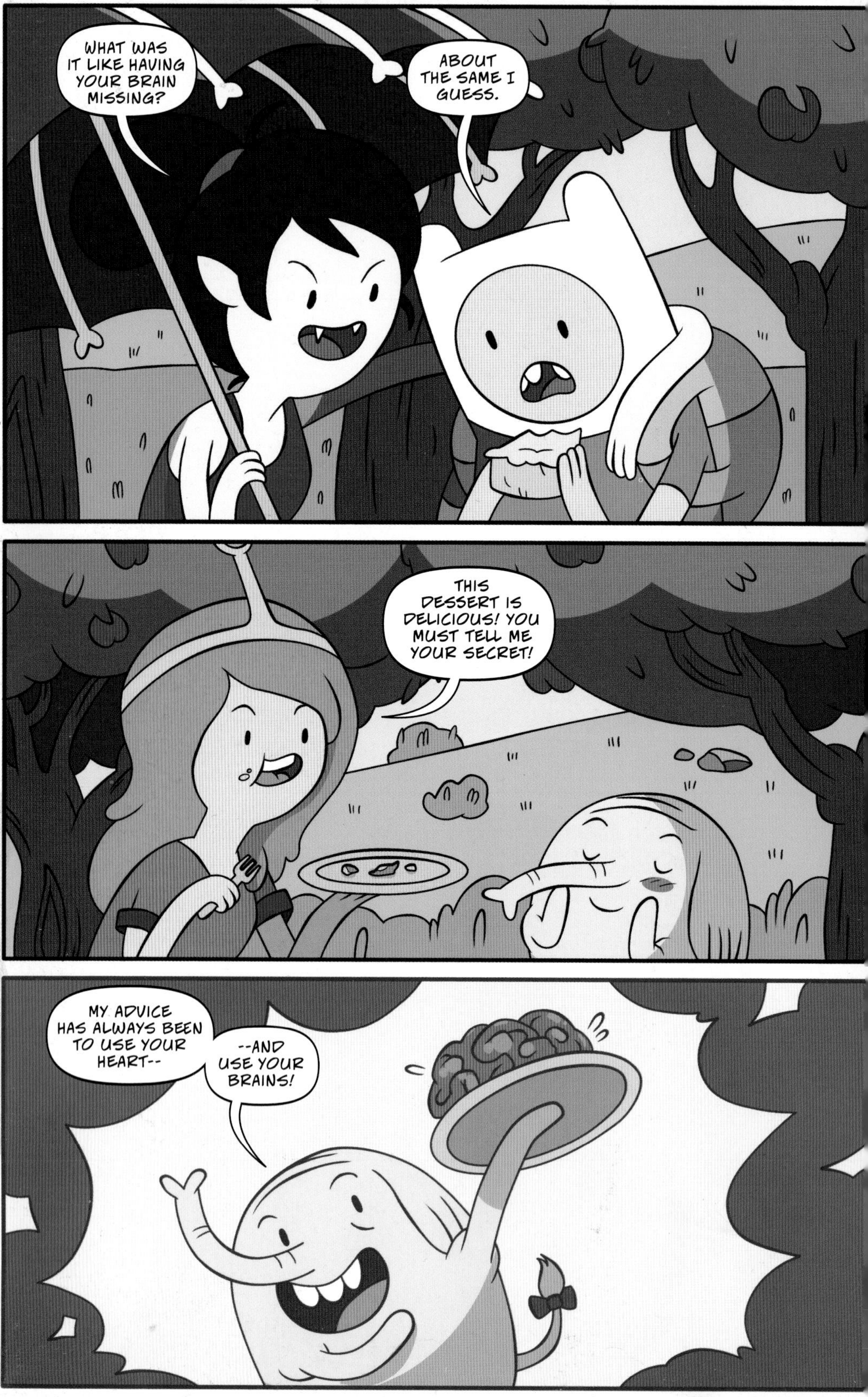
WHAT WAS IT LIKE HAVING YOUR BRAIN MISSING?
ABOUT THE SAME I GUESS.
THIS DESSERT IS DELICIOUS! YOU MUST TELL ME YOUR SECRET!
MY ADVICE HAS ALWAYS BEEN TO USE YOUR HEART--
--AND USE YOUR BRAINS!

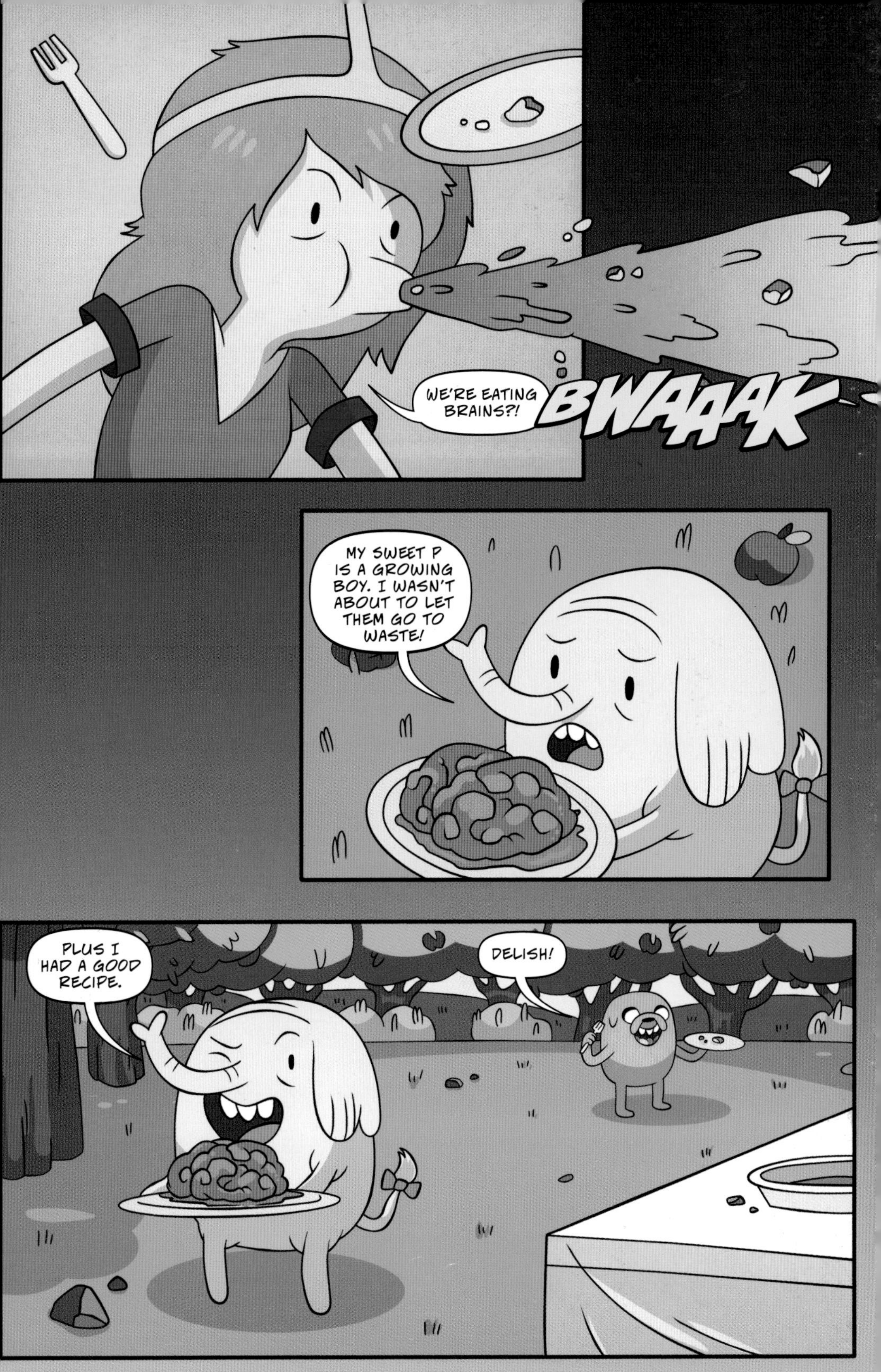
WE'RE EATING BRAINS?!
BWAAAK
MY SWEET P IS A GROWING BOY. I WASN'T ABOUT TO LET THEM GO TO WASTE!
PLUS I HAD A GOOD RECIPE.
DELISH!

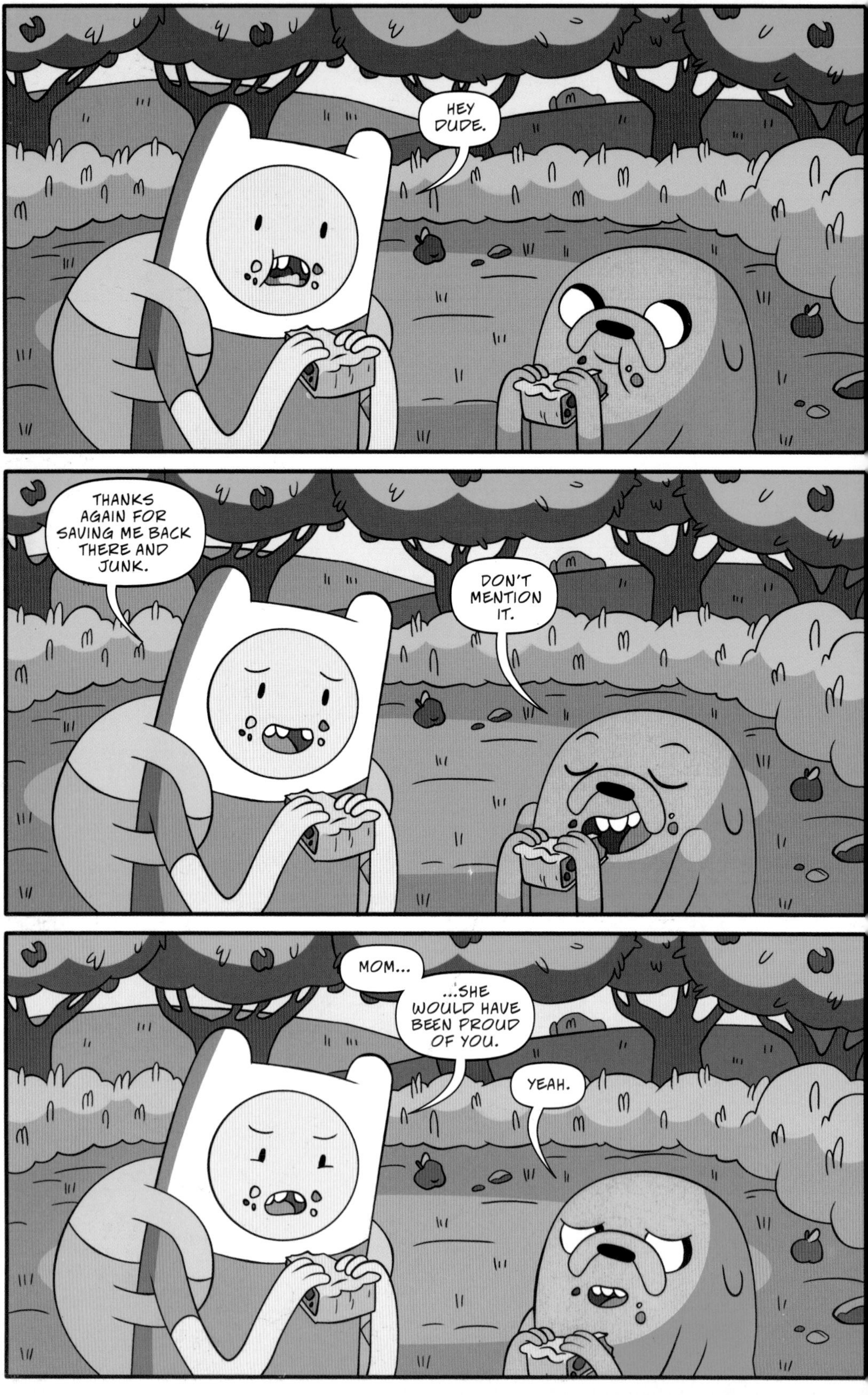
HEY DUDE.
THANKS AGAIN FOR SAVING ME BACK THERE AND JUNK.
DON'T MENTION IT.
MOM...
...SHE WOULD HAVE BEEN PROUD OF YOU.
YEAH.

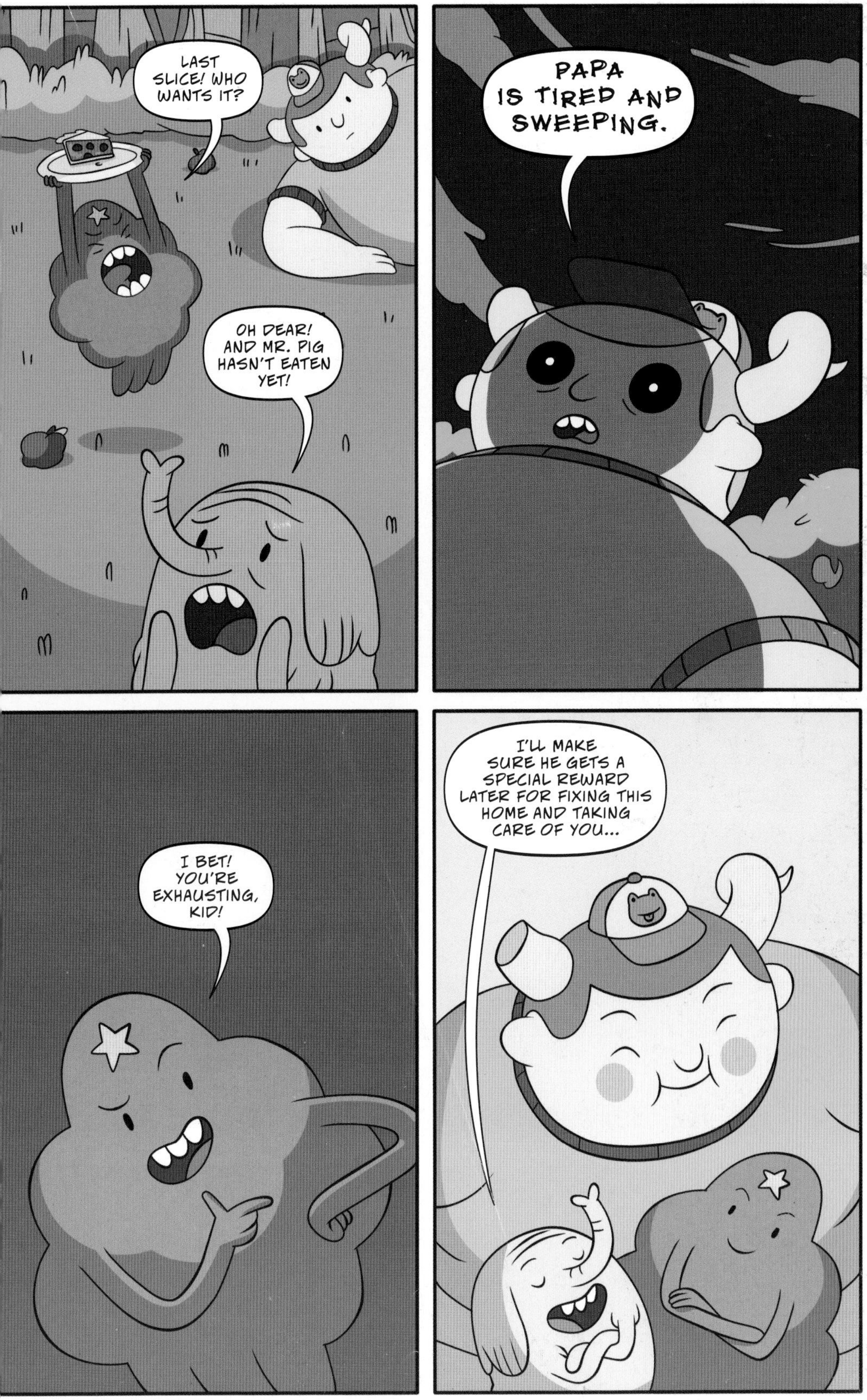
LAST SLICE! WHO WANTS IT?
OH DEAR! AND MR. PIG HASN'T EATEN YET!
PAPA IS TIRED AND SWEEPING.
I BET! YOU'RE EXHAUSTING, KID!
I'LL MAKE SURE HE GETS A SPECIAL REWARD LATER FOR FIXING THIS HOME AND TAKING CARE OF YOU...

"...HE IS ALWAYS SO GOOD WITH CHILDREN!"

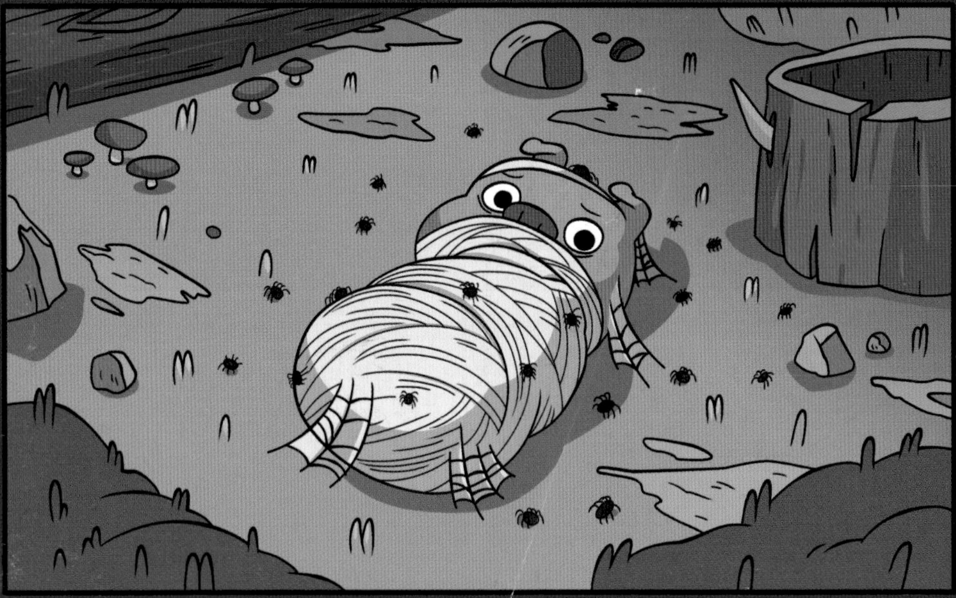

end!

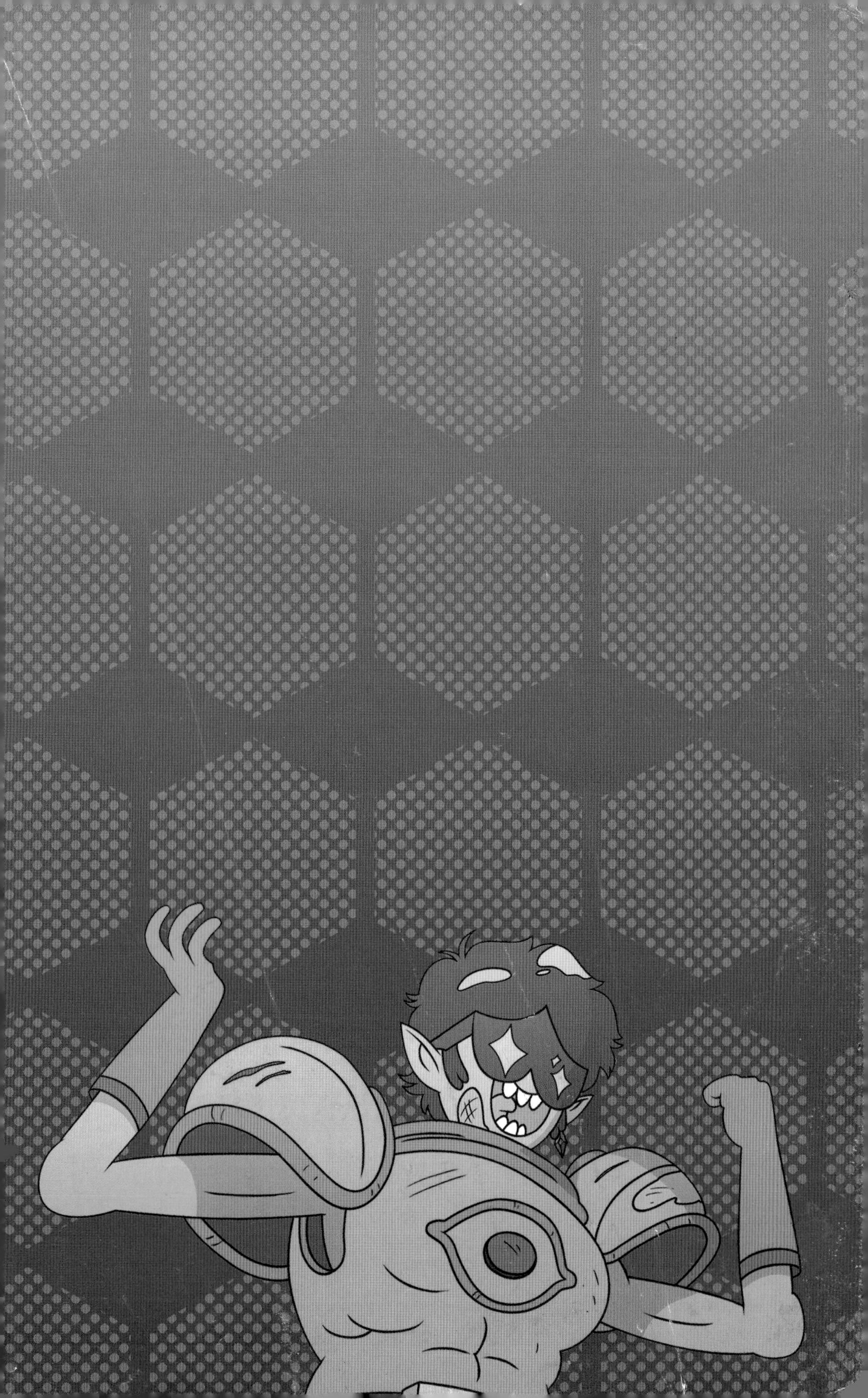

The Ooorient Express

Spring 2017

Written by Jeremy Sorese
Art by Zachary Sterling